W9-AVS-262

Born in Scotland in 1910, Jane Duncan spent her childhood in Glasgow, going for holidays to the Black Isle of Inverness. After taking her degree at Glasgow University she moved to England in 1931, and when war broke out she was commissioned in the WAAF and worked in Photographic Intelligence.

After the war she moved to the West Indies with her husband, who appears as 'Twice' Alexander in her novels. Shortly after her husband's death, she returned to Jemimaville near Cromarty, not far from her grandparents' croft, which inspired the beloved 'Reachfar'. Jane Duncan died in 1976.

Also by Jane Duncan

MY FRIENDS THE MISS BOYDS
MY FRIEND MURIEL
MY FRIEND MONICA

and published by Corgi Books

My Friend Annie

Jane Duncan

CORGI BOOKS

MY FRIEND ANNIE

A CORGI BOOK   0 552 12877 5

Originally published in Great Britain by Macmillan London Ltd.

PRINTING HISTORY

Macmillan London edition published 1961
Macmillan London edition reprinted 1969, 1971, 1978, 1983
Corgi edition published 1987

This book is set in 10/11pt Plantin.

Corgi Books are published by Transworld Publishers Ltd.,
61-63 Uxbridge Road, Ealing, London W5 5SA, in Australia by
Transworld Publishers (Australia) Pty. Ltd., 15-23 Helles
Avenue, Moorebank, NSW 2170, and in New Zealand by Transworld
Publishers (N.Z.) Ltd., Cnr. Moselle and Waipareira Avenues,
Henderson, Auckland.

Printed and bound in Great Britain by
Cox & Wyman Ltd, Reading

TO
MY BROTHER

CHAPTER ONE

I set out to write this story of my friend Annie and I gave it the title 'My Friend Annie' in all good faith and for what are, I think, three good reasons. The first is that I like to write stories; the second is that, to me, Annie seemed to be an unusual and interesting person; and the third is that I chanced to know more of her life than most other people – particularly people who like to write stories.

But, now that I have written down all that I know about Annie, I find that I know very, very little about her. All I know is the outward seeming of a few salient events in her career and I find that comparatively few of all the pages that follow are about Annie. A few salient events, even if one knew more than the mere outward seeming of them, are not a life, any more than one shower of rain or one bright day can be described as a climate and, instead of writing the story of Annie, as I set out to do and thought I was doing, I find that I have described some seasons in the cycle of my own life which came under the influence of Annie, as the climate of a country may be affected by an area of high or low barometric pressure that is many hundreds of miles away. The weather of the life of an individual can be affected by the life of a fellow-being without that individual having any deep knowledge of that other being, just as the country on which the sun shines or the rain falls has no knowledge of the intimate nature of the cyclone or the anticyclone which affects its weather. I am in this position with relation to Annie. I know nothing of her or of her nature although, in the careless way of ordinary conversation, I can say to you, and with truth: 'Annie? I have known her since I was nine years old.' Yes. That is true. I first met Annie when I was nine years old. . .

If you happened to read a book I wrote about some friends I came to know when I was eight, you will probably know that, up to the age of nine, I was one of the happiest children in the world, living, dearly loved, in the centre of my family at my home, Reachfar, in the north of Scotland. But very shortly after my tenth birthday, I came to know that a whole world, without warning, can disintegrate and that the grown-up people of that world, whom the ten-year-old child had regarded as being as fixed, certain and sure as the stars in their courses, are not fixed, certain and sure at all, but as lost and groping in their struggle with life as any child of ten can be in her own smaller dimension of struggle. It was out of this upheaval that began shortly after my tenth birthday that I came to know Annie and, as the best way to tell a story is to begin at the beginning (if one can find it), I will tell you about it.

When the year 1919 turned into the year 1920, my world was bounded by my family, our small agricultural holding of Reachfar in Ross-shire, our local district, our village, Achcraggan and its village school, but the main pivot was what I thought of as My Family, which consisted of my grandparents, my parents, my uncle, my aunt and My Friend Tom, who was also our handyman about the place. For me, this world of Reachfar, with these people in it, had always been there and would always be there and, that being so, no real harm could ever come to *me*. I was looking forward to having my tenth birthday early in March of 1920, for this would mean that, in June, I would leave the village school, have the long days of the summer holidays wandering around our moors and fields and, in the autumn, go to Fortavoch Academy to start what was called the 'Higher Eddication', for I was what was known as 'clever at the school' and my family had been saving money since my birth to 'give me a chance'.

Because of the prospect of Fortavoch Academy, I had been looking forward to my tenth birthday for three years, for,

8

having gone to the village school at the age of five, I had, at the age of seven, calculated that, if I went through its five classes at the rate of a class per year, without the scholastic disgrace of being 'kept back', my tenth birthday would herald in the year of the 'Higher Eddication'. Towards the end of 1919, however, I discovered that my tenth birthday was going to be an event even more remarkable than I had expected, for there was to be a baby born to my mother and it was expected to arrive almost on my birthday. I remember no emotion about this, other than a feeling of wonderment. I had been an only child in this grown-up household; I had accepted this as the natural order of things; I could not imagine what it would be like to have a brother or sister and I simply waited, wondering, upon events. The events came and the wonder ceased.

I had my tenth birthday, my brother was born the next day and, two days later, I came downstairs, dressed, ready to go to school, to find all my family in the big kitchen, dressed not for work but as if it were a Sunday, and all looking strangely afraid. As I came into the room, all of them except my father turned away from me and he looked down at me and said: 'Janet, you have to be a brave bairn. Mother died during the night!' Having said the dreadful words, he put his hand on my head for a moment and then walked past me, out into the harsh, windy sunshine of March. I remember my grandmother saying: 'Come, Janet,' and after that I do not remember any more.

I have no clear memories of that year until about July. I do not know by what process I came to accept the death of my mother as a fact. I had always known that her health had been delicate – that had been one of the features of that former world of mine, that on certain days you moved quietly about the house, that on other days Doctor Mackay came to see her and my grandmother's temper varied in accordance with his report. I know, however, that the process of acceptance must have been all-absorbing, for, before that day, I had been a keen observer of my little world and have detailed memories of its doings, but for this period from

9

March to July I must have lived in some isolated vacuum. It is as if the stream of my memory had suddenly, that March day, flowed into a cavern in a dark hillside to emerge, about mid-July, on the other side in a different world, and the detail of memory takes up again with My Friends Tom and George (my uncle who dislikes the title of Uncle) and myself walking, one Sunday, across the Reachfar moor, which was our favourite Sunday pastime. When we reached the Juniper Place beside the spring where the heather gave way to an area of short, springy grass, George sat himself down beside a juniper bush, took out his pipe and said: 'Well, this is as good a place as any to be holding our Parlyment.'

Tom, George and I had many amusements that the rest of my family did not know about and, had they known of them, they would not have approved of them, for we used to preach sermons in imitation of the Reverend Roderick Mackenzie, the minister, and 'waste our time' composing songs and poems about all sorts of local affairs and interesting subjects. We also, when some family crisis demanded it, held 'Parlyments' at which we decided what our policy as a group would be in the said crisis, such as whether or not we would lend our support to my young aunt's request for a new dance dress or whether we would table a vote of censure on the fact that, after we had picked all the brambles to be made into jam, we were being allowed bramble jam only once a week at Sunday tea while my grandmother was giving most of it away as 'compliments' to our friends and neighbours.

'Well, what's this Parlyment about?' I asked, after we had all sat down and Tom's and George's pipes had been lit and seemed to be drawing satisfactorily.

'This is a terrible important Parlyment,' said Tom, 'and everybody has to be listening careful and there's not to be any losing of people's tempers.'

I had a strange, forlorn feeling of being in a new world, for this was not like the opening of any Parlyment I had ever attended at before.

'Silence now for the Prime Meenister,' said Tom.

'The thing of it is,' said George in his character of Prime

Minister, 'that there's been a lot of changes about Reachfar lately. We will not be speaking about the big change that is past, which was very sad for us all – what we are speaking about is the changes that is still to come. Aye. We all thought, the way things used to be, that Janet would be going to the Academy at Fortavoch in September, but now we know that she will be going to a far bigger and better school – down in the south.'

My mind was in a turmoil and I drew breath to shout some protest, but Tom reached out and laid a silencing hand on my knee.

'You see, it's this way,' George continued, holding his pipe in his hand and staring at its bowl. 'Since the war, things is not the same up here in the north. Sir Torquil canna afford to pay your father as his grieve any longer.'

My mind could not encompass this, so I sat on the grass in a stunned silence, but now, forty years later, I do not find it surprising that the mind of a child of ten years old could not encompass the facts and effects of revolution, for that is what this was.

All my life that I could remember, my father had been 'grieve' or farm manager to Sir Torquil Daviot, our local baronet, just as my grandfather had been grieve to old 'Sir Turk' who had been Sir Torquil's father, just as George, now, was grieve to Mr Mackintosh of Dinchory, our neighbour on the west march. It was an economic fact, of which even I was aware, that our own croft of Reachfar could not support us all and that what had made our comfortable life – not to mention our ambitions for my schooling – possible was the money earned and brought home to the family pool by my father and my uncle. That Sir Torquil could no longer 'afford' my father was a revolutionary blowing-up of one of the foundations of our economy and, in my life at that time, as unlikely and as much of a shock as the City of London of today would suffer should the Old Lady of Threadneedle Street suddenly close her doors.

'What – what about Dinchory?' I asked.

'Dinchory is all right,' said George. 'Mr Mackintosh has

11

more money behind him. It's a smaller place than Poyntdale and he has no bairns and their future to be thinking of like Sir Torquil – and us.'

'I – could work in the holidays, maybe?' I asked.

'Wheesht, now, pettie,' said Tom. 'Wait you, till George tells us a-all about it.'

'So this is the way of it,' George continued. 'It has been very hard and lonely-like about here for Duncan – your father – since – since your mother died. It's been bad enough for the rest of us, but far worse for him, and Sir Torquil and us all thought if he could go to a new place, among new people, it would be better, especially when Sir Torquil canna afford to be keeping him. So Sir Torquil and Leddy Lydia know a gentleman that lives down Glasgow way, that got wounded in the war so that he can't be going to his town business any more and this gentleman has bought a big farm and is going in for dairy business. Sir Torquil has arranged for your father to go to be his manager, as they call it down there.'

'Near Glasgow?' I asked.

George dropped something of his uneasy Prime-Ministerial character and became more like himself now that my first shock was over. 'Aye, but not in the *toon*, of course. You canna have pedigree milking cows in the middle o' yon smoke an' stink. No. It's a real bonnie place, your father says. Cairnshaws, it's called.'

'Dad has seen it?'

'Och, surely – that's where him and Sir Torquil was last month, down there seeing this chentleman, Mr Hill,' said Tom.

'Oh!'

'But the great thing about it is,' George went on, 'there's a great big monster o' an Academy not a mile from the house – not *twelve* miles away, like Fortavoch is from here.'

'The *house*?' I asked.

'Surely! There's a house for you and your father—'

'An' a bathroom in it with hot water running oot o' a tappie intil a bath—' Tom put in.

12

'Who will make the dinner?' I asked.

'Och,' said George, lighting a match and applying it to his pipe, 'that's a-all arranged. There's a leddy coming to keep house and make the dinner and a-all.'

'What about Baby John?' I asked.

'Baby John, poor little fellow, will be stopping here with Granny and us,' George told me quietly. 'It's better – and him so sma-all.'

He was silent for a moment and then continued in a heartier voice. 'But for *big* people, that have got sense, like you and your father, it's a fine thing to be going venturing off into the world down south, although we would not care for either of you to be going off all on your own. No. It is better for the both of you to be going together and be a help and company for one another.'

I could not visualize myself as either help or company to my god-like father, but if My Friends George and Tom said that this was expected of me, I suppose that it must be within my capabilities. I think that I have always lived largely by blind faith and, in those days, most of my faith was vested in Tom and George. We went on to discuss all sorts of points, I remember, for I was, although unconsciously, searching for some flaw in the arrangements – anything that would stop the terrifying flow of events – but, apparently, during the long time that I had been in that dark tunnel under the hill between one world and another, it had all been arranged. Every question that I asked in my efforts to find something that would form an obstacle in the path of this fearsome change was countered with a concrete assurance against which I was defenceless. After many of these questions and many concrete answers, George stared away into the fir trees that surrounded the Juniper Place and said: 'Of coorse, it is a-all very hard to get used to. Tom and me is going to find it kind o' funny here at Reachfar with you not here, but we must a-all chust try to make the best of it.'

'That's what I think too, forbye,' said Tom. 'We have to mind that your father is doing what he thinks is the best thing for the whole of us and we must not be worrying him more than he is worried already by looking doon-in-the-mooth aboot things.'

'That's right,' said George. 'And anyway, Janet, we always knew that if you did all right at the Academy — even if it was Fortavoch — the time would come when you would have to be going off to the University, for God knows there's no university doon at Achcraggan yonder.'

Achcraggan was our local village, and in spite of everything the thought of its having a university made me laugh.

'And there'll be the holidays, whateffer,' said Tom. 'When you'll be coming home for the holidays, George and me will be meeting you at the train at Inverness with a bittie heather in oor bonnets . . . In a way, I wish it was myself that was going south to this Academy. It is a wonderful place that is of it, from what your father was telling us.'

I was passionately interested in school. 'Has Dad seen the Academy too?'

'Surely!' said George. 'And the Dominie of it is called Mr Lindsay, but he's not called the Dominie like Mr Stevenson at Achcraggan — what was the word for him, Tom?'

'Rector,' said Tom. 'Rector — I minded it special, when Duncan was telling us aboot him sitting in this roomie where he saw him that had 'Rector's Study' pented on its door, and him with a black robe on him on the top of his suit of clothes, just like a Minister.'

'That's a pack of lies!' I protested, for if you were not careful Tom and George could take a fearful rise out of you when they got to their story-telling.

'No, no lies!' Tom swore. 'It's the Bible truth and chust you ask your father at tea-time if you'll not be believing me. And there's *hundreds* of bairns at this school and them all marching to their class-rooms to a piano playing!'

'Ach, away with you!' I rose to my feet. 'I'm going home to speak to Dad about this myself!'

'Och, what's your hurry?' George lay back on his elbow. 'Apart from bairns, there's aboot a hundred *teachers* in it, I am thinking, what with the mannie for the singing lessons and the leddy for the jimmynastics and—'

14

'What's jimmynastics?'

'Drill,' said Tom and rose to his feet. 'Like this – hands on hips! Knees bend! Arms outwards, stretch!'

Tom, who was about fifty at this time and dressed in his second-best suit which was a little tight and his heavy boots, overbalanced and fell sprawling on the grass, but that caused hardly an interruption in their panegyric about 'the Academy in the south'. My Friends George and Tom were, and still are, two simple-hearted countrymen, but their hearts are so essentially good and their kind cleverness so subtle that, an hour later, I walked into the home that all my family had been afraid to tell me that I must leave and said: 'Dad, is it true that there's a jimmynasium with ropes for people to climb at this Academy that I'm going to?'

At the time, I did not know why my father's mouth twisted or why his eyes looked curiously different as he smiled and said: 'Aye, that's true enough, Janet. Was Tom and George telling you about it?'

'Yes. And Dad, the – the Rector – he is in a black robe?'

'Aye, he wears a robe like the Minister. Mr Lindsay, a very, very fine man that was a major in the war.'

'Did you ask him if I could come to his school? What did he say?'

'He was very nice and asked me to get Dominie Stevenson to write him a letter.'

'And did you, Dad?'

'Surely – and I had a letter from Mr Lindsay since then saying he was looking forward to seeing you.'

'Then it's all right?'

'Yes, Janet. I think it is all right.'

I have a better memory for people and conversations than I have for scenes and events and this may explain the fact that I remember clearly only one incident in the course of the first train journey that I ever made. I had never seen a train at close quarters before, but the trains and the station made little impression on me. What did amaze me, when I alighted from the local train at Inverness to board the large train for Glasgow, was the number of people there were in

15

the world. Utterly bemused, I walked through the noise, smoke and bustle beside my father, while a porter wheeled our baggage ahead of us on a large barrow. It seemed very strange to walk among all these people, bidding nobody 'Good morning', for at home one spoke to everyone one met and I thought that this big world was an ill-mannered, unfriendly place, so that I was pleased when my father stopped at a queer, doorless shop that seemed to sell nothing but books and newspapers and spoke to the lady behind the high counter.

'Good morning,' I said to her too, in order to make myself feel more normal.

'Good morning,' she replied pleasantly.

'And now,' my father said, 'we'll get you a book to read in the train. Tell the lady which one you would like.'

I looked with wonder at her well-stocked shelves and straight away saw a copy of *Alice in Wonderland*.

'That one, if you please,' I said, pointing.

Dominie Stevenson had read it to us in school and I had hitherto regarded it as a miracle thing that only remote, godlike people like schoolmasters could own − not as a book that might belong to *me*.

'You are sure?' my father asked. 'You didn't take much time to think.'

'I am quite sure, please, Dad − if it doesn't cost too many pennies.'

'Then that's all right,' he said and the lady took the book from the shelf and handed it to me.

'Thank you very much indeed,' I told her with emphasis.

As I turned away, my eyes on the book between my hands, its jacket with the picture of Alice with her long, serpentine neck that carried her head away above the tree-tops, I suddenly found myself, book and all, entangled in a large tartan rug that hung over the arm of a fierce-looking old gentleman.

'Janet! Look where you're going!' said the too-late voice of my father as I looked up into a pair of bright, fierce old eyes in a ruddy, wrinkled face.

'I beg your pardon, sir,' I said and made the curtsy that

16

my mother had always insisted that I make to old people. 'I hope I did not hurt you?'

'Not at all,' he said. 'And that's a splendid book you've chosen. What is your name?'

'Janet Sandison, sir.'

'And where do you come from?'

'Reachfar, Achcraggan, sir.'

'That is in Ross?'

'Yes, sir.'

He looked at my father. 'The ladies at Reachfar have good manners, apparently. Your daughter?'

'Yes, sir,' said my father.

The gentleman turned to the shop lady and said: 'Hand me the other half, please – *Through the Looking-Glass*.'

'Certainly, your Lordship,' she said and handed him a book similar to the one I was holding, whereupon he took out a fountain pen, opened the book, wrote something in it and handed it to me.

'There you are – that is a memento.'

'Thank you, sir. Please, what is a memento?'

'Janet—' my father began, but the old gentleman held up a hand, silencing him.

'A memento is something to remind you of a certain person, a certain place and a certain time. You will remember that?'

'Yes, sir.'

'Thank you, sir,' said my father.

'Thank you, sir. Good day,' I said and made my curtsy again.

'Good day, Janet,' the old gentleman said and my father and I went to take our seats in the train.

'Could I have a look at the gentleman's book?' he asked when we were settled.

He opened it, but I could not read the fast, grown-up writing on the flyleaf.

'What does it say, Dad?'

'A memento to Janet Sandison, a lady,' my father read. 'Inverness, August, 1920. Farness.'

'What is Farness?'

'The gentleman's name. It was old Lord Farness that was in it.'

'But I'm not a lady – I'm only a girl. Why did he give me the book?'

'I think maybe he liked your manners – you mind how Mother was always so parteeclar about manners? And I think he wrote that hoping that you would mind to have good manners always. There's the guard's whistle! We'll be off in a minute.'

I do not remember any more of the journey except a few small details, but I have the clearest memory of the incident at the bookstall, for it was my first experience of spontaneous kindness from a stranger who did not know me, and it has had a far-reaching effect on my life, as you will see, if you read to the end of this book. Since that time, I have learned that Lord Farness was an irascible old man who became known as eccentric because of his strong and strongly expressed views on a wide variety of subjects, but his eccentric action at the bookstall was one of those small incidents that are destined to have what seems to be an out-of-proportion effect on the course of a life.

I remember little more of the journey except that the rhythm of the train's wheels set itself to a song I had made during August when I was playing around the moor with my dog, Fly, and which went to the tune of 'Riding down from Bangor'. I quote the song here because it gives the mood which Tom and George induced in me to ease the wrench of leaving the home which I loved so dearly.

'I am going to Glasgow in the south-bound train,
Down across the Grampians – I hope it does not rain.
Tom and George aren't coming but staying at Reachfar,
And I will write them letters, saying how things are.

When I get to Glasgow, I shall go to school,
At the *Academy*, which is very full
Of pupils of all ages, up to seventeen,
And try to be a credit to the school where I have been.'

CHAPTER TWO

When George and Tom had talked of Cairnshaws as being 'near Glasgow' and 'down Glasgow way', their geography had that vague world-wide-ness which it had about any place that was beyond the limits of our own district at home. To them, the Suez Canal was 'east Egypt way'; France was 'south London way and across the water'; Canada was 'down to Glasgow and west across the sea in a big boat where Willie Mackintosh went', while the North Pole was 'up over the Firth and away further north than Shetland and terrible cold'. Miles of distance and degrees of latitude and longitude meant nothing to George and Tom. Their geographic principle – and mine – was that Reachfar was the hub of the compass, the centre of the world, from which lines radiated to certain main points such as Edinburgh, Glasgow, Canada and Australia, and that a place pin-pointed between Reachfar and one of these main points had been geographically located in a way quite adequate for our needs or its own minor importance.

Cairnshaws, in actual fact, was about twenty miles north-east of Glasgow, in a greenish-grey valley with a meandering stream known as 'the Burn' which rose at 'the Cairn' at one end of the valley and debouched into the Forth and Clyde canal at 'the Bridge' at the other end. Starting at 'the Bridge' was 'the Toon', an ugly community of drab, grey, stone houses with three outstanding features, namely a railway junction a mile from its centre, a large and very old church at one end and the huge, fairly new Academy at the other.

That description that I have given you of a pocket of central Scotland is a portrait such as an airborne camera might give, but, at ten years old, I had no such panoramic, unfeeling or dispassionate vision and the valley called the Cairn Glen which will emerge from these pages may bear little resemblance to what I have described in that paragraph up there. Selection is a law of life and the living eye and memory see and remember what they select and do not, like the dead camera, record with equal stress everything that passes before their lenses.

All my life, the words of my language have extended over me a fascination and, at ten years old, this fascination was canalized, temporarily, into an interest in place-names, so that the first thing that absorbed me about my new home was the domination of the word 'cairn'. In this district, it seemed, the little heap of stones – the Cairn – on the Cairn Hill at the top of the Cairn Glen dominated everything, for through the valley the Cairn Burn ran down to Cairnton, where the Academy was and all the farms on either side of the burn had names such as Cairnshaws, Cairnyetts, Cairnriggs, Cairnbrae, Overcairn, Nethercairn, Biggs o' Cairn and Cairn in a hundred monotonous varieties. There was no end to the influence of the Cairn and, of course, there was the paradox which is so characteristic of life in general. The presence of the Cairn was so all-pervading that it would be left out of speech, so that, instead of Cairnton, people spoke of 'the Toon' and no farm was given its full name, but was known as the Riggs or the Yetts or the Over or the Nether.

When, at the age of five, I had first gone to Achcraggan School, I had come home and had made reference to the village baker's wife as 'Katie Donny' as she was known to the rest of the schoolchildren. My gentle but firm mother at once said: 'Mrs Donaldson, Janet. It is extremely ill-mannered to trifle with names to suit yourself and please don't do it.' The result of this and other similar comments was that, at the age of ten, I found all the Braes and Overs and Yetts and especially 'the Toon' vaguely offensive. The abbreviations, it seemed to me, carried a double-edged insult, especially in the case of Overcairn, for if people called it 'The Over', it was a rude contraction of its own proper name which also gave it the importance of being the *only* 'Over', which was extremely insulting to 'Overnewton', a big, neighbouring farm to Reachfar in Ross-shire. These Something-Cairns should remember, I thought, that their cairn of stones on that hill was part of their identity and not think that all the world knew when they said 'The Brae', they meant 'Cairnbrae'. There were other, and maybe better, braes, notably the croft of Seabrae to the east of Reachfar.

This absorption of the local geography and the early beginnings of my own attitude to it took place during my first few days at Cairnshaws -- locally known as 'The Shaws', of course -- which I spent mostly in our house and in our garden and its immediate surroundings, for I have always been a slow-moving, slow-witted creature who takes a long time to explore a new environment and this was the first time I had ever had to adapt myself to a major change.

The housekeeper who had been found for my father by his employer was a native of the Toon, a pretty, fair-skinned, reddish-haired woman and very much the clean, efficient, sonsie, house-proud Lowland Scots housewife. She was about thirty-five years old, named Jean Gray, and I called her 'Miss Jean'. She was, to me, extraordinarily different from the women of my family in every way and notably so in her attitude to *me*, for she made comments *on* me *to* me, a thing which my family never did except when they said; 'You are a very bad girl to do that and you ought to know better.' Miss Jean did not tell me I was a bad girl, but she told me all sorts of queer things in those early days, such as that I was 'as Heilan' as peat', that I was 'old-fashioned as tea' and that I 'knew far more than was good for me'. And then, when I assured her that there was no peat in my part of the Highlands and that our fuel was mainly wood; that tea was not as old-fashioned as porridge when you came to think about it, and that my family said 'Nobody could ever be knowing too much and that was what education was for', she stared at me in a nonplussed way, which none of

21

my family ever did, gave a rippling laugh and then said philosophically and as if she were talking to herself: 'Och, well, when the school goes in she'll learn to get a wee bit mair like ither folk.' I found this the strangest comment of all and I longed to make a detailed inquiry into it, but I learned very early that there was no point in going into a question like that with Miss Jean. At the point where George or Tom would have sucked at their pipes and stared away into the distance before giving words to their considered opinions, Miss Jean would do her rippling laugh and say: 'I'll never get the parlour turned oot bletherin' tae *you* a' mornin'!' and disappear in a whirl of dusters, carpet brushes and furniture polish.

The house allotted to us was a pleasant one, built originally as a farm-house in the days when the farms in the valley were smaller and more numerous. It contained five rooms all told and had a low wing jutting out at the back which housed the more recently built scullery, bathroom, wash-house and coal-cellar. The house had garden plots on all sides and these were surrounded by a wall with an iron gate in the front on to the road and a little wooden gate at the back that led out on to a long, upward slope of rough grass with outcrops of rock here and there which was known as 'the Shaws hill'. This hill was part of the farm of Cairnshaws, but an unimportant part, for it was infertile and never used except to graze a flock of sheep. Nobody went up there, among its rocky gullies, its bracken, its big boulders and few scattered, wind-twisted trees, and I claimed it more or less for my own. From its summit, you could see a long way in every direction; I had been born and bred on the hill of Reachfar, so this green hill relieved the cramped feeling that could overtake me down there in the valley with its dominating stone cairn and its walls of grey rock.

In the course of that week at the end of August, before the school 'went in', I explored the hill very thoroughly, for I went there each day as soon as I had reduced Miss Jean to the dusters and furniture-polish stage, the which event took place progressively earlier each morning. When my father came home for mid-day dinner or tea about five-thirty, he would say: 'Well Janet, what have you been doing since I saw you last?'

And I would reply: 'I've been up the Hill, Dad.'

Then, Miss Jean would say, from her place at the end of the table: 'Aye, she's been up there by her lane a' day. Ah tellt her she should go an' play wi Annie but she widnae go.'

By about my fifth day at Cairnshaws, Annie was an irritating – though personally unknown – figure in my life. My hearsay knowledge of her, through Miss Jean, was that she was 'an awfu' nice an' bonnie wee lassie'; that she was the 'fair worshipped' only child of the owners of 'The Nether' which was the nearest farm to Cairnshaws and that she was about my own age. On the skeleton structure of these bare facts, Annie arose in my mind as a person of whom I was a little afraid, because she seemed to keep on being so different from myself all the time, for if she were 'bonnie', that made her different, for I was not particularly bonnie with my long colt's legs and long, straight plaits of hair and, of course, to be 'fair worshipped' made her more different still. In All My Born Days, in my family, I could not think of anyone who was 'fair worshipped' except God at church on Sundays and, indeed, I had felt sometimes that the Reverend Roderick Mackenzie, when worshipping, had been a little too fulsome and there was a chance that God might suspect him – and us who worshipped with him – of 'protesting too much' so that we would all be written down in Heaven's Big Black Book as a pack of hypocrites.

Out on the hill, when I thought about Annie, she would appear as a little angel with her 'bonnie fair curls', then she would change herself into a silly little thing that was 'sae prood o' a' her braw claes ye would hardly credit it', and then she would change herself again into 'Annie, that is sic a pride an' joy tae her folk', and the sum total of it all was that I was in a muddle about Annie, I did not want to hear any more of Annie and I was simply terrified of the day when I would have to meet Annie face to face.

At ten years old, I was much more shy and afraid of other

children than I was of grown-up people, because I had known fewer children than I had adults. The only child friend with whom I had played a great deal was My Friend Alasdair, our village doctor's youngest son, and even my playing with him had been limited to a few pranks on our way home from school during the last year. Alasdair was the late-coming 'tail-ender' of a large family, which gave him some of my own 'only child' status, while all the other children at Achcraggan School had been members of large families, which made them seem subtly different from myself. I do not know whether I was basically and by nature a 'solitary' or whether I became one by accident of my birth and upbringing in a remote place, but a 'solitary' I was and quite happy to be left so.

Life, however, does not leave people 'so'. No. Life seems to work on the principle that if someone is doing very nicely 'so', it has to poke that person in the ribs and see what she will do if she is placed in a 'thus' position for a change, and, at ten years old, Annie became my prevailing 'thus'.

The Saturday of my first week at Cairnshaws was a tremendously exciting day, for in the morning my father did not go to work at all but was dressed for 'going out' at breakfast and said to Miss Jean: 'The school clothes came all right, you said?'

'Aye,' she told him. 'They're a' ready for Tuesday.'

'She needs them today,' he said. 'I am taking her down to see the Rector.'

'Oh, she's better pit on her Sunday coat an' hat the day,' Miss Jean said.

'Why?' My father frowned thoughtfully at her and then: 'No. No, I don't think so, Jean. Let her put on the school clothes.'

'She cannae dae that!' Miss Jean protested. 'The ither bairns will a' be dressed—'

'Oh?' My father frowned again, puzzled, and I felt sorry for him because my mother was no longer with us to help him with these details and although Miss Jean was doing her best, that was not quite the same. She was 'different' from my mother and could not be relied upon not to be 'different' about things like what clothes to wear too, and my mother, I somehow knew, would not like me to be 'different' in Miss Jean's way.

'I would have thought it more suitable—' my father began again and then he turned to me: 'What do *you* think, Janet?'

I had never been asked for an opinion of this nature before. 'If I am going to the school,' I said slowly, 'surely I should wear my school clothes and not my church clothes?'

The worried look lifted from his face and he smiled: 'That sounds like reason. Give her the school clothes to put on, Jean.'

Miss Jean brought the cardboard box with the white blouses, the underwear and the dark green tunic to my bedroom and laid it on the bed and then she laid beside it the round, dark green hat with the badge in front and the dark green coat.

'There ye are,' she said and gave a frowning, irritated little sigh.

'Mind ye, ye'll no' be like ither folk,' she said and then she went away and left me to change.

Miss Jean was perfectly correct. When we arrived at the huge building and were taken by a man with a peaked cap that my father said was 'the Janitor' into a big hall and up the first flight of a staircase, we came into a room where there were about a dozen boys and girls, all dressed in obviously their best clothes, sitting with their mothers and fathers. At a desk in a corner, though, there was a lady in a dark skirt and a severe white blouse who looked less 'different' than the girls in their flower-trimmed hats and she rose and said good morning to us.

'And so, Mr Sandison, you have brought Janet Elizabeth?'

She looked down at me. She was very tall, with dark hair going grey at the sides and bright dark eyes. She was not a 'different' person like Miss Jean. She was more like the ladies who came to stay for the shooting with Lady Lydia at Poyntdale House, in spite of being so severely dressed.

'How do you do, Janet?' she asked.

I made my curtsy and held out my hand, but before I could speak, a little girl who was leaning against her mother's knee began to giggle. The lady took my hand and then looked over my head very sternly and said: 'No silly giggling here, please,' and the little girl's mother looked angry, gave her shoulders a shake and resettled her big handbag in her lap. The lady smiled at my father: 'You are punctual for your appointment, Mr Sandison. We'll go in. Mr Lindsay will be ready.'

She led us through another door and, all alone in here, in majesty, behind a large writing-table was Mr Lindsay, 'black robe on the top of his suit o' clothes' and all, but as we went in, he rose and came towards us and I saw that he had bright blue eyes and that he limped a little. He said good morning to my father, then pushed the robe back, put his hands in his trousers pockets, rocked to and fro from his heels to his toes a little, twinkled his blue eyes at me and said: 'Well, you have come a long, long way from the Highlands, haven't you, Janet?'

'Yes, sir.'

'And what did you see on the way?'

I told him there were so many things that I could not remember them all — 'but', I ended, 'I remembered a very, very queer thing this morning, sir.'

I saw my father give a little frown but Mr Lindsay said: 'Oh? And what was that, Janet?'

'I'll show you, sir.'

I picked up a pencil from his desk, whereupon he pulled a piece of paper towards me and he and the lady watched while I said: 'There was a big chimney like this just before we came to Glasgow and it had writing like this—' and having drawn the chimney, I wrote down it:

F
I
R
E

'Did you ever see writing going up and down like that instead of along, sir?' I inquired.

'Only once or twice,' he told me solemnly. 'Interesting, isn't it, Janet? And how did you like Glasgow?'

'I couldn't see it, sir. It was too dark and full of people and very, very dirty.'

'Janet, that will do,' said my father, but Mr Lindsay laughed like anything and sat down behind his table.

'Sit down, Mr Sandison. Well, Janet, we had a letter from Mr Stevenson at Achcraggan and from what he says we are going to put you into what we call the First Year, Higher Grade. I hear that you have been doing some Latin?'

'Yes, sir.'

He turned to my father. 'There are five sections in our First Year, Mr Sandison – classes according to the aptitude of the pupils and the parents' plans for them.'

'I have no particular plans for her, sir,' my father said. 'Her mother and I wanted her to have a good schooling and I would put her on to a University in time if you thought she was fit for it.'

'Good. That's easy.' He turned to the lady. 'Register her for 1A, Miss Hadley. Janet, when were you born?' I told him. 'And what is your address?'

'Reachfar, Achcraggan, Ross-shire, sir.'

'No. Not that one.'

I glanced at my father and understood what was meant. 'Oh, you mean Cairnshaws, Cairnton, by Glasgow, sir? All right, but, of course, Reachfar is my *proper* address.'

'Janet,' said my father firmly, 'that will do.'

When we came out with Miss Hadley into the other room again, there were more children and parents than ever in

27

there, and one group of father, mother and little girl was very noticeable because the girl had long fair curls and was be-ribboned, be-frilled and bedizened as if she were going to a party.

'Good morning, Mr Sandison,' the father said to mine.

''Morning, Mr Black,' my father replied.

'And this is your wee girl, the wee soul?' said Mrs Black, staring at me, and then she interrupted her own stare in a curiously rude way, turned to Miss Hadley and said: 'Can we go in? We've been waiting about half-an-hour already.'

'I am sorry,' said Miss Hadley. 'Quite a number of people are ahead of you. We *do* ask parents to make appointments, you know.'

'Come, Janet,' my father said. 'Good day, Miss Hadley, and thank you.'

'Good morning, Mr Sandison. Tuesday morning, Janet – remember!' She smiled and went away to speak to a mother with a little boy.

When we were out of the, to me, sacred precincts and on to the street, I said to my father: 'Dad, was that Annie?'

'Who?'

'The little girl with all the ribbons with Mrs Black?'

'Is Annie the Black bairn's name? Aye, that would be her, likely. Didn't Miss Jean say she was going to the Academy too? Aye, that would be Annie. You've never been over to play with her yet?'

I wondered if my father also thought it desirable that I should play with Annie. 'No, Dad.'

'But you haven't been wearying, though?'

'Oh, no, Dad! – Dad, would you have time to come for a Look Round up my hill tomorrow when it's Sunday?'

'I would like that just grand,' he said with enthusiasm and I felt that it was all right about Annie.

It was nearly dinner-time when we got back to the house and Miss Jean was bustling about cheerfully, laying the table. Miss Jean talked a great deal more than the women of my family – indeed, she talked so much that my grandmother would probably call her a 'clip cloots' I thought, for when I asked too many questions, my grandmother always said:

'Be quiet, now! That tongue of yours would clip cloots!' or: 'Be quiet with your ask, ask, asking! You'll have your tongue worn as thin as a threepenny bit!' So, Miss Jean talked all the time she was laying the table and then, as soon as my father had said grace, almost before the 'Amen', she said: 'Did you see the Blacks? They went doon by the road jist aboot hauf-an-'oor efter ye left. They said they were takin' Annie for her interview.'

'Aye, we saw them outside Mr Lindsay's room,' my father said.

'Did you see Annie?' Miss Jean asked me.

'Yes,' I said.

'And did you see the nice dress *she* had on?'

'Yes,' I said. 'And blue bows in her hair and white shoes.'

Miss Jean looked at my father triumphantly. 'There ye are!' she said. 'Ah *tellt* ye!'

My father stared thoughtfully out of the window for a moment before he said: 'Well, I'm no judge of these things, but I thought the bairn looked kind of out of place, myself.'

Miss Jean sniffed. 'I suppose things are different if ye're Heilan',' she said, but as she served the milk pudding she was off again: 'Anyway, Annie's a nice wee thing an' ye'll see her this efternune, Janet, because Mrs Black has asked us doon for a cup o' tea.'

My heart sank and I looked up the table at my father, searching for guidance.

'That is very kind of Mrs Black,' he said, which made me realized that I had to go.

It turned out, however, to be very interesting at Nethercairn as long as we were at the tea-table in the cosy, over-furnished parlour. The parlour itself was of surpassing interest, for it contained more ornaments than I had ever seen in All My Born Days and there were no less than three lots of curtains and a blind on the window. The blind was close to the glass and had a deep edge of crochet lace; then, progressing inwards, came a pair of frilly muslin curtains that were wide at the top and came to a point at the bottom; then, inside those, came two long lace curtains hitched back with pink ribbon bows and then, inside those, long red velvet curtains, hitched back with green embroidered bands. The floor was as decently clad as the window, having a layer of linoleum which showed only at the edges, then a carpet on top and then a number of rugs on top of the carpet. When you took into account the serried ranks of pictures on the walls, I thought, what My Friend Tom would call 'the usable, breathin' size' of the room was considerably reduced. There was, however, plenty to eat on the table among the embroidered tea-cloth, lace doilies and fancy china, so I ate a considerable amount with concentration and was only half-aware of the conversation for a long time, until Mrs Black said: ' – jumped-up incomer, that's all he is. It was Hill at Cairnshaws and them that voted him in there. It was this Lindsay and Willie Begg that belongs to the Toon that was on the short leet for the Rector's job an' it was Willie Begg that belongs here that should have got it. Well, I just told him to his face today – Annie is rising thirteen, I said, and it's time she was moved up, I said, and moved up she's going to *be*, I said, even if I have to see the Commy*tee* about it, I said.'

'And what did he say?' Miss Jean asked.

'Oh, he gave in in the end. Very uppish, of course. It is against my advice, says he, but she's *your* daughter. I know that, says I, and I'm not in need o' your advice. The im*pid*ence!'

I glanced sidewise at Annie, who was beside me at the table, to see what she was thinking about all this, for it must all be dreadful for her. I was careful not to let her see me look, for I was sure that she must be suffering black, burning disgrace at being a person who had been 'kept back' at school so that her mother had to ask the Rector that she be 'moved up', but I need not have taken such great care to be unobserved. Annie was not paying any attention to her mother and Miss Jean. She had taken the lace doily from an empty plate, folded it into a semicircle and had put it round her arm so that the frill of lace fell over her pretty wrist with its gold bracelet. With a look of blissful content on her angelic face, she was turning her dainty, dimpled hand this way and that, admiring it.

'And how old are *you*, Janet? Mrs Black asked me.

'Ten and a half, Mrs Black.'

'The poor wee motherless soul,' she said aside to Miss Jean.

This made me very, very angry. I was *not* poor, for not any Sandison of Reachfar was ever poor or in need of pity and certainly no Sandison would accept pity, even if in need, from a fat, loud-voiced person like Mrs Black.

'She's as auld-fashioned as tea,' said Miss Jean. 'But what can ye expect? Brocht up away up there?'

'Och, she'll alter,' said Mrs Black complacently, 'when she gets to the school and gets among the rest and you get her dressed more natural.'

I became still angrier. Annie was, I supposed, what they meant by 'dressed natural', but my mother would never have approved of clothes like that. 'Plain clothes are always best,' my mother used to say, 'especially for someone like you with long legs and straight hair. And it is always better for clothes – or anything else – to be too plain rather than too fancy.' My mother was always right. I had never known her to be wrong about anything and she was *still* right although she was no longer here. What was wrong with this room we were in was that it was far too 'fancy', so that it was piled up, layers deep, to a stifling degree in fanciness.

'Yes, very nice,' Miss Jean was saying. 'And eats everything – very easy to please. Terrible careful an' thrifty, of coorse, but I aye heard Heilan' folk were like that. Never thinks o' the Pictures in the Toon or onything – he's never been twice in a picture-hoose, he tellt me. Jist imagine!'

They were talking of my father now.

'What can ye expect?' said Mrs Black. 'There's nothing much up there where they come frae but heather. Annie, pet, are ye not goin' to take Janet up an' show her your dolls?'

Annie looked at me and I looked at Annie. No two people could have been less interested in one another.

'That's right,' said Miss Jean. 'Away ye go, the two o' ye, an' have a nice play.'

We went upstairs together to a big bedroom which was even more be-frilled and be-curtained than the parlour we had

31

left and which contained more dolls than I had ever seen in one place in All My Born Days. I do not remember Annie speaking a word to me, nor did I speak a word to her. She waved a hand at the dolls, then sat down at a small, frilly dressing-table and began to comb her long, ash-blonde ringlets, combing them out, one by one, lovingly, and then retwining them into long tubes round her pretty fingers. I looked about me with interest, although I was not interested in the dolls, for although I had a room at Reachfar and another one, now, at Cairnshaws, I had never seen a room like this one. *My* rooms had in them a bed, a chair, a chest of drawers and a cupboard and, after that, they had in them things that I had brought there, such as my books, a jar of flowers I had picked, my school satchel and some odds and ends, such as my Big Dish for growing my winter hyacinths in (at Reachfar), or the queer-shaped stone I had found on the hill (at Cairnshaws). I had never before been in a room that looked and felt as if it had been specially built round the idea of someone as this room looked and felt, and the queer thing about it was that the room looked and felt different from what Annie looked and felt, so that, in a queer way, they did not match and the idea behind the room felt all wrong. It was all very interesting, but odd, in a queer way that I could not explain even to myself, so, having examined the room in detail, I returned my attention to Annie.

She had finished with her ringlets for the moment and was taking off her dress. She pulled it over her head, dropped it on the floor and went over to a wardrobe with a full-length mirror in its door, where she stood gazing at herself for a moment, turning this way and that. She was about my height, for I had always been tall for my age, but Annie was more pink and white than I was and, where my arms and legs were long and bony, Annie's were rounded and plump and boneless-looking. As I watched her, she opened the wardrobe where what seemed to me to be hundreds of dresses depended from pink and blue hangers and she began to leaf through them as one would search for a book on a shelf. At last, she made up her mind, took down a pink dress with many frills and a long sash and laid it on the bed. She then returned to the wardrobe, closed the door and had another long look at herself in the glass. This time, she raised her plump arms above her head, pushed her chest out, leaned close and made a careful inspection of her reflection. Then, I think, she spoke for the first time.

'Have you got hair?' she inquired.

'Of course I have!' I said, leaning forward and jerking so that my long pigtails swung to the front, one on each shoulder. 'Are you blind?'

'You're daft!' she said. 'I don't mean *that*. Look *here*!'

She pointed to her naked armpit where a few hairs were visible.

'Oh, that!' I said. 'Everybody gets that when they grow up!'

'They do not! – It's only girls that the *boys* like that get it!'

'That's a pack of lies!'

'It is *not*!'

'It is!'

'It isn't!'

'It is! And you're just a silly vain little brat!'

'I am *not*! Mah-mee!' yelled Annie. *'Mah-mee-ee!'*

In a rush, Mrs Black and Miss Jean were in the room.

'What is it, pettie?' Mrs Black gathered her ewe lamb to her bosom.

'What's wrong wi' Mammy's lassie? What did she do to ye?'

'She *hit* me!' said Annie, crying now, beautifully, with large crystal tears welling from her blue eyes to flow down over the smooth pink and white cheeks.

'Janet!' said Miss Jean. 'I'm black affrontit at ye and Annie showin' ye her nice dolls an' a' her lovely dresses! Say you're sorry!'

I called into my mind the thought of My Grandmother at Reachfar. I silently asked the tall vision of her what to do in this predicament and with calm certainty the answer came into my mind and decidedly and coldly the words left my lips: 'Annie tells lies. I want to go home, please. Thank you for the nice tea, Mrs Black. Good day.'

I ran down the stairs, out of the house, and then really

took to my heels and did not stop until I was safely in a nice cranny on the side of my hill above our own house. For the first hundred yards or so, down the road from Nethercairn, I had heard Miss Jean's voice calling after me, but I took no notice. I was not going to answer any questions until my father was present and, even then, I decided, only such questions as I thought fit, for Tom and George, my Friends, had told me that I must try to be a good girl 'and not be a worry in any way' to my father.

'If you ask me,' said Miss Jean, about two hours later, 'she's a thrawn, determined little brat!'

'Nobody asked you, Jean,' said my father. 'Just clear the table.'

Miss Jean shook her shoulders, pursed up her mouth angrily, but began to carry the supper dishes through to the scullery. As she came back for a second trayful, she said: 'Annie is such a nice wee thing. It's a pity she had to go and fight with Annie the first time they—'

'Bairns often fight. There's no need for grown-up people to make fools of themselves too.'

'But you cannae *blame* Mrs Black for bein' angry! An' Annie would ha' been such a nice wee pal for her! She has to have *some*body like hersel'!'

'Like myself?' I thought miserably, for I *was* miserable, for here was my father being worried after all.

'Och, maybe Janet can manage without Annie,' he said easily.

He did not sound too worried, which was comforting. 'Yes, Dad. I can manage fine!' I encouraged him.

'That's right,' he said and clapped me on the bottom. 'Off you go to bed now.'

'But what am Ah tae dae aboot Mrs Black?' said Miss Jean shrilly.

'Do? Och, well, you'll just have to manage the best way you can, Jean. We are not in debt to Mrs Black in any way.'

'She's a neebor — an' somebody tae speak tae!' Jean protested, the butterdish in one hand and the jam in the other.

My father opened his evening newspaper. 'Och, well, I

34

hope she hasn't been knocked altogether speechless,' he said and began to read.

Miss Jean sniffed and went into the scullery, pointedly closing the door behind her. My father looked at me over the top of his paper:

'Janet, you are *sure* you didn't hit that Annie?'

'Quite sure, Dad.'

'So it was honestly a lie she told?'

'Yes, Dad.'

'All right. Get off to your bed. We'll have a big walk on the hill tomorrow. Goodnight.'

'Goodnight, Dad.'

I put myself to bed and lay comfortably thinking of my cranny on the hill and my 'Thinking Place' among the fir trees in the home moor at Reachfar and other favourite thoughts and then I made a 'song' before I went to sleep. It was a spiteful ditty, but it must have been a comfort to me, for I went to sleep after writing it down on the fly-leaf of my *Alice in Wonderland*, and it is only because it is written down there that I am able to quote it word for word, now. You may realize, if you read to the end of this book, why I have taken the trouble to quote it at all:

'Annie is a lying girl and Annie is a fool,
And Annie is a dunce because she was kept back at
   school.
Annie is a bonnie girl with long and curly hair,
But the awful thing about it is that Annie doesn't care.
She does not care if telling lies might cause her Mother
   worry,
She does not care if other folk are told to say they're
   sorry
For something that they did not do. No. Annie does
   not care.
For Annie's mind can only think that she is getting
   hair!'

CHAPTER THREE

My father and I had our walk the next day – the fore-runner of many Sunday walks – and I remember it, in particular, as the beginning of my adult relationship with my father, who, hitherto, had been a distant member of the grown-up world whom I loved and respected, but did not expect to pay any attention to *me* or to take part in my world. I was much impressed, now, to find not only that he was prepared to pay attention to me, but that he was also prepared to share a world with me, and that the sharing should take place through a relationship on *his* level, as if I were an adult – what I called in my mind 'a real, grown-up person'.

Not only did he expect me to have opinions – he was also prepared to listen to them. We climbed to the top of the hill, sat down and he took out his pipe and his tobacco.

'You like Miss Jean?' he asked.

This question was typical of the new relationship. Hitherto, I had never been asked for an opinion about a grown-up person and had I volunteered such an opinion at Reachfar, I would have been given very short shrift.

'She is very nice,' I said, 'but Different, of course.' This was added cautiously, because I did not want to 'worry' him in any way.

'She is a fine cook and very good about the house,' he said.

'Oh, yes!' I was learning the weather of the grown-up world now.

Miss Jean was what My Friend Tom had called a 'housekeeper leddy'.

'And she is a grand baker!' I added with enthusiasm.

'Aye.' He stared out across the countryside. 'She's kind

36

of simple, of course. Nearly foolish about some things, you would think, but never heed her.'

This 'nearly foolishness' was something of what I meant by 'different'.

'Why is she like that, Dad?'

'I don't know right. I think myself that people that has always been near the town and the pictures and the shops and had things always made easy for them get kind of foolish like that. It's rich country, this – not like Reachfar. Coal and quarries and all. The people here get their living easy – even the farmers with their milk for Glasgow – they don't have to think much about it, so they'll be thinking a lot about the picture-house and lace curtains and hair ribbons. I think it's something of that that is in it, whatever. But a person doesn't have to take any notice. Mr Lindsay is a fine man, isn't he?'

'Yes, Dad. And I liked the lady – who is she?'

'She is the head lady teacher, I am told, and next to Mr Lindsay at the head of the Academy.'

'Dad, Mrs Black fought with Mr Lindsay yesterday.'

'*Fought* with him? What about?'

'Because he wanted to keep Annie back.'

'Oh? Mrs Black must be a foolish kind of craitur. Well, if *you* are ever kept back, I'll not be down there fighting about it, mind, so you'd better try not to be kept back.'

'I'll try, Dad.'

He looked at his watch. 'It will soon be time for the afternoon milking. You haven't seen the dairy yet – like to come over with me?'

'Yes, Dad.'

We came down the hill, past our own house and went along to the big farm, where I had not been before because My Friend George had counselled me not to go 'sticking my nose in' when my father was at work and I had remembered this. We went into the biggest, longest byre that I had ever seen, with twenty cows down each side, and it was full of the smell of milk and the sound of cows chewing, mingled with the foamy spurt of milk flowing into

37

six pails under the hands of six milkers in white overalls.

'Mercy me!' I said. 'What a lot of cows!'

My father smiled. 'There's another two byres this size as well.' He turned aside to the man who was standing near a row of big churns. 'Put that cigarette out, Garvey. I won't tell you again,' he said quietly, and the man looked sulky but threw the cigarette into the wet gutter. 'Do you know this breed of cattle, Janet?'

'Ayrshires?'

'That's right.'

'Ugly brutes!' I said, quoting My Friend Tom, for whom the Aberdeen Angus, the Shorthorn and the Highland are the only breeds of cattle worthy of the name.

My father laughed. 'Look at the milk, though!'

The milk was unbelievable. A boy was employed constantly going from milker to milker, exchanging an empty bucket for a full one topped with white froth.

'But who *drinks* all that milk, Dad?'

'Glasgow,' he said. 'Do ye remember all yon miles and miles of houses and all yon thousands and thousands of people when we came through? And not a cow in all the miles of it. Aye, the Glasgow bairns have to get their milk from somewhere.'

'But how?'

'As soon as the milking is over, the lorries will come round and take the cans down to the station and put them on the train. The Glasgow bairns will get this milk for their breakfast. Then, when we milk tomorrow morning, it will be the same thing again and the Glasgow bairns will have it for their supper.'

'Mercy me!'

'Come and see the young heifers.'

This tour, of course, was in actual fact my father's evening inspection of his charge, for, as a family, we have never been able to work at any job for pay without treating it as if the enterprise were our own and the profits entirely ours. The attitude was summed up by my father on the occasion when he sacked the sullen, cigarette-smoking Garvey, when he said: 'Be off! Come-night, come-ninepence men are not the kind I want!'

We were just about to go home when Mr and Mrs Hill came round the end of the dairy buildings, walking very slowly, and I remembered that My Friend Tom had said that Mr Hill had been wounded in the war. He did not lack an arm or a leg, like the soldiers who used to come as convalescents to Poyntdale House, nor did he limp a little like Mr Lindsay, but he looked very, very sick and delicate. His skin was a waxy, yellow colour and his grey eyes were sunk in deep, dark hollows in his thin face.

'Good evening, Mrs Hill,' my father said. 'Good evening, Mr Hill.'

'And this is the wee girl, Mr Sandison?' Mrs Hill said.

'Yes. This is Janet.'

I made my curtsy. 'What a nice wee thing!' said Mrs Hill.

They *were* 'different' sort of people, I thought, in this part of the country. My father would be right – it was too much milk and going to the pictures that did it, probably. Nobody at Reachfar would think of referring to a person as a 'nice wee thing' in that way!

'And how do you like being at Cairnshaws?' she asked next.

'Quite well, thank you,' I replied.

'And are you going to the school?'

'Yes, to the Academy, on Tuesday.'

'What a shame! No more playtime until Christmas!'

I did not say anything. I could think of nothing to say, for never in All My Born Days had I heard a grown-up person say it was a shame to be going to school.

My attention was distracted by the arrival of a big, fat boy on a bicycle, who rode almost between us all before jumping off.

'This is Tommie,' said Mrs Hill. 'Tommie goes to school in Glasgow and he's going back on Tuesday too. Tommie, this is Janet, Mr Sandison's wee girl.'

Tommie glowered at me and did a long pinging peal on his bicycle bell.

39

'Been out for a run on your bike, Tommie?' my father asked.

'Iphm,' said Tommie, did another ping, gave his bicycle a push, jumped on and rode away.

I was dumbfounded. If I, at Reachfar, had dared to say 'Iphm' like that in reply to a question, there would have been a bother of fearsome magnitude, but Mrs Hill simply gave a tinkly little laugh and said: 'Boys will be boys!'

This struck me as being inordinately silly. It was so obvious that a boy could not be other than a boy. The tired-looking Mr Hill, who had not spoken until now, said: 'The place is looking a lot better, Mr Sandison.'

'It's coming on a little, Mr Hill,' my father said in a comforting sort of voice, 'and it'll be a lot better yet before we're done with it.'

On the way back to our own house, I asked: 'Is Mr Hill still sick with his wound?'

'Yes,' my father said.

'Where is it?'

'Inside him – in his lungs. He got some of this poison gas, poor man.'

'I am glad you weren't at the war, Dad.

He stopped and looked away over the green pastures of the valley.

'It was Sir Torquil that got me kept at home to grow corn and tatties.'

He sighed. 'Maybe it was as well. I doubt if I would have been much use at the war anyway. I hate fighting and rows between people.'

And then we walked back to the house and our supper.

On Tuesday morning when school opened, the face of my small world changed again and so much seemed to happen in a week that my memory is blurred like a crowded landscape seen from an express train. When I set out with my satchel in the morning, I found that this was not at all like the field paths between Reachfar and Achcraggan where, for most of my three and three-quarter miles to school, I was the only child on the way. No. Here, the road was dotted with people from the age of five up to what seemed to me to be 'grown-up people' of seventeen and eighteen and I would not have believed that they were going to school at all but for the satchels of the male ones and the attaché-cases of the female ones. Nobody spoke to me, for which I was grateful, and I arrived at the school gates alone. I felt a little lost, now, in the big playground which was full of groups of boys and girls, until my attention was attracted by a boy of about my own age, with a new satchel on his back, who was squatting down talking to a mongrel dog. I had been missing my own collie, Fly, a little during this past week, so I went closer.

'No, Paddy,' the boy was saying to the sad-eyed mongrel. 'You know fine that you don't get coming to the school.'

'Is that your dog?' I asked.

'Aye. He's needing to come in to the school. He's aye like this for the first week after the holidays.'

'Poor Paddy fellow!' I said.

As my American Friend Martha says: 'Nothing like a dawg for recognizing a sucker for a dawg', so Paddy turned his sad liquid eyes on me and held up a hairy paw. I squatted down too and patted the drooping head.

'What's your name?' the boy asked.

'Janet Sandison. What's yours?'

'Hughie Reid.'

'Have you been to this school before?' I asked.

'Och, aye. Since I was five. I'm to go up to the First Year now, though.'

'So am I.'

'Come on, you two!' said a male, authoritative voice and I looked up to see the peaked cap of the janitor. 'Iphm, so Paddy's here again. All right, Hughie. Run in and I'll take Paddy back to your Granny.'

'Come on,' Hughie said to me and then I noticed a very odd thing. The boy had no left arm and the empty sleeve of his jacket was neatly pinned into the side pocket.

I do not remember a great deal about my first week at the Academy except that, at frequent intervals, Hughie said: 'Come on!' and I came. In the classrooms, the teachers

41

would say: 'Boys that side and girls this side,' but at the end of the lesson, or at a break, Hughie would be in the corridor outside with his 'Come on!' Without Hughie I would never have been present at a quarter of the places where I was supposed to be, for I had never been in a building so large, never among so many people, and although I was what was known as 'clever at the school', I was a very slow-witted child who became easily dazed in the midst of crowds, noise and bustle of any kind. Indeed, the child being mother of the woman, I can still lose my way with great ease inside a building, though never out-of-doors, and the crowd, noise and bustle of a large cocktail party can render me deaf, dumb and senseless in a way that the cocktails themselves never could.

When we came out of our class-room for lunch on the first day, however, Hughie said: 'Are you going with the rest of the lassies to eat your dinner? Because if you are, you have to go *that* way,' and he pointed to a lobby which was full of chattering girls of all ages.

'Where are *you* going?' I asked.

'Home,' said Hughie.

'Oh!' I looked at him.

'Come on,' said Hughie.

Carrying my satchel which contained my sandwiches in its front compartment, I came on beside Hughie down the road a little way to a small, detached cottage with a strip of garden in front. It had a door in the middle, a window on each side of the door and two dormer windows in the slate roof. It was an older building than most of the others I had so far seen in the town and when I went inside, behind Hughie, it was the most remarkable house I had ever been in, for one end of the downstairs was a shop, with rows of sweet-bottles, tins of biscuits and trays of pancakes, scones and toffee apples on the counter beside a set of shining brass scales. Behind the counter was a pink-cheeked old lady in a white apron.

'Granny,' said Hughie, '*she's* from far away and she's never been in a town before so I brought her home to eat her dinner.'

'*She* is the cat's mother,' said Granny. 'What's your name, pet?'

'Janet Sandison, Mrs Reid.'

'Och, aye.' She smiled. 'Your father has come to the Shaws?'

'Yes.'

'There now. That's fine. Hughie, for goodness' sake go ben and let Paddy out before he breaks the door! And are Hughie and you in the same class?'

'Yes, Mrs Reid.'

'That's fine. Och, well, you'll get your dinner with Hughie an' me in a wee while.'

'I *have* my dinner, I said, patting my satchel.

'That's fine. Then you'll give us a wee taste o' yours and we'll give you a wee taste of ours.'

By way of striking the bargain, I took out my packet of sandwiches and bottle of milk and handed them over the counter.

'My, that's fine! Just you run ben to Hughie while I serve the school bairns with their sweeties and then we'll get our dinner.'

From the other window, which had pots of geraniums on the sill, I watched the school children in twos and threes come up the path with their pennies, and a brisk trade in toffee-apples, scones and jam, sweets and slabs of toffee went on for about half-an-hour and then Granny turned the key firmly in the door as she came past from the shop end to this cheerful kitchen where Hughie, Paddy and I were.

'That's fine,' she said, beginning to lay the table. 'We'll soon get our dinner now.'

She opened my packet of egg and lettuce sandwiches and put some on each of the three plates, she shared the milk between Hughie and me and filled three large plates with soup from the pot on the fire.

'Come now,' she said. 'We're real stylish the day with sandwiches to our soup instead of just plain bread.'

The soup was very good and when we had finished it we each had a large plateful of milk pudding and stewed rhubarb and then Hughie and I were told to go to the shop end and choose two sweets each.

'That's fine,' she said then. 'Run away back to school now and come and see me the morn, Janet.'

'It was a splendid dinner, Granny,' I told her, 'and thank you very much.'

I meant this, for I have always been a great appreciator of good food.

When school was over at quarter-to-four in the afternoon, I suggested to Hughie that we might fetch Paddy and go for a walk before I went home, but he rather hurt me by saying: 'No. You'd better just get away home.'

'Why, Hughie?'

'Your folk'll be wondering where you are when it's your first day.'

I had to agree that this might be true. 'Another day, though, Hughie?'

He kicked a stone with the toe of his tackety boot. 'I don't know. You see, I have the papers.'

'What's the papers?'

And then he explained to me that before he came to school in the morning and after he came out in the afternoon, he and Paddy went all over the town delivering newspapers.

'Could I not be helping?' I inquired.

He stared at me. 'You would have to ask your folk first,' he said and then suddenly ran away from me down the road that led to the nice house with the shop.

I too went home, thinking of my new friends and this first exciting day, but I did not go by the road where all the other pupils were, shouting and kicking balls and clouting one another with their satchels. I had observed that by climbing a fence, crossing a field or two and going through a small wood, I ought to emerge somewhere on my hill near the back of our own garden, and, sure enough, I did, having found on the way a most delightful place, a disused quarry, but a much bigger one than the Old Quarry on the ground of Reachfar. This quarry had a big, deep, block loch in the centre and a towering cliff of greyish-black stone. It was a

weird, uncanny place, but very pleasant in a shivery kind
of way. By the time I arrived home, my father was home
from work and it was suppertime.

'Well, Janet,' he said, 'and what sort of day did you have?'

I told him all about the Academy and how, at the end of
each class, we moved to another room to have the next
lesson, and how Latin was in Room I and French in Room
IV and Mathematics in Room IX.

'And you found your way all right in that big place?'
he asked.

'Hughie helped me.'

'Oh? And who is Hughie?'

'A boy that has a dog called Paddy and only one arm.'

'Well, Ah'm blesst!' said Miss Jean. 'It's Auld Sweetie
Maggie's Hughie she's talkin' aboot!'

'And is Hughie in your class?' my father asked, taking
no notice of Miss Jean in a pronounced way.

'Yes,' I said, 'and his name is Hugh William Reid.' I added
with emphasis, looking at Miss Jean, to indicate that it is
not polite to refer to people by names like 'Sweetie Maggie's
Hughie', but Miss Jean did not seem to notice. 'And I had
my dinner at Hughie's house, Dad.'

'Well, Ah'm blesst!' said Miss Jean again.

'But you mustn't do that, Janet,' my father said. 'You
mustn't go and be bothering Hughie's mother at your
dinner-time.'

'He hasn't got a mother – just a granny – and she said
I was to come again tomorrow. And she's nice. And we had
soup and semolina and stewed rhubarb and my sandwiches
and two sweeties from the shop afterwards.'

'You mean you *shared* Hughie's dinner?' My father
frowned.

'Yes, and they shared mine.'

'Well,' said Miss Jean, 'I never heard the like!'

'Do you know Hughie and his granny, Jean?' my father
asked.

Miss Jean sniffed in a superior way. '*Every*body kens auld
Sweetie Maggie!' she said. 'She keeps the wee shop near the

45

shule where the bairns buy their sweeties.' She looked across the table in a way that meant that she was about to mention something that ought not to be mentioned in the hearing of people of my age. 'As for wee Hughie – he was her dochter Jeanie's bairn, but Jeanie dee'd when he was born. Hughie was aye an objeck, wi' jist the wan airm – folk never expectit him tae live – but auld Maggie focht for him in spite o' the disgrace. Auld Maggie's aye been kin' o' saft an' no' like ither folk.'

'I see,' said my father and turned to me. 'And who else did you get to know at school besides Hughie, Janet?'

'Nobody yet, Dad. Just Hughie.'

'What about Annie?' Miss Jean asked. 'You and her should be speakin' again – ye're only bairns. Did she no' speak to ye?'

'Oh, yes. In the cloakroom. But I am not in Annie's class,' I told her.

'She's in the First Year Higher Grade!' said Miss Jean indignantly. 'Her mother tellt me on Setterday that she was! Dae ye mean tae say that that man hasnae moved her up efter a'?'

'Mr Lindsay, Jean!' said my father sharply.

'Yes, Annie's in the First Year,' I broke in hastily. 'Yes, she's been moved up.'

'An' *you* are in the First Year so ye are *so* in the same class!' snapped Jean.

I realized that if I said that Annie was in IE, the section of the First Year that also had the frightening girl with the slobbery nose and the mouth that hung open as if she could not remember to close it, I would get into deeper and still more dangerous waters, so I allowed the entire subject to drop and engaged the attention of my father with a description of the ceremony of morning prayers in the school hall.

After supper, when my father had gone out into the garden, Miss Jean trapped me in the scullery where she was washing dishes and said, 'I'm fair surprised at ye tellin' lies like that aboot wee Annie Black!'

'What lies?' I asked.

'Saying she wasnae in the First Year.'

'I didn't say that,' I said, 'What I—'

'Ye wicked wee leear!' she broke in. 'Ye did so!'

'I'm *not* a liar!' I was very angry at her interrupting me, giving me no chance to explain, and I now made up my mind that I *would* not explain. 'I am *not* a liar,' I repeated, 'and you are just an ignorant fool talking about something you know nothing about.'

'The im*pid*ence!' she said and I ignored her and marched defiantly to the back door. 'You're a thrawn bad wee besom!' she called after me. 'An' ye are *so* in Annie's class!'

I went into the garden and slammed the door shut in case my father would hear her, full of resentment and ashamed at her lack of dignity in calling after me like that as if she were a street child. My father was away at the far end of the garden, completely unconscious of the incident and, thereafter, the subject was never re-opened. Jean, at table, persistently referred to Annie and myself as being in the same class, in a baiting way, but out of some innate cussedness I would never rise to the bait. As far as the five sections of the First Year went, Jean always remained in ignorance.

During my first week at the Academy, I continued to be directed by Hughie and I continued to go home with him at dinner-time and contribute my carried sandwiches and milk to the family pool, for, each day, Granny sent me off after lunch with the words: 'And mind an' come in with Hughie the morn, Janet!' but I was still coming home by my quarry route without being allowed to accompany Hughie and Paddy on their paper-delivery round. I had said no more on this subject to Hughie, because I intended to discuss it on Sunday with my father when, I hoped, we would have another walk on the hill and Miss Jean would not be there. When Hughie and I came out of school on the Friday, however, who should be at the gates but my father.

'Hello there,' he said. 'And is this your friend Hugh?'

'Hello, Dad. Hughie, this is my father.'

'How are you, Mr Sandison?' said Hughie, holding out his hand.

'Fine, man, fine,' said my father, shaking hands. 'I was in the town on a little business for Mr Hill so I thought Janet and I could walk home together. But I thought we would buy some sweeties first.'

'Hughie's Granny has nice sweeties, Dad!'

'Come on,' said Hughie.

Hitherto, Granny Reid's shop had seemed to me to be quite a large place, but when my big father was standing at the counter it seemed to be much smaller, and I suddenly noticed that Granny too was a very small old lady as she stood looking up at him.

'This is my father, Granny, and he wants to buy some sweeties.'

'That's fine,' she said. 'How are ye, Mr Sandison? I'm real pleased to meet ye.'

'And I've been needing to see *you*, Mrs Reid, for I hear that this one of mine has been bothering you quite a bit.'

'Ach, away, She's no bother! Her and Hughie gets on like a hoose on fire. Look, come on ben and get a cup o' tea, Mr Sandison. It's just my time for a fly cup before the papers come in.'

We all trooped through to the room with the geraniums in the window and my father shook hands with Paddy before sitting down in the big armchair by the fire.

When he had drunk a cup of tea and had eaten a piece of Granny's excellent gingerbread, he said in the shy way of the men of my family: 'Mrs Reid, I am not very used to the ways of the people about here and I don't want you to be offended, but I wondered if we could come to a kind of arrangement.'

'I'm no' easy to take offence, Mr Sandison, when folk means well,' said Granny.

'Well, it's this way. The one thing that I'm not pleased about with Janet's schooling here is this business of a few sandwiches for her dinner. Of course, my housekeeper has a dinner for her at night, but I would rather that she had a right meal in the middle of the day, and there's nothing in the town but the fish-and-chip places and the hotel. Would it be a nuisance to you to give her her dinner every schoolday? You must be busy with your toffee-making and your shop and all—'

'Och, I'm never too busy! It's not that – it's – well, Hughie and me doesnae live very fancy, Mr Sandison – that's the truth of it.'

'Janet isn't used to anything fancy,' he said.

'Please, Granny, have me for my dinner!' I said.

'Come on, Granny!' said Hughie.

'Away oot the back an' play, both o' ye!' she said with a laugh. 'And let me speak to my visitor in peace. It's no' often I get a visitor.'

Hughie said. 'Come on!' and I came, but as we closed the back door he said, 'It's all right. She's going to say you can come. Come on down to the burn!'

And so it was arranged that I went five days a week to Granny Reid for my dinner and my father visited her every Friday, with a 'present' – some eggs, some boiled ham from the butcher of which she was very fond or a dressed fowl for her Sunday dinner – and, at the same time, he bought some sweeties. He used to tender what I called 'a lot of pennies' for the sweets and never took any change across the counter, but I did not connect this money in any way, at that time, with my dinners. I have told you already that I was a slow-witted child. It did not occur to me then that hospitality could be sold and I now *know* that it cannot. The hospitality I received from Granny Reid was not bought with the few shillings extra that my father paid for the sweets – it was something that came from her heart and that no money could buy.

The arrangement suited all parties admirably, with the exception of Miss Jean, who sniffed and said: 'It's no' the thing at a'!' When pinned by the ears against the wall (to use the idiom of my friend Twice) on this statement of hers, she never could explain exactly why there was a fault in the arrangement, but simply became quarrelsome and said: 'Ither *folk* widnae send their bairns tae get their dinners there!' Further pinning of her ears to the wall did us no good and got us no further, so my father and I gave up and I continued to have my dinners in comfort and with great pleasure at Granny Reid's.

Hughie and I continued to go from class to class together in school – separating only for gymnastics – and in school we were a force to be reckoned with, for we both had an equal aptitude for the absorption of learning. Out of school, we became a force to be reckoned with still more seriously.

After discussion with my father, I was allowed to stay one evening to 'do the papers' with Hughie and when I arrived home, and Miss Jean discovered what I had been doing, there was a tremendous sniffing and a large volume of acid comment which was stopped in the end by my father opening his newspaper and saying: 'Honest work never hurt anybody', and beginning to read with exaggerated concentration. But he had no idea, just then, of the 'honest work' that had been done that September evening. By this time, I should mention that I had prevailed on my father to the extent of having had my collie Fly sent down from Reachfar with a label in My Friend Tom's handwriting attached to her collar, in spite of Miss Jean's protest that 'a dug wid mak' sic a mess o' the hoose', and on the big day when I was to be allowed to 'do the papers', Fly went with me to Granny Reid's and stayed there while I went to school. In the evening, she and Paddy, Hughie and I set out on the paper round. I felt with pride that I was a really well-equipped paper-deliverer, now that I had my dog, for Hughie had impressed on me in some oblique way that he would never dream of delivering the papers unless he was accompanied by Paddy. It was a Thursday, the 'big' day of the paper-delivery week, for nearly every house took a weekly periodical which was dated Saturday but blossomed into print, and delivery, on Thursday, so we left Granny Reid's with more than twice Hughie's normal load, even for a Thursday, for I was bigger and stronger than Hughie although he was two years older than I was.

We 'did' the High Street first, in great style, I obeying Hughie and going to the doors he indicated, ringing the bells or knocking the knockers and handing in the papers, and everything went well until we reached what was known as 'the top o' the Toon', where the Italian ice-cream shop was. Outside it was a group of boys and girls of fifteen or so, but among them was My Friend Annie and I think hers was the first voice to be raised.

'Paper! Paper! Penny for a paper!' came the cry. 'One-wing Hughie! Auld Maggie's Hughie! Whae's yer faither? Penny for a paper!'

'Never heed them,' whispered Hughie. 'Ye just have to walk on and never heed them.' Hughie, with Paddy behind him, crossed to the other side of the street, saying over his shoulder: 'Come on!'

Somehow, this was one time when I did not come on when Hughie said so. I was big and strong for my age, compared with Annie and other products of Cairnton, but, aside from that, I had a dog such as they had never imagined, a Shetland collie bitch – and there is no bitch more courageous or more vicious – trained by my grandfather – and there has never been a better trainer of collies.

'Take them, Fly!' I said quietly and then the fun began.

Fly 'took them', boys and girls impartially. Paddy with quick monegrel instinct, realized that this was a day for dogs and joined in. In two minutes, the High Street was full of screaming Annies and Willies and Lizzies and Archies running for their lives, while Hughie and I stood with our papers in our arms 'on the crown of the causeway' and Mr Cervi, the Italian ice-cream man, hopped up and down in his doorway shouting: 'Chase-a-dem from ma door! Das *nize!* Alla time rounda da door make-a da rude-a noise! Bite-a dem, dag! Bite-a dem good!' When Annie and her friends had disappeared still yelling round the bend a quarter of a mile down the street, I called: 'Fly, here! Fly, in!' and Fly came back, closely followed by Paddy who looked twice the dog he had been before. Paddy, obviously, had been waiting for this evening all his life.

In the way that children have of regarding life as a mere series of events, some happy, some sad, some amusing, some terrifying, but all separate and unrelated, I went happily on my way, very, very interested in the paper round, although I noticed that Hughie was unusually silent, and when we had finished I went straight home, with Fly at my heels, as I had promised by father I would do.

We had just started supper when Mrs Black arrived, with Annie by the hand, and all I remember of the storm of words that ensued was that Mrs Black kept on shouting that my dog had bitten Annie and my father kept on saying: 'All right, Mrs Black – just show me the bites.' This was a deadlock. My father knew nothing of what had happened, but he knew with certainty that Fly would not bite. He knew that she could make a terrifying display of savagery, that in extreme circumstances she would take a hold on human clothing, but he was confident that Annie had not been bitten. He was equally confident, though, that Fly had not even looked at Annie without being so instructed and he knew too that Fly would obey no-one but himself or me. And Fly was not, during this time, helping matters any by studying Annie out of golden, narrowed eyes and then cocking her head at me as if to say: 'Shall I have another go?'

While my father coped with the infuriated Mrs Black, I could see events piling up ahead of me. At last, after having told us several times that we would 'hear more o' this', she went away and my father came back to his place at the supper-table. I continued to eat in silence. This was not the first time in my life that I had been in trouble and My Friends Tom and George had made me understand long ago that speech does not always strengthen a position. Indeed, they went further and claimed that silence was a far more reliable weapon. Miss Jean, however, did not subscribe to this theory.

'Ah tellt ye ye shouldnae bring that dug here tae mak' a mess o' the hoose an' bite folk!' she said. 'This is no' the Heilan's.'

The silence took over again. 'An' Ah *said* she shouldnae be trailin' aboot wi' that Hughie – deliverin' papers – Ah never heard the like!' The silence continued. 'A perfect disgrace, frichtenin' poor wee Annie an' a' the ither bairns oot o' their wits! An' jist you wait till that Mrs Mathieson comes up here aboot Teenie – Mrs Black is no' a *patch* on *her*!'

'Are you finished, Janet?' asked my father.

'Yes, Dad.'

'Come with me then.'

He rose and went through the back door, through the little back gate and out on to the bright, moonlit, frosty hill.

'Now, then,' he said, 'what have you been doing?'

I told him, as exactly as I could, what had happened and when I had finished he sat down on a big boulder, took out his pipe and said: 'Well, I don't know *what* to say.' He looked round him into the black shadows in a lost way, as if looking for advice from someone who was no longer there and, realizing now how I was 'worring' him, I began to cry. He looked at me for a moment and then: 'Ach to the devil with them!' he said suddenly. 'Indeed, I'm not sure I wouldna' put the dog on them myself and them shouting things at the poor, hardworking laddie and him cripple. Never mind, Janet. Only, just mind that people like that Annie is different from us and have as little to do with her as you can.'

'Miss Jean is always wanting me to play with her and walk to school with her.'

'Ach, never mind that. Chust you do the best you can among them all and we'll be all right.'

On Friday evening and all day Saturday, Miss Jean talked on and on about the scene in the High Street which, she said, 'was a fair scandal an' the talk o' the hale countryside' and my father and I let the talk flow into the absorbent sponge of our silence. I do not know what *he* was thinking, but on the Saturday, out on my hill with Fly for company now, I gave a lot of thought to Miss Jean.

I simply could not understand her. I could not understand her relationship with Mrs Black. At the moment, you would have thought, hearing her, that Mrs Black was the most angelic woman in the world and the most wronged, but the trouble with Miss Jean and Mrs Black was that their relationship to one another did not stay the same from one hour to the next. With me, when I liked somebody, I *liked* that person, as I liked Hughie, and would set my dog on people who were nasty to him. But Miss Jean and Mrs Black were not like that – at least, Miss Jean was not. What Miss Jean felt about Mrs Black and Annie seemed to depend on the person to whom she was talking about them. When she was talking to Mr Black's ploughman's wife I had heard her say that Mrs Black 'was getting that stuck-up she thocht ither folk was dirt', and when she was talking to the man in the butcher's van I had heard her say that 'the way the Blacks went on aboot that Annie, ye wad think that naebody ever had a bairn before.' But when Miss Jean was *with* Mrs Black, she spoke to her in a flattering way and admired her new curtains and told her that she wished that I was more like Annie. Why could not Miss Jean make up her mind, I inquired of Fly. Fly stared at me for an instant out of her golden eyes and then turned her head away, as if in scorn.

On Saturday afternoon, my father and I were doing a little autumn clearing-up in the garden, when who should arrive at the front gate but Mr Lindsay, looking quite different from what he did in school, for he was wearing plus-fours, a tweed cap, and had a walking-stick.

'Good evening, sir,' my father called, pushing his fork into the ground. 'Come in. Janet, just you load that rubbish into the barrow for me.'

My father and Mr Lindsay sat down on the garden seat and I began to load the rubbish. I liked garden work and was interested in loading the barrow, wheeling it away, tipping the rubbish on to the bonfire heap and trundling back for another load.

'I thought you might have had some trouble. That's why I came up,' Mr Lindsay was saying, as I came past with the barrow to pick up another load. 'But they'll calm down.'

'I don't want her to get a reputation as a hooligan,' my father said.

They were talking about *me*. My father was calling *me* a hooligan.

'Don't you worry,' said Mr Lindsay. 'You know my house?'

'No.'

'It is very well placed for observation of the High Street. My wife and I saw the whole thing – we haven't laughed so much for years!'

My father smiled shyly. 'Still, I'm sorry about all these letters and complaints you've had, Mr Lindsay.'

'Oh, the letter in the *Chronicle* will put an end to that. Have a look at it on Thursday.'

They began to talk of gardening and I ceased to eavesdrop, but the *Chronicle* was the local newspaper, the *Cairnton Chronicle*, and I had been able to read since I was four. I would see this letter for myself.

When the letter appeared, I thought it was extraordinarily dull and that I could myself have written something much more telling and dramatic. It was a formal letter to the Editor from T. D. Lindsay, MA, BSc, Rector, Cairnton Academy, which informed the Editor that there seemed to be some misunderstanding in Cairnton as to his sphere of activity as a school-master and begged the courtesy of his columns to clarify the position. As Rector of the Academy, Mr Lindsay was, he felt, directly responsible for the behaviour of his pupils only while they were within the Academy precincts. He and his staff, however, did their best to influence all pupils towards that fair-mindedness that was an essential part of good citizenship and it was a matter of regret that a recent occurrence in Cairnton High Street seemed to indicate that certain pupils left their fairmindedness behind at the school gates of an evening. Nevertheless, the behaviour of pupils in the High Street was a matter for home discipline and the responsibility of the parents. Mr Lindsay would like all parents to rest assured, however, that savage dogs would not be countenanced within the Academy precincts, any more than would be the bullying of the younger and weaker by the older and stronger pupils, and he hoped with all sincerity that the occurrence in the High Street would not be repeated.

The occurrence in the High Street was not repeated. From that time on, Hughie, Paddy, Fly and I delivered our papers on Thursdays unmolested and Mr Cervi of 'the Kafe' always gave us a few sweets to help us on our way.

CHAPTER FOUR

I was now established with a small world of my own with which I was content. At home, I had my father, Fly and Miss Jean; at school, I had Hughie, Mr Lindsay and Miss Hadley (I have no distinct memories of the other teachers except the Latin master who had fascinating tufts of grey hair sprouting from his ears and nose) and at lunch-times I had Granny Reid. Of course, there were plenty of other people that I knew, and always Annie skirmishing on the outskirts, for her suitability as a friend for me was almost an obsession with Miss Jean, but the people I have mentioned were the pillars of my world for the first two years at Cairnshaws. I think my school-work was my most absorbing interest and the Academy had a good library which was in the charge of Miss Hadley and I read a great deal. I also spent a lot of time on my hill and in the disused quarry and, every Sunday afternoon, I went for a walk and visited the farm with my father.

It was an uneventful way of life and the isolated incidents that I remember following that of the dog chase in the High Street are all connected with Miss Jean, for there was a basic difference between our basic attitudes to life and all it contained which caused us, repeatedly, to astonish, irritate and, even, hurt one another. I continued to be governed by the principle that my father must not be 'worried' and, because of this, he remained unaware, I think, of these cross-currents of feeling between us, for I saw to it that we never came to an open argument in his presence, while Miss Jean, who was a housewife flesh and bone, kept the house and everything connected with it in magnificent order.

57

The housewives of Lowland Scotland are justly famous for their meticulous cleanliness and domestic economy, but for anyone who does not believe that vice is closely allied to virtue-carried-to-extreme, let me commend a month or two spent in a working-class household in Cairnton in the 1920s.

The main industry of Cairnton, apart from the farming carried on in its valley hinterland, was the quarrying of its very hard, ugly, greyish-black stone, which was shipped away by rail and canal barge to the cities as street-paving blocks, kerb-stones for much-used steps and pavement edges, and as crushed stone, it was shipped all over the country for road metal. The thud of blasting and the rattle of stone screens and crushers were always in the air, and the town lay, always, under a pall of grey dust. At school, the paper on which we wrote was gritty with the dust, and the men one met, morning and evening, on their way to or from work – the sett-hewers, the blasters, the labourers from the quarry faces – seemed to be impregnated with it. It was embedded in their skins, it discoloured, grotesquely, their eyebrows and it rattled in their lungs as they coughed.

They were a hard-working people, but I could not find them worthy of love or respect. It seemed to me that, down their generations of working with this stone, it had penetrated to their very bloodstream so that, in time, their hearts and brains had become part-petrified by the grey dust that lodged in them. Even before they had begun to quarry their stone, too, I came to know later, the people of this district had been harsh, recalcitrant and just plain cussed. They had been Covenanters – the hollow behind the Cairn Hill at the head of the valley had been the site of their conventicles. A lot of romantic slush has been written about the Scottish Covenanters and how they would die for their religion and it may be more or less true of some of them, but the Cairnton people whom I knew, while still proud of their covenanting background, were not religious in any true sense. What I do believe of them, and am willing to swear to, is that almost any one of them would have to be threatened with death before he would admit that someone else could possibly be right and

58

he could possibly be wrong. Their confidence in Cairnton's code of morality and the essential rightness and importance of every Cairnton custom, and their belief in the essential wrongness and unimportance of every other moral code and custom practised anywhere else on earth was unassailable.

A dominating factor in the moral code of Cairnton was the duty to acquire possessions. I know that this statement looks absurd, but it is true. It is summed up in Miss Jean's main and oft-repeated criticism of old Granny Reid: 'Och, the Reids were never any *good*! Look at auld Maggie there – no' a ha'penny tae her name!' Then, the most desirable possession to acquire was a house, and, having acquired that, it had to be filled with as many other possessions as it would hold. At this stage, the true worship began. The man breathed dust all day in the quarry, brought home his weekly pay packet and, out of it, what the hoose needed' came first. The needs of that god 'the hoose' were monstrous at times, such as the time when Mrs Findlay's uncle left her thirty pounds when he died and she bought the piano. There was no peace in Cairnton until all the wives of all the sett-hewers – for Tom Findlay was a sett-hewer – had equipped their houses with pianos.

Apart from the Friday-night pay-packet sacrifice to the god in the form of new linoleum for the kitchen or a new stair-carpet, the god required daily, even hourly, propitiation. If it was not having its windows cleaned or its chimneys swept, it was having its curtains washed or its carpets beaten from daylight till dark, and Miss Jean would pause, sweating and panting, in her black-leading of our kitchen stove to say: 'That auld Maggie Reid is a fair disgrace, but the Reids never were ony guid an' neither were *her* folk. That kitchen winda o' hers hasnae had new curtains this five year!' There was an ugly, literal truth in the term 'household gods' as applied to the houses of Cairnton.

Miss Jean, having been bred out of the grey stone of the district and left an orphan at fifteen years old whereupon she went as a general servant to the maiden sister of one of the quarry-owners – they lived in grey villas on the Station

Road, the quarry-owners – was a true daughter of the religion of 'the Toon'. She worshipped this little house that we lived in, which, far from being her own, was not even the property of my father. At Reachfar, where I had been reared, the hierarchy of a household was very different from that of a Cairnton household. At Reachfar, as on most well-run farms, the animals and crops came first and the people served them, and after that, the people were served and made comfortable by the production of the farm, the house and its contents. Miss Jean could not see things in this way. She resented the fact that my father, instead of spending money on the embellishment of the house, chose to save it anent my education and other things. She resented the fact that he would not remove his boots in the scullery at midday and eat his meal in his slippers or stockinged feet 'like ither folk'. To protect her polished linoleum, she spread newspapers on the floor, but this he would not tolerate, in spite of her assurance that '*every*body did it – even the big hooses doon the Station Road'.

'Pick them up,' he said, in a voice that brooked no argument.

She did so, but when he had gone back to work she complained that her back was 'fair like tae breck wi' a' the polishin'.'

'I wouldn't polish it, if I were you, Miss Jean,' I said. 'At home, we just wash the floors and they always look clean.'

'That's the Heilan's!' said Miss Jean with scorn. 'That's a different thing a' thegither!'

Then, she and I would get into trouble over my bedroom. At Reachfar, my attic room had always been my own and I was allowed to arrange it to suit myself. I also had to make it tidy before I left it in the mornings and hang my bedclothes to air and this I continued to do at Cairnton. Miss Jean, however, would arrange it to 'look nice'. She would re-arrange my books according to size or the colour of their covers; she would stuff my writing-paper into a drawer and put a pot plant in its place in the middle of the table and she bought out of the housekeeping money what she called a 'Duchess Set' of 'art' silk mats – three in number, two round and one oblong – which she spread on my small dressing-table. It happened to be a pleasing mahogany table which had been discarded from the farmhouse of Cairnshaws, and, on Saturday mornings, I would polish it myself in order to feel the silk of the dark red wood under my hands. And there would be the 'Duchess Set', removed every Saturday and replaced, as soon as I had gone to school, every Monday. It became a right royal King Charles's head between us.

These irritations between us were caused by our utter inability to reach any understanding of one another on any plane, high or low. I could not understand Miss Jean's need to talk all the time that two people were in the same room – or even in two different rooms that communicated – and she could not understand my need to be silent. I could not understand how sometimes she was 'speaking to' Mrs Black and sometimes not, and when I asked questions about this sort of relationship, she merely became impatient and said she could not see why I 'never got fed up with that Hughie'. Then, when she related the newest local gossip to me, the questions I asked were always the wrong sort which made her cross, then I would become bored and my boredom would show so that Miss Jean would then accuse me of 'bein' ower stupit tae tak' a richt interest in onythin' that was gaun on' and this accusation, which I felt to be unjust, would, in turn, make *me* cross. She could not understand why I would not gossip to her of my time spent with Granny and Hughie and I could not understand why she should be interested in such gossip, when she declared so frequently her disapproval of both Granny and Hughie.

I found that the easiest way to deal with the situation was to spend as little time alone with Miss Jean as possible and this was simple, even in winter, for I was practically impervious to cold or rain and could always find plenty to interest me out-of-doors at the weekends, while, on the evenings of schooldays, I had a fire in my bedroom so that I could do my lessons in peace.

At the end of June, the school closed for the summer

holidays and, as I walked home by my quarry route with the three books that I had been given as the First Year Prize (Hughie came second), I was looking forward to going home to Reachfar, a journey which I was to do from Glasgow to Inverness all by myself. When I had told Hughie and Granny about this, they had been very impressed and I was planning to send them a postcard, telling them of my safe arrival. My father was home when I came into the house and Miss Jean was in the act of making tea, so I said 'Hello' as usual and put my prize books on my father's knee, for he always read my prizes.

'Well, well,' he said, '*three* of them?'

'It's just all the one prize, though,' I told him.

'A *prize*?' said Miss Jean and squinted over my father's shoulder.

'*First* prize, First Year, Higher Grade—' She stared at me, very sharp-eyed. 'An' ye never *told* us?'

I stared back at her, astonished at her rising voice. 'I always get the first prize,' I said.

This was true. To me, it was a natural law of life, like the sun rising in the morning. I had always had the first prize in my section ever since I went to school.

'Ye conceited wee brat!' Miss Jean exploded.

'Now, now!' said my father. 'Janet, what you mean is that you have always had the first prize up to now. Maybe somebody will beat you for it next year. Who was second?'

'Hughie.'

'Well, he might get ahead of you next year.'

I absorbed this new idea and nodded. Hughie was very quick at geometry. 'He might,' I agreed cautiously.

But Miss Jean had sunk on to a chair with the teapot in her lap and a stricken look on her face. 'What in the world will folk *think*?' she said.

'Think?' my father asked, looking up from the books with a puzzled frown.

'Look at her!' Miss Jean almost screamed. 'In that same auld gym frock an' the same auld blouse! Folk'll say Ah'm no' lookin' efter her richt! What a disgrace! Ah niver was sae ta'en doon in front o' the hale toon in a' ma life!'

'Och, away with you, Jean!' said my father easily. 'She was clean and tidy as usual.'

'Clean an' tidy! An' you up there at the fairm a' day – no' even at the schule tae see her gettin' it! What'll folk *think*?'

My father scratched his head. 'I have my job to do, Jean. I canna go running away to things like a bairns' prize-giving. Och, up at Achcraggan, when she was little, we all used to go, but it was different up there – a wee school and all youngsters.'

'But what'll folk *think*?'

'I don't care a damn *what* they think!' he snapped suddenly. 'For goodness' sake, go and make the tea, Jean!'

I have no doubt that my father thought that the incident ended there, for it took him many years to realize that incidents between Jean and me did not end at all, ever. Our non-understanding of one another was a permanency. For three days, over the weekend between the school closing and my departure for Reachfar, every moment that we were alone, Miss Jean renewed her attack about my 'conceit' and my determination to disgrace her by appearing on Prize Day in my ordinary school clothes. Being no more of an angel than any other child – probably less of one than many – I lost all patience in the course of a diatribe which ended: ' – an' Mrs Black there an' everybody! I bet ye *Annie* was dressed!'

'Yes!' I bawled. 'She was all dressed up like a dish o' fish, but she didn't get a *prize*!' and I ran out of the house and slammed the door.

Once I was in the train for Inverness, where Fly and I were in the charge of the guard, I forgot all about Miss Jean and the tribulations of Prize Day and when I saw My Friends George and Tom on the platform, I practically forgot even about Hughie and the Academy. Reachfar was, for me, what it had always been, a sunlit slope above the blue water of the Firth, where there were no nagging problems about the clothes to be worn for this or for that, no incomprehensible undercurrents of relationship with Mrs Black, blissfully there was no Annie and, of course, 'the hoose' did not matter and there were no 'Duchess Sets'. I spent a carefree six weeks, then my father came north for the last fortnight of August, which made a final peak of perfection before we travelled back to Cairnton together at the beginning of September.

Automatically, on our return to school after the holidays, Hughie and I moved up into the Second Year and at the end of the first week of school, high drama broke loose again. Annie, 'rising fourteen' now, was 'kept back' in the First Year. Mrs Black came down to the school in high dudgeon and, this being of no avail, she began to call on the Minister, Mr Hill, and various other people influential in education circles to air her grievance. I do not think that these visits were of much avail either, and eventually she called on Miss Jean one afternoon and gave vent to much dark muttering about 'favouritism' on the part of Mr Lindsay, the other teachers and the County Education Committee. Miss Jean, in the curious, malicious way that I could never understand, repeated the burden of Mrs Black's discourse at the supper-table, saying one moment that Mrs Black was 'rinnin' aboot makin' a perfeck fool o' hersel'' and, the next moment, that 'still it was funny that Annie who was nearly fourteen was kept back when some that she could mention that was only eleven was bein' moved up', until my father, becoming tired of the endless rigmarole, said: 'There's nothing funny about it. Mr Lindsay either reckons a bairn fit to tackle the Second Year or he doesn't.'

'Hughie Reid'll be fourteen next month for a' he's sae wee,' Miss Jean persisted. 'An' Mary Dickson is thirteen an' Peggy Findlay must be nearer fourteen – Ah cannae think o' anither o' them that's only *eleven*!'

'It doesn't matter,' said my father, leaving the table and opening his newspaper.

'Ye can say whit ye like – she's a wee oddity. She's queer. She's jist no' like ither *folk*!'

My father gave Miss Jean a long, stern stare before concentrating on his newspaper and Miss Jean, with an angry sniff, began to clear the table. I went to my room and tried to concentrate on my lessons, but it is not pleasant to have been described as 'a wee oddity'.

The year rolled round into the Spring, Annie had her fourteenth birthday with a lavish party which I did not enjoy, and with a great furore Mrs Black removed her from the Academy altogether. Miss Jean told us all about it.

'She's to go tae a commercial college in Glasgow to learn shorthan' an' typin',' she said.

'They have shorthand and typewriting at the Academy,' I volunteered as general information and to get away from the subject of Annie. 'All the "C" classes up to the Third Year do them. I had a look at Minnie Paton's shorthand book, Dad, and when you write a word like photograph, you write as if it started and finished with "f".'

'Is that so?' said my father.

'Weel, Ah dinnae see why Annie's being' sent tae Glesca!' said Miss Jean. A moment ago, she had pronounced the name of the city as 'Glasgow', but when Miss Jean became malicious or angry she invariably lapsed into the dialect of Cairnton at its broadest, I had noticed. 'Jist swank, likely, so that the Blacks can show folk that they can pey for her!'

I knew why Annie had not been learning shorthand at the Academy, but I did not say aloud that Mr Lindsay had an unshakeable belief that a pupil must be able to write, before learning to write in shorthand.

Annie, after Easter, began to travel by train to Glasgow every day and less was heard of her in our house, for which I was thankful, and Hughie and I were much too busy, now that summer was coming on, exploring round in the old quarry when we were free from school or our paper round, for me to think of Annie at schooltime or out-of-doors. Instead, I thought more about Hughie. When I had first got to know him, he had seemed to be no older than myself, but, during the last year, he had grown a lot in stature and, in his mind, he was growing away from me. It was not that he was ahead of me at school work. Without effort, I was still the top of my Year with Hughie coming second, but

I was now vaguely conscious that school work was not 'everything'. There were things that, at fourteen and a half, Hughie seemed to know by instinct that I, just turning twelve now, had no instinct for at all. He put a point on this one day by saying: 'I like how your father calls me Hugh and not this Hughie. I wish my Granny would call me Hugh. Hughie is a kid's name.'

'You want *me* to call you Hugh too?' I asked.

'fcourse!' he said and then stared at me with a frown because I was giggling. 'What are you laughing at?'

'Me saying "You Hugh too" like that – it sounds so funny, like an owl hooting.'

'You're a daft wee baby!' he said scornfully and not in the least kindly.

'I am *not*!'

'You are *so*! Only kids laugh at something like that.'

'I am *not* a kid! I'm in the Second Year just the same as you!'

'You're a kid all the same! You're not twelve yet – and Second Year! That's nothing!'

'I can't help being just about twelve, Hughie!' I said and began to cry, for I was deeply hurt.

'Oh, stop that crying, you silly wee baby! And *stop* calling me Hughie!'

He ran away from me down the hill, leaving me feeling very lonely, and I continued to cry for a bit before climbing into an old twisted tree that I liked, settling myself in my 'armchair' branch and staring surlily out over the country. I thought that Hughie – Hugh – had been extremely nasty but, at the same time, I was not surprised now that I considered matters that he had been a little scornful of me. He was no longer the small bullied person to whom I had first spoken at the school gates; no longer the scorned, illegitimate, crippled grandson of 'auld Sweetie Maggie' who delivered newspapers out of school hours. In a manner for which I could not find words, Hugh Reid had become a boy who was respected by the other children of the school; a person regarded as a 'proper person' by the householders to whom he delivered newspapers from Mrs Reid's shop.

From my armchair in the tree – though still with a sob catching my breath now and then – I accepted the fact that he would probably prefer to spend his spare time with the other boys rather than with me, and he did not spend it with the boys of our own year either, now that I thought of it. No. He was 'in with' the Big Boys of the Fourth and Fifth Years who, to me, were practically men. It was queer, I thought, that Hugh should be 'in with' them when he only came second to me in school work, no matter how hard he tried, for the Big Girls would never have been seen with *me* and would never invite me to share their giggling walks through the 'toon' home from school. Oh, well. Maybe Hughie – Hugh – was right. Maybe it did not matter if you were in the *Sixth* Year, if you were not yet twelve, big people of fourteen could not be bothered with you.

Hugh and I did not come to a dramatic split or sudden ending of our relationship, of course. I continued to have my dinners at Granny Reid's and, quite often, we went to and fro together at lunchtime and, frequently, we would meet on Saturdays to go for an exploratory walk together, but Hugh's attitude to me changed. Part of the time, now, he was a grown-up person talking to a child and I did not object to this, because, at these times, talking in this way, he really *was* grown-up and not 'just pretending and putting it on' like Chrissie Martin who was thirteen and talked and sighed in the voice of her mother, without being really grown-up inside, as her mother was. No. Parts of Hugh's mind were suddenly more grown-up than mine and I accepted this truth.

I have always liked the company of my friends, but this does not mean that I become a victim of loneliness when I am parted from them, and as long as Hugh was *there*, in the background, to think about when I felt the need, I was content. And I had plenty of other things and people to think about, too, for there was always this paradoxical business that the older I became and the more things and people I knew about, the more things and people there seemed to be in the world to *get* to know about.

The end of my Second Year and Prize Day came along, but this time it caused no trouble in our household, as an edict had come forth from the school that *all* pupils would wear uniform on Prizegiving Day. I do not think that this was in any way connected with my dress of the year before, but that it was a development that was bound to arise out of the absurdities perpetrated by a few mothers, such as Mrs Black, especially in a school where it happened that some of the cleverest children were also some of the poorest, financially. In this year, when the reform in dress for Prize Day was introduced, the Dux of the school was the eldest daughter of a cattleman, who had another eight children, and the school uniforms alone must have strained the limits of the family budget. I suspect, now, the fearless hand and mind of Miss Hadley in the pushing-through of the edict, for Lisbeth Lithgow, the Dux, was brilliant at modern languages and, naturally, a favourite pupil with Miss Hadley.

Although I, with my liking for my plain uniform, Prize Day or no, was now in line with 'ither folk' from Miss Jean's point of view, the edict did not pass without adverse comment on Mr Lindsay and Miss Hadley and, of course, when history repeated itself on my return with the first prize in my Year again, Miss Jean did not know whether to be pleased or annoyed and settled the matter by being something of both, which led to a tremendous spate of words that lasted throughout the weekend until I left for Reachfar.

My early July departure for Reachfar now, too, became a matter for comment. According to Miss Jean, on the Sunday evening: 'It was a' richt enough last year, goin' tae see her Granny efter livin' up there in the Heilan's sae long, but noo that she's gettin' bigger it wid be mair like the thing to go for a fortnicht tae the seaside – Dunoon or Rothesay – like ither folk.'

I was appalled at this as an idea and stared at my father in silence, for I was tending to argue less and less with Miss Jean with every day that passed. She became cross so easily.

'What would she do at Dunoon or Rothesay?' my father asked.

For a dreadful moment, I thought that he was considering the idea seriously and I visualized myself being sent to lodgings at Rothesay for a fortnight to be fed on bread and margarine as Mrs Black had said had happened to her Annie the year before, so I said quickly: 'There's a seaside at Reachfar, Dad!'

'Whit wid she dae!' said Miss Jean scornfully. 'Whit dae ither folk dae? There's the sands an' the band an' the prommynaid an' the pier-*rots* an' everything!'

'Would you like that, Janet?' my father asked with a smile that made me know he was teasing.

'I'd rather go to Reachfar, Dad,' I said, smiling back at him.

'All right. And George and Tom will be glad to see you.'

I felt, though, that I had had a narrow escape and, to this day, I cannot think of the white overalls and pointed pompommed caps of the old seaside concert party without thinking of piers, rotting, with trails of dank seaweed trailing from their wooden piles, while I walk disconsolately, in an exiled loneliness, along the 'prommynaid'.

It seemed nowadays, though, that, like Hughie changing into Hugh, my father was changing too, for he listened more carefully to what Miss Jean had to say; gave more consideration to her views, more credence to some of her opinions, especially with regard as to what was fitting and suitable in the treatment of *me*. This worried me, for it led only to friction between Miss Jean and myself which I did my best to conceal from my father. I did not like the out-of-school clothes which she was commissioned to help me choose; I did not like or wish to accept the advice she gave me about the friends I should have and the parties and amusements that I ought to attend, but, at the same time, I did not wish to be outwardly scornful of her, for that would make her ill-natured and that, in turn, would 'worry' my father. I consequently pursued a policy of uneasy compromise which was constantly fretting at me. I have little natural genius for compromise.

CHAPTER FIVE

Even my careful policy led me into serious trouble shortly after I returned from Reachfar to begin my third year at the Academy. Every Saturday afternoon, it was the habit of my schoolmates to 'go to the Pictures' at the cinema in Cairnton and, one Friday evening, Miss Jean came home from her weekly shopping expedition and was sniffing in obvious ill-temper as she prepared the supper.

'What's wrong, Jean?' my father asked with a glance of amusement, for now that he knew Jean and had become accustomed to her ways and moods, he would often, when she was indulging in displays of sniffing and bridling, inquire as to the reason for them.

'That Mrs Mackie from the Upper!' snapped Jean.

'What's wrong with her?'

'I walked intae the Toon wi' her for the messages.'

'Well?'

Jean swung round dramatically. 'She speired at me if ye were ower mean to send Jinnit tae the pictur's on Setterdays like the ither bairns!'

My father threw back his head and roared with laughter and so did I.

'It's naething tae laugh at!' said Jean indignantly. 'Hoo wad *you* like tae be asked the like o' that?'

Seeing that the matter was serious to her, for she was almost in tears, my father stopped laughing, for he did not like to see people unhappy and he and I had learned that such remarks made by her peers caused Jean a genuine unhappiness – unwarranted, maybe, but still genuine and painful.

'Like to go to the pictures tomorrow, Janet?' he asked me.

'Or had you other plans?'

'No, Dad, I hadn't planned anything,' I said. I had an open mind about the pictures, although I do not think, left to myself, that I would have asked for permission and the money to go.

'We'll see what picture they have,' he said and opened the *Cairnton Chronicle*. 'Oh, *The Hunchback of Notre-Dame*!' he read out.

'That's not a *picture*, Dad!' I said. 'That's the book we read last year from the school library!'

'But that's what the pictures very often do,' he explained. 'They take a story from a book and make a picture of it.'

'I'd *like* to see that,' I said.

The next afternoon, with sixpence in my pocket, part of it to enter the picture-house, part of it to buy sweets (like ither folk), I set off to the cinema. I found some school companions at the door and had no difficulty in buying my ticket and entering the stuffy place with all the dusty seats, but was fascinated and repelled all at once, in the hallway, by dozens of children, some of them less than half my own age, all carrying jam-jars. Some of the jars had not been washed and the sticky, glutinous remains of mass-produced, sub-fruit-standard, raspberry and plum jam still clung to them. The children laid them in a large box at the ticket office and, in exchange, received an entrance ticket to the cheap front seats of the cinema.

Chattering to my companions, I stared at the white screen with the black edge to make sure that no words of the story appeared on it when I was not looking and, suddenly, all the lights in the place went out, which seemed to me rather ill-organized and inhospitable of them, especially after I had paid fourpence to come in. Then a long arm of light struck the white screen and a piano began to play. After that, I remember nothing except that I was appalled. Picture after picture appeared in front of me, so fast that the figures seemed to be moving in a jerky sort of way, but there was no illusion of reality. Then the screen would go blank, except for a few written words – and never the words that had been

71

in the book I had read – and then the flickering, artificial figures would come back again and then they were flogging with a big whip a deformed man who was tied to a post. And it was all dark, except for the swinging arm of light, and there were people all round me eating sweets amd shouting and the piano was tinkling and the beam of light was buzz-buzz-buzzing and – after a very long time, it was over and the lights came up along the dirty walls. Dazed with panic, I ran for home over my own route through the old quarry and the back-garden gate.

By supper-time, I had got myself sufficiently in hand to be ready for questions, for it would not be polite to say that I had hated it all, for that would mean that a precious sixpence had been wasted and such a thing would be sinful and, also, Miss Jean would make a fuss. So, when my father said: 'Well, Janet, what did you think of the pictures?' I said: 'It was very nice, Dad, thank you.'

'*There* you are!' said Miss Jean in a pleased voice.

'But I wouldn't want to go very often,' I added cautiously.

'No, nor me,' my father agreed. 'The pictures always make my eyes sore, somehow.'

'Ach, awa' wi' ye!' said Miss Jean.

'My eyes too,' I said firmly, for I had a feeling that, now, my father was on my side. 'Besides, the pictures of it weren't as good as what you could imagine for yourself when you were reading the book.'

'That's the way I never cared much, even, for a book with pictures in it,' my father agreed. 'Like yon one of the Fair Maid of Perth at Reachfar – I think it was Aunt Mary that got it for a school prize once. The Fair Maid was far too fat in the pictures in it!'

'I know, Dad!' I agreed fervently. 'The people in the pictures aren't like the real people at all and they weren't at the Pictures today, either.'

'So you still like the reading best?'

'Yes, Dad.'

'Och, well,' he said comfortably, 'when you've been all through Miss Hadley's library, we can see about the Town one and the one at the tobacco shop. You could get your sixpence for that instead of for the Pictures, if you like.'

'Thank you, Dad.'

Miss Jean sniffed. 'Books! She does ower much book-readin' already! Whit she needs is tae be mair among ither folk!'

'But you're not *among* them at the Pictures, Miss Jean!' I argued. 'It's all in the dark!'

'But they're *there*, beside ye!'

'But if you can't *see* people and *talk* to them, they might as well not *be* there!' I argued.

'Ach, dinnae be sae stupit!' said Miss Jean and flounced through to the scullery.

In these small incidents in my life, Miss Jean, always, and my father, to a large extent, were under the impression that the flounce through to the scullery which ended the conversation was also the end of the incident, but my experience 'at the Pictures' did not end there. I began to dream at nights, a recurring nightmare, that I was shut up in a dark place with something cruel and hideous, where there was a moving shaft of white light that never illumined the source of my dread, but stabbed uselessly and spent itself against the surrounding darkness —

It was part of my home discipline from far earlier days that, before I washed to go to bed, I had to clean my shoes and put them ready to wear to school the next morning, and about five days after the cinema visit I woke up to see my shoes, side by side under their chair, coated with mud. I then discovered that the hem of my nightdress was also mud-splashed. I was badly frightened by these things which I could not understand, but contrived, by some means, to keep them secret. Three mornings later, I awoke to find that my shoes had again been worn, although this time they were not muddy, and there was a small thorny twig in my bed. Again, I kept my secret, but about a week later my father woke me while it was still dark outside and the gas lamp in my room was alight. He was sitting on the end of my bed, wearing trousers and a mackintosh, and was busy filling his pipe. My glance went at once to my shoes. They were in their place under their chair, but they were wet and a little wave of mud lapped over the black toecaps. I looked, fearfully, at my father.

'Aye,' he said calmly, lighting a match and applying it to his pipe, 'that was a nice walk up the hill we had.'

'Up the hill?' I whispered.

'Aye.' He studied the bowl of the pipe for a moment. 'Don't you be frightened, Janet. You've been taking a bit of a prowl in your sleep – quite a lot of folk will be doing it. Somnambulism, they call it – that word will be from the Latin, I am thinking?'

'Yes. Sleep-walking,' I whispered.

'Och, it's a common enough thing, a kind of dreaming. What were you dreaming about? Can you mind?' He laughed a little, a comforting little laugh. 'I'll often be dreaming at night and, in the morning, I'll be danged if I can mind what it was all about!'

It might have been George or Tom speaking to me. His voice was quite different from when he spoke to Miss Jean or the people about Cairnshaws and it was like Reachfar, the way he said: 'I'll be danged' like that.

'I didn't have the dream tonight,' I told him.

'What dream? You'll be having one that you can mind about?'

'Yes, Dad.'

I told him all about the dark, sinister place of the recurring nightmare and how, on the nights when it came, I would wake up cold and shivering and be afraid to go to sleep again.

'I'm not surprised that a person would be frightened of the like o' that,' he said, when I had finished. 'I would be right frightened of it myself. But I'll tell you what to do. Next time you get it and you waken, chust you come ben to my bed and climb in and pack into my back until the morning.'

'But what about – about the walking, Dad?' I asked, staring at my shoes.

'Och, I wouldna worry about that. Of course, it's a danged pest to have to clean your shoes twice instead of chust the

74

once, but we canna help it. It will soon stop, ye know.'

'Will it, Dad?'

'Och, aye. Especially if a person will not be worrying about it.' He rose to his feet. 'Do you think you can go off to sleep again?' he asked.

I yawned. 'Yes, Dad,' I said.

'That's fine.' He gave my bottom a pat through the bed-clothes, turned off the light and I think I was asleep before he had left the room.

At breakfast, he behaved as if he and I had never met since the evening before and so did I and I do not think that Miss Jean knew anything of what had happened, but, a few mornings later, when I was re-cleaning the tell-tale shoes, I saw her darting strange glances at me although my father was behaving just as usual. That evening, I was home from school before my father came back from the farm and Miss Jean was behaving very oddly. Instead of chattering in her usual way as she went about the preparations for supper, she was strangely silent, and she would dart these queer glances at me as she passed the chair where I sat as if, behind it, there stood some spectral figure which only she could see and of which she was afraid. She maintained the same strange silence throughout supper but now I noticed that my father was silent too and I realized that, at the dinner-hour, while I was at school, something had happened between them and that it was connected with *me*. It must – it could only be, my sleep-walking. Miss Jean was 'worry-ing' my father about it, although he himself had said that it was nothing to worry about. My father would not tell me a lie like that, I was certain, and if he and I were not worried about it, why should Miss Jean be making a worry of it?

I sat at the supper-table, looking out of the window at the garden and wondering about it all in the strange silence until, suddenly, I was startled nearly out of my wits by Miss Jean springing to her feet, her eyes staring at me, while in a high, harsh voice she shouted: 'Look at her! Sittin' there starin' at nothin'! Ah tell ye, Ah cannae bear it; she's no' like ither bairns!'

'Be quiet, Jean!' said my father sternly.

'It's no' naitral! Ah dinnae care whit ye say! *Ither* bairns dinnae dae it! Ye'll hae tae get the doctor!' She began to cry, noisily and messily.

I gazed at her and felt rising in me fear of a kind that I had never known before, for this was the first time that I had seen a grown-up person of my household lose her self-control. I had seen women cry before; I had seen them sad and angry and hurt, but never had I seen any sane person, male or female, in this state of babbling, incoherent disintegration. I felt no pity for her, but merely a nauseated disgust and yet I could not look away from her wild eyes and her twisted, distorted face. Through the sobs and the gulps the words forced themselves out of her in a disorderly cataract.

'Ye'll hae tae get the doctor tae her! She's no' richt, Ah'm tellin' ye – ither bairns dinnae walk aboot in their sleep like ghosts an' clim' trees a' day an' play a' their lane an' niver speak tae folk! She's no' *richt* – that's whit she's no'! An' she – she's at a bad age for lassies – she's gaun aff her heid – she'll hae tae go tae the *Asylum*!'

On the final word, her shrill voice which had been rising in a rapid crescendo hit breaking point, became a piercing, shuddering shriek and, in the midst of it, she dashed out of the room, through to the back of the house, the shriek stretching behind her in a vibrating streamer of hideous sound which eventually seemed to break into fragments and fall all over the room in jagged splinters around and between my father and myself.

When the last splinter of noise had died to silence, I raised my eyes to my father's face and, in a single second, as I looked into his frightened, puzzled, worried eyes, I became aware of the heart-pang that is the real loneliness of the human soul. My father, I knew with dreadful certainty, believed what Miss Jean had said. He was afraid that I was going mad and would have to be shut away in the County Asylum.

'I am all right, Dad,' I assured him shakily.

He stared at me and I saw a convulsive movement in his throat.

'I'll get the doctor,' he said. 'I'll go and 'phone for him now.' He spoke as if to himself.

I felt a surge of panic in my lungs. 'No, Dad! I'm all right!'

'I – I'll get the doctor,' he repeated and, in a blind way, he stumbled out of the house.

I stared at the half-eaten food on the table, I stared round the room, I heard Miss Jean give a snuffling cough in the bathroom and I rose and went out-of-doors, through the back gate and on to the hill.

Young people are often cruel and people who are afraid are often cruel and on that evening I was both young and afraid. It did not occur to me to think that, out of his love for me, my father by fetching a doctor was taking what he thought was the safest and best course. All that I thought was that he was no longer the man I knew, but some stranger who had withdrawn his support from me at the signal of a few hysterical words shouted by a woman whom I regarded as a fool. *He* was a fool too – not the wise, kindly, big man on whom I had been taught to depend! Let them think I was going mad! What did *I* care? What did I care what any of them thought? Defiant question after defiant phrase, my mind churned the words out on to the twilight breeze of the hill, but behind it all – the dark root from which the questions and phrases grew, of course – was fear. Maybe they were right. It was true that other girls did not walk in their sleep. Annie did not walk in her sleep. Annie did not like to wear old clothes and climb in trees and spend her time alone. Neither did Minnie Paton nor Teenie Mathieson. None of the 'ither folk' liked the things I liked. I was 'different' – that is what people were always saying – Jean and all of them. I, Janet Sandison, was different, different, different —

When I heard my father's voice calling me, I called back, quite calmly, that I was coming and made my way back to the house. Doctor Blair was there, standing with his back to the fire.

He was a man I liked, the same red-faced sort of doctor as Doctor Mackay of Achcraggan, and precisely what I thought a doctor who came to your house should be like. A doctor who was a 'specialist' who worked at a hospital was, in my mind, quite a different sort of man – dark and tall and lean and serious, with a white coat or a dark, well-pressed suit instead of these baggy, comfortable, hairy clothes that Doctor Blair wore.

'Well, Janet,' he said, 'your father tells me you are off walking about on the hill at night – I would have thought you did enough walking all day without setting off at night too.' He sat down on a chair and ran a hand down my leg from the thigh to the ankle as I stood in front of him. 'It's these long, hardy legs. They need a lot of exercise, legs like that. You like to do gym?'

'Yes, sir.'

'That's right. Take off your tunic and blouse and let's see your arms and shoulders. How old are you?'

I told him as I pulled my tunic over my head.

'You are in Robert's class, aren't you? Comment vous portez-vous, Mademoiselle?'

'Ca va très bien, Monsieur le Docteur, je vous remercie,' I replied.

He glanced up at my father and Miss Jean. 'It's a wonderful thing how two people, if they are clever enough, can be quite alone in the midst of company,' he said mischievously, 'isn't it, Jeanie?'

Miss Jean gave one of her angry sniffs, but my father's eyes became less worried and puzzled.

'Does it take you a long time to do your homework at night, Janet?' Doctor Blair asked next.

'Time!' Miss Jean snapped before I could say anything. 'It's not much time *she* spends on homework! Sits and reads books, that's whit she does. An' writes her weekend composition at the scullery table on Sunday when she's shellin' the peas for the dinner! Mary Lennox an' the ither bairns take the hale o' Sunday for their compositions!'

Doctor Blair sat me on another chair and hit my knees with a little hammer, which made me giggle.

'So homework's easy, eh, Janet?'

'I quite like doing it,' I told him.

'That's fine. And you like to read. Tell me, do you like the Pictures?'

'No, sir!' I said at once, without thinking of the sniff that this would – and did – elicit from Miss Jean.

'Neither do I,' said Doctor Blair, producing his stethoscope and turning to my father. 'I went to *The Hunchback of Notre Dame* because I've always liked the book – never saw such damned rubbish in my life.'

'Is that so, Doctor?' said my father.

'Pure rubbish! D'ye know what I think? I think the people that made the picture had never read the book at all.' He turned back to me. 'Let's see how big a breath you can take and how long you can hold on to it.'

As the final act of his examination, after he had looked at my throat, my teeth and peered into my eyes, Doctor Blair untied the ribbon on the end of one of my waist-length pigtails, undid the plait and spread the hair out over the broad palm of his hand.

'Her hair should be bobbed like the ither lassies',' said Miss Jean. 'Ah've aye said that – half her strength gaes intae it!'

'Rubbish, woman! You and your old wives' tales! Cut it and she'll put the strength into growing it again – she was designed to have long hair – she's not a Hottentot!' He looked at my father and slapped me on my school knickers. 'She's a grand specimen, Mr Sandison, but faster-growing mentally than physically. Puberty is a long way off, but you haven't a thing to worry yourself about.' He looked at Miss Jean with a firm, beady eye. 'And if she goes out for a walk at nights, there's not much harm in that either. It's a free country, except for the folk I choose to certify for Asylum and the ones the police lock up.' He scratched his head thoughtfully with the earpiece of his stethoscope. 'I've been trying for years to come to an arrangement with the police to certify or lock up all the silly, gossiping women round Cairnton, but we haven't a big enough building to put them in.'

'Ye can say whit ye like, Doctor Blair, but—' began Miss Jean.

'But what?' he barked.

'She – she's *different*!'

'Great God Almighty! *I'm* different! So are *you*, only *you're* daft enough to think you're not! Maybe I ought to certify you after all.'

'Well!' said Miss Jean, drawing herself up and heaving her chest indignantly, and dramatically.

'Don't be a fool, Jeanie,' said the Doctor and whipped her over the firm, round buttocks with the stethoscope. 'If you had any sense, you'd be proud of her. You couldn't get a better advertisement for a bairn that's well fed and looked after!' Unwillingly, Miss Jean began to smile, but in another five minutes she was making a cup of tea for the doctor and chattering on in her usual scattered fashion about anything and everything. I did not pay much attention, for I was thinking of something else and waiting for a pause in the grown-up talk so that I could ask my question. As the doctor rose to go home, it came.

'Please, Doctor Blair, what is puberty that you said I haven't got yet?'

'Jinnit!' said Miss Jean, her face scarlet, as she swung round on the doctor. 'There – ye see? Whit *ither* lassie wid—'

The doctor barely glanced at her. 'Puberty, Janet? Well, you see, when a female person grows up, she changes from being a girl into a woman and—'

Miss Jean, with a loud shriek of outraged modesty, fled from the room, followed by a 'Bloody fool!' from Doctor Blair before he continued his explanation.

I did not see her again until the next morning at breakfast. She did not look scared when she looked at me now, but she avoided looking at me at all for a day or two because it always made her face get red, especially when my father was present. However, this blushing phase passed over and I co-operated with everyone by taking only two more night walks and then giving up somnambulism as a pastime altogether.

I do not know how the psycho-analysts would explain what happened. I can merely describe what actually happened to me, which was that I ceased to have nightmares about the film I had seen at the cinema and ceased to walk in my sleep because of this disturbance because I was far too busy hating Miss Jean to remember the film or the cinema at all.

Until the time of the hysterical incident which had resulted in the calling of Doctor Blair, I had regarded Miss Jean, in an unemotional, patronizing way, as an unimportant, slightly irritating feature of Cairnton life – something in the nature of the quarry dust – who had no real potential for either good or evil, as long as she was kept in her proper place, but, on the evening that she cast doubt on my sanity and caused my father to call the doctor, I considered that she had stepped out of that proper place of hers. It is only now, nearly forty years later, that I can see this in perspective and recognize it as the actual grain of sand that formed the real hard core of my hatred for Miss Jean which, like the irritant in the pearl oyster, has been walled and coated and rewalled and recoated down the years by layer after layer of bruised feeling caused by incidents for which I have laid the blame at her door. The hard grain at the seat of the trouble was not the misery of that evening before Doctor Blair's arrival, when I wondered if I were really becoming insane. No. The hard core was formed at that moment when my father left me and our house to telephone to the Doctor. In that moment, for me, Miss Jean had achieved what I had not believed to be possible. She had caused one Sandison to lose faith in another. She had convinced my father that I was going mad. What she had done, in my eyes, was to reduce my father, by a few hysterical words, from the status of an omnipotent, omniscient god to the human plane of a vulnerable, ignorant man. Men go to the stake in martyrdom at the scorning of their gods; nations go to war for their religious beliefs; empires have been shaken by the falling of their idols. It is, perhaps, in the light of these facts, not surprising that I declared subconscious war on Miss Jean for what she did to my mental image of my father.

I believe now, as a result of experience, that no emotion is barren. Love, however concealed and obscured under the froth and bubble of daily life, will bear fruit, and hatred, even a childish hatred like mine for Miss Jean, although decently hidden under a convention of 'peace' in the household, will also bear its fruit. Because this story is written by me, Miss Jean may emerge from its pages as something of a monster, but the reader must bear in mind the bias of the writer. As surely as Miss Jean had an effect on my character, I had an effect on hers and it should be remembered that from the time of this incident I was a 'hate-full' little girl in relation to Miss Jean and hatred breeds hatred as surely as night follows day. If Miss Jean truly was something of a monster, I did my hateful part of making her so.

As usual, the sleep-walking incident did not end with the sleep-walking itself. At some time during the period of the nightmares and prior to the visit of Doctor Blair, Miss Jean had unburdened her mind of its terrors of me to Mrs Black, which, Mrs Black being what she was, was the equivalent of publishing my sleep-walking peculiarity in the *Cairnton Chronicle*. Talk became rife round 'the Toon'. The 'wee lassie fae the Heilan's' who had 'aye been different fae ither folk', who 'curtsied tae that uppish Miss Hadley fae Edinburgh' and who was 'ower clever at the schule tae be naitral' was now a 'real daftie an' it wid be safer if she wis locked up in the Asylum'.

I am sure that none of these remarks were made directly to my father – for Miss Jean I would not vouch – but for some weeks at school my life became a child's hell, than which there can be no hell which is worse. In the cloakroom, there would be the audible whisper: 'She's a' right as long as she's no' sleepin' – it's when she's sleepin' that she might–' and the silence that remained was fraught with my potentiality for frightfulness. In the playground, there would be: 'No, she's no' comin' in *our* game, for my mither says ye just never *ken* with folk like her – she might–' and on the way home from school, on days when I had not Fly with me, there were the cries of: 'Daftie! Daftie! Daftie Jinnit! Daftie Jinnit that walks aboot a' nicht!

82

Wee daftie Jinnit rins through the Toon,
Up the stair an' doon the stair,
In her nicht-goon!'

My misery was so great that I do not remember the details
of it or how, at last, it came to an end and the catcalls and
the whispers died away. I only know that I was aware, all
the time that the shrill voices or the cruel-curious glances
were surrounding me, that they had originated with Miss
Jean. I knew that if she had held her gossiping tongue, this
would never have happened to me, for I did not 'run through
the Toon' – I walked only on my beloved hill where Cairnton
would never have seen me. If Miss Jean had not succumbed
to her degrading need to talk to her dreadful crony, Mrs
Black, I thought, this terrible humiliation would never have
overtaken me. Perhaps unfairly, but naturally enough, I
think, I held the behaviour of the schoolchildren against
Miss Jean.

Both my father and she, of course, remained unaware of
these whispers in school and catcalls on the way home, for
I did not speak of them. I know, now, that Miss Hadley and
Mr Lindsay were aware of something of them and that they
were instrumental in stopping them, but at that time I knew
nothing of this. The important thing was that stop they did,
before too long.

But to return in time to the visit of Doctor Blair – after
he had drunk his tea in our house that evening, with the
lavish praise of Miss Jean's scones and cake, interlarded with
anecdotes of the many brilliant people he had heard of who
habitually walked in their sleep, Miss Jean forgot, in the way
that was typical of her, all that had gone before. She forgot
her fears of me as someone who 'wasnae naitral'; she forgot
that she had unburdened herself of her terror of me to Mrs
Black; she forgot, indeed, everything that she had ever said
before about me, even *to* me, and she veered round before
a stiff breeze of 'being proud of me', a breeze whistled up
by Doctor Blair out of kindly diplomacy.

Miss Jean was proud of me, as My Friend Martha would

put it, in no ordinary way. She boasted to everyone of my size for my age, the length and thickness of my hair and my prowess at school. She even boasted of how I was not 'like ither bairns' and how I could spend hours by myself reading books or 'awa' up on that hill with nobody near her'. There was no end to the things that she could find to boast about, but all the boasting did not mean that she and I were any less, fundamentally, opposed to one another in character.

And, of course, inevitably, as is the way of life, if one force is fundamentally opposed to another force, the crash came and from the least expected quarter. It came through the kindly, well-intentioned diplomacy of Doctor Blair, which led to all Miss Jean's boasting. In telling her that she should be proud of me, Doctor Blair meant well, but, as is often the case with diplomacy, even between nations, it had results far different from what the well-meaning diplomat had intended, although, again like the results of diplomatic activity between nations, the results did not come to their full flower of effect until over a year later.

CHAPTER SIX

The school year went round again and shortly after my thirteenth birthday, in the spring, Mr Lindsay came once more to call on my father. Hugh – as even his Granny called him now – and I were nearly at the end of our Third Year in the Higher Grade of the school, the 'intermediate' year, as it was called, when pupils were, as a rule, in their fifteenth or sixteenth year of age, as was Hugh, and parents were required to make up their minds whether the children were to stay on at school or be taken away to be apprenticed to some trade.

Jean, in her new role of being proud of my 'difference fae the ither bairns' and my 'cleverness at the schule', was interested in what Mr Lindsay might have to say and, when my father asked me to leave the room, I felt that my banishment was grossly unfair, for anything connected with school I regarded very much as my affair and certainly more mine than Miss Jean's. However, it is not essential to be inside a room to hear what is being said there. The window was open at the top.

'I'm in a quandary, Mr Sandison,' Mr Lindsay began.

'Oh?'

'Have you ever heard of the Jarvie-Kerr Bursary?'

'I read about some boy in Dumbarton winning it last year,' my father said.

'That's it. Old Jarvie made a pile of money in the last century out of shipping and coal and he left a fair sum of it to provide a bursary in memory of his wife who was a Miss Kerr. It is open for competition to pupils at non-fee-paying schools in the five counties where old Jarvie's businesses were – but the City of Glasgow is not eligible. The pupils competing have to be in their third year of the Higher Grade, not less than thirteen and not more than sixteen on the first of April of the year in which they sit. It is a very valuable prize – a money grant allotted to the pupil every year for six years – it is also something of an honour to the school which can bring it home.' Mr Lindsay paused for a moment and then continued: 'You see before you, Mr Sandison, an unfortunate schoolmaster who has two pupils who are in the Jarvie-Kerr range.'

'And you can't enter both?' my father asked.

'I could, but the wrong one, from my point of view, would almost certainly win it!' He laughed, but when he spoke again his voice was very serious. 'The two pupils, Mr Sandison, are Hugh Reid and Janet. I do not say that either of them can top the list – I don't know what the other schools are sending up. But I *do* know that if Janet goes in, Hugh might as well not bother. It is a question of which child is in most need of financial help. You see what I mean?'

'Aye. I see. I can manage for Janet, Mr Lindsay.'

'If she's cleverer than Hughie Reid – an' everybody in the place *kens* she is – she has the richt—' Miss Jean began.

'This is between Mr Lindsay and me, Jean,' said my father sternly and I heard Jean give her snort and flounce out of the room, closing the door in a pronounced way.

Having made sure that she had gone no further than the scullery where she began to rattle pans about, I returned to my listening point, for it was being borne in on me that I was on the verge of Serious Bother. I had read a big, long notice on the school board about this bursary, had decided that it was an excellent chance to earn some money for my education and had written my name on the paper provided below the notice without delay. My father had told me repeatedly that I must always take serious thought before putting my signature to anything and I was now feeling that my thought had not been serious enough and that, even, being a minor, I should have asked my father's permission before writing my name on that paper at all.

'That's the attitude – that Janet is *cleverer* than Hugh,' Mr Lindsay was saying, in reference to Miss Jean's remark. 'I know you won't object to my saying this, Mr Sandison. Janet, in my opinion, is *not* cleverer than Hugh Reid – she has a different type of brain and she has a natural flair for examinations. She seems to have no nerves, she turns in beautiful papers, and at a *viva* I've never seen a child put up a better performance. She approaches it as if it were a friendly conversation and it is extraordinarily appealing. The *viva* is a big part of the Jarvie-Kerr and if she gets in there in front of that committee, Hugh Reid, who has a fine brain, might as well not try at all.'

'Don't enter her, Mr Lindsay,' said my father.

He laughed. 'She has entered herself!'

'She has? The brat! But I'll soon sort that!'

I swallowed hard – the wrath was undoubtedly to come – but I continued to listen.

'That's very generous of you, Mr Sandison. You see, the boy's whole future turns on it. I wouldn't have come to you at all but for the fact that he is a cripple. If he had been physically normal, he could have left school now and fought his own way. But—'

'Give the poor laddie his chance,' said my father. 'I'll see to Janet, Mr Lindsay, for money and every other way.'

'There's another side to this,' Mr Lindsay said. 'I would like to put Janet forward for the City and Western Counties when she is the age for it, if she goes on as she is doing now. If she happened to win the Jarvie-Kerr, she wouldn't be eligible. I'm not entirely altruistic, Mr Sandison. By dividing my forces, you see, I have a chance of getting *both* for my school within three years.'

'I wish ye luck!' said my father. 'But, especially, I hope that Hugh makes something of the Jarvie-Kerr one. You would be helping him all you can, Mr Lindsay?'

'Certainly! What do you think I approached *you* for? With that little clip of yours out of the way, he has no competition from schools in our own county, anyway.'

'Little clip is right, sir,' said my father and called: 'Janet!'

I ran from my listening point away around the kitchen garden and the clothes green to the back of the house.

'Your father's callin' ye!' shouted Miss Jean from the scullery window.

I went into the living-room. 'Yes, Dad?'

He frowned sternly at me. 'What's this that Mr Lindsay is telling me about you entering for examinations without asking me or Mr Lindsay or Miss Hadley or anyone?'

'Well, Dad, it said on the notice-board that anyone who was thirteen and in their Third Year could enter and I'm thirteen now and in my Third Year and I – well, I just wrote my name down.'

'I see. And what makes you think that you might be clever enough to go in for a thing like that?'

The hypocrites that they were! The roundabout way they went at you to get what they wanted! I became smug. 'Well, there's no harm in trying, is there, Dad? Miss Hadley says there's *never* any harm in—'

'Never mind that just now. The thing is that you shouldn't have done that on your own. Mr Lindsay and I don't want you to sit that examination.'

'Why not, Dad?'

Miss Jean sidled through the door behind me and I had the feeling of her tacit support, which, although it did not mean much to me, made the two powerful men less terrifying.

'I want to hold you back for another exam later on, Janet,' Mr Lindsay said, 'and your father agrees with me.'

Just imagine, I thought smugly, the awful lies grown-up people will tell, even the Rector, sitting there telling them, Absolutely Bare-faced. It was only a lie of omission, of course, saying nothing about Hugh, but a lie all the same.

'I would like to have a try for the bursary,' I said, just for Pure Badness, for I did not really care whether I won a bursary or not, as long as I could continue to go to school.

'Well, you're not *going* to!' my father barked. 'And that's all about it!'

'You might, if you won it,' said Mr Lindsay, 'be taking it away from someone who needs it more than you do, Janet.'

'Like – like Hugh?' I asked. I would make them tell the truth, just for the good of their souls, I thought. I cannot think where this smugness in me came from, but am inclined to blame it on an infection that I caught in Cairnton. I outgrew it later and I think this was the last occasion on which I interested myself in the state of anyone's soul.

'Well, yes. The Jarvie-Kerr would be very useful to someone like Hugh.'

'That's fine, sir.' I was smugly delighted, feeling that I had earned a good mark from God for getting at the truth. 'Hugh can have it! I'll wait for the next one!'

From that moment, I espoused Hugh's cause and directed much of my energy to trying to help him with his preparations for the examination. I did not dare to confess, even to him, that I had eavesdropped on the conversation between my father and Mr Lindsay and consequently could not encourage him by telling him how good the Rector thought his chances were. But I did everything else I could to encourage him and although he called me a 'silly kid' now about most things, he listened with respect to all I had to say on the technique of examination-sitting.

Perched on a slab of rock in the old quarry in the evening sunshine, I would put Hugh through *viva voce* examination after *viva voce* examination. His answers to my questions were unimportant – Hugh could answer correctly most of the questions I could think up – I was concentrating on his manner.

'Where is the seat of government of the United States of America situated?' I would ask and Hugh would look away across to the quarry face.

'Washington, sir.'

'Who is asking you the questions? Me or the quarry?'

'Don't be an ass!'

'Don't *you* be an ass, Hugh Reid! I wouldn't give a single mark to someone who is afraid to look at me!'

'I'm not afraid!' Hugh would glare fiercely into my eyes.

'Well, then – has there ever been a Jewish Prime Minister of Great Britain?'

89

Hugh would look down at his hand. 'Benjamin Disraeli, sir.'

'That's all wrong! And *look* where you're looking!'

'It is *not* wrong! Disraeli was Prime Minister and he was a Jew!'

Hugh would glare at me again.

'It's a wrong answer to the *question*, you ass! If they want you to name him, they will ask you. Don't give them anything for nothing.'

'Oh.'

Then, one day: 'Can you describe the main characteristics of the Aberdeen Angus breed of cattle?'

Hugh looked wildly round him like a hunted beast, from his own feet to the quarry face and over his shoulder as if trying to see the back of his own head and then gave a deep, sad, defeated sigh.

'Do you *know*?' I pursued. He stared at me as if terrified. 'Ach, *Hugh*! If you don't know, *say so* – and better still, look interested and say: 'I don't know, sir. What *are* the characteristics, please?'

'You can't do that in an *exam*!' Hugh protested. 'You have to *know* the things before you *go* there!'

'Don't be stupid, Hugh Reid! *Nobody* can know all the general knowledge in the world!'

'Well, anyway, you can't go asking *them* questions!'

'You can so! *I* do it all the time! They like it – it makes them feel all pleased and clever to sit there explaining things to you and it uses up the time.'

'But – but that's *awful*!' said Hugh, aghast with horror at what was, to him, sheer double-dealing and immorality – and probably it was, at that, too—

The great week came along and every day, for three days, Hugh went away in the morning train to Glasgow where the sittings took place, on neutral ground as it were, and every afternoon I was at the station to meet him when he came back. In Mr Lindsay's study, we would go over the question papers and by the end of the third day Mr Lindsay and Miss Hadley could decide that, at least, Hugh had not disgraced himself. But everything turned on the *viva* on the fourth day. On that third evening, before the *viva*, the Rector and Miss Hadley surprised me by not talking to Hugh of school work or scholastic matters at all. Instead of going to the Rector's study as we had been doing, we went to his house and his wife brought a tea-tray with biscuits and cake into the sitting-room. The talk was all about all sorts of general subjects, but just before Hugh and I came away, the Rector said: 'Hugh, what sort of job would you like to have when you are grown-up?'

Hugh flushed scarlet, looked wildly about the room and then glanced at his own left shoulder where no arm was.

'Never mind that!' the Rector said, 'Of all the jobs in the world, is there one that you would particularly like to do?'

'Yes, sir,' Hugh said quietly.

'All right.' Mr Lindsay rose and we all walked towards the door of the house. 'At the *viva* tomorrow, don't think about the people round the table. Don't give your whole mind to them. In the background, just keep thinking of that job you want to do. And listen, Hugh, so far, on paper, you look like a winner. Goodnight, my boy.'

Nobody said goodnight to me. Nobody remembered that I was there and neither did Hugh. At the end of the road that led to his home, he turned away in silence and left me and I walked to my own home in a semi-trance while my footsteps held to the rhythm: 'Hugh is a winner! Hugh is a winner!'

From that time, I have never been able to believe in the vanity of human wishes. I do not intend, here, to embark on a treatise on the subject, but I am prepared to say, with conviction, that all our wishing helped Hugh in some way that cannot be catalogued.

Three weeks later, all Scotland knew that Hugh was, in material fact, a winner and no-one was more surprised than Hugh himself. Also, no-one was more pleased than I was. I was more pleased than if I had won the bursary myself and so was my father.

'Of coorse,' said Miss Jean, 'if *Jinnit* had been sittin' — '

'Hold your tongue!' barked my father. 'The boy is a grand scholar – the Rector himself knows more about it than you or me!' Miss Jean snorted and retired to the scullery.

Once again, my father thought that the matter had ended there but it did not. A week later, Hugh walked past me at the school gates and would not look at me, and Granny Reid sent a letter to my father saying that she 'could not manage' to feed me at lunchtime any longer. On the Friday evening, my father went down alone to see her, came home and was terribly and terrifyingly silent. The silence persisted until the Sunday afternoon, when he and I left the house for our usual walk on the hill and round the farm. I did not at this moment know of the letter from Granny Reid, of course, for lunch at her house on Friday had seemed to me much as usual, Hugh and I being still too much excited about the bursary to have thought of anything else.

'Dad,' I said at last, into the silence, 'is anything wrong?' He stopped and looked at me, his eyes hard, his forehead frowning. 'Wrong?' he asked. 'I am black, burning ashamed of you! I never thought to be disgraced by one of my own in a way like this!'

'But, Dad, what have I done?'

'Ach, Janet!' He spat my name out as if it were unspeakably disgusting to his mouth. 'Why in God's name did ye go saying the like o' that?'

'But *what*, Dad? *What* did I say?'

A look of puzzled doubt now came into his eyes as he looked down at me. 'That if you had been in for that examination, Hugh would never have got his bursary! Janet, that was a terrible thing to—'

'I didn't! I haven't! Dad Sandison, how could you ever *believe* I said—'

'Don't deny it! Don't dare deny it, you damned, boasting little liar!' he shouted at me.

I recoiled from him, not in fear but in horror. 'That's not fair!' I shouted. 'You are wrong, all wrong! I did not do it!' I began to walk away from him, across the face of the hill.

'Janet, come back here! If you didn't say these things, who

92

did? No-one was concerned but you, Mr Lindsay and me—'

'Who do you *think* said them?' I shouted. 'Who do you *think*? Who has the longest tongue in *our* house?'

'Jean?' he asked, on a wondering questioning note. 'But why should *she* say the like o' that? She's not concerned at all. Janet, are you real *sure* you didn't say—'

I was blazingly angry now because he could think so easily that I might have done the shabby thing and that it was so unlikely that Jean could have done it.

'*Why* should she say it!' I mocked him. '*Why* does she say any of the things she says? There's no reason for saying half that she says! Just wait till I get down there!'

I set off, running, down the hill. All thought of 'not worrying' my father had left me, was lost in the red flush of fury that was staining my brain and in vain did he call after me to come back. Down over the grass helter-skelter I went, with him behind me, and by the time he arrived in the house the battle was in full swing. Miss Jean was huddled, bellowing and sobbing, in a chair while I, beside myself with rage, stood over her: ' – you long-tongued, interfering, gossiping, old trollop!' I bawled and followed it with a great deal more until Miss Jean began to kick her legs in the air and scream and sob in senseless, unhearing hysterics, with which I swung round on my father.

'*There's* who made the trouble!' I shouted. 'How dare you blame *me* for what *that* did?'

'Janet Sandison!' he yelled back at me through the screaming din. 'You damned little termagant! Jean, stop that noise for God's sake! People in Cairnton will hear you! Janet, get her a glass of water!'

'Get it for her your blooming self!' I shouted back and dashed out of the house and back on to the hill.

When I was alone in the hill breeze, my rage did not sustain me for long, but dissolved in an acid flood of shame, mingled with the bitter waters of disillusion, born of the fact that my father could automatically suspect me of being the cause of the trouble with Hugh and his Granny. To me, with my view of Miss Jean and my knowledge of her constantly wagging tongue, it had been immediately obvious that she was the author of the hurtful remarks about Hugh's bursary and I could not understand how my father could ever have suspected myself. He ought to have known, I felt, from his experience of me and his knowledge of my friendship with Hugh that I was incapable of saying such things. He ought, equally, to have known, I felt, from his experience of Miss Jean that the nature of the remarks was characteristic of her. It did not occur to me that, ever since we had come to Cairnton, I myself had been at pains to conceal much of Miss Jean's uglier side from my father that he might not be 'worried', nor did it occur to me that, in common with many big, physically powerful men, he had an inherent leaning towards people who were in some way weak. In mind, Miss Jean was unstable; she could be swayed by any personality in whose company she found herself and she had a flattering respect for the male of the species and his opinions. My father regarded her, indulgently, as something of a fool, but an amiable, harmless fool – a nonentity capable of no real evil. I do not think, even at this early time in my life, he regarded me as a fool or a nonentity, probably for no better reason than that family pride would not allow him to believe any Sandison to be a fool or a nonentity. This attitude of mind in him was proved, I think, when, late on that evening, he found me in my hidden cranny on the hillside.

'I'm not surprised that you are ashamed to come home,' he said. 'I never thought to be disgraced by two women fighting in my house.'

I rose and began to walk homewards beside him, saying nothing. 'And I'm surprised too at old Mrs Reid listening to Jean's nonsense and the nonsense of the Cairnton gossips. I thought she would have more sense.'

The implication was, I see now, that it would have been in order for Mrs Reid to listen if I, Janet Sandison, had made the remarks, but mere stupidity that she should have taken Miss Jean seriously, but as we walked down the hill, I was not thinking of this, but of the injustice that I should have been suspected of the remarks in the first place.

'I don't know how you got the idea that *I* would say things like that,' I said.

'Och, I see now that it was just some o' Jean's foolishness,' he said easily, but he continued in a sterner voice: 'But you needn't put on an insulted voice and try to make out that you are an angel. Not after that exhibition in the house today. That's no way for a young person to behave to a grown-up woman and don't you forget it!'

I walked on in silence, aware of nothing but bitter injustice. We were almost at the back gate into the garden and I could not collect my thoughts and find the words to question what he had said, to ask why Miss Jean could cause an uproar through 'her foolishness' and why, at the same time, I had to treat her with the respect due from a young person to a grown-up woman who should have 'known better'. The waters, then, were too deep for me and I floundered miserably in their bitter tides, but the hard core of my hatred for Miss Jean became enlarged by several more layers of gritty deposit. What my home should have in it, I told myself, was not a person like me, but someone like Annie, who could not win a prize to save her life. *That* is what would suit Miss Jean, I thought, and be the only thing to stop her from making trouble.

A short time later, I brought home my Third Year First Prize (Hugh came second) and put the books away in my room without even showing them to my father in case they would remind everybody of the 'Bursary Trouble'.

I was glad to get away to Reachfar for the summer, away from 'the Toon' which, split into two factions, stared at me in the street and whispered in corners; away from the school which, split into two factions, made, one half, derisory calls after me, and the other half, derisory calls after Hugh. I do not know whether my father ever discovered precisely what Miss Jean had said or to whom she had said it, but she had certainly quoted, out of its context, out of its mood, my childish, careless, ill-expressed: 'Hugh can have it!' Now, many years later, I am sure that Miss Jean has never realized the far-reaching misery that she caused to Hugh, Granny

95

and me by her ill-judged, boasting gossip, for, true to my principle of 'not worrying' my father, I did not mention in the house the catcalls of my colleagues or my own unhappiness and, very soon, for Miss Jean and my father, the matter fell into that limbo that is full of blown-out tea-cup storms.

I remember, however, that this storm and its unhappiness was one of the things that accompanied me home to Reachfar that year and, one Sunday, when My Friends George and Tom and I took a walk up to the Juniper Place to sit 'yarning' in the sun, I told them something of it. George had made some remark about life at Cairnshaws and in the course of my reply the name of Miss Jean was mentioned.

'She seems to be a fine woman,' George said. 'Your father writes that she is a grand housekeeper. You were lucky to get her, for to have the house comfortable and the food good chust makes all the difference.'

'That's what I think too, forbye,' said Tom. 'A house with a good woman in it is a-all the difference between being a house and not being a house at a-all. She's a nice woman, Janet?'

'She's all right,' I said.

'What's wrong with her?' pounced George who, though reputed to be a 'clown', has always been the sharpest-witted member of my family.

'She talks too much,' I said. 'She just gabs on all day and never thinks of what she's saying.'

'Och, that's not much harm,' said Tom comfortably. 'Some folk will speak everlasting – especially weemen – but a body doesna have to be listening to them.'

I did not see any point in telling George and Tom that the people of Cairnton were only too fond of listening and repeating what they had heard and there the matter dropped.

Shortly after my return to Cairnshaws, Mr Hill died, leaving his wife and Tommie, the loutish only child, with the large dairy and a great deal of money, but no business acumen or farming knowledge of any kind. Tommie, who had been whiling away his last two years at a Glasgow Technical School of some kind, gave up his so-called studies, coaxed a rakish-looking sports car out of his besotted mother and came home to take up his position as a gentleman farmer. My father, who liked most young people, had never been able, as he put it, to 'take to' Tommie and I believe that but for the pleadings of Mrs Hill, supported by her lawyers, and a natural liking for the model dairy which he had done much to create, he would have left Cairnshaws at that time, in spite of the fact that such a change in our economic situation would have rendered my future education a burden.

However, two years rolled past, with Miss Jean – whom I now, at her own request, called simply 'Jean' – talking as hard as ever, Tommie Hill scouring the country in his sports car from bar to bar, my father running the farm, Annie Black working in an office in Glasgow and Hugh and I progressing through our Fourth and Fifth Years without ever addressing a word to one another. The local talk about the bursary competition had died away long ago, but the breach that the talk had corroded in our young friendship had merely grown deeper and wider through time.

Towards the end of our Fifth Year, Hugh and I, among others, were eligible to sit the examination which would determine our entrance to a university or other higher form of education, and shortly before this Mr Lindsay called me to his study.

'I have entered you for the Higher Leaving, Janet,' he said, 'but you will have to stay on with me here next year nevertheless. You are too young for the university.'

This was a severe blow to me. My father's life was one long battle against extravagances of Tommie Hill, combined with a tedious series of rescues from one drunken scrape, after another, and the longer I took over this education business, I felt, the longer would be my father's purgatory. Also, the time was coming when Reachfar would need him, for my grandfather and Tom were getting too old for the long, hard, unremitting days of work and my father was the eldest son whose duty it was to hold the home together.

'And what about the City and Western Counties, sir?' I asked.

'That again,' he replied. 'You are not eligible until you are sixteen.' He smiled at my disappointment, for, of course, he did not know all that lay behind it. 'Come, Janet, there's no hurry, you know. You will enjoy a sixth year here with your Higher Leaving in your pocket. There will be no curriculum for you. You will study mostly by yourself with a little special tuition from Miss Hadley, Mr Adair and myself. I think you will enjoy yourself.'

Mr Lindsay, with his usual flair, was right and during that sixth year at the Academy I did indeed enjoy myself, more than I had enjoyed any other year of the some eleven that had been devoted to my education and all the years of it had been pleasant for me. Hugh, at the end of our fifth year, left school to go to his university and thus the daily reminder by his presence of the breach between us was removed. Miss Hadley opened up two new worlds for me by taking me, one Saturday afternoon, to a Beethoven concert in Edinburgh and, on another Saturday afternoon, to a performance of *Twelfth Night* given by a touring company in Glasgow. Mr Lindsay paid another call on my father and told him that my liking for music and the theatre should be encouraged and, thereafter, I was given five shillings every Saturday to cover my train or 'bus fare, the price of a theatre or concert ticket and my afternoon tea and I had to return to Cairnton, without fail, by a 'bus that arrived at seven-fifteen. These were the most enjoyable theatre-goings of my life, for the week built up like a pyramid to the glorious peak of Saturday afternoon. In the Monday newspaper, there would be a choice of at least six entertainments for the Saturday to come, and by Tuesday evening, after much pleasurable consideration, I would have reduced the choice to five and so the process went on until, by Saturday, there remained only the proud performance that was to have my three-shilling patronage (four shillings, if I did without tea). And the theatre performance, or the concert, was not all. At that time, it was customary for young girls to be adjured, before leaving home, 'not to speak to any strangers', but my father did not think of this, and Jean, who had taken up a stand-offish

98

attitude to me ever since she had been scolded so severely over the bursary affair, made no comment except to say that she could not see why 'the Cairnton pictur's are no' guid enough for her, like ither folk'. So I was quite uninhibited about 'speaking to strangers' and would 'speak' in 'bus, theatre foyer or teashop when I was in the mood to anyone who was kind enough to 'speak' to me.

Also, in an adventurous way, I never went twice to the same tea-shop or café, but tried a new one each week, which was easy to do, for, as anyone who knows Sauchiehall Street, Glasgow, and its environs will agree, they are more than rich in tea-shops.

One Saturday, I decided to give the benefit of my shilling to a certain Sauchiehall Street café which differed from any that I had visited before in that it was approached from the pavement by a long, narrow, wooden staircase that led to the first floor. (It was really a side entrance to the lounge of a hotel, but I did not know this at the time.) It was about six in the evening when I walked into the room and there was about the place a difference from the other tea-shops which I was, at first, at a loss to identify. Having ordered my modest cup of tea and sweet cakes, I sat back and looked about me. In Glasgow, six o'clock was the hour of the 'high tea', but here there were no respectable couples enjoying fish and chips or bacon and eggs before going to their Saturday evening pictures. Here there were no pretty mothers, with shopping baskets, trying to control the avid greed of a healthy young son and daughter who were arguing shrilly about who was to have the cake with the pink icing. No. The clientele of this place, apparently, was entirely female, and ladies such as I had never seen before, who had a strange uniformity about them. They had faces that were neither young nor old, but all bearing a queer, indescribable resemblance to one another, and there was, too, a uniformity about their style of dress. They all wore the same pattern of coat, with a long, rolled collar of light-coloured fur, into which was pinned an artificial flower. They all had small hats, high-heeled shoes and large handbags. They all had painted faces and they were all smoking cigarettes. Actresses off duty, I wondered. No. That could not be. I myself had just come from the theatre and the players could not yet have had time to change their clothes, while, from the evidence of the used cups in front of them and full ash-trays on the tables, these ladies had been here for some time. I studied the various groups of four and five while I ate my cakes. They were not like friends who had met for tea, either. They were not chatting to one another, more than to exchange a word now and then. They did not look amused by one another – indeed, the air seemed to be full of a critical distrust and dislike that seemed to radiate from them, as they exchanged their brief, desultory remarks and then resumed their bored stare at the entrance.

Suddenly, another of them came through the door at the top of the stairs, wearing the same fur-collared coat, the same hat, shoes and large handbag, and I watched her cross the room to join a group in the corner who greeted her with a bored: 'Hello, Annette.' I could hardly believe my own eyes and ears, for the newcomer was none other than Annie Black.

Jean had told my father and me, many times and with much undercurrent of feeling that 'long schooling wasnae everything' and that Annie Black was earning 'good money' as a secretary in Glasgow although she had 'different workin' 'oors fae ither folk'. Annie, Jean said, worked for a gentleman who was away travelling through the week so that, instead of being able to come home for weekends, Annie had to work on Saturdays and Sundays and came home to see her people, usually, on Tuesdays or Wednesdays. I was giving all this my consideration, now, while the café was beginning to fill up with gentlemen, gentlemen of all ages, wearing what my father would call 'counter-jumpers' suits, flashy ties with breast-pocket handkerchiefs to match, coloured socks and pointed shoes. I now discovered that the place was not an ordinary tea-shop after all, but was licensed, for a large screen was suddenly rolled up to the ceiling at one side, disclosing a bar backed by shelves of bottles and glasses, from which drinks were dispensed to the gentlemen at the tables. I had just finished my observation of this new development when an oldish gentleman, fat, with a purplish face and small eyes, came in and sat at a table near the centre of the room. He ordered a drink, looked around him for a moment and then gave a glance of curious significance at the table where Annie was sitting. A few seconds later, Annie nodded to her companions, rose and walked across the room to sit down, her back to me, and begin to talk to the gentleman. It must be her employer, back from his week's travels, I thought.

I went back to Cairnton in the 'bus as usual, but when I reached home I did not mention having seen Annie, for she was a subject in which I found as little interest as ever, and which, I knew from experience, was only too liable to 'start bother' between Jean and myself.

As the year 1925 turned into the year 1926, in March of which I would be sixteen, Jean went off on a new tack when she and I happened to be alone in the house and she talked to me a great deal, in a giggling way, of what she called 'the boys'. All this talk came to a head – a pimplish, suppurating sort of head, as were most of the heads developed between myself and Jean – one week in late February or early March, just before my sixteenth birthday.

On a Friday evening, Jean cut her hand quite badly with the vegetable knife and my father called Doctor Blair to dress the wound, whereupon the doctor told Jean that the hand must be kept dry in the dressing until Monday, when he would pay another visit, so that she was immobilized in a chair by the fire with the arm in a sling. She was, of course, in tears and, after the doctor had gone, she looked at my father with despairing eyes and said: 'But whit are we gaun tae *dae*? There's the bakin' the morn an' the cookin' an' the washin' on Monday an' – '.

'Good God, calm yourself, Jean!' said my father. 'Janet is here – we won't die of starvation or dirt!'

She looked at me with eyes full of tears and disparaging doubt.

'There's the schule on Monday,' she said.

'I'm not in curriculum at school, Jean,' I said. 'Dad can send a note to Mr Lindsay and I can stay at home until you are better.'

'Now, stop crying, Jean,' my father went on. 'Is the hand comfortable?'

'Aye—'

'Well, that's fine. Just you sit there and calm down. Make some supper for us, Janet – something that Jean can eat one-handed.'

'Cheese pudding?' I asked. 'You can eat it with a spoon—'

'Whaur can *you* mak' a cheese puddin'?' Jean broke in.

'She can try,' said my father. 'She'll never be younger to learn and if it's not good she can stop home from the theatre tomorrow!' He gave me a jocular smile.

I made the supper and even Jean had to admit that the cheese pudding was light and highly edible although she continued to wonder aloud how I had learned to make it, in spite of the fact that she must have been aware that I had watched her make it a hundred times. The next day, being Saturday, I cleaned the house, did the meals and arranged a quick supper that I could serve immediately I came in from my visit to Glasgow, where I forwent my teashop tea and came home by an earlier 'bus.

By the following Thursday, when the doctor called for the third time, Jean's hand was entirely healed and he said that she could now work normally again, but I went about preparing the supper as usual on the grounds that another twelve non-working hours would do the hand no harm and I had planned the meal in any case, so she and my father sat at the fire while I went about my duties. I picked up the kettle to refill it if necessary, tilting it forward with my left hand and lifting the lid off with my right hand that I might look inside.

'Ye stupit fool!' Jean screamed. 'You'll scald yersel' wi' that steam!'

'No, Jean,' I said, standing between them, the tilted kettle in one hand, the lid in the other. 'If you tilt it like this, the steam goes straight up in the air and misses your hand.'

'That's right enough,' said my father, looking with interest at hand and steaming kettle. 'You can see it.'

'Oh, her and her bliddy science!' said Jean and flounced out of the room.

I was not – and still am not, for that matter – a very sweetness-and-light sort of person and if it had not been for the old inhibition about 'worrying' my father, I would have hurled kettle, steam and all at Jean's flouncing, departing back, but I said nothing.

'Och, never heed her, Janet,' said my father. 'She doesna' like being idle like she's had to be for the last few days.'

This seemed sensible and true enough and when, a little later, supper was ready and my father called to her to join us, her mood, in her typical way, had completely changed.

As I have tried to tell you, I did not, from the beginning, understand Jean's temperament and I do not understand it even now, so that I can only tell of her behaviour without attempting to interpret it fully. One of the strangest things, to me, about her mind was that she seemed to expect that any words spoken by herself, no matter how scornful, insulting or hurtful, should be at once forgiven and forgotten, but, at the same time, any words spoken by another person that she chose to interpret as scornful, insulting or hurtful towards herself, she felt herself to be justified in remembering for ever. It was as if in some queer, subconscious way, she was aware that her own words and thoughts were completely valueless and without meaning, and without knowing that she did it, she acted in a manner logical to this awareness.

Having come to the supper-table in her changed mood, therefore, her remark about my 'bliddy science' was forgotten and she began, in a giggling way, to say that it was about time I took an interest in 'the boys' and what about Tommie Hill? *He* would be a good catch – he had plenty of money – and Cairnshaws was a fine farm and he was just the right age for me. My father sat eating in silence, while I, who had not yet forgotten the remark of a few minutes ago, became more and more irritated. Jean chattered unconsciously on, genial, generous – even fulsome now –

103

in her complimentary attitude towards me. 'An' Tommie could go a lot further an' fare a lot worse,' she said, smiling benignly at me. 'Goodness knows whaur ye picked it up, readin' books all the time like ye dae, but Ah *will* say ye mak' a fine job o' the hoosekeepin'. Am' whaur did ye learn tae iron like that? The parlour curtains are jist lovely. An' this pastry—'

She was being very generous, lavish with the richest praise she could bestow for the only craft for which she had any respect, but I was sick and tired of the sound of her voice and I could see that my father had been irritated at her suggestions about Tommie Hill, so as I rose to pour more tea, I said lightly and carelessly: 'Oh, dry up, Jean! Any able-bodied person can do a little washing and cooking – there's nothing to it!'

Her prattle ceased, her face became stony and, thankful for the respite, I paid no attention, but at supper the following evening, she placed a perfect savoury soufflé on the table and said: 'Help yourselves while it's hot. It's nothing much – I've got nae book-learnin' but any fool can cook!'

Jean and I had now known each other for nearly six years. The situation was not improving between us.

CHAPTER SEVEN

All these petty incidents of which I have told, and there were many more besides, were another crumbling away of the land between Jean and myself so that the gulf between us became ever wider and deeper and, as is the way with forces of destruction, the hurtful remark, on either side, in this year, caused a landslide much greater than the same hurtful remark would have caused if spoken a year ago, when the gulf was less wide.

My sixteenth birthday came and went, but I was still a lanky, coltish schoolgirl, showing little sign of the adolescent development that had been Annie Black's pride at the age of twelve, and Jean now, when my father was not present, began to make suggestions that not only was I not like 'ither folk' in general ways, but that there was definitely something 'terrible wrang aboot' me. The old grey nightmare of the gaping jaws of the County Asylum began once more to lurk about the house.

It is difficult to describe the state of mind that she induced in me. In an inward, arrogant way, I despised her for her passive lack of intelligence and active silliness and I despised her still more for a cunning, feline malice that I could feel behind what she said. At the same time, though, my early training in my own family was strong in me and, from my youngest days, I had been aware that country women had an instinctive knowledge of many mysterious matters. Certainly of the women of my own family, this was true. At one moment, then, I was confident that Jean was talking nonsense out of her sly, morbid prudery and that Doctor Blair had spoken truly when he had said that I would be late in developing, while, the next moment, I would be thinking of Annie Black and all the other girls I knew and their giggling walks in the evenings along the Glasgow Road in the company of a band of boys. All this was further aggravated by more secret observation of Annie on Saturday evenings in the café in Sauchiehall Street. The first time I saw her there, I would have spoken to her had she not gone to join the fat man, but when, out of curiosity, I revisited the café a fortnight later and saw her join, in a similar way, an entirely different man, I realized for the first time, in a vague way, the true nature of Annie's 'work'. The realization was a shock. To some minds, and mine is one of them, prostitution of any kind is so repellent as to be almost mentally unacceptable, and 'the oldest profession in the world', as practised by Annie, apparently from choice, was doubly repulsive.

Her cunning, in the leading of her double life, was amazing. At Cairnton, that hotbed of gossip, Annie's reputation was quite unsullied. Dutifully, she came home every Tuesday or Wednesday to spend a night with her people and she would carry back to Glasgow the fresh butter, eggs and gifts of clothing that her doting mother loved to lavish upon her. Hitherto, I had not been interested in Jean's stories of Annie, how well she was doing at her 'job' and the new cami-knickers of crêpe-de-chine that Mrs Black had given her this week, but now I listened to these tales with quiet, concealed interest. I also began to walk abroad on Tuesday and Wednesday evenings in the hope of seeing the Cairnton version of the 'Annette' that I had watched from behind the potted palm on the previous Saturday. Annette to Annie was an interesting transformation. Annie did not wear the coat with the long, white fur collar and the artificial flower. Oh, no. Annie wore a coat with, admittedly, a small fur collar and she wore a neat felt hat similar to those worn by all her local contemporaries. At Cairnton, she was simply one more farmer's daughter, walking about in the evening with the other farmers' and townspeople's daughters and 'the boys'.

Hugh, now, was travelling up and down to the university

every day and I saw him hardly at all until I began my local observations of Annie and then I noticed that when Annie was in a group, Hugh also tended to be in the same group. When, with a nauseated misery, I had established Hugh's interest in Annie beyond all doubt, I ceased to haunt the Glasgow Road on Tuesdays and Wednesdays and returned to my 'own' places – the old quarry and the hill which were beginning to burgeon with all the clean freshness of Spring, but I invariably was at pains to give Jean the impression that I had been out along the Glasgow Road with the 'ither folk', for this curbed, to some extent, her remarks about my 'difference'.

Ever since my early childhood, I have liked to sit in trees. At Reachfar, I had a number of favourite trees for sitting in, all with names, such as the 'Waving Tree' which was a slender birch that responded to every wayward breeze and the 'Stalwart Tree', a big fir with many crooked branches that hardly moved a single one of its needles even in a November gale. When I had first come to Cairnton and had explored the hill and then the old quarry, I had climbed as a matter of course all the trees, and half-unconsciously, had selected certain ones for sitting in. At Reachfar, I had a 'Thinking Place' on the moor which was a dark dell among the firs, but at Cairnton I had a 'Thinking Tree', a huge ash which stood on the cliff above the dark pool in the old quarry. This Spring, I spent many hours in its comfortable forked branches, among its bunches of young green leaves that overhung the cliff face and the dark pool.

On an evening late in May, I was reclining in a forked branch in this tree with somewhat the feeling of ease and freedom, I thought, that fat cupids must have when riding on their fat clouds of puffy cumulus. I suppose that the feeling of ease and freedom when tree-borne above the earth was symbolical of some youthful need to escape from the many things I did not understand – from Jean's constant and cruel little pricks of malice, from the sordid picture of Annie's work in Glasgow, from the sense of loss that I still suffered in regard to Hugh and, above all, I realized on this evening that I had a need to escape from my own home, which now had a queer indefinable atmosphere that was making me bitterly unhappy. All I knew was that something 'different' had entered there; something that I could not identify, yet something that seemed to be eating away at the roots of my own security. I lay in my tree and wished that the month of June, with the bursary examination, was over, so that I would be free to go home to Reachfar.

I suddenly heard voices coming from the direction of the field path which led towards the quarry from Cairnton and looked down through my branches to see Annie Black and Tommie Hill come down the green slope that led to the quarry floor. I felt a rush of indignation at this invasion of a quiet place which I had always regarded as my own, and where, indeed, I had never seen another human being except my father and Hugh, and I lay back along my branch, ignoring them, waiting for them to cross the quarry basin and take the path that would lead them on to Cairnshaws. They did not, however, pass straight through. Instead, they first sat down and then lay down on the grass, in a thicket of wild rose and hawthorn, so that they were invisible, probably, from every point except the one that I occupied, high in my tree on the summit of the cliff. Repelled and sickly fascinated, all at once, I was privileged, to all intents and purposes, to see Annie Black 'at work'.

I was no stranger to the acts of sex. I had been brought up at Reachfar where we made our living, largely, by breeding animals, and that apart, once before as a young child, in a similar lonely place, I had been the accidental witness of the antics of a couple of grown-up people in the toils of the uglier lust. But Annie Black was, for me, now, the incarnation of the falseness that I found so dominant in Cairnton life, while Tommie Hill was a 'worrier' of my father, in addition to being a loose-mouthed, fleshy lout that few young girls or women would have cared to touch, I thought.

There was nothing of the lingering of lovers between Annie and Tommie. The transaction between them was over in a very short time, whereupon they parted, Annie going in the direction of Cairnton and Tommie going along the other path that led to his home. Quite suddenly, I, my tree, the quarry and the rose and hawthorn thicket were alone again and it was difficult to believe what I had seen. I settled back in my forked branch, gazed at the sky and gave myself up to wondering how long it would be before the secret of Annie's profession was an open one in Cairnton. This red light of hers, surely, was not one to be hidden much longer under a bushel.

Strangely, however, the truth about Annie did not leak out, although all Cairnton and its district were more interested in her this Spring than in any other single individual, for it became generally known that several of the boys were 'after her' and, in particular, that Tommie Hill and Hugh Reid were in hot competition for her favours.

'It's not to be surprised at,' said Jean, with a side-glance at me over our supper-table. 'She's an awful bonnie lassie an' aye sae bright and cheery. That's what the boys like.'

I made no comment.

'An' Mrs Black was tellin' me that she has a boy in the office in Glasgow, forbye. He gave her a lovely bottle o' scent for her birthday. Imagine that Hughie Reid thinkin' *he* has a chance wi' her! The puir silly sowl, as if a bonnie lassie like Annie wid be bothered wi' the likes o' him!'

This was the only side of the eternal commentary in praise of Annie that worried me and hurt me. My groping, adolescent mind could not grasp why My Friend Hugh was interested in Annie, perhaps because it was unwilling to accept the fact that Hugh and Tommie Hill were interested in Annie for the same reason, for that would put Hugh on a par with the revolting Tommie.

When I look back upon it now, it seems to me that the mental life which I lived at this time resembled a flat, pleasant enough, but featureless plain, in which I wandered about, happily enough, but with a sense of waiting to return to the hills behind from which I had come – Reachfar – and, after that, make a new departure by going to the University. I could see and feel the hills behind me and I could look forward to the new departure that lay ahead, but, on either side, there lay what would always be, for me, terra incognita. On one side was the world in which Annie, Tommie Hill, Hugh and the Cairnton people lived, and on the other was the world of Jean, which seemed to creep ever closer, hemming me in and yet remaining unknowable. The explored plain compassed by my understanding was limited on either side by these steep cliffs and dark forests that defied all my efforts to gain knowledge of them and establish an understanding of them.

Early in June, the examination for the City and Counties Bursary came along and it seemed to me that everyone was much more excited and anxious than I was. The pupils of the senior forms at school talked a great deal of embarrassing rubbish about 'the honour of the school' and how, if I were successful, 'what a one in the eye it would be for all the big Glasgow schools'. Mr Lindsay, Miss Hadley and Mr Adair said little, but there was a strange, uncomfortable tenseness about them. On the Sunday evening before the examinations started on the Monday, the Minister called and outraged by father's Highland modesty by talk of his 'brilliant' daughter and also offended his religious sensibilities by saying that we must all 'pray for success'. Jean, having caught the local infection, talked of nothing else, but from her own curious point of view, which led her to tell me that 'it would be a queer-like thing if a lassie fae the Heilan's was to win the City and Counties' and she hoped aloud that 'that man Lindsay kent whit he wis daein'' in entering me and had not done something that 'wid mak' a public fool o' a' Cairnton'. Indeed, had the candidate for the examinations been a finely-balanced, nervous scholar, instead of the cold-blooded, stolid repository of academic information which was myself, the said candidate would have been a screaming, drooling lunatic by the dawn of the fateful Monday morning. As it was, I ate a good breakfast and went calmly off to the station to catch the train for Glasgow.

Sitting in the train that carried me through the industrial smoke that rings Glasgow on all sides, I fell to wondering

110

what the essay subjects would be, for the first day was devoted to the examination in English, an important part of which was the essay, and as I walked down to the ticket barrier at my Glasgow station, I was still engaged with these thoughts.

'Janet,' said a voice behind me.

I turned round to face Hugh Reid. I said nothing.

'You going to the C. and C. exams?' he asked.

'Yes, Hugh.'

'Good luck,' he said. 'I feel for sure that you'll win it!'

He turned away, ran out of the station and sprang aboard a tramcar headed for the university.

It was strange that, when I sat down at the table that carried my name and number in the large, table-filled hall, and when the doors were closed and we were allowed to open the folder that contained the first examination paper, the first essay subject from the choice of six should be the word 'Friendship'. My pen travelled across the book of paper all morning without my conscious effort.

All the week, from Monday morning till Thursday evening, I concentrated on nothing except the examinations and, as if my essential self had disappeared, and temporarily, I had become nothing but a question-answering automaton, I have no precise memories of these four days from that moment when I read the word 'Friendship' on the Monday morning until I awoke on the Friday morning to the consciousness that, for well or ill, the examination was over. My father asked me how things had gone and I replied that I did not know. Mr Lindsay, Miss Hadley and Mr Adair, on the Friday, asked me for details of the question papers and of the answers I had made, but I was so vague and unintelligent in my replies that they gave up after a short time and retired, trying unsuccessfully to conceal their disappointment. I was aware of their belief that I had probably not only failed, but had demonstrated myself to be a complete idiot, and because I respected them and believed in their beliefs, I too accepted the idea of failure. I was neither ashamed nor disappointed. I had no feeling of any kind in the matter, beyond the thought that my going forward for the examination at all had been slightly ridiculous. I remembered the scholarly-looking young man with the incipient moustache who had sat at a table two yards to my left and the earnest, pimply young woman who had scribbled with a knowledgeable air at a table two yards to my right. I had not seen, in all that scholarly company, another female with pigtails with ribbons at their ends. Oh, well. It did not matter. I was more fortunate than My Friend Hugh. My goal of the university would not be affected by my failure in this examination.

As I prowled about on the hill on Sunday morning in the lark-song-sparkling, early-June sun, I was happier than I had been for many months as my mind played about round the thought of Hugh and how, now, when next I saw him, I would be able to talk to him again. We would have many months to rediscover together and Hugh would be different, just as I was different, but basically he would be the same, just as I was the same. It was the wee Hughie Reid whom I had always known who had looked at me out of the maturer eyes and had spoken in the man's voice the words 'I feel for sure' at the Glasgow station on Monday morning. I turned the thought over and over in my mind and as it turned it seemed to make a sweet, soaring song like the song of the larks. As I walked down the green slope towards the house at lunchtime, I was aware of a curious change in myself, a strange change that was accompanied by a vague physical discomfort and, in my bedroom, I discovered that the long-delayed change from girlhood to womanhood had, this morning, taken place. I joined my father and Jean at the table in a mood of secret, almost drunken, exhilaration, with the thought that I could have *real* fun with Jean now, by keeping the change a secret and letting her prattle on about people who 'were fair by-ordinar', no' like ither folk an' heidit for the Asylum'.

My withdrawn attitude to my home, Jean and even my father, which had been developing gradually over the years, became manifest to me in the course of that meal. I had come to this house, among these Cairnton people, as part of the Reachfar entity which was known in my mind as 'My Family'

112

and, at Reachfar, I was still part of that entity, but, here at Cairnton, I belonged to no-one but myself. My 'Cairnton father' even was not an intimate of mine. Among these people – with the sole exception of Hugh Reid – I was merely a sojourner and a stranger.

On the Sunday evening, my father and I went for our usual Sunday walk which we had taken together almost every Sunday for the last six years. Constraint was strong between us, so strong as to be almost material in essence, so that the air was turgid with it and as I walked in silence beside him I realized that this constraint was no new thing, but something which had been growing and gaining strength ever since my father had 'gone over to Jean's side' about the sleep-walking episode of four years ago.

'I wonder how you got on in that exam,' he said at last.

'I just don't know, Dad. There were nearly a hundred entrants. They all seemed much older than me. It wasn't like an exam at school, where you know the other people and what they are good at and where they are weak. So I just don't know.' I was speaking jerkily, but I could not help it.

'I can see that,' he agreed. 'But did you find any of the questions hard to answer?'

'No. But then, I never do. You either know a thing or you don't. And there was plenty of choice of questions. It was as if – as if they weren't interested in *what* you knew so much as how – how you *thought* about things.'

'I see. An' what about the *viva* as the Rector calls it?'

'They were very nice.'

'What sort of things did they ask?'

'Where I was born—'

'Oh? And what had they to say about that?'

'They asked all sorts of questions about the trees and flowers and birds and animals at Reachfar—'

He smiled a little. 'That would be easy – and then?'

'A man asked me what I thought of Communism.'

'Good God! What did you say?'

'I said I didn't know much about it and had never read Karl Marx or anything, but I understood the theory was that

113

all people were alike and on a common level and that I didn't agree with that. And he said why didn't I agree and I said because people just *weren't* all alike and that was the end of it. And he said but mightn't it be better for Scotland, say, if there were no rich and no poor, like Russia. So I said I didn't see how that could be managed, really, because here he was with the other ladies and gentlemen trying to choose the likeliest person to have the C. and C. Bursary, for instance, and even if you made Scotland into a country that didn't have bursaries, there would still be people who could win them if you *had* them, because no matter what you did on the surface people were not all alike underneath, and then they all laughed.'

'They laughed? Och, Janet!'

'I laughed too,' I said.

'And what then?'

'Then a lady asked me if I could knit socks.'

'God Almighty!' said my father. 'Likely she thought that was all you were good for?!'

'No, it wasn't like that, Dad. They *all* started to talk about knitting and a gentleman said that it was a mystery to him and very, very clever. So I told him about Danny Maclean.'

'Danny Maclean?'

'Yes. I told him how Danny knitted his own socks and how Danny said that to knit was easy but that the person who *invented* knitting was a genius.'

'And what then?'

'They started to ask all about Danny, so I told them about Danny's bees and how they would come and sit on him and not sting him and how Danny plays the fiddle. And then they all started talking about music.'

'How long were you with them, for pity's sake?' my father asked.

'About an hour, I think.'

'Well,' he said, 'I don't know. I just don't know.'

And that, I thought, made two of us, and neither of us would know until a certain name was published in the leading Glasgow newspaper a fortnight hence. From what I had seen of the candidates, it would probably be the name of the scholarly young man with the incipient moustache, I thought.

'I haven't a chance,' I warned my father now. 'The others were so much more grown-up. They are just *bound* to know more than I do. I'm sorry, Dad.'

'Och, it doesna matter. It's not as if we were in sore need of the money. It's not like it was with the Reid laddie.'

I wanted to tell my father of how Hugh had spoken to me at the station on the Monday morning, but his face was closed and distrait and I felt the constraint again so that I could not break the silence. It clouded about us all the way round the dairy and across the fields on our way home, right to the last gate into the pasture where our house and garden occupied a corner. Here, my father did not at once open the gate but leaned on its top bar and stared across the grass at the house.

'I—' he began, and paused and then: 'I want to tell you – tell you that Jean and I are going to be married.'

The rectangular green field with its enclosing fence, its brown and white cows, our neat house at the corner and the spreading elm tree in another corner tilted crazily before my eyes as if house, cows, tree and fence were a child's toys stuck to a rigid green board, and across the surface of my mind flashed a phrase that Jean used so frequently that it had long ago become meaningless: 'Ah nearly faintit!' The phrase was not meaningless at this moment. I think that I was about to faint, but I clutched the top bar of the gate and stared hard at the tilted field to which the brown and white cows were sticking like flies on a slope and waited for it to come back to the horizontal.

'Oh. When?' I managed to say at last.

'Next Friday.'

'Oh.' I stared away across the field, past the house, to the cairn at the top of the glen.

'We plan to go away for a week and then come back here and we'll all go up to Reachfar together after the school closes.'

'I see.'

'Where would you like to go while we're away?'

'Go?' I asked stupidly.

'Mrs Hill has invited you and so has Mrs Black.'

I swallowed something bitter. 'Do I *have* to go anywhere, Dad? I'd rather stay in our own house. I can manage for myself.'

'That's true,' he agreed. 'You'll not be lonely, though?'

'Lonely? Oh no, Dad.'

I wanted to get away by myself. I did not want any more discussion but I could see that my father wanted to have all his arrangements clear-cut and settled. I must not 'worry' him.

'I'll be fine, Dad,' I told him. 'We can tell Mrs Hill and Mrs Black that I've got studying to do or something like that.'

I opened the gate, walked through and stood waiting for him to follow me. Before he moved, he stared at me for a moment, his forehead wrinkled and puzzled.

'Janet, you're – you're not pleased?'

I could not look at him. I did not want him to be worried or puzzled by anything that I might think or feel, but, at the same time, I could not simulate the pleasure and approval that he wanted from me. I did not speak.

'She is a nice woman,' he said in a pleading tone, 'and has been very good to us. I know that she can be foolish, whiles, but she is a lot more settled than she was—'

'I – I hope that you will be happy, Dad,' I managed to say at last and we began to walk across the field to the house.

During supper and for the short time after the meal that I spent in the living-room, I looked at Jean with more attention than, probably, I had concentrated on her for several years. I found myself comparing her with the woman I had first talked to and tried to understand when, as a child of eleven, I had first met her. She had changed, outwardly, very little. She was still the pretty, buxom, fair-skinned, reddish-haired woman I had first seen, and still as 'trig' (to use a Cairnton adjective) of figure as ever. But her face, now, this evening, had the smug, satisfied, complacent look that was worn by the prosperous housewives of Cairnton, a look very different from the blinking, uncertain glance of Miss Laidlaw at the Public Library or of Miss Aitken who played the organ in church. I could not find words, then, for the look on Jean's face, but I know, now, that it was the look of the woman who had Made Her Mark, Achieved Her End and was proudly satisfied with both.

I do not remember a great deal of the ensuing week, but I remember that on the Thursday evening – the wedding was to take place quietly at the Manse the next afternoon – Jean, with a tentative, touching, shy pride, asked me to look at her wedding clothes. I went with her into the bedroom she used where, laid on the bed, in proud panoply was a 'costume' of light saxe blue cloth, a blue hat with a pink silk rose in it, a red fox fur, brown kid gloves and shoes and a pink frilly blouse. I thought of my mother's plain hats, her quiet grey and deep blue coats and skirts and dresses, her plain blouses that were usually white and the slim-lasted shoes that were so different from these fat little brown things that were too high of heel for Jean's buxom weight.

'It's all very nice, Jean,' I said. 'I think you'll look lovely.'

I felt that I was touching the slimy depths of hypocrisy and longed to get away, out on to the green hill in the evening sun.

Jean fingered, lovingly, the frills of the blouse.

'You'll be – all right – while we're away?' she asked hesitatingly.

'Of course!' I said.

Neither of us had any more words. Jean, so garrulous about minor things, so full of words for petty gossip, was, I see now, trying to make some contact with me. I so full of thoughts – jealousy, probably, and ugly resentment, certainly – and yet aware too of Jean's blind urge towards some rapprochement, would, if I could, have tried to come to sympathy with her, but I was too young and gauche to find the words that would establish the contact. The moment passed over us, leaving me with nothing but the urge to escape, and Jean, having exhausted her ability to express herself, was, I think, glad to see me go. I went out on to the hill, came home and went to bed and, the next morning,

I went off to school as usual. I came home in the afternoon to the empty house with no sense of anything other than relief. I was glad to be alone, glad that the awkwardness was over and behind me. I did not spare a thought for my father and Jean. I cooked my supper and sat down beside the fire with Chaucer's *Canterbury Tales* and had a delightful evening. I did not happen to read the tale of Chaunticleer and Pertelote that evening. If I had, perhaps Chaunticleer's 'Mulier hominis est confusio' might have made me think of them.

This week was my first experience in life of being in a house entirely by myself and I enjoyed it. I realized that I had always had the need to be by myself, and had supplied and indulged that need, both here and at Reachfar, by my excursions to hill and moor, but instinctively and unconsciously, supplying the need without realizing its nature. I had pursued solitariness all my life, I saw now, as primitive man must have pursued the food that would satisfy his hunger and keep him alive, without recognizing that he was in fact pursuing the essential means of his survival.

For, I think, five evenings, my solitude was unbroken, although Mrs Black called one evening and I made my escape by the simple ruse of keeping quiet and not opening the door, but on the following evening Mr Lindsay's car drew up at the gate and out of it stepped the Rector and Miss Hadley. I went to the door to greet them.

'Janet!' said Miss Hadley. 'You've done it!'

'What?' I asked. I had no idea what she meant.

'The City and Counties!' Her deep voice vibrated in a way I had never heard it do and she gripped me with both hands by the upper arms with tense fingers. 'Oh, *Janet!*'

I looked from her to Mr Lindsay and his mouth was shaky, his eyes glittering. 'I just heard by telephone!' he said. 'Janet, we are very, very proud of you!'

I could think of nothing to say, so I thought of my grandmother, which always helps me at such times and the words came: 'Won't you come away in?' I said. 'I don't know why we are all standing on the doorstep.'

They both broke into a burst of laughter which sounded

as if some long-tensed spring had been released and then
came in and I shut the door. When they were sitting down,
I went to put the kettle on for that cup of tea which, in
southern Scotland, meets every occasion and, as I went
about, I looked at them with a new, strange detachment.
Mr Lindsay and Miss Hadley, the god and goddess of my
last six years, had suddenly turned into the most ordinary
human clay. They had become people for whom I, Janet
Sandison, could do something – could do, apparently, a great
deal. I, Janet Sandison, had made these two people almost
unbearably proud and happy. They quivered with it. It was
very strange. It had been so easy. All I had done was to go
to Glasgow and travel my pen over paper for three and a
half days or so. I had then talked to six very pleasant ladies
and gentlemen for an hour or so. There had been no effort,
and yet, here was the result! These two kind, clever people,
who had always been so good to me, were sitting there in a
trembling sort of rapture, and yet, here at home, with Jean, I
had made all sorts of efforts for no result. Why? Why? Why?

'Your essay, Janet—' Mr Lindsay asked as I handed them
buttered scones. 'Can you remember what you wrote?'

'Not in detail, sir. Why?'

'Made a great impression – you took "Friendship"?'

'Yes, sir.'

He nodded. 'That – and the *viva*, of course?' And
he laughed.

'And don't forget the French essay!' said Miss Hadley.
'That was the other highlight. What *was* the set subject,
Janet?'

'I chose "My Favourite French Author",' I told them.
'There was a choice of three—'

'And who did you write about?'

'Alphonse Daudet, Miss Hadley.'

'*Daudet*? Why?'

'Because I really enjoy him. I could write about Reachfar
– that's my home – as he wrote from his windmill in
Provence. You – you sort of *like* the things you feel you could
do yourself.'

'Then some day,' said Miss Hadley, 'you must write letters from Reachfar for us!'

They both then indulged in another burst of joyous laughter and I, pouring more tea for them, felt that the whole thing and their pride and joy in it was away beyond my comprehension. I was glad to hear the interrupting knock on the panels of the door. When I opened it, Hugh Reid stood there.

'Hugh! Hello!' I said.

He jerked his head at the little car at the gate. 'I was in the High Street. I saw the Rector and Miss Hadley driving out here like anything. You've won the C. and C.?'

'Iphm,' I said. 'Come in, Hugh.'

He stared into my eyes. 'I knew you would,' he said. He stepped into the house. 'Good evening, Miss Hadley. Good evening, sir.'

'Now this is a *real* Cairnton Academy party!' said Mr Lindsay.

'Sit down, Hugh.'

After a short time, Mr Lindsay and Miss Hadley drove away and when Hugh and I had seen them off, I walked across the fields as far as the old quarry with him on his way home. We did not talk a great deal on the way, but when we had crossed the quarry and the houses of Cairnton were in sight across the fields, he said:

'Will you come and see Granny some night, Janet?'

I looked at him. 'If you think she would like it,' I said.

Hugh sat down on a large boulder beside the path and I sat down beside him.

'She would,' he said. 'Janet, yon was a bad thing that happened when I won the Jarvie-Kerr—'

'I couldn't help it, Hugh,' I said.

'I don't mean anything to do with *you*. What I mean is, what Granny and I did was bad. But I was a senseless kid at the time and Granny – well, she belongs to Cairnton and you know what the Cairnton folk are like – the women coming into the shop and telling her that you and your people were going about saying that if you had gone in for the exam I wouldn't have had a chance—'

120

'It wasn't *my* people who said it!' I burst out. 'It was *Jean*! I – we would never have said a thing like that even if it had been true!' And suddenly a black silence descended over me. I fought my way out of it. 'Hugh – you know my father and Jean are – are married?'

'Yes. I heard that.'

'Hugh, what should I do?'

'Do? You don't like her?' he asked.

'No. You know I never have. I have tried my very best, but I can't.'

Hugh stared at the ground. 'It's a pity,' he said after a moment. 'But, you know, it really doesn't matter and you don't have to do anything. Things at your home will be pretty much the same. And you'll find that, next year, when you are going to the University, the world will get bigger and Cairnton things don't matter so much. Like this thing of being hurt about the Jarvie-Kerr and not speaking to you. I – I've been ashamed of that for over two years, but it was difficult to speak again for the first time and wondering if, when I did speak, *you* would speak to *me*. You see, even if you *had* gone round Cairnton saying that you could have taken that bursary from me, I would have had no right to take offence. It would have been perfectly true.'

'Hugh! That's a lot of rot and—'

'It isn't.' He grinned at me. 'Mind you, I am not admitting that your brain is any better than mine – but it is different – and you know yourself that your pure flair for exams is outstanding. You could have lifted the Jarvie-Kerr from under my nose all right. What you might have done with it after you got it is a different thing. What *do* you intend to do?' he asked.

'Go up to the University, of course!'

'For what?'

'I don't know yet.'

'Medicine? Teaching? What?'

I stared at him. 'I've no idea, Hugh. Have *you* got plans?'

'Of course!'

'Since when?'

'Since I got the Jarvie-Kerr. I had them even before that, but I didn't dare to think about them.'

'Would you tell me?' I asked. 'I won't tell a soul if you don't want me to—'

'You'll be the first person to know,' he said quietly. 'Granny thinks I am going to be a teacher or a minister – Granny thinks that's what universities are for – making teachers and ministers. Well I *do* hope to turn into a teacher of a sort, but not the usual kind.'

'What kind then?'

He looked at me and, for the first time in our years of friendship, he touched with his right hand his empty left sleeve. 'Dozens and hundreds of people in the world are like me – incomplete. People like you – especially *you*, because you are so very complete in body and brain – don't know what it is like to have some – some deficiency, like this.' He touched the sleeve again. 'One is aware, always, of being basically different and people remind you of it all the time. You know something, Janet?'

'What?'

'You were the only kid I ever met until I was over fifteen who never asked me in one way or another if it didn't feel funny to have only one arm. Funny!' He stared bitterly at the houses of Cairnton that were sending up their smug, comfortable cloud of evening smoke. 'I don't know whether you held your tongue out of sensitivity or mere good manners – in your case I think it was sensitivity, but I wish that the insensitive ones of the earth could at least have good manners.' He smiled. 'Anyway, what I am trying to do is turn myself into a person who will be half-doctor, half-teacher so that I can help children who were born as I was.'

'Hugh!'

'You see, I don't think they'd want a cripple as a teacher in an ordinary school for kids. And of course, I can't *be* a doctor with only one hand. But I can learn how to teach and I can learn the brain side of medicine and I am going to Technical School as well to learn about jobs and crafts that can be done one-handed or one-legged. But the main

thing of all is that I know already – for I was born with
the great gift of knowing – exactly how it *feels* inside your
mind to be born – incomplete.'

'Oh, Hugh!' My eyes were full of tears so that the Cairnton
smoke was a blurred grey cloud. 'Oh, Hugh! It's a wonderful
idea! Thank you for telling me.'

We both stared across the fields for a moment.

'It will be grand when you are coming up to the University,' he said next. 'We can travel together and quite likely
we'll be doing some of the same classes. I attend every one
that I can get my nose inside – except some of the divinity
lectures.' He grinned with some mischief. 'I made my peace
with the Almighty long ago and I'm not all that interested
in the learned divines' opinions of Him. Besides, *He* knows
that I've got other things to do.'

I laughed. 'I'm looking forward to it all, Hugh. I'll be
glad to get away from the Academy, although I'll miss the
Rector and Miss Hadley.'

'Fed up with it?'

'I am a bit. Hugh, it's not much fun to be like me – to
be supposed to be so ''clever'' as they call it. It – it puts
distance between you and the rest.'

He nodded. 'A bit like having only one arm. Freaks, that's
what we are!'

'We are *not*! Besides, I'm not all that clever. You know
what I think? I think the Cairnton lot are pretty dull-witted,
that's all.'

'What about the crowd that sat the C. and C.?'

'Never mind that now,' I said. 'It's just that here in
Cairnton I got the habit of being first in exams because the
local crowd gave me no competition.'

'Anyway, you don't *look* all pimply and spectacly and
clever,' Hugh said. 'And that's a help. And later on, if you
made a bit of a study of playing the fool, you are clever
enough to get quite good at it.'

'What do you mean?'

'I should think that, later on, someone like you could have
herself a grand time by playing the fool cleverly on purpose.

123

But as you often say, never mind that now – I'll have to come to the Academy on Prize Day and cheer like anything when you get your Dux Medal and your C. and C. parchment and all the rest of it!'

'Hugh Reid! If you do, I'll never speak to you again. I couldn't bear to have a claque!'

CHAPTER EIGHT

My father and Jean came back from their honeymoon-holiday round of visits to Jean's aunts and cousins who lived, mostly, in the area between Glasgow and Edinburgh, on the day before the prize-giving and, of course, by that time the announcement about the City and Counties Bursary had been published (complete with an unrecognizable photograph of me which had been extracted from a school group taken two years before) and the talk was of little else.

'I aye kent she wid get it!' said Jean, with her customary lack of memory of what she had previously said or done. 'And jist imagine there not bein' a richt photo o' her for the newspapers. Annie Black's had her photo taken every year since she was a baby. Imagine, no' wan photo in the hoose! Sic a disgrace!'

The next morning, I left for school as usual, not thinking of the holiday atmosphere that would prevail or the speech-making or prize-giving that would take place in the afternoon, but thinking, instead, that on Monday I would be in the train for Inverness and Reachfar. The forenoon passed very quickly, for I, together with a group of the senior girls, had to help Miss Hadley and the other women teachers to decorate the platform in the school hall with flowers and evergreens, while the senior boys, with much bustle and noise, carried chairs and forms from schoolrooms and set them in place.

'There will be a tremendous crowd today,' Miss Hadley said. 'Will your father be coming, Janet?'

'Oh no, Miss Hadley. He has been away and has a lot of work to catch up.'

'I can understand that. He is a very conscientious man,' she said and hurried away about some new task.

By two o'clock in the afternoon, there was indeed a tremendous crowd. All Cairnton and district seemed to be cramming into the big hall of the school and as I stood with Miss Hadley in a corner near the platform, I began for, I think, the first time in my life to feel nervous. There seemed to me to be something reasonless in this mob of people who had gathered here mainly to see me, someone of whom they knew nothing, receive the unassuming roll of thick white paper which represented the C. and C. Bursary. I realized, of course, that they were here out of some bastardized, mistaken sense of civic pride. In their eyes, the 'C. and C. had come to Cairnton' and they were here to receive the honour, if honour such a thing can be called, unto themselves. It struck me that they were receiving the 'honour' with far more enthusiasm than they had ever received *me*, the stranger, the one who was 'aye different an' no' like ither folk'. I stood in the corner half-embarrassed, half-ashamed, but wholly ill at ease, as I watched the bright, proud faces of the populace who were jostling for the seats. I was suddenly startled by a voice at my elbow: 'Oh, there ye are, Janet!' and I turned to see Jean, right beside me.

I had seen the wedding finery lying on the bed ten days or so ago, but now it was lying, resplendent, upon Jean. Above the pink frills and under the blue hat, her face was flushed crimson with excitement and triumph and the shiny kid gloves were stretched tight with satisfaction round the handle of the brown handbag that was held before her stomach. I stared at her, astonished and stricken dumb.

'And who is your friend, Janet?' said the gentle voice of the neatly-tailored, dignified Miss Hadley at my side.

'It – it's Jean,' I gasped. 'She was our housekeeper and—'

'Oh, Mrs Sandison!' said Miss Hadley. 'How very nice to see you! This is a great day, isn't it? You must come and meet the Rector.'

'I know him already,' said Jean stonily. 'I've seen him at the hoose.'

126

She glared at me from a face redder than ever and Miss Hadley glanced quickly from the one of us to the other before she said hastily: 'Let me give you a chair in the front row, Mrs Sandison!' and led Jean away talking amiably, while Jean, stiff with rage, waddled in her wake on the too-high heels. I sank into my own chair in the corner by the platform with a dreadful, sick consciousness of doom. Why had she come? What had I said? What was I going to do? What if she made a scene? Why had she come? She knew I did not want people! And that terrible pink blouse and red fur! Why had she come? Would she make a scene?

She was not more than four yards away from me, staring at me, from under the drooping brim of the blue hat, with eyes of flint in a face as red as rage combined with humiliation could make it. I could not look at her, after that one frightened glance. I was too afraid of her temper and that she might create some dreadful public scene. I stared at the floor.

The ceremony began, prizes through all the classes of the lower school were handed out, pupils came to the platform and went away until nothing was left on the big table except the roll of white paper, the black velvet box that contained the gold Dux Medal of the school, and the pile of books that formed the Dux prize. Mr Lindsay rose, raised his chin, took a firm grip on the front panels of his black gown and began to speak. 'Ladies and gentlemen, I am proud today to stand on this platform and to be able to tell you all of the great honour that has been brought to Cairnton Academy—'

I stared in utter misery at the floor, aware, without looking, of Jean's stony yet rage-swollen face, and all I could think of was the return home, the atmosphere in the house and the puzzled, worried look that would come to the face of my father. Why had she *come* to the prize-giving, unexpectedly, like this? If only she had said that she wanted to come, I would have been prepared, had the neat phrase ready, instead of being surprised into those gauche words which had led to this dreadful impasse.

'I and my colleagues here on the platform behind me,'

Mr Lindsay was saying, 'take a little of the credit, but only a very little. As I told you three years ago, when Hugh Reid brought the Jarvie-Kerr bursary to Cairnton, teachers, like other men and women, work within limitations.' He picked up the roll of white paper. 'This is the work of Janet Sandison – Janet Elizabeth Sandison – and but for her–'

If only Jean had not worn that *fur*. It was a hot June day and her face looked like the boiled lobsters in the fish-monger's window. *Why* had she worn the fur? What would happen when we got home?

'As you all know, Janet has been a scholar all the way. You have seen that on successive Prize Days. But, although I am a schoolmaster, I wish to tell you that scholarship is not all. You all know the phrase "a scholar and a gentleman". It has been a pleasure to all of us here to teach Janet, who is a scholar and a lady.'

What would happen when we got home? What sort of a fishwife row would there be in the house this time?

I became aware that the Rector was facing in the direction in which I sat. 'Janet, it gives me great pleasure to hand to you the parchment of the City and Counties Bursary. Ladies and gentlemen, Janet Elizabeth Sandison.'

I was somehow on the platform, beside the table, and all the people were some four feet below, all applauding, and on the stairs and galleries round the hall my school-fellows were madly cheering. But in the very centre of the front row was one figure, immobile as a monolith of hard, grey, Cairnton stone, a monolith absurdly clad in saxe blue, pink and red fox fur, a fat pair of non-clapping, kid-gloved hands grip-ping, as in a vice, the handle of a showy, shiny handbag. It all went on – the Rector's voice, and the cheering, and the applause. The black velvet box with the medal came into my other hand and then the pile of books was laid in my arms. I stood there, sick at heart, my brain numb, my eyes blind, my ears deaf. At last, I could turn away from the table – please God? Where are the steps down to the hall floor? Miss Hadley stood at the foot of the steps, but from the other side of them came a voice: 'Come on, Janet! – Carry your books for you?' and Hugh's eyes were smiling up at me. I 'came on' and he took the heavy books from my arms. 'It's all right!' he whispered. 'It's all over!' and then, in a louder voice: 'I said I wouldn't applaud, but I cheered like all the rest!' He paused and added: 'But one.' I managed to smile at him, I think.

After the ceremony was at long last completely over, Jean disappeared and I, semi-dazed still, clung to Hugh because I was afraid to go home.

'Come and see Granny and show her your prizes,' he said. It was comforting to 'show Granny my prizes', for they had no false significance of any kind for her. In her old, comfortable way, when Hugh called to her from the door of the house that he had brought me to see her, she called back her old, comfortable phrase: 'That's fine!' and then came bustling through the passage from the shop to the kitchen.

'I'm pleased to see ye, lassie! It's far too long you've been away from us,' she said and, after that, she did not refer again to what had happened three years ago. She took the burden of prizes in her stride, commented that the bursary would be 'a big help' to my father, that the medal would 'make a real nice locket' if I got a chain for it and that I would be busy in the holidays reading all these books 'and just put them over there on the dresser oot o' the road and we'll all have a cup o' tea'.

Hugh walked home across the fields with me later in the evening and, as we left his home, I said: 'If all women were like Granny, everything would be much simpler.'

'What *was* wrong with that blooming Jean today?' he asked. 'Why did she come at all if she felt like that?'

'It was all my fault, Hugh,' I told him. 'I didn't know she intended to come and I was with Miss Hadley and she suddenly appeared, dressed up like that and – well, I was so taken aback that I'd said it before I knew what I was doing—'

'Said what?'

'I – I introduced her to Miss Hadley as our housekeeper, Hugh.'

'Oh, God!'

Hugh deposited his share of my books on top of a boulder in the old quarry, sat down beside them and began to laugh as if he would never stop.

'It's *not* funny!' I was almost in tears. 'It sounded snobbish and dreadful—' I sank down beside him. 'And the worst of it is, it's the *truth*! I *am* a snob about her. I was furious at her for arriving there in those awful frills and roses, with that smug Cairnton look on her red face as if *she* had had some part in winning the prizes! Mind you, I didn't say the housekeeper thing because of that – it just came out because I hadn't got used yet to thinking of her as anything else. But now that I *have* thought about it, I'll never think of her in relation to myself as anything *but* a housekeeper or something. Coming there as if *she* had helped in any way over the prizes – she's been telling me for months that I hadn't a chance!'

'Bitch!' said Hugh. 'But listen, she didn't come there because of the prizes.'

I stared at him. 'Then why?'

'Don't be an ass! She came there to parade her marital success before more of Cairnton and district than will be gathered together in one place again for ages! Hence the frills and the fox fur and the tight shoes. I bet she has corns and blisters before she gets home again.'

'Oh, Hugh! But that makes my housekeeper thing to Miss Hadley a million times worse!'

'Of course it does! But you always *were* a slow-witted dope about some things.'

I stared across the dark pool in the quarry floor. 'Hugh, what on earth shall I do?'

'Do? I don't see that you can do anything definite – just the best you can.'

'If I apologized to her? If I explained that in all the excitement and not expecting her, I *forgot* they were married? That is *true*, you know, Hugh—'

'Honestly, I think that would make her angrier than ever,' Hugh said. 'Listen, you know I was telling you the other night about the work I want to do? I talked about people

130

being incomplete. Very few people are what you could call as complete as they might be – they all have terrific limitations. Jean's mind is very limited. You know that yourself. She would not believe for a moment that you could forget her marriage, the most important thing in her life. Besides, in an instinctive way, she knows you don't really like her – she has always known since we were kids that *I* didn't like her. I could feel her knowing it, and feel her thinking that I was a cheeky little brat for daring not to like her. She will believe that you set out deliberately today to hurt and humiliate her and that's that.'

'But that's not true!'

'Jean doesn't care whether it's true or not. That is how she will see it, I bet you.'

'But, Hugh, if I *explained*!' I argued. 'You know I would never set out deliberately to hurt and humiliate anyone! You know how I loathe nasty and embarrassing situations when people's faces get red and everything is awkward. I don't mind a good fight, like that time I clouted Teenie Mathieson in the High Street for throwing stones at Paddy –' we smiled at one another bleakly, in memory of Mrs Mathieson's infuriated attack on Mr Lindsay – 'but that's different from saying things to hurt the inmost bits of people! I've clouted Teenie Mathieson to stop her throwing stones at Paddy, but I would never tell her how she smells in spite of her scent because I don't suppose she can *help* that! So just in the same way, I couldn't tell Jean about that awful fur – it's her *taste* and she can't help it. Hugh, I wouldn't be nasty to anyone about something they can't help and I wouldn't be a snob out loud about Jean—'

Hugh sighed and I had one of these moments of realization that he was very, very much older than I was – really older, and not just in years.

'Janet, listen carefully,' he said. 'Your whole approach is all wrong for people like Jean and Teenie Mathieson. You try to sort things out, so that you know that Jean likes that awful red rabbit-skin she was wearing and that Teenie hopes that nobody notices her what the advertisements call B.O.'

He gave a lewd chuckle. 'Jean and Teenie don't take the trouble to sort things out as far as *you* are concerned – they don't even sort things out for themselves. I bet you Jean always tells you point-blank what she doesn't like about *your* clothes and taste and so on and, believe me, if *you* smelled, Teenie Mathieson would shout it after you in the High Street, just as she used to shout "Hughie One-Wing" after *me*. The Jeans and Teenies don't discriminate about weapons. Anything goes. And they believe that everyone else is just as they are. They have no standards except their own. Jean would never believe that you spoke in admiration of her blooming rabbit-skin when you first saw it just to make her happy, because she would never do such a thing to make *you* happy. Jean is not interested in you and your happiness and neither is Teenie. They are interested in the happiness of Jean and Teenie and – remember this – when you have a limited mind you derive a certain amount of happiness out of causing *un*happiness to a person you are jealous of. *I* know that, terribly well.'

'What do you mean? You talk as if you made a habit of being mean-minded and—'

'I hope I am not mean-minded, anyway, not now. But remember that I am mean-bodied.' He tapped the empty sleeve and then extended his right arm. 'You don't know this – but I am a hell of a good table-tennis player, although I say it myself.' He gave a snorting laugh of scorn. 'I tell myself I play it because I like the game. That's only half true. I play it, largely, because a bloke with *two* arms always looks so crest-fallen when I beat him. It's one of my attractive little ways of getting back at life for my own limitation, see?'

'Hugh!' I said on a note of protest.

'Accept it. It's the truth,' Hugh said harshly. 'The important thing about it is that I *know* why I like to play table tennis. What is so *wrong* in my opinion with the Teenies and Jeans is that they don't know *why* they do the things they do. They do them by some terrifying, blind, ungoverned instinct. For instance, I am certain that Jean, today, didn't really know why she dressed herself up in her wedding

132

clothes and went to the prize-giving. She probably thought
– quite sincerely, mind you – that she was doing it in order
to be an audience for *you*. She probably doesn't know that
the real drive behind her was the triumphant appearance
before all Cairnton of the woman who, a bit late in life, had
made a good match. Deficiencies have to be made good –
a limited mind has all sorts of false horizons. When the truth
is unpalatable, any delusion will do – like my trying to claim
that I like table tennis because I am a sportsman. I don't
give a damn for sport. My true mind would rather read a
good book than waste an evening at a table-tennis game.
What Jean wanted, to make up for her quiet wedding, was
the public acclamation of Cairnton – the crowd round the
church door for the young bride of twenty. She is nearer
forty and there was no church door, but she had a grand
chance today. All Cairnton would be there, she knew. She
saw you as a pawn in the game – subconsciously, I mean
– the 'poor wee motherless soul' – oh, let's face it, we've
heard her at it often enough – that she could *support*, for
that's how it was away down deep in her. She was all set,
rabbit-skin and everything, for a double kill of Cairnton,
the only community she has ever known, and what happens?
In two minutes flat, the awful truth is rammed down her
throat in public by the poor wee motherless soul. She is
introduced to Miss Hadley – she is afraid and jealous of
Miss Hadley anyway and loathes her on principle – as the
"housekeeper" which – and this is the truth that she is
hiding from – is what she really is. Your father did not
marry her as his first choice – she knows that but she
doesn't think about it – she was hit bang on the Achilles
heel by the poor wee motherless soul.' Hugh stared at the
dark water of the pond. 'You get used to the idea, Janet.
Accidentally, you have hit that woman where it hurts her
most and nothing you can do, now, will make any difference.'
He gave me a quick sidewise glance and a fleeting smile.
'Do you ever hear any jazz?'

'Not much. Why?'

'There's an American woman who sings a song with very

133

little tune and a lot of appeal – goes like this: "Your step-mam*ma* is gwan ta *hate* ya, honey—" The words are mine, not hers, of course.'

I detached myself from Hugh and went home at last, but before the evening was over, I knew that his reading of the situation was acutely accurate. Jean was never going to forgive me. She was also going to hate me, and as publicly as possible, for Jean with a wedding ring on her left hand was not quite the same woman as the Jean who had been my father's paid housekeeper. If, hitherto, my father had been unaware of how little Jean and I had in common, he was left in little doubt before the evening meal was over, and my mind was tortured by the look of worried amazement that settled more deeply on his face at every malicious comment that Jean threw in my direction.

In times of stress, the mirror of my mind seems to become distorted, like those bent looking-glasses at fun fairs that enlarge the image of the head or the feet, and now, as the atmosphere around the table became more tense, the image of Jean as seen by my eyes became distorted until it consisted of nothing but her eyes and her hands. It seemed that I had never noticed before how small and fat her hands were, how short and thick with flesh were the fingers, so that they seemed stiffened into a permanent curve, as if they were holding something even when empty. Nor had I noticed before how small were her hazel-coloured eyes in relation to her face. Hitherto, Jean's face, to me, had been vaguely featureless, consisting of two eyes, a nose and a mouth, a combination normal enough and pleasant rather than ugly, but unremarkable for size of mouth, shape of nose or colour or setting of eyes. Now, it was dominated by the eyes, in which a light seemed to be snapping on and off, as if crazed fingers were playing with a concealed electric switch. I had read, often, the verb 'snapping' in connection with eyes, but had never been able to visualized what it meant until now. There was something in those eyes that appalled me, as the hazel pupils went from fiery brilliance to blank dullness – in and out – with no intermediate stage of flicker or half-light that indicated any thought process in the brain behind them. As I watched, I became more and more terrified.

Eventually I ventured to say: 'Please, Jean, let's try not to quarrel. Dad can't stand silly fusses in the house and—'

She sprang erect, holding on to the table edge with both fat hands. 'Silly fusses in the *house*! Very lah-di-dah! Public insults in front o' your fancy freen's are a' richt, Ah suppose?'

'Jean, I'm sorry. I did not mean to be insulting. I was taken by surprise – I didn't expect you—'

Her voice rose to a shrill scream, such as my father had never heard from her – or from any woman connected with him – before.

'So ye didnae expect me! Common hoosekeepers have nae business at yer fancy affairs, Ah suppose! Jist you listen tae *me*—'

'Stop that damned skirling!' said my father. 'Half Cairnton can hear you! I will not have two women fighting and disgracing my house and me—'

'Disgrace! *Whae's* a disgrace?' Jean shrieked and then, through her rage, she saw something in his face that seemed to frighten her. She burst into howling tears, dashed through to the bathroom, slammed the door and locked it.

Stern, but more worried than stern, my father turned on me. 'What the devil happened down at Cairnton today?' he asked.

I told him as exactly as I could and I told him how sorry I was about the accidental – but hurtful – words. When I had finished, he startled me by barking: 'Tell the truth, damn it! What happened next?'

'Next? Nothing, Dad. Miss Hadley put her in the first row as I told you.'

'And afterwards?'

'She had left the school before I got down off the platform.'

He stared at me. 'Are you asking me to believe that all this row is because you said to Miss Hadley that Jean was our housekeeper?'

'But that was all that happened, Dad,' I assured him shakily.

His anger left him with a deflated sigh and was replaced by a look of lost non-comprehension.

'But God be here,' he said, 'she's been a housekeeper all her life. There's no disgrace in it! Every married woman in Cairnton is a housekeeper and everybody in Cairnton knows that she was my housekeeper before we married!'

He looked at me in a searching way, as if to ask whether I could see any flaw in the logic of this reasoning, and this is where a very queer thing happened in my mind. I suddenly felt sorry for Jean and, at the same time, for the first time in my life, completely and utterly out of sympathy with a member of my family, and my beloved father at that. I felt slightly sick. I could find nothing to say and, after a short silence, he continued: 'Something more than this must have happened between you. Janet, in a way, I don't blame you. It is always difficult, I have heard, for folk to have step – stepmothers. Tell me – I'll not be angry – what *did* you say to Jean?'

'Dad, I said nothing but what I have told you. And my mother doesn't come into this – does she?' I jerked out.

'Och, your mother was a different person altogether,' he said, and his worried eyes became soft and filled with dreams for a moment. 'What else did you *say*?'

'Nothing, Dad. On my Bible oath, all I did was to say the housekeeper thing to Miss Hadley. I shouldn't have done it, and I am very, very sorry. I wish—'

He interrupted me. 'Well, you've never been much of a liar. And if that was all that happened, that one through there –' he jerked his head in the direction of the bathroom – 'can come out of her tantrum the way she went into it. I've never heard such a damned carry-on about nothing in all my born days.'

I stared at him in silence and wished that I could think of a way of comforting Jean, for now, in my mind, she was a woman who needed all the comfort that anyone could give her except that – I felt this very strongly – there *was* no comfort for someone in her situation. She had achieved what, in the eyes of the law and Cairnton, was marriage, but in a vague, wordless way I knew that a marriage that depended on the law and Cairnton for its existence was a poor thing, with no human comfort in it and, worse still, no possibility of comfort in it or to be brought to it by me or by anyone else.

'I think I'll go out for a walk, Dad,' I said.

'Aye, just you do that,' he said and, almost incredibly to me, calmly picked up his newspaper. 'I'll see to that nonsense through there.' He glanced again in the direction of the bathroom and turned to his paper, but before I left the room he said: 'Oh, by the way, you'll be travelling to Reachfar alone on Monday as usual. Jean and I will be up later on, I hope.'

I stared at him. 'Why?'

'It's that shit, Tommie.'

My father had never used such an expression in my hearing before, but I was so relieved that the crisis was a business and not a family one that I could have burst into hysterical laughter.

'What's he done now?' I asked.

'Got some lassie up at Stirling in the family way. Her people are threatening to take the case to court.'

I felt sick again. In the last few weeks, I thought, there had been far too much of sex and its turmoils in my life, what with Annie Black and my father and Jean, my own development to womanhood and now this mess of Tommie's. I wanted to be out in the air, in a tree in a high wind for preference, where I could think, perhaps, of something else.

'I'm sorry, Dad,' I said. 'It's very hard for you.'

'It's Mrs Hill I'm sorry for,' he said. 'She is a poor, silly craitur and I have to do what I can for her. Sometimes I wish I had never promised Mr Hill I would try to look after her. Off you go for your walk, Janet. At least, it needn't bother *you*.'

He opened his paper and, thankfully, I went out on to my hill. Life was suddenly much better. On Monday – only two days away – I would be off to Reachfar on my own and none of these hideous problems would have a place on that lovely sunlit moorland slope. . .

I spent the greater part of the two days with Hugh, for the atmosphere of my home was heavy with the sullen hatred and noisy with the angry snorts of Jean, although she curbed both and behaved more reasonably as long as my father was in the house, for which I was grateful to her. Jean had no longer any power to hurt me except through my father, and apparently he had made her understand that he would not accept her exhibitions of rage. This led to a curious situation immediately and it was a situation that was to persist down the years.

In so far as Jean was capable of loving anyone, she loved my father, I think, and she was also aware that his feeling for her was less strong than hers for him. He was in no way a cruel man, but inadequacy of love or affection leads always, inevitably, to moments of inadvertent cruelty and to intense suffering. When these moments came to Jean, by some instinct of self-defence and self-preservation, she concealed her hurt from my father, transmuted it into a new aspect of hatred for me and vented it upon me with all the force of screams, tears and every ugliness for which she could find words, as soon as my father was out of earshot. At these times, her rage was maniacal in its fury, due probably to the iron control of herself that she tried to maintain in my father's presence. She was unable, as I have said, to hurt me; she did not even make me feel afraid, and when she stood, raving, in mid-floor, I would look at her with something of the cold, clinical attitude of a doctor and wonder at the underlying cunning that made her know that I would not report her behaviour to my father. It is superfluous to say that this attitude of mine merely increased her fury and, although I was aware that it did so, I was capable of no other. In my way, I was as cruel as she was — more so, for of the two I think I was the more intelligent person and should therefore have been capable of more understanding behaviour — but if Jean hated me, I also hated Jean. In my own defence, I can only say that I did not ever try, deliberately, to rouse her. On the contrary, I did my best towards our sharing of the same roof without the occurrence

138

of these storms, but I now know that they were a condition of Jean's married life and that they had to happen as inevitably as the tide must ebb and flow. The tragic summary of the matter was that, in Jean's mind, she had achieved marriage, her future was assured and she could allow the frustrations of the past years as well as those of the marriage itself to have full rein because she knew I would never 'tell'.

I spent the Sunday afternoon and evening before leaving for Reachfar with Hugh and I remember telling him how right he had been in his reading of Jean's attitude and unburdening myself by telling him of the scene that had taken place that forenoon when my father had left the house to go up to the farm.

'She didn't expect him to go out this morning, and she wanted them both to go to church,' I said. 'And she took her disappointment out on *me* after he had gone.'

'Of course she did,' said Hugh. 'She had to take it out on *some*body!'

'Not very fair, is it?'

'Stop talking like the fifth form at St Fanny's!' said Hugh. 'You are a big girl now and going to the university in the autumn.'

I felt hurt. 'What d' you mean?'

'All that half-baked rot about fairness. A thing like you and Jean is life, not a game of hockey. There isn't any fair or foul and there's no referee – nobody to appeal to and say: Howzat? Jean is there and there she is going to stay and you have got to accept life with her in it – unfairness and all.'

'I don't have to accept one damn thing in my life that I don't want!' I argued.

'That's true enough. You can pack up and clear out,' – he grinned at me – 'but you won't do that. You'd be a fool if you did, if you cut yourself off from all your family means to you, just because of Jean. What you have to do is achieve some sort of compromise, a sort of working basis. That will come, but don't go clobbering yourself up with ideas of Jean being unfair to you and looking on yourself as a martyr. As a martyr, you are purely comical.'

From being hurt, I moved towards feeling very angry. I do not think that any sixteen-year-old is capable of accepting the idea of herself as comical. 'How do you mean – comical?' I snapped.

'Just what I *say* – *comical*!' he said, laughing at me. 'You as a martyr are as comical as Teenie Mathieson would be if she fancied herself for the C. and C. bursary. You are no poor little bullied step-child of anybody and don't you go thinking so. You are a great big hefty hunk of bone and muscle and about as impervious to bullying in any way as an odd chunk of the Grampians. You are not even amenable to ordinary influence. Look at you! Six years you've been living here – you've been through the sausage-machine of that school down there, you've been rubbing shoulders daily with Cairnton and all it means and in essence you are not one whit different from the first morning that you walked through the school gates!'

I was now both angry and hurt, for I felt that Hugh was criticizing me very adversely, that his pointing out of these things that I was meant that he wished I were different, for it was seldom that young people of my generation, class and country were told anything about themselves without the implication being present that that thing required alteration and improvement. Looking at me as if I were a specimen on a microscopic slide, Hugh added: 'It's queer that you seem so different from the ordinary run of girls. I wonder what it is?'

He could not have said anything more unfortunate, for this was too like Jean's well-worn 'no' like ither folk'. I blazed into rage – hurt, incoherent rage.

'I am *not* different! I'm taller, but that's only because these people here are short compared with us in the Highlands. What's *wrong* with me?'

'I didn't say there was anything *wrong*—'

'You did! You're as bad as Jean, always *saying* things and *wondering* and carrying on!'

'Oh, stop acting the baby and dramatizing yourself! I didn't say there was anything wrong with you. I said that you were unlike the ordinary run of girls around here but I can't find words for the difference — that's all. Dash it, that's a *compliment*!' he laughed.

'It's a pretty queer compliment!' I snapped, determined to take offence.

He might not have heard me. 'You seem to be impervious to mass things, like fashions and local patterns of behaviour and so on. You seem to work out all your own standards. Look, you've been six years down at school there and never once have I seen you walking home with a friend like any of the rest.'

'Hugh Reid! You're dotty! When you and I were kids we were together all the time! *You* were the one who started leaving *me* for the other boys when we were in the Third Year.'

'Yes, but you never took up with any of the girls, did you?'

I was still angry, but arguing a losing battle now, for I knew that Hugh was right in saying that I had nothing in common with the Cairnton girls.

'*What* girls? Annie Black, I suppose?' Annie's face came to my mind and her name to my tongue merely because she was the main symbol of my 'difference'. In my fury, I had momentarily forgotten Hugh's interest in her, but remembered it, of course, as soon as I had spoken her name. This only made me the more angry and defiant. 'You are as bad as that old Jean with her "Annie, such a nice wee pal for you!" '

'I wasn't thinking of Annie, particularly,' said Hugh quietly.

'I thought you did a fair amount of thinking about Annie Black!' I said tartly.

Hugh looked at me solemnly. 'Maybe I do, but not in connection with *you*,' he said. 'And anyway, why don't you like Annie?'

'She makes me feel sick,' I said.

'Why?'

I drew breath to speak, swung round to face him and suddenly the words died in my throat. I did not know the reason, but I knew that I could never tell Hugh of Annie's

141

Glasgow life or of her activities with Tommie Hill, here, in the old quarry where we were sitting.

'She just does!' I said. 'Jean fed me up to the back teeth with Annie Black years ago.'

Hugh stared at the ground. 'Janet, do you like Tommie Hill?'

'No.'

'Why not?'

'I don't *know* why!' I still felt cross. 'You either like people or you don't. I think he's awful-*looking*, with that red, fat face and that loose mouth of his. Besides, he gives my father a lot of trouble.'

'What sort of trouble?'

'Oh, always getting drunk and things and spending too much money. And he gets in messes with women too. Don't repeat all this though, Hugh. After all, Mrs Hill is my father's employer. I wouldn't say anything about Tommie to anyone else.'

'That's all right,' he said. 'I don't like to see Annie going about with him.'

This made me angry again. 'Oh, Annie can look after herself!' I snapped.

'You think so?'

'She always has. She's had lots of practice and she is very single-minded about it.'

Hugh changed the subject after that and we did not speak of Annie any more. It would be inaccurate, I think, to say that I was merely jealous of Hugh's interest in Annie, although there was jealousy in some measure in my feeling. What I felt was mainly an irritated resentment that someone like Hugh should 'waste his time' over someone like Annie, for I was full of the arrogant, clear-cut, black-and-white judgments of youth. I had formed an opinion of Annie when I was ten years old and since that time I had never thought of changing or revising it, for, since that time until very recently, I had thought of Annie as seldom and as little as I could. For me, therefore, she was still pigeon-holed in my mind as the vain, silly, kept-back-at-school little ninny who

142

had preened herself before the glass in her frilly room and had now turned into a common prostitute, a thing about which I hesitated to think at all. My Friend Hugh, whose development and progress I had studied down the years, had turned into a personality to be respected and, in my opinion, he was 'far too good' for the like of Annie.

CHAPTER NINE

On Monday morning, I boarded the north train out of
Glasgow for Inverness and gladly left all of Cairnton behind,
and, when I met Tom and George at Inverness, the only
people there who, in my memory, had any reality were my
father and Hugh. In a mood of high holiday, we made our
way to a restaurant where George and Tom had several drams
of whisky and I was deemed old enough to have a glass of
sherry (which I enjoyed greatly) and then we all had a large
high tea.

'What I think,' said Tom, as he sat back from the table, at
last, to light his pipe, 'is as follows. Now that we have this
big bursary behind us, there is no reason in the world why
the whole of the three of us should not go to the University.'

'That,' said George, 'is a very, very good idea, Tom. I
daresay they would still take us at our age – they'll not take
you if you are too young, but I never heard of them objecting
to a person as being too old for it.'

This was conversation in the true Reachfar style and spirit.
It meant that George and Tom were congratulating me on
having won the bursary, although I had been the youngest
entrant, and I accepted their congratulations in similar
Reachfar fashion.

'Och, if the bursary wouldn't pay for us all, we could
always pawn the Academy's gold medal,' I said, and this
suggestion having been accepted with acclamation, the entire
subject of the bursary and the medal was relegated to the
archives of our past. They had been put, duly honoured in
the passing, into their place in the scheme of things.

We then caught the little train to Fortavoch, went to the

inn to get the horse and trap that had been stabled there all day, and, naturally, George and Tom had another few drams and I had another glass of sherry. We came rollicking across the moor by the short way into Reachfar about nine in the evening singing '*Over the Sea to Skye*' in hilarious voices. My grandmother, my grandfather, my aunt and my shy little brother were at the moor gate to welcome us and my grandmother's face was stern, although her eyes were twinkling, when she said: 'So here you are! It's well seen that Duncan and Jean didna travel north the-day, I'm thinking. Come, Janet! Mercy, you're still growing! You look fine, though – in spite of everything!'

After I was in bed that night, in my own attic room where the sheets smelled of the whin bushes on which they had been spread to bleach, that phrase 'in spite of everything' echoed in my mind. Eight or ten years ago, when I had been a small child, I had often heard some of the older local people say that my grandmother was a witch or that she was gifted with 'The Sight', but, this apart, there is no doubt that she was a very worldly-wise old woman with uncommon sensitivity of observation.

The everyday lines of thought are the permanent ways laid down by humanity out of its experience and, like the permanent ways of the railway system, they tend to go straight from one profit-point or station to another, by a process of 'if I do this, that will result', without paying much attention to the intervening countryside across which they run. My grandmother's mind did not ride upon the permanent way that had been hastily thrown up or laid down by common human experience and it did not run at the normal human speed or by the normal human rules. Oh, no. My grandmother's mind had constructed its own way and, as it moved along that track, it took note of the ground below, the sky above and the terrain on either side. It was more interested in these things 'by the way' than it was, very often, in the destination towards which it was, at the moment, going. At the time of my arrival at Reachfar, then, her mind was on the way to meeting Jean and welcoming her to our home, but, on that way, it was inspecting everything that led to the station that was Jean – the earth below, the sky above, and it was now taking a pause to inspect, in detail, as part of the terrain, the small, wild, thorny bush that was known to the world at large as her grand-daughter, Janet Sandison. This was quite clear to me before I fell asleep, as I repeated in my mind that phrase: 'in spite of everything'. I was not surprised, therefore, when, the next morning, after the men-folk had gone out to work and my aunt was upstairs cleaning the bedrooms while my grandmother baked scones in the kitchen and I washed dishes in the scullery, the Ould Leddy (as George, Tom and I often called her behind her back) said: 'Your father tells us that Jean is a grand baker.'

'She is, Granny,' I said. 'She is a first-class housewife in every way.'

'And she's a bonnie woman, I hear?'

'Yes, Granny. Very bonnie. Reddish-fair hair and she has a beautiful skin.'

She took some scones from her girdle, set them up on edge against the side of the baking-board and spread the white cloth over them. 'It is a wise thing your father has done, Janet. It must be lonely for him, away down there in the south – he is better with a woman of his own in his house.'

'Yes,' I agreed, as I hung the clean cups from my tray on their hooks on the dresser shelf.

She swung the girdle with its new load of scones over the fire, dusted a little flour from her apron and said: 'It is a pity that you and Jean don't get on.'

'Who said we didn't?' I asked.

'Said?' she asked. 'There doesn't have to be *saying* for everything.'

'Did Dad say anything?'

'Him? No. Oh, no. He tells us she is very good to you and always at him to see that you have the right clothes and everything you need.'

'That is quite true, Granny,' I said and went back to the scullery for more dishes.

When I came back with my tray, she had turned her

146

scones on her girdle and she now turned her back to the fire and looked directly at me. I stopped in mid-floor and looked back at her. We are a tall family, and now I was about my grandmother's height, so that our eyes were on a level. Brilliant blue, in her proud, West Highland face under its white hair, the eyes looked into mine. 'It is a pity, in a way,' she said, 'that you are so like your mother.'

The words were about the last that I expected. With a release of tension, I put my tray on the end of the table and began to put away the cutlery in the drawer. '*Am* I like Mother? Everybody says that I am more like *you*, Granny.'

'They say that you are like me in nature.' She gave a little smile that was youthfully mischievous in spite of her age. 'I wouldn't have said I could ever be as thrawn and determined as you can be, but maybe a body won't be seeing themselves as plain as others do. But the face is your mother's. This very morning, now, you are the image of the lassie that your father first brought to Reachfar, but you're not so delicate-looking. Your health is all right?'

'Goodness, yes, Granny.'

'Maybe the Sandisons have given you that. Your face is not as fine of the bone as your mother's, but you have the hair, the forehead and the eyes. She had as fine a pair of eyes as I ever saw in a woman and the good width of an eye between them, like you. But hers were better than yours. They were soft, always – you never saw the Sandison rage in them, to spoil them. – Has your father still got that big photograph of her that was taken in Inverness?'

'Yes,' I said. 'It hangs in the parlour. But last week, the cord broke and it fell and the glass got broken.'

As I spoke, I was bending down to put a bowl into the low cupboard of the dresser and I was suddenly arrested, bent from the waist, bowl in hand. I suddenly knew that that picture cord had not broken of itself. This may make clear to you why the local people used to say that my grandmother was a witch and why, also, so many of them said that I resembled her so strongly 'in nature'. This conversation between us, which I have quoted, without need of any more

147

direct words between us, opened up a complete new vista for me of the mind and heart of Jean. I had been too young and undeveloped to understand that Jean would, naturally, be jealous of my father's first wife and it had never occurred to me that I was a permanent, flesh-and-blood reminder to her of that deeply-loved woman.

'It is a pity about the glass,' my grandmother was saying calmly as she re-loaded her girdle with fresh scones. 'But these big photographs is out of fashion in houses these days, whatever. Next time you come home, bring it with you and we'll get it mended for your roomie here. We have always been a little old-fashioned and behind the times at Reachfar, so it will be all right here.'

'All right, Granny,' I said, put my bowl into the cupboard and closed the door.

My father and Jean arrived at Reachfar at the beginning of August and the last days of July were given over to a tenseness – though not admitted by my family, of course – of expectation. Indeed, the tenseness showed itself in the main in the fact that Jean's name was never mentioned, which was typical of the Reachfar attitude and approach. On the day that they were due to arrive, I spent my afternoon alone in my 'Thinking Place' on the moor and I think that I actually prayed to God that Jean would not arrive in the pink blouse, the hat with the rose, the blue 'costume' and the 'rabbit-skin', but in her nice, plain tweed, going-for-the-messages coat, so that she would make a good impression on my family. This was not because I had any more liking for Jean than formerly, but because I could not bear the thought of 'family difficulties' at Reachfar. Such things were scarifying enough to the mind and spirit at that unimportant place, Cairnton, but at Reachfar, where my family had always been a solidly welded unit, they were impossible to contemplate. If, as I think, I did approach God in detail on the subject, it was one of the times when He was busy elsewhere with more important prayers. The trap came over the moor to the gate with George and Tom in front and my father and Jean – pink blouse, hat with rose, blue costume and rabbit-skin and all – in the back. In addition, the hat now had a pink veil which reached to the tip of Jean's nose, which was red, as was her whole face, with the exertion of the jolting over the twelve miles from Fortavoch. As the trap approached, I was aware of my grandmother's deep-drawn breath and straightening of her shoulders which always betokened moments of crisis and then, I think, I must have gone into the merciful coma which tends to overtake me in desperate moments, for I remember no more of that first evening except Jean's opening remark: 'In the name o' God! Whit a place! Ah thocht we wis never gaun tae get here!'

On my way through life, observing the age in which I live which, up to the moment that my pen is crossing this paper, is mostly the first half of the twentieth century, I have noticed that people, in the main, tend to live at greater and greater speed and consequently in less and less detail. This may seem, at a quick glance, to be a crashing statement of the obvious, so I will now drive home what I mean by 'detail' by citing in, I hope, a few short phrases, what Jean's opening speech meant to the people of Reachfar, my family, to wit – my grandfather, my grandmother, my father, my Uncle George, my Aunt Kate, Tom and me. I do not count my little brother, John, who was only six at the time and has no part in this story.

a. The entire speech was offensive to all, with the improbable exception of my father, because it was spoken in a loud, shrill voice, was ill-mannered, was disparaging of Reachfar and was indicative of ill-content.

b. My grandfather as a separate unit took exception to the familiar use of the name of the Almighty.

c. My grandmother as a separate unit took exception to a woman who could be so abysmally stupid about a place that obviously meant so much to the man she had married.

d. My aunt as a separate unit was an avid student of the better fashion journals which were handed on to her by Lady Lydia Daviot of Poyntdale and, in addition, herself possessed that indefinable quality which the French call 'chic', which made her wear even her milking apron with a flair of elegance. As a highly skilled charmer of the male sex, she would have been horrified by the lack of charm in Jean's speech had she not been stricken dumb with horror as she gazed upon Jean's 'honeymoon-outfit' with an expression that was compounded of amusement, embarrassment and barely-believing wonder.

e. My uncle and Tom, never very separate units at any time, probably did not hear the speech at all, so firmly welded together were they in the irritation and dislike of Jean that had been born in them over the twelve miles from Fortavoch Station and so busy were they bending on me, from behind the horse, a joint look which said, more clearly than any words: 'Why the devil didn't you *warn* us?'

As the trap passed the gate, my mind went into a turmoil and the lens of my memory does not come into focus again until about two days later, when I have a picture of my family, bemused, but determined to do its best. My family, indeed, had its back to the wall, fighting in the last ditch, holding its ground and no more and, although nobody spoke the words, the essence of them: 'Och, well, it's only for ten days!' was in the air. My family had set itself to be civil for the ten days of the visit and when my family sets itself for something, it takes a lot of *un*-setting. It can stand up to anything, almost, and it was now standing up to having Reachfar, lock, stock and barrel, reorganized by Jean, so that it would be 'mair like the thing'. She told my grandmother and my aunt how to re-arrange the parlour and a better way of baking oatcakes, and was prepared to advise my grandfather and Tom on the feeding of cattle, in blissful unawareness that she came from 'milk' country and was now in 'beef' country. Jean was having a fine time, putting Reachfar to rights, and Reachfar, unbeknownst to Jean, was having a fine time letting her think that she was putting it to rights. 'Only for ten days!' said their faces, that is, of course, if you could read the faces, but it was Jean's weakness that she was not – and never became – Reachfarliterate.

For eight days, all went merrily. My grandmother, who was locally recognized as the best butter-maker in the district, had listened with a fine display of respectful wonder while Jean instructed her as to how butter should be made; my aunt accepted with humility Jean's dictum that the people at Achcraggan Church — including Lady Lydia, whose clothes were always impeccable — were 'awfu' countrified an' auld-farrant in their dress', and my grandfather, who was a silent man by nature, said nothing to Jean at all except an oft-repeated; 'That will be quite right, Jean,' which pleased her very well. I think she was quite unaware that, most of the time, her words were not penetrating to his consciousness, for it did not occur to her that he lived largely within his own mind and seldom took any notice of the spoken word unless it happened to be uttered by my grandmother. George, Tom and I, for our part, contributed to the happy home atmosphere by absenting ourselves as frequently and for as long periods as possible.

The Ninth Day of Jean's stay at Reachfar, which has lived for ever under that name in the minds of George, Tom and myself, was a Saturday and Jean and my father were to return to Cairnton on the Tuesday. In the forenoon, my grandmother, grandfather, father and Jean had driven down to Achcraggan to visit an old lady, known as Aunt Betsy, a remote relation of my grandfather. We had heard that Aunt Betsy had fallen the day before and my grandparents were anxious about her, but Jean insisted on going with them on the grounds that 'it was aye an ootin'.'

Tom, my aunt and I had had a fine, lazy, comfortable morning until, just before dinner-time, George came home from work at Dinchory and Tom said to him: 'Ye know, George, it is myself that is a little suspeecious o' the young heifer.'

'What? She's not due for about six weeks yet!' said George.

'Well, I've brought her in to the byre, anyway,' Tom told him.

'Why is she so late in calf anyway?' I asked as I poured the water off the potatoes.

'It's her first year at the bull,' said George and glanced bawdily at my aunt. 'When a lass is young, she will aye caper

151

a bittie before she will be making up her mind. We had to take her to Poyntdale three times before we got her served and her going on as if she didn't know what the bull was there for!'

'Whit a wey tae gang on!' said my aunt, in flouncing imitation of Jean. 'No' wan bit nice or polite, that's whit it's no'!'

'It is very, very vulgar' said Tom solemnly, 'to be making fun o' these refined, clever people from the south. Come on out and take a look at the heifer, George.'

By the time they came back, the Achcraggan party had returned and, during dinner, the talk was mostly of Aunt Betsy who, it had been discovered, had broken her thigh.

'The pare auld sowl!' said Jean, fluffing up the frills of her blouse.

Jean had a way of speaking this phrase which had always irritated me when she applied it to Granny Reid, and now I was interested to notice the rising of the family hackles round the table as it was applied to Aunt Betsy. I had it in my wicked heart to wish that Aunt Betsy herself could have heard the remark and the patronizing tone in which it was spoken in order to see what would happen to Jean. Aunt Betsy was no subject either for pity or patronage. She had started her working life at the age of twelve as kitchen-maid at Ulldale Castle and had ended it at the age of seventy, at the death of old Sir Gordon Ulldale, her eccentric, irascible, bachelor employer to whom she had acted as housekeeper for forty years. Sir Gordon was the only member of the Ulldale family and the only person on the Ulldale Estate who did not go in mortal terror of Aunt Betsy and even he had had his moments of uncertainty when he overstepped the mark in a way that she considered Going Too Far. The scenes between them were reputed to cause a quivering of the pepperpot turrets of the Victorian castle and someone of Jean's mental stature would have been chaff in the wind to Aunt Betsy.

'Jean didn't come into the house,' said my grandfather, for the general information of the rest of us, to indicate that

Jean had spoken of what, to her, was an unknown quantity. 'The doctor said it would excite Aunt Betsy too much to see a stranger.' (Doctor Mackay was always a diplomat.)

'I must say, it's a real nice hoose,' said Jean. 'Ah wis fair surprised – her bein' a pare auld maid body an' everything. Of coorse, the rents'll no' be high in Achcraggan.'

'Rents?' said my grandfather in a wondering voice.

'The house is Aunt Betsy's own, Jean,' said my father suppressively.

No more was said of Aunt Betsy, but, as had been demonstrated during this period at Reachfar, if my father suppressed Jean on one subject, she seemed to feel a need to assert herself on another. As a rule, on Saturday afternoons, my aunt would amuse herself by baking a cake or some buns or some biscuits or something 'special' for Sunday tea and as this baking was usually by a new recipe culled from a neighbour or some housekeeping magazine, it was known as Kate's 'expeeryment'. When the dinner-table had been cleared, my aunt said briskly: 'Well, you men, outside! I'm going to bake,' and she pointed to the door.

Tom jumped up. 'Come on, George; come on, John, boy. Make way for the expeeryment! See and make it a good one, Kate!'

The men went out and my grandparents retired to their room for the short rest they were now taking every afternoon.

'What's it to be?' I asked.

'Strawberry Shortcake,' said my aunt. 'American. I got the recipe from the cook at the hotel.'

'Och, that's jist sponge-cake an' strawberries!' said Jean.

'It doesn't *look* like an ordinary sponge mixture,' said my aunt, frowning at her recipe book.

'That's whit it comes *oot* like!' Jean was authoritative. 'Mrs Mathieson at Cairnton mak's it. Can ye mak' a Cairnton loaf?'

'What's that?' my aunt asked.

'Ye've niver heard o' a Cairnton Loaf?' Jean squealed with amazement at such ignorance.

This concoction known as Cairnton Loaf was a sort of cake spiced with ginger and cinnamon and carrying a few currants and raisins, but it was quite local to the Cairn Glen, which was not surprising, for it had not the gastronomic distinction of the Edinburgh Shortbread, the Cornish Pasty or the Stilton Cheese, that was likely to earn it world-wide fame.

'I'll show ye hoo tae mak' it!' said Jean and snatched the mixing-bowl from my aunt's hands.

For a second, my aunt and I stared at one another tight-lipped – we *still* wanted to make strawberry shortcake – but, in the end, the principle of 'peace in the house of Reachfar' triumphed and we allowed ourselves to be lectured by Jean on the virtues of Cairnton Loaf, the cleverness of Cairnton cooks and attended meticulously to her instructions on the preparation of the delicacy. At long last, it was in the oven, the top of the big stove was shut down and the dampers set to keep the oven at the high, steady heat, prolonged for three hours, which was required. Having observed the amount of coal which Jean piled on to the fire, my aunt and I agreed, without words, that there would not be many Cairnton Loaves baked at Reachfar. Cairnton was within ten miles of the coal-mines, Reachfar was about two hundred miles away. Different places have different economies.

The three of us were having a 'fly cup' of tea when Tom appeared at the open window.

'Kate, come out to the byre for a minute, will you?'

Kate ran out and was back at the window inside a minute. 'It's the heifer, Janet. Go and call Granny. Something's far wrong.' She flew back to the byre.

My grandmother was the best amateur veterinary surgeon in the district, so, having called her, I came back to the kitchen to restrain Jean from any attempt to render assistance or give advice in the byre. I need not have troubled, however, for Jean did not seem to be interested. A few minutes more and George ran past the window and into the kitchen, a bucket in each hand.

'Boiling water, Janet! As much as you can boil, the Ould Leddy says!'

I threw the oven dampers in, seized the poker, tore the top plates off the stove and swung the kettles on to the roaring, open fire. Tom and my aunt were now also in the kitchen, filling pans with water and bringing them to the stove.

'Whit the bliddy hell are ye daein'?' squealed Jean. 'Whit aboot ma loaf?'

She picked up the poker and tried to replace a stove-plate.

'Oot o' the road, Mistress,' said Tom, shouldering her aside and swinging a bucket of water to the stove-top.

My aunt had been out to the byre and in again. 'Granny wants you, Tom. They can't hold the heifer down.'

Tom ran out and my aunt rushed to the bedroom and came back with an armful of towels which she threw into the sink. 'Fomentations, Janet. Help me to wring them!'

We splashed boiling water into the sink, wrung out the towels, threw them into a basin and my aunt fled to the byre.

'Ah niver saw sic a cairry-on in ma life!' bawled Jean. 'The loaf'll be ruint an' jist look at the mess on the flare!'

'Oh, damn the loaf and the floor!' I said, refilling kettles as fast as I could. 'Put some dry wood on the fire, Jean!'

'If you think Ah'm here tae tak' *your* orders, ye're daft!'

'Oh, *Jean*, don't be so silly!' I began to put the wood on the fire myself.

'Don't you dare ca' me a fool, ye uppish bitch!' Jean yelled.

I turned to face her, saw beyond her my grandmother and Tom in the doorway and, in that moment, the large, sharp cooking-knife which had been lying on the table whistled past my ear and stuck, quivering, in the wooden wallboard above the stove. For a long moment, the silence was broken only by the crackle of wood and the hiss of steam from the kettles and then came the voice of my grandmother, like the crack of doom: 'Jean, go to your room and stay there.'

'Ah didnae mean it? It niver hit her! Ah didnae mean it!'

'GO TO YOUR ROOM!'

With a hysterical bellow, Jean fled from the kitchen.

'Great God Almighty!' said Tom on a long, sighing breath.

My grandmother, inhaling long and deeply, came calmly forward and took my trembling hand. 'Steady now, Janet,' she said gently. 'I need you to help me with the heifer. My

155

hands are not as good as they were and yours are fine and long and narrow and strong. Look, I'll show you what's wanted and there's nothing to be afraid of.' She took a tumbler from the dresser, laid it on its side and laid five matches inside it. 'That's the calf — the body and the four legs. That's the way it *should* be lying, but it isn't. It's like this.' She broke two of the matches in half and replaced them in the glass, demonstrating how the calf's legs on one side were bent the wrong way for birth. 'What I want you to do is get your hand in — but not till I tell you — and try to straighten the legs. You can do that?'

'I — I'll try, Granny.'

She poured water into a basin. 'Wash your hands well, rinse them in clean water, but don't dry them,' she said.

We went to the byre with its agonized young animal and its worried people.

'Wait now, till I tell you when, Janet,' my grandmother said. 'And as steady and gentle and quiet as you can manage, Janet. The steadier you are the less you will hurt her.'

I gritted my teeth and knelt down behind the heifer who gave a sudden, dreadful, convulsive heave and the calf's head and one leg appeared.

'Now,' my grandmother said quietly. 'See the knee there? Push back a little — canny, gently, that's right — fine, can you feel the little hoof?'

'Yes.'

'Push it back a little more and then try to bring it forward, but keep your hand between the hoof and the mother's body.'

The heifer groaned, the sweat started on my forehead, but I got my hand back into the warm, slippery cavity and, with what seemed an age of slow movement, I at last drew my hand forward and the small hoof came into the light.

'Hold tight, George!' said my grandmother and my uncle's big hands closed round the calf's body, arresting the birth process.

'Now the hind leg, Janet. It's far easier. You're doing grand. Put your hand in and try to hold the hoof back as the body comes forward, so that the leg comes to birth last.'

The heifer heaved. 'Now!' she said and moved up the stall to the animal's head and squatted in the straw beside her. 'There, now, poor lassie, it will soon be all over.' Her voice was gentle and encouraging and, as if the heifer understood the words, she sighed and gave a great heave. Inside, my hand against the hoof went back and I suddenly knew that the leg was in position. 'It's straight, Granny!'

'Good – take your hand out, canny, now!' She concentrated again on the heifer. 'Now a little more, my poor young craitur.' She took the suffering head in gentle old hands, there was another heave and the calf lay panting on the straw.

Tom picked it up and began to massage it with clean sacking while my aunt ran to the house for a hot drink for the heifer and in an unbelievably short time the calf struggled up on to four wobbly but sound legs and stared at us all and this strange world with big, wondering, brown eyes.

'A bonnie wee heifer, Mistress!' said Tom.

My grandmother, with the mother's head still between her hands, looked over her shoulder. 'That's Janet of Reachfar that you have there, Tom. Janet is due that the calfie should get her name!'

'It's not many crofts in Ross-shire that has *two* vets o' their own!' said my 'clown' of an uncle.

The mother animal now gave a low croon and the calf tried to escape from Tom and struggle towards her.

'No, ye don't, ye wee devil!' said my father, and picked it up in his arms. 'You are going to drink your milk out of a pail like a proper leddy!' and he carried the calf away to the prepared pen.

The heifer who, a short time ago, had been *in extremis*, had now had her warm drink, wanted her baby and was prepared to fight for it as my agile young aunt edged a milking stool into position, preparatory to drawing off the first, heavy flow of milk. She lashed out with her hooves and sent the pail flying into the manger and then made a good try at trampling my aunt into the straw of the stall.

'She'll do!' said my grandfather with pride. 'She's doing fine!'

'Get out of here!' my aunt panted. 'Leave me alone with her, the devil, or we'll never milk her!'

'That's right,' said my grandmother. 'Come into the house the whole of you. Kate will be better on her own.'

'We've all worked for a cup of tea,' my father said. 'Come on, Janet,' and we all trooped into the house.

We were all filled with a sense of achievement and it seemed to be a very long time since I had left the kitchen with my grandmother, my wet hands and arms held out in front of me. We all gathered, chattering, round the sink to take turns with the kitchen soap in washing our hands.

'Who the devil put that knife into the mantel-board?' my father's voice suddenly asked.

We all turned from the sink to form a half-circle in the doorway of the scullery and it seemed, in that moment, as if the old kitchen contained nothing but the big varnished board in which the knife stood like some pointing, accusing finger. Calmly, my grandmother dried her hands and handed me the rough kitchen towel. 'Make some tea, please, Janet,' she said. 'Duncan, come with me.'

My father followed her through the passage to her room and the door closed behind them. My grandfather, George and Tom looked round at one another and I turned to the fire and set a kettle to boil. Tom scratched his head a little and then looked at my grandfather.

'Ye see, Reachfar,' he said, 'it was this way . . .'

I do not think that Reachfar was a satisfactory place to Jean in one solitary aspect. It did not even provide her with a noisy, recriminating, parting scene which she might have enjoyed. When my grandmother returned calmly to the kitchen to drink her tea, my father went to the room that he and Jean were occupying and for some ten minutes the air was rent with a wild howling. My grandmother behaved as if nothing unusual were afoot and we all, as we always did, took our cue from her and behaved likewise. Jean, swollen-eyed, appeared at the supper-table and the talk was of our fine new calf and which of the family would attend church in the morning, as the trap would carry only four. In the

158

end, my grandparents, my father and Jean went to church.

'It's aye an outing,' said my mischievous aunt as the trap drove down the hill.

The next morning, the trap drove away across the moor in the direction of Fortavoch and the railway, and Reachfar saw Jean no more for many, many years, but that is away ahead of this point in this story.

CHAPTER TEN

My classes at the university were not due to begin until about mid-October, so that I had a fine, long, late summer and autumn at Reachfar and I do not remember that Jean's name was mentioned during the entire period, until the last evening before I travelled south. George, Tom and I had been round the sheep on the moor and had come back as far as the gate that led down the yard to the house when, by common consent, we all stopped, leaned on the top bar and looked away past the house, down the long slope to the firth and away to the hump of the Ben.

'You would hardly believe what I am going to tell you,' said George, puffing at his pipe. 'Tom and me has been at the letter-writing.'

'You are quite right,' I told him. 'I don't believe you. I don't think that either of you *can* write any more.'

'Och, we can still make a bit shape at it if we are fair desperate,' Tom said.

'And who did you write this desperate letter to?'

George gave the back of his neck a rub with his left hand as he always does in a situation that he finds embarrassing. 'Well, it was like this – it was to your father.'

'My *father*? What about?'

'Well, Tom and me has been thinking a bittie about Jean and the way she doesna seem to like you and we was thinking that things wouldna be very nice likely, at this Cairnton place, so we made up our minds to write to him. So we wrote to him. In my opeenion, that Jean is a wicked thrawn limmer but your father has married her now – mind you, I believe that she is nice enough to *him* –

160

and we all chust have to make the best of it.'

'That is chust what I will be thinking too, forbye,' said Tom.

'So Tom and me had a Parlyment,' George continued, 'and then wrote to him and it was this way. We said that we had the bursary now and Tom and me has a bittie in the bank and I have yon few hundred that ould Uncle Kenny left me and your father has a bittie in the bank too and we chust said that it would be far handier for you to have nice lodgings near the University, like all the other students from the north here, and none o' this running up and down in the train or the 'bus to this Cairnton place.'

'And it's *my* belief,' said Tom with emphasis, 'that it is a *saving* that will be in it, instead o' spending a lot o' good money on train fares.'

I had been dreading the return to Cairnton. This was like a hope of Paradise.

'And did my father write back to you?' I asked.

'Aye. And he said that he could see that we had made up our minds and that he thought it maybe was the best arrangement.'

'Except that it's not arranged yet,' said Tom. 'For with Mrs Hill dying last Monday the way she did, poor woman, your father won't have had time to see about the lodgings, so it's to Cairnton that you'll have to go tomorrow, chust for the meantime but not for long.'

'That Jean will not be very nice, likely,' George added thoughtfully, 'but I don't think she will be at the knife-throwing again. Man, Tom, I never heard of a woman doing the like of yon!'

'No, nor me neither,' said Tom.

'Oh, it wasn't really *knife*-throwing,' I told them. 'The knife just happened to *be* there, that's all. It was really a sort of accident.' The incident had not been mentioned until now and I was now embarrassed by the very memory of it and wished to be rid of it.

'Accident!' said Tom. 'If I hadna seen it with my own eyes, I would never have believed it. And, by God, George, the

Ould Leddy was wild! You could feel the rage coming out through her skin like sweat off a horse! I was standing there beside her and I was feared of my life to move!'

'Aye, the Ould Leddy can get angry, right enough,' George agreed. 'I mind once when we were loons – Duncan would be aboot eleven and I was ten – Duncan was aye a good, big, soft, decent lump and no wickedness in him o' the world, but I don't know the way it was – the wickedness would get into *me* whiles and one day I took my knife and cut a big bit out o' the stack tarpaulin to build a tent or some caper like that and when I was found out I said that Duncan had done it. Lies is bad enough, but a danged silly lie like that was chust plain foolishness, for the Ould Leddy knew fine that Duncan would never *think* on cutting the good tarpaulin. Man, what a bliddy row was in it! The Ould Leddy broke a bittie branchie off that ould rodden tree round at the back there and you could see her rage sparking out o' the end o' it like forked lightning when she came at me! I never forgot it. No. And I never went out o' my road to make her as wild as that again either,' he ended thoughtfully.

'The Ould Leddy is far coorser o' the temper than that woman Jean for all Jean's bawling,' Tom said.

'Aye.' George was thoughtful. 'But the Ould One's temper is like a well-trained horse. You'll always make a quicker, more thorough job with a well-trained horse than you will with a wild one, however strong it is.'

'And anyway, besides an' apart from all else,' said Tom, 'to be throwing knives at people is terrible poor manners.'

On this note of understatement, the subject was relinquished.

When I returned to Cairnton and went to bed on my first evening after a three-cornered meal during which Jean tried to pretend that I was not present, I discovered that Jean and, indeed, all Cairnton were utterly unimportant to me. In my mind, I discovered, Cairnton was a place where nothing happened. I can understand, now, long afterwards, that this attitude in me, which for six years had been an unconscious one, was a large part of the cause of Jean's basic dislike for me, for Cairnton, to Jean, was the hub of the universe, just as

Reachfar was to me. However, I was impervious to Cairnton and might be said to have left more mark upon it than it had left upon me, for, as Miss Hadley annoyed Jean very much by telling her, my name was now painted on the Dux Medal Board in the school hall while, on another wall, a small brass plate had appeared, beside the one that carried the name of Hugh Reid, which told the world that the C. and C. Bursary had been brought to the Academy in 1926 by So-and-So, aged Such-and-Such. Hugh said that the school hall was getting to look quite like a war memorial, with all the names of the fallen hung around, which caused Miss Hadley to give us the 'look' which she used to bend on us during our First Year and say: 'Quite the university wit, Mr Reid.'

But if, unconsciously or subconsciously, my attitude for six years had been that Cairnton did not matter and that Cairnton was a place where nothing happened, this does not mean that during the six years Cairnton had had no effect on me. I do not know – and probably I never shall know – the full extent of its effect, but a straw will show the way the wind blows, and straws themselves, sometimes, are quite interesting things. Down my six Cairnton years, every time I went home to Reachfar on holiday, Tom would choose a quiet moment to have with me a conversation something like this: 'Ye know, I have been chust a little disappointed this last year back. Aye.'

'Oh? Why, Tom?'

'Well, it's a long time since you sent me a bittie poetry. I am a great hand for the poetry and a person misses it when he has always been used to it.'

'Och, Tom! That was a thing I did when I was only a bairn—'

'Och, I can see that with the Latin and the French and the matheemateeks an' a-all you'll not be having much time, but still, it's kind of funny not to be having a bittie poetry now and again.'

'But, Tom, that stuff I used to write *wasn't* poetry!'

'Och, maybe it wasn't as good as Shakes-fear' – Tom

invariably called the great man 'Shakes-fear', conjuring up an absurd vision of a shaker-in-his-shoes – 'but it used to suit me fine. It would stick in my mind and I could be saying it to myself when at some chob that is monotonous-like, like the turnip-hoeing. Aye. It is myself that misses the poetry.'

I loved Tom very deeply. I would come back to Cairnton, write him a letter and hard, hard would I try to 'do a bit of poetry' to put in it for him, but not a rhyme would come. Since I wrote my spiteful little song about Annie Black that evening on the fly-leaf of my *Alice in Wonderland*, I had never written, and could not write, another rhyme. My early childhood had been spattered and punctuated with rhymes. Any small experience, any childish occasion, the acquisition of any new bit of knowledge had been celebrated naturally and as a matter of course with a 'bittie poetry', which was, in the end, written out in my fairest hand and given to Tom, but out of the grim, grey stone of Cairnton, apparently, 'poetry' did not come.

But, on the evening of the day when Hugh and I visited the Academy and Hugh made his remark about the names of the fallen, when I went to bed, instead of going to sleep I found myself sitting up, composing a poem. It was not a good poem and it had not the humour of the childhood rhymes and I am not going to quote it here, but I tell of it because it was a straw in the wind. It was a straw that, by its drift, made me aware that some part of my essential self which had been dormant had come awake again and was actively seeking for and believing in its right to claim its own happiness. A bad poet even – indeed the very worst poet – is at his happiest and is his truest self when trying to grasp with his clumsy fingers the filament-fine, ever-fleeting skirts of the muse.

However, if, in my opinion, nothing had happened in Cairnton for six years, something happened now, although to this day I have never been clear as to the details of it all. Just a day or two after my return, we had a telegram from George telling us that Old Aunt Betsy had died of pleurisy and asking whether my father could come north for the funeral. My father went up to the farm to see Tommie, who was now the owner – or it would be more accurate to say that he went up to the farm to inspect Tommie's condition, for, since the death of his mother, Tommie had been on one long drunken spree. This spree was not induced by sorrow at the death of his mother, but was more in the nature of a celebration of the taking-over of his inheritance and took the form of sodden alcoholic stupors, alternating with a wild exercising of his new authority, which he demonstrated by sacking out of hand this man and that without glimmer of excuse.

On the evening of the telegram, my father arrived at Cairnshaws to find that Tommie was not there at all, but that the house servants had just finished putting out a fire which had started in his bedroom and had destroyed the bed, the carpet and several pieces of furniture. The only information that could be derived was that Tommie had left in his car at mid-afternoon. My father went from the farm to Cairnton to try to trace the car, which was well known in the district, and heard that it had been seen a short time before headed back in the direction of Cairnshaws, so he then left Cairnton by my school route through the old quarry. At this point, obscurity sets in. When my father reached the old quarry, Annie Black was lying on the ground with her clothes torn and disarranged and the heavy, drunken Tommie Hill and the one-armed Hugh Reid were engaged in mortal combat. The combat came to a sudden end with Hugh Reid sitting breathless and bruised on the ground while my father laid about his employer with his ash-plant and finally picked him up bodily and threw him into the cold, dark quarry loch with the words: 'Maybe that'll sober ye, ye dirty bugger!' He then ordered Hugh to take Annie home to Nethercairn and came, himself, home to our house.

I was in my bedroom, reading, when I heard him come in, his stride more rapid than usual.

'Better start packing, Jean,' he said. 'We're finished here.'

'Are ye aff yer heid?' I heard Jean yell.

I suppose that she had seen his face and knew that he meant the words. I laid aside my book and decided that this was a time for Sandisons to stand together. I was completely mystified as to what had happened, but Jean was not going to yell like that at my father without question. I went into the living-room.

'The stinkin' rotten brute!' said my father

'Whae?' Jean squealed.

'Tommie Hill!'

'Duncan Sandison, whit hae ye been an' dune?'

'Done? I threw him in the quarry loch!'

'Ah-ow-ow!' yelled Jean and collapsed, still yelling, into a chair. 'Aw, whit'll we dae? Whit'll we dae?'

'Hello, Dad,' I said. 'What happened?'

He was quite incapable of telling a coherent story, and his speech was spattered with 'the poor innocent lassie and her clothes all torn' and 'the poor cripple laddie and him doing his best' and 'the dirty raping brute and him like a wild beast with drink'. And through it all Jean rolled about in her chair howling like a tortured banshee.

I put the kettle on the fire. 'Sit down, Dad,' I said.

He obeyed me and then looked at Jean. 'What the devil's wrong with you?' he barked at her. 'Stop that bliddy bawling, for God's sake.'

She gulped and stared at him. 'But whit are we tae dae? Ye'll get the sack!'

'The *sack*?' he shouted. 'God Almighty, I wouldn't work for that brute any longer for all the money in the bank!'

'Ye're aff yer heid! Whit'll we *dae*?'

'Ach, hold your tongue! Cairnshaws is not the only place on the face o' the earth!'

'It's the only *big* place there *is*!'

He suddenly became calm, staring with narrowed eyes at her blotched face, and I do not believe that, until that moment, he had realized just how limited to the Cairn Valley was the mind of Jean.

'By good farming standards,' he said brutally, 'Cairnshaws isn't a place at all. There's nothing in it but a stee-owl o' thin Ayrshire milk and a few petrol lorries!'

'Ye're aff yer heid!' gasped Jean and then gave herself up

to a fresh fit of howling.

I have no further clear memories of my home during the next few days. I know that, in the fore-ordained fashion of my family, I set out on schedule for my first class at the university which seemed to Jean to be a flying in the face of Providence now that my father had gone and 'made a fool o' himsel' an' lost his job'. I know that my father did not go north for Aunt Betsy's funeral, but remained to look after the farm at Cairnshaws, for, after he emerged, dripping, from the cold autumnal waters of the quarry loch, Tommie had gone somewhere and had some more to drink and, eventually, about midnight, drove his car through the canal bridge and finished up in the cottage hospital, while the car in the canal caused quite a deal of trouble to an old grey horse which was trying to tow a barge laden with Cairnton stone along a route by which it had been towing such loads for a quarter of a century.

Gossip, as can be imagined, was rife in Cairnton, but this latest affair had one great unusual feature from 'the Toon's' point of view. None of the principals in the affair would contribute any information. Tommie Hill, being unconscious, could not, while my father would not and neither would Hugh, but, what was so extraordinary, Mrs Black would not either. Gossip and rumour developed like a cancerous growth, stretching octopus-like tentacles in every direction. I went up and down to Glasgow each day and, in my slow-witted fashion, was not aware of half that was being said in the district. All that concerned me was that the atmosphere in my own home was less tense, for Jean was in such a ferment about the rumours concerning Annie Black that she had, temporarily, forgotten her own troubles and how my father 'had made a fool o' himsel' an' lost his job'.

Annie Black had 'disappeared'. The morning after Hugh had delivered her to her home on the instructions of my father, she had left, ostensibly, to return to her 'job' in Glasgow, and her mother, being overcome about mid-day by anxiety, took the afternoon train to the city and called at the address where Annie had said she had been working all these years. The respectable insurance brokers had never heard of Annie, and Mrs Black, in the train back to Cairnton, which also happened to be carrying Mrs Mathieson, broke down and told the latter what she had discovered. From there, the landslide began and it was not long before the bright light of the truth – in all its lurid red – about Annie had broken over the malicious minds of Cairnton. They were all the more malicious, of course, because they had not seen the light about Annie long ago.

The next thing that happened was that Tommie Hill was released from the hospital, whereupon he got into his car and drove away and two days later my father received a letter from his lawyers which informed him that they had been instructed to sell Cairnshaws.

'Ah kent as much!' said Jean. 'Him an' Annie's thegither an' a bonnie pair they'll make, for there's no' yin o' them tae mend the ither!' She then added one of these veering-wind pronouncements of hers which never failed to astonish me, although I had heard so many of them on all sorts of subjects. 'Ah aye kent since that Annie was jist a wee thing that she was a bad, wicked we bizzom!' and then: 'An' serve that Mrs Black richt for the way she went on aboot her! A fine thing! The hale o' Cairnton kennin' that yer dochter is a street wumman!'

'Oh, be quiet, Jean, and go and get the supper!' said my father.

But this month of events had not yet ended. After Aunt Betsy's funeral was over, it was discovered that she had left in the hands of the Achcraggan bank manager a most competent will which she had drawn up under his guidance several years before. She had left her house, complete with contents, to me and sums of money, greater than anyone expected, to my father, George and Tom. My father told me in private of the terms of the will and then said: 'It's funny the way things come out. I've made up my mind to go home and I've had Tom and George looking quietly about Achcraggan for a cottage, for God knows I can't take Jean to Reachfar.'

I could not bear now, any more than I ever could, the note of worry in his voice. 'I'm sorry about what happened that day, Dad. If only Granny and Tom hadn't come in at that very moment, it would have been all right.'

'It's awful the temper that's in her,' he said. 'The funny thing is, though, that she never flies up at *me*, no matter what I say or do.' He spoke the words in genuine wonderment, as one puzzled by a great mystery. 'Och, she loses her head, of course, like the night I threw Tommie in the loch. That's her nature. She seems to think there's no other place to make a living except here.'

'Will she like Achcraggan, do you think?' I asked.

'If she doesn't,' he said, 'I doubt she will have to lump it, for that's where I'm going, if you'll lend me your house, Miss Sandison! By the way, there's something else, but I don't want Jean to know about this. She is foolish and loud-mouthed about money and the less she knows about everything of that kind, the better. Mr Hill made some sort of arrangement about a pension fund for me. He was a business man and the way of it is a little above my head – it is something to do with insurance – but it appears that I will get between three and four pounds a week from his estate for the rest of my life, so the lawyers tell me.'

'Dad! And you never knew?'

'All I knew was that he once said to me that if I would look after Mrs Hill I would never regret it and I promised him I would do my best. He was a fine man. Mrs Hill was a silly little craitur and in a way it's a blessing she died when she did, although she wasn't that old, poor woman. I could not have been doing with Tommie much longer, pension or no pension. It's hard to see how such a fine man – and she was a good enough woman, though foolish – had a son like Tommie. He was a dirty little rag from when he was a boy.'

'They always spoiled him,' I said.

'That's true – and then they were old before he was born – I believe she was over forty before she had Tommie. Old parents will often spoil a bairn, the way a granny often will.'

'*My* Granny never spoiled *me*!' I laughed.

He laughed too. 'No. That's true. But Granny is a little out of the ordinary run. Mind you, she is inclined to be soft about wee Jock, though.'

When Jean was told about the house at Achcraggan being left to 'the family' by Aunt Betsy and the plan to move there, she naturally began to cry, but my father and I were accustomed now to this reaction and waited in silence for the tears to subside. Since the upheaval of my father 'having made a fool o' himsel' ' and the *débâcle* of Annie's and Tommie's disappearance, Jean's short memory had forgotten that she was 'not speaking' to me. I think, perhaps, that although I could never be anything to her but a thorn in the flesh, I was at least a steady pain in a frighteningly changeable world, leaving every day, as I did, no matter what happened, for the university and coming back by the same train every evening. When the ceremonial of the tears was over, therefore, she turned her blotched face to me and said: 'Ah niver wis in the hoose that day we went doon tae see the auld wife – hoo mony rooms is in it?'

'I haven't been in it, except for the parlour, since I was a kid,' I said. 'Wait a minute.'

I had to send my mind back to my childhood and Saturday mornings when I would be sent off from Reachfar with one of my grandmother's 'compliment' baskets for Aunt Betsy, with many adjurations not to spill the jam or chip the eggs or 'Aunt Betsy will fairly sort you!' The first time I went, I remembered, I went to the back door, for, in Achcraggan, any house that had a front door had it merely for show, like the parlour. It was never used and I doubt if a number of them could be opened at all without the assistance of a joiner. When Aunt Betsy opened her back door, she glared at me sternly and said: 'Since how long do the Reachfar Sandisons sneak round to the back doors as if they were that rascal Jock Skinner collecting rags? Go round to the proper entrance and learn to behave yourself fittingly as the representative of your Grandmother!' I had to trot fearfully round the house with my basket and present myself again at the 'proper entrance'.

'There's a little glass porch at the front,' I told Jean now.

'Then there's an inner door that opens into a longish, narrow passage. At the left end of it, there's a parlour — quite a big room with a smaller room opening off it, to the back, behind the passage, as it were. To the right, there's the living-room, and opening off *it* behind the passage, there's a kitchen and a sort of scullery, wash-house place. The back door goes out through the scullery and there are some coal-sheds and things, I think, out there. The staircase is very pretty—'

'Hoo dae ye mean?'

'Well, it's wrought-iron, the banisters, I mean—'

'Iron?' Jean squealed. 'Like a Glasgow tenement? That'll niver dae!'

'Oh, no,' I said. 'Not like that. They were made by old John-the-Smith to Aunt Betsy's design—'

'Ah'm no' fur nae iron stairs. Ah dinny care *whae* made them!'

I did not argue further. 'The staircase takes two bends, right and then left and the landing is long and narrow like the passage downstairs. There are one, two, three — yes, four rooms up there, but Aunt Betsy cut a bit off one of the bigger ones to make a bathroom.'

'A bathroom?'

'Yes.'

'Whit wis an auld body like that awa' up there in the Heilan's needin' wi' a bathroom?'

I let this pass, wishing that the question had been asked of Aunt Betsy herself. Not only did she bathe every day herself, but on more than one occasion she had been known to have seized the boy who delivered her groceries, have accused him of being 'unfit to handle food with ears like that' and have dragged him bodily upstairs to be forcibly washed all over.

'It's a nice little cottage,' I ended.

'Cottage!' said Jean and turned to my father. 'Ye wid think it wis a wee but-an'ben cottar hoosie tae hear her!'

'We always referred to it as the Cottage,' I excused myself. 'Its name is Jemima Cottage.'

Jean gave a raucous squeal of laughter. 'God sake! Whit a name!'

'I'm danged if I could mind on its right name the now,' my father said. 'But that's right. It was the old Minister that put it up for his sister and she called it Jemima in memory of her mother. Aye, Jemima was her mother's name – that's right.'

'We'll sune change that, though!' said Jean in a business-like voice.

'You could call it Seaview Villa,' I said solemnly, 'or maybe something French and swanky, like Mon Repos.'

Jean, dreaming of the new house, paid no attention to me, but my father, in a voice as solemn as my own had been, said; 'It's time you Mon Reepoh-ed yourself off to bed if you're to catch that train in the morning.'

Very shortly after this, the day-to-day face of my life changed completely. In the end, when my father and Jean left the south for Achcraggan, I did not go to lodgings near the university as had been planned originally, but went to an old couple, who were very remote relations of my family and who lived in a ship-building village on Clydeside, to the west of Glasgow. In another story I have told of Aunt Alice and Uncle Jim, as I called them, and of my 'bus journeys daily to the university.

My years with them and at the university were fairly peaceful and happy in the main, but life at the university did not work out as Hugh and I had planned it in our talks at the old quarry. At the end of my second year, Hugh took a very creditable degree in Arts and, after the graduation ceremony, he treated me to sherry and a slap-up dinner at a hotel. We had a lot to say to one another, for despite our plans we had seen little of one another during the two years. Hugh, although he had taken an Arts degree, had spent most of his time in the medical faculty or down at the Technical College, which was a quite separate institution, and I had gone my own way, mostly around the libraries of the university.

'All right,' I said to Hugh over the sherry. 'Tell me about

the great surprise,' for he had indicated to me that something wonderful had happened to him.

'You know Farness?' he asked.

'Professor Farness, you mean?'

'Who else?'

'There's another Farness in my life!' I laughed at Hugh and told him of the incident at Inverness Station long ago. 'I shall never forget him,' I ended. 'I thought he was one of the most magnificent and wonderful men I had ever seen. Isn't Professor Farness related to him?'

'Yes. A nephew. Professor Farness comes into the magnificent and wonderful category too,' Hugh said. 'He is sending me, largely at his own expense, although he has managed to get a special grant for me too, to study under Sir Humphrey Collins at his clinic in London.'

'Sir Hum — that's the big paralysis man?'

'That's right.'

'Oh, Hugh!'

As always, I derived an inordinate amount of joy from what I privately called 'a good' happening for and to Hugh. It seemed to me that it argued a basic justice and balance in life that Hugh, born at a physical disadvantage, should have given to him, out of a clear blue sky, favours that did not come to his physically normal fellows and now I called down blessings on the heads of all the Farness family.

We went on to talk of Granny Reid and our early days at the Academy and eventually I said: 'Of course, to me, now, Cairnton is so far away that sometimes I wonder if it ever existed at all. It doesn't seem real, except for a very few things and people.'

'Such as?' Hugh asked.

'Well, I remember every detail of *your* home but hardly anything about our house at Cairnshaws. I remember the detail of the class-rooms at the Academy and every inch of the hill and the old quarry, but I remember hardly anything else.'

'Happy and lucky one!' Hugh laughed at me across the table. 'To remember only the things you liked and loved and to forget all the rest.'

'I suppose that's it – except that I haven't forgotten them. It is simply that the hooligans outside Cervi's Café in the High Street and Teenie Mathieson and Annie Black don't seem *real*. By the way, did Cairnton *ever* find out what happened to Annie Black and Tommie Hill?'

'I can't speak for Cairnton,' Hugh said.

'But *you* know?' He had a repressive air but I pursued the subject.

'They did clear out together, didn't they?'

'Yes,' said Hugh.

'And where are they now?'

'They have been apart for ages. I don't know where Hill is.'

'Where is Annie then?' I asked a little snappishly, for I now could understand less than I ever could Hugh's interest in her.

'Edinburgh, at the moment,' he said.

'You – you see her?'

'Now and again.'

He was becoming more repressive and more unwilling to discuss the subject and, although I very much wanted to understand him, I was too proud and too shy and too resentful and too full of all the other things that muddle the minds and curb the tongues of eighteen-year-olds to pursue the matter any further. The only thing that I can say to my own credit is that I did not give way to sheer spite and tell Hugh what I knew of Annie's character – which was more detailed and circumstantial than any knowledge that had ever come to Cairnton knowledge – together with my own views on it, but this is no great credit at that, for I refrained from giving rein to my spite merely because my grandmother had told me long ago that spite never 'paid'. So, instead of saying any more about Annie, I said instead: 'Fancy you going off to *London*! *I'm* going to London, one day!'

'To do what?' Hugh asked.

'Oh, I don't know. I'd just like to go to London.'

Being only eighteen, I did not know then what I know now, which is that I am not a do-er, I am a be-er. I did not know, then, that some people are born primarily to 'do' and to 'make', while others, like me, are born simply to 'be' and 'become', or that, for the weal of the world, the Hughs are by far the more valuable people.

'Anyway,' I continued, 'when you get to London, you must write to me. *Promise* you will write to me, Hugh!'

'I promise, but only if you will write back. I *know* you, Janet. You are rich and careless.'

'Hugh Reid! Rich! Me? If I hadn't won the C. and C., the way things are with Jean grudging every penny that is spent on me and everything, I wouldn't even be at the university, probably!'

'Oh, that! I don't mean that. You are rich in human interest and if, tomorrow, you run across someone who engages your attention, you wouldn't bother to answer my letters. Three is the limit. If you don't answer after the third one, I won't write any more. What's the address?'

'Better write to Reachfar,' I said. 'That will always find me. I might have to leave Aunt Alice's and they might forget to forward the third letter!'

CHAPTER ELEVEN

My father and Jean were now, of course, settled at Jemima Cottage, but I still regarded Reachfar as my home and spent all my vacations there. My father, too, regarded Reachfar as the centre and Jemima Cottage as an outpost. He spent every day except Sundays at Reachfar, walking up in the morning to arrive about seven in summer and a little later in winter and walking back in the evenings in time to have supper at the Cottage. On the face of things, there was no rift in the Sandison family. The local people knew that my father was the eldest son who would inherit Reachfar and whose duty it was, by tradition, to help his parents in their old age. They also accepted the fact that his wife, naturally, being a stranger from the south, would like a home of her own that was less remote than Reachfar, especially when the family happened to own a suitable house, as Jemima Cottage was. My grandmother and my grandfather did not go out a great deal now, but they called at the cottage occasionally and my aunt, George and Tom and my brother – and even I – would go there for short visits if we happened to be in Achcraggan.

Among George, Tom and myself, in private, Jean was something of a family joke, as had been, a few years earlier, a cockerel that refused to grow. At the time of this unfortunate bird's short existence, the Irish Mayor of Cork had indulged in a prolonged hunger strike as a political protest, and George christened our pining cockerel 'The Mayor of Cork'. The joke was not entirely unkindly, for the name denoted a certain sympathy with the cockerel – and with the Irish mayor – and was, also, a family comment on life and the times. In our minds, there was some similarity between Jean and the cockerel. She was someone that had been wished upon us; someone whose well-being we could not improve; someone whom we tried to accept as she was, and to laugh at her a little, in private, made the acceptance more easy.

I think that Jean, in Jemima Cottage, was very happy according to her lights. When she first arrived there, she had plans for ripping out the wrought-iron staircase and for getting rid of some fine Regency chairs, a walnut sofa-table and a few other pieces that she described as 'as auld-farrant as the hills', but Lady Lydia Daviot did me and my family an unconscious – or perhaps a conscious – service by calling at the cottage within a few days of Jean's arrival and saying, in the course of conversation: 'Why, there are the Regency chairs from Sir Gordon's study at the Castle! He always said Miss Betsy was to have them, but he was so careless that I never expected he'd remember to put it in his will. And that staircase, *how* I have envied it! It is a *far* more graceful design than the one at Poyntdale.' Lady Lydia also straightened out the renaming of the cottage question with the words: 'I *quite* see your point, Mrs Sandison. Jemima Cottage *has* got an old-fashioned sound, but you know what country people like the people of Achcraggan are. If you renamed it and friends from the south came to visit you, the Achcraggan people would say: "Cairnton Villa? Och, yes, that's Chemima Cottage!" which would sound so *silly*!' Lady Lydia gave her light, musical laugh. 'Country people are so *slow* in these ways.'

I do not know – nor, I swear, does anyone else – how much co-operation and collusion there was between my grandmother and Lady Lydia in these matters, for these two had a close, dignified friendship, the ways of which were obscure to all except themselves. To Jean, in particular, were its ways obscure. Before Jean had met Lady Lydia, but had heard us all speak of her, her attitude had been: 'Duke's dochter or no', she's nae better nor onybody else!', but when Lady Lydia called at Jemima Cottage Jean invariably entertained her in the parlour, out of which Aunt Betsy's old furniture had been taken for storage at Reachfar, while Jean had made the room 'mair like the thing', with a three-piece suite upholstered in brown plush brightened up with many cushions in pink 'art' silk with tassels at their corners. Jean was appalled to discover that my grandmother invariably entertained Lady Lydia in the Reachfar kitchen, and commented that 'that wisnae the thing at a'. ' To begin with, Jean thought that she had been singled out for Lady Lydia's attention because she, Jean, was, in her own words, the 'mistress o' the best hoose in Achcraggan', but she was sadly disillusioned one day when Lady Lydia called on her on her way home from a visit to Bella Beagle, the old fish-wife who lived in a two-roomed cottage in the fisher town. In course of time, Jean acknowledged herself defeated by the social rules that governed Lady Lydia but, in spite of this, she was always pleased and flattered to welcome that lady to Jemima Cottage.

As I have said earlier, Jean was a highly accomplished housekeeper in the Cairnton tradition and Jemima Cottage became the pride of her soul. She was content for my father to be at Reachfar all day to be 'oot o' her road' as she put it, while she 'thurry-ed oot' the parlour or a bedroom or had a washing of curtains or a scouring of the kitchen and scullery. From top to bottom, Jemima Cottage gleamed with paint and polish, and from early morning until supper-time Jean hardly sat down from her labours of propitiating her household gods. George began to refer to the house as 'Castle Chemima', my aunt said that she felt at ease only in its scullery and hardly so even there and Tom would add: 'An' me too, forbye and besides. The last time I went intil the roomie, I was fair feared to sit down. I felt I should put my feet over my shoulder to be saving the carpet.' For myself, I found the atmosphere of the cottage oppressive. Even in Aunt Betsy's day, I had thought it over-full of furniture and now that Jean was adding another cushion here, another vase there and yet another layer of curtains on the windows, reminding me of Mrs Black's parlour at Nethercairn, I could not be in it for long without being overcome with near-claustrophobia, for I have always liked breathing space.

Jean, however, seemed to be heavenly happy and everyone was content. As the years passed, I came to understand that, according to her lights, Jean had the best of several worlds. I think that in Jemima Cottage she found the achievement of a life-long ideal, for it is impossible to overestimate or overstress what such a home of her own meant to her. And, along with the home, she had achieved a small but respected standing in the district, for my family was a long-established one which had always been known for its good-neighbour-liness and fair-dealing and, as the wife of my father, she shared in this respect. In addition to her position at Achcraggan, she had maintained some of her contact with Cairnton where the status that she had attained on marriage now increased, the more her Cairnton friends came to know of her establishment at Achcraggan. And Jean was at pains that they should know of it. In the first years there, she had friends to stay at the cottage the summer long, although parties seldom remained for more than a week, for Jean's relations with most of her women friends were of the veering-wind type that had prevailed in the past between her and Mrs Black, so that they could not be under the same roof for more than a few days without coming to a quarrel. Then, at least once a year, usually in the Spring, my father would take up residence at Reachfar, the cottage would be closed and Jean would set off on a round of visits in Cairnton and district. She saved the money for these jaunts from her housekeeping allowance, for, since her marriage, she had begun to practise domestic economy to a degree that verged on meanness. As Tom said, every penny was a prisoner with her and every spending that did not benefit herself or the house was eschewed.

She was under the impression that my father earned his total income out of Reachfar and was therefore content that he should 'stay at his work' and not accompany her on her holidays. Although she was very astute in many ways, she was extremely gullible in others. It always amazed me that she could believe that our few acres of marginal land could provide for us all, but believe it she did, for my father never saw fit to tell her of his pension from Mr Hill or of his legacy from Aunt Betsy and, indeed, never gave her any financial information of any kind that he could possibly withhold. Jean was 'loud-mouthed' about money and possessions, a trait which my family deprecated and, with her grandeur at 'Castle Chemima', she was embarrassment enough without further encouragement.

The years rolled on. I took my degree and left the university, my life broadened to new horizons and the people I knew changed and developed as people do and my relationships with them changed and altered and adjusted themselves, but one thing in my life remained completely static – my relationship with Jean. It did not change, develop, ebb, flow or do any of the other things which are characteristic of life and its relationships. Jean and I remained at a deadlock of basic non-sympathy and non-understanding of one another, which tended to flare into a pointless, unresolvable scene if we were together for any length of time.

But we were seeing less and less of one another. Shortly after I took my degree, I went away to the southern counties of England to earn my living, then came, as most Scots ultimately do, to London, and during the years from 1931 to 1939 I came home to Reachfar only once or twice a year and then, in the main, for comparatively short periods. I would pay a courtesy visit to Jemima Cottage; admire all the latest acquisitions in the way of curtains, vases and wallpapers; listen to Jean's malicious gossip about her neighbours and the populace of Achcraggan in general; listen to her tales, also malicious and gossiping, of her latest visit to Cairnton, and then climb back up the hill to Reachfar to release my pent-up irritation and dislike of Jean and all she had said and all the things about her in a riot of mimicry and laughter with George, Tom and my aunt.

What lay between Jean and me now was no longer a relationship of any kind. Even the hatred of her that I had once felt had died. If a relationship between two people can be likened to the meeting and mingling of two tributaries of personality to form a river of common feeling, it has to be imagined, with Jean and myself, that, at the point of confluence, the fluid of our personalities changed into solidified lava. When we met, there was no mingling, nor was there, any more, a clash of opposition. It was as if two barren rocks were, for a moment, moved mysteriously into juxtaposition on some arid, desert plain, by some antic, inexplicable, unnatural force, such as a lunatic giant moving boulders of lava about, without purpose, on the cold, dead landscape of the moon. Jean, for me, was coming to have no reality as a person, even when I was in her presence, and this frightened me when I thought of her, so I avoided the thought of her as well as her presence as much as I possibly could.

In 1939, when war broke out, I joined the Women's Auxiliary Air Force and from 1940 until 1945 my service was spent in the South of England. My leaves were short and infrequent, and sometimes in the course of them I did not visit Jemima Cottage at all, for Jean against a background of war was even more improbable and unreal than she had been against the background of peace. She would contribute to no war charity; she would work for no war organization and, indeed, I question if she allowed herself to believe that the war existed at all. The fact that soap was rationed and in short supply incited her to fury and even my father, with his deep love for peace in the family and a smooth family face turned to the world, smiled a rueful agreement when, in the course of one of my seven-day leaves, Tom said: 'It is myself that would be sorry to see you putting off your short whilie at home listening to that one down there girning about the soap.'

'Soap?' I asked.

'Soap rationing,' my aunt explained. 'The soap ration for the whole of Achcraggan isn't enough to clean Castle Jemima.'

'It's not chust ordinary soap,' said Tom. 'It's carpet soap she is wild about now, for it seems that they are stopped making it.'

'Carpet soap?' inquired George the clown. 'Och, tell her

181

chust to send the carpet over to this mannie Hitler – he'll eat it for her, dirt an' a-all!'

But in 1945 the war came to an end and, as if some gigantic revolving stage had turned again, as it had turned before in September 1939, we all found ourselves at new points in space and time, in a different light, among a new ebb and flow of relationships and, in this new world, Jean at Jemima Cottage was, for me, less of a reality than ever. She might as well, by this time, not have existed at all.

Down the years, however, I had continued to keep in touch with Hugh Reid, although, for a long period, our contact was no more than short letters exchanged at Christmas, but in the summer of 1945, a short time before I was demobilized, I met Hugh in the flesh after a gap of some fifteen years. In that time, he had gone from strength to strength in his chosen work and, for his services to the maimed of the war, he had been knighted, so that I was honoured to meet my friend Sir Hugh Reid for dinner in London one evening. And a most distinguished-looking escort he made, too.

I recognized him immediately in the foyer of the restaurant, but I could only stand and stare at the clever, thin, strangely dedicated face with the hair greying at the temples.

'Oh, *Hugh*!' I said at last.

'Janet! You are the most satisfactory person! You *look* just the same and you say just the same right old thing!'

'It isn't right any more. I should say Oh, *Sir* Hugh!'

'Come on!' said Hugh, took me by the arm and led me to our table.

I came on across the fashionable restaurant, remembering the while the long tiled corridors of Cairnton Academy where I had first 'come on' alongside Hugh.

We had plenty to talk about but, in the end, our minds inevitably went back to Cairnton. For me, the little grey town at the end of the valley was less real than it had ever been, but Hugh had only recently broken his contact with it at the death of his grandmother less than a year before.

'I had bought that house in the High Street, where the

182

Murrays used to live, for Granny,' he said, 'but I sold it after she died.'

'So you have no ties there at all now, Hugh?'

'No. I have none anywhere.' He gave his quiet, sweet smile. 'No ties with places, I mean, only with people. I don't care where I eat or sleep as long as it's within reach of my patients of the moment.'

'And you have never thought of marrying?'

'No.' He smiled again. 'I'm not surprised at myself for not marrying, but I am amazed that *you* haven't married. Why, Janet?'

'Oh, I took some early advice of yours about learning to play the fool and, as you said I would, I got quite good at it, so I grew up into something of a flibberty-gibbet, I think. I've got to the brink of marriage several times and then I've always thought the better of it and drawn back. It's such a risky sort of business.' I grinned at him. 'I've had the example of Jean constantly before me, not to mention the odd effects of marriage that I have observed in several other women. I'd hate to turn into a Jean.'

'How is she, the old devil?'

'Oh, very much the *grande dame* of Achcraggan and worse in temper and tongue than ever. She and my father sleep in the same house, even in the same bed, but that is all. He spends all his waking time at Reachfar; she spends all hers polishing the furniture and washing the curtains. It is a hideous relationship, I think. I get filled up to the ears with a sort of barren, stifled mockery every time I go near the cottage. I don't go very often, though. Jean loves me no better than she ever did. But when I do go, I always come away with my weather-eye cocked at marriage in general.'

'A pity,' Hugh said. 'I wouldn't like to see you turn into an old maid.'

'It depends on what you mean by "old maid". In my opinion, that is precisely what Jean is in spite of having had the marriage service spoken over her. She isn't even an honest tart. Talking of tarts, I wonder what happened to Annie Black?' I have a friend called Freddy and My Friend

Freddy always says that the amazing thing about people is that you never know which way their cat is going to jump, and there are times when I utterly agree with him. This was one of them.

'Annie is still a tart,' said Hugh calmly, offering me a cigarette.

By this time I was thirty-five years old and had attained some small measure of self-control, so I told myself that if Hugh Reid could be that calm about his early love, there was no need for *me* to get into a tizzy of excitement. Still, I was slightly rattled. 'You – you always *knew* about Annie?' I asked.

'Oh, lord, yes. Only a fool like Mrs Black could have believed in that fictitious secretarial job of Annie's from the very beginning.'

I had a feeling of having been cheated, having been made a fool of and generally victimized. 'But I thought you were in love with her!' I protested.

'No. I loved her,' he said quietly. 'I still do.'

'Great God, Hugh! Why?'

'I don't know why. But she is my sister.'

'Sister?'

'Half-sister, then. We had a common father in Willie Black.'

'You knew that – away back in the Cairnton days?'

'Granny told me when I was fifteen – around the time of all that row about the bursary, when Cairnton managed to come between you and me, Janet.'

'Cairnton being what it was and Jean being what she is and always was, it is odd that I never learned that Mr Black of the Nether was your father.'

'Secrets can be kept, even from Cairnton.' Hugh gave his quiet smile. 'I think only my mother and Granny knew and after my mother died that left only Granny. I feel sorry for Willie Black – I never refer to him as my father. Granny always called him Willie Black. He is one of these people who seem to be born to be the victims of defeat.'

'Tell me what you mean, Hugh.'

'There isn't much to tell. It's simply that Willie Black seems to have been caught in a vicious circle of self-defeat. He came to Cairnton from Midlothian to work as a ploughman at Biggs o' Cairn where my mother was a dairymaid, and Granny told me that they began walking out together and that she was pleased, for Willie seemed to be a nice young fellow. Then, old Galbraith of Nethercairn died and his daughter Maggie was his sole heiress. She became the Mrs Black you knew and the mother of Annie. Even as a young girl, Granny used to tell me, she had the tongue of a viper and the temper of a termagant, but Nethercairn was a good farm and a number of young men began to take an interest in Maggie. Maggie had never liked my mother – my mother was a pretty girl – maybe you remember her photograph? So Maggie set her cap at Willie. I think myself that in the first instance she probably only wanted to cause a rupture between him and my mother, but Willie saw the value of the Nether and Willie made sure of things. Annie and I are practically twins.' Hugh's smile was as gentle and free of bitterness as ever. 'But Annie was legitimized – I wasn't. It killed my mother, but Maggie lived on. She is still alive and so is Willie, in the sense that he still breathes and moves. Willie has paid for Nethercairn in blood, sweat and tears, to quote Mr Churchill. Maggie has bullied him ever since they married, he has never been anything other than a ploughman in her eyes and, of course, she blames his "bad blood" for everything that Annie has done. Nethercairn is a madhouse inhabited by two people who are only technically sane now and hardly that.'

'Hugh! What an appalling story! You go to see them?'

'I did, periodically, to let them know about Annie. Not that it did any good. They regard her as being dead.'

'Then why did you bother?'

He stared away across the crowded restaurant. 'Because I kept hoping that if I could bring her to life for them they would be happier.'

'But would Annie go back to Cairnton even if they would have her?'

'Oh, lord, no!'

'And where is she now?'

'In Paris at the moment. She got herself over there shortly after the liberation.'

'How have you contrived to keep tabs on her all down the years?'

'Oh, there are all sorts of ways and means. It hasn't been difficult. And she turns up of her own accord when times are hard for her, of course.'

'I'm sorry, Hugh. I don't understand any of this one bit,' I said. 'I think it's all simply horrifying and all so – so foreign to your own nature and everything that you are that it doesn't make sense and I don't see how you can be so calm about it.'

He smiled again, that gentle, compassionate smile. 'Apart from our father, Janet,' he said, 'Annie and I have a lot in common. We were both born at a disadvantage, I physically and Annie mentally. To me, there is nothing horrifying in Annie – she needs helping, that's all. Just as your father helped *me* by agreeing not to let you sit for that bursary in 1923.'

'Hugh! There is no comparison or resemblance at all! Besides, bursary or not, you would still have achieved your end.'

'I don't think so,' he said. 'The severely handicapped need a flying start and a lot of help. Cairnton being what it was and I being young, it took me a long time – *too* long – to work out in my own mind what you and your father did for me. It was not only the giving of the chance to win the Jarvie-Kerr – the important thing was the knowledge that the strong could sometimes stand back, which developed into the knowledge that real strength lies in just that *ability* to stand back for a moral reason. Your father, by sheer moral strength – which he would call mere decency – did a great thing for wee Hughie Reid, Janet.'

I wanted to cry and took refuge in the attitude normal to women in uniform in 1945. 'Oh, balloons!' I said. 'If ever you go up north, go to Reachfar and see Dad. He is as lively

186

as ever in spite of Jean. Talking of people who gave you opportunities, what happened to Professor Farness?'

'Still teaching, still helping lame ducks,' Hugh replied.

My mind went back to the morning at Inverness Station when old Lord Farness had given me the book, and then travelled in a flash, as the mind can do, over that journey to Cairnton and all that came after.

'What an extraordinary place Cairnton was!' I said. 'A *killer* of a place!'

'You always hated it,' Hugh said thoughtfully, 'and yet it wasn't particularly cruel to you. It couldn't touch you, really – not as it could touch and hurt people like me, who were born in it, at a disadvantage. And there are thousands of places just like it, you know.'

'Not just like Cairnton!' I argued. 'I have never seen another place that was so deadly destructive. It was a sordid little hole that tried to taint everyone and everything that came into it and grit up their hearts and brains with its own grey dust. The Toon! And its smug, complacent pride in itself! With respectability a lurking, grim spite behind lace curtains, peering out to look for other people's sins to be indignant about; with sex something filthy that was most at home in the stinking outhouses at the bottoms of the gardens; where the decent friendship – like the one between Mr Lindsay and Miss Hadley – was construed into a leering lewdness; where–'

'I had no idea you felt so strongly about the Toon, Janet!'

I stopped in mid-tirade. 'Neither had I, till now,' I admitted. 'It has just come to me, after all these years, as a hatred I have always had but can now find words for. I'll tell you something, Hugh. I've just newly discovered this too. You asked me why I have never married. I got engaged to a bloke, once, back before the war – Alan Stewart his name was – and suddenly, one night, I threw him over, told him it simply would not do, left him and walked home. Before I went to my flat, I went down to the river and tried to think out why I had done it. Silly, wasn't it? There are millions of reasons for doing a thing and they are all mixed up. But now I've found another of my reasons for jilting Alan Stewart. He was a Lowlander and he reminded me of Cairnton. He had Cairnton's holy respect for the so-called well-to-do and he had Cairnton's sexual leer that made me think of dirty little outside lavatories.'

'Poor fellow!' smiled Hugh, with his indulgent air of being a great deal older and wiser than I was.

'You can laugh,' I said, 'but it's true. Cairnton has left a permanent mark on my character!'

'What an indignity!' teased Hugh. 'That *you* should be influenced by the Toon!'

'And Jean, of course. Now, Jean is Cairnton personified. They both give me an Irish feeling of whatever their government is, I'm agin it.'

'Their government is always the favourable wind, that's all,' Hugh said.

'That's right, and scuttle the small craft that can't get their sails filled, just for sheer fun and spite. Remember our dog-fight in the High Street?'

'One of my most treasured memories – that, and the time you felled that girl in our shop with the string of onions because she was rude to Granny.'

'I was always meticulous about manners. One of the worst things about Cairnton was its basic bad manners and bad taste. Awful hole. What are you going to do now the war's over, Hugh?'

'For me and people like me, this war won't be over for the rest of our lives,' he told me. 'I'm going over to the Continent for a bit fairly soon to see what can be done about the crippled and homeless children.'

'Hugh, it must be a heartbreaking job!'

'No. No, it has tremendous satisfactions too. What about you? Going home to Reachfar?'

'For a bit, anyway. Later, I don't know. Something will turn up – it always does.'

Something did. At thirty-five, I was a light-hearted, careless woman with a large number of very good friends scattered here and there about the world and, as I have told in another story I wrote, through one of these friends I found my postwar job in an engineering works in Scotland and, through the job, I found the man I decided to marry.

Away back at the beginning of this chronicle, I told you in connection with the Cairn and Cairnton that I have always been very interested in words and place-names and the like and I am also interested in phrases. I have a friend who, when she tries to tell one what she thinks on any subject, always prefaces her remark with: 'I am a person like this – I think . . .'

Well, at thirty-five, thirty-six, thirty-seven, which was my age when I took this decision about marrying this man, I was a person like this: when I decided to marry, I decided to marry. So, the man seeming a bit shy about the thing, I told him first of my decision and he seemed quite agreeable – I have told all this in detail in that other book – then I told my family and then, one way and another, by telling one woman friend called Mrs Slater of my decision, I found that I had inadvertently told the whole town of Ballydendran, which was the name of this place in Scotland where this man and I were working for this engineering firm.

What I have *not* told in any other book so far, for the very good reason that it has not been relevant to the story, is that this is the point at which the contrariness of life caught up with me, for as soon as he could catch up with me and keep me quiet for long enough to listen to him, this man, whose name is Alexander Alexander and we call him 'Twice' for short, told me, as nicely as he could, that he could not marry me just yet because he had a wife already.

I have told this here in this silly, lightsome, quipsome way because that is the easiest way for me to tell it, but I will admit that on the evening when he told me of this legal impediment to my plans, while we were sitting in his car on top of a hill in south Scotland, there was not a light quip in the whole lovely landscape of a world that was pitching and heaving before my eyes like a storm-swollen ocean.

'But, Twice,' I said, 'it's two whole years since I've known you and you never even said—'

'Dinah is not one of my favourite conversational subjects,' he told me grimly.

'But—'

I stopped speaking because I found that I had nothing that it would be fair or just for me to say. I had been in love with him for two years, yes – but he had never given me the slightest reason for being in love with him. Forty-eight hours ago, I had decided that he was in love with *me*, and I had been right, but where I had gone wrong was in taking over from there. *I* was the one who had gone shouting to my family and to Mrs Slater about getting married. But I have told all this in that other book.

'Where – where is she?' I asked at last.

'Belfast.'

'You – see her?'

'I saw her a year ago for the first time in fifteen years.'

'Only a year ago?' I was terribly hurt at this for some silly and queer reason. 'But you said—'

'I flew over there at a weekend to ask her again for a divorce.'

'And she won't?'

'She is a Roman Catholic. And apart from that, she prefers the status of married woman to that of divorcée.'

'She – she loves you?'

'No.'

'You are sure?'

'Certain, Flash. In fact, I think she hates the very sight of me.'

'Could you – tell me about it?'

'There isn't much to tell and it is all shameful.'

'I must know what there is,' I told him.

'It was my first job after I qualified – I was only twenty-two – and my firm suddenly decided to send me to Belfast to take charge of the erection of a factory. It was a big job and a big salary for a youngster – I suppose I got swelled head and then lost my head altogether. Before I knew where I was, I was stepping out with the factory-owner's daughter and being quite the bright boy about town. One thing led to another and, at the end of six months, we were married. I was madly in love – you know by now the kind of bloke I am when moved by emotion of any kind. At the end of three days, Dinah went home to mother. Three days! That's how long it can take from being madly in love, as I was, to being frozen to the point of death.'

'And Dinah?'

'A born nun, but she prefers smart clothes to a habit and coif, and dance music to Hail Marys. It's quite simple, if a little ludicrously sad. There is a child of the marriage. I only saw him once. He didn't know who I was. He means nothing. You hear a lot about blood ties and how blood tells. Blood by itself is not enough – it makes no tie and it does not tell. The child had been biased against a father who went away; an idea had been planted and nurtured – *it* told. That's what tells, the idea, not the blood. Flash, I am not going to try to apologize to you. That would be insulting and ridiculous. You know how this thing overtook us, down at the Works, there. I did my best to—'

'None of it is your fault, Twice,' I said. 'And Dinah being there doesn't alter anything. I still love you – I think I always will. What can we do?'

'Do?' Twice stared away across the countryside. 'It's simple enough. We'll carry on for a week or two with this engagement –' he laughed in a peculiar way – 'that you've announced so blithely. Then you'll throw me over and I'll clear out and that will be that. Nobody will be any the wiser.'

'We will do damn-all of the sort,' I heard myself say.

'What then? For God's sake, Flash, don't let's have a long-drawn-out thing about this. I can't stand it!'

'Can you stand *me* all long-drawn-out for the rest of your life?' I asked.

'I tell you she won't even *consider* divorce. She is fanatical about it. You simply don't understand people like Dinah—'

'To hell with Dinah! Listen, if nobody will be any the wiser about a broken engagement, nobody will be any the wiser about a non-existent wedding if we work it properly.'

'What in God's name do you mean?'

'We'll tell Ballydendran that we are being married quietly up at Achcraggan and tell Achcraggan we were married quietly at Ballydendran – except for my family, that is. I have to tell them the truth. Thank God *you've* got no family!'

'You're mad!' said Twice.

'Who's mad?' I snapped. In those days, Twice and I could lose our tempers and rage at one another in a fish-market fashion that I now find almost incredible. 'Of course, if you don't want me, *say* so! There's absolutely no compulsion to—'

'Shut up!' said Twice, seizing me by the shoulders and shaking me till my teeth rattled. 'Think of the risk, you idiot! There is always somebody bound to—'

'Do *what*?' I bawled. 'And let go of me! Are they going to ask to see my marriage certificate before they ask me to tea?'

Twice let go of my shoulders and expelled a long, hard breath. 'I never know whether you are more full of generosity or moral courage,' he said. 'You mean, you would readily take that sort of risk?'

'There's no risk in it. Marriage is a private thing between you and me. If people find out that it isn't legal, they find out, that's all. If it's all that important to them, they needn't know us. If I get *you*, I can manage without the rest.'

'By God, you're right! Oh, Flash – I really *do* love you so – But what about your family?'

'Think nothing of it,' I said airily. 'I'll fix *them*.' I took thought for a moment. 'The family will be all right – except for Jean, but she needn't know any more than any other outsider.'

Twice, at this time, although he had been to Reachfar, had not met Jean, for, at the time of our visit, she had been on one of her periodic trips to Cairnton. In any case, had she been in residence at the cottage, it is doubtful if he would have met her, for, at the end of 1945, there had been a major quarrel between her and my aunt, and relations had been completely broken off between Reachfar and the cottage – or, rather, between Reachfar and Jean, for my father and my brother were as solidly welded to the rest of the family as ever and went to and fro between the two houses as if nothing had happened. As usual, this quarrel was rooted in me, although in no way did I instigate it. The events that led to it were beyond my ken and control.

During the war, I had discovered among the bomb debris My Friend Monica, a beautiful and wealthy young woman who was, and is, a law unto herself. In the autumn of 1945, she went on a visit to Skye and, on her way south to her home in England, she called at Reachfar and spent a weekend with my people. I was not there, having gone to Ballydendran after a short visit home when I came out of the Air Force. The weekend, apparently, was a tremendous success from all points of view and my father wrote, in terms almost ecstatic for him, to tell me how charmed he, George, Tom and my aunt had been with Monica, 'who was as nice a lassie as he had ever met for all she was Lady Monica and everything'. Indeed, they all had a fine time at Reachfar, so fine a time that they forgot, or deliberately omitted, to do one thing – they did not arrange for Jean to make the acquaintance of Lady Monica.

'Apparently the balloon went up absolutely vertical,' I told Twice now. 'Jean was convinced that I had instructed them to keep her in the background because I did not think she was good enough to meet My Friend Monica. I don't expect you to believe me when I tell you things like this about Jean, because they are barely credible, but I tell you a little about her in the hope that some of it will sink in and break the shock when you encounter her in the flesh for the first time.'

'But,' said Twice, 'I *do* believe you. The whole thing is just like Old Home Week to me. Didn't I tell you once that my father remarried after my mother died? A woman so ill-natured that I always wondered why he never murdered her?'

'Why, so you did,' I agreed.

From that time forward, Jean became one more bond, one more awareness that formed common ground between Twice and me, which was a blank contradiction of all her inmost desires, for of all the 'successes' that Jean had ever grudged to me, she grudged me most the 'success' of achieving marriage – or what she believed was marriage, and what

193

I also believe is marriage, although Jean's views and mine on this subject were, at bottom, as widely diverse as were our views on any other subject under the sun.

And, whenever I think of Jean in relation to Twice and myself, I find myself face to face with the paradox that seems to be at the root of life and to be its main driving force. I think that, but for Jean, I would never have had the courage to 'go away' with Twice, as such liaisons as ours are described. I had been brought up fairly strictly, I think, within a framework of rigid convention, which regarded the legal certificate as the most important fact or in any marriage. This is no exaggeration. By the year 1900, to which year the social-moral ideals of my family were truer than to any other, all ideas of mating, companionship and even happiness or well-being, mental or physical, had become submerged under and dominated by the legal factor. I suppose it was the extreme of the swing of the pendulum which had begun in the early days of Queen Victoria, but whatever the social or historical explanation, the ruling fact was that the young woman who was brought up as I was, thought first of her marriage certificate, sweetly sugar-coated, sure enough, with white satin, tulle and orange-blossom and washed down almost unnoticed in a flood of organ-music and champagne, but, none the less, the hard pill of the legal contract was there with its satisfactory after-taste of: '*Now* let him try any nonsense!' I had seen, at close quarters, Jean react to the legal pill; I had seen her, armoured with a marriage certificate, come to the certainty that she could behave as badly as she pleased, and it was this that made me say to Twice now: 'You know, in a way I am actually *glad* that we can't be married. This marriage thing is an attempt to make everything sure and certain. Life was never designed to be sure and certain and when people think they have made it so, it is bad for them. It makes them vegetate and eventually degenerate, like people in jobs they don't like who are sweating it out because of the pension at sixty. They don't do the job well because they are not interested; because they are not interested, they're not happy and when they get to sixty and get the pension, they usually die at sixty-one or so because they are no longer *able* to be either interested or happy. Besides, if we're not married, I'll know that you are staying with me just because you want to. As the Americans say: 'Ya don' hafta!'

'On the contrary,' said Twice, 'I do hafta for the right reason, which is that I wanta and I'll go on wanting ta for as long as *you* wanta, which I hope will be for ever.'

We talked on the hillside that night until long after darkness had fallen of the children we might have; of the passports we would need if we travelled abroad; of the filling of Income Tax returns and of all the other practicalities that society builds like a thorny hedge round a man and a woman who want to live together, but the talking merely made our decision all the firmer.

'On the surface of my mind,' I remember saying, 'this that I am doing is a very queer and unlikely thing, but deep down in my mind, which is the part that matters, it has a terrific certainty of rightness. I have always regarded unlegalized liaisons as rather squalid, but nothing between you and me could be as squalid as the thing between my father and Jean, for instance. It's an arid, desert sort of squalor they have, with no bond except that she looks after the house in return for so much money that she saves some of to go to Cairnton with to impress her former neighbours with her grandeur. She doesn't even know what his income is and she doesn't know where it comes from and she doesn't care. They never talk together or make any plans for anything – I don't think they ever even *think* about one another. All the things about them that I say sound silly and trivial, but taken all together they add up to – well, just plain squalor!'

'After all, there *is* nothing more squalid than a corpse,' Twice said, 'and a corpse is a body from which the spirit has departed. I suppose the corpse of a marriage is very similar to any other squalid, rather smelly corpse.'

'That's it – that's it exactly!' I agreed.

'I have often thought of my marriage to Dinah as a corpse – like the corpse of a chicken hung round the neck of a chicken-worrying dog to teach him a lesson.'

'It was a corpse that it took me two years to get past,' I said, 'a serious loss of time. And you'd better stop thinking about Dinah for good and all, for I'm not setting up house-keeping with an odour of corpse permanently in the air. You are sure you want to risk this, Twice?'

'To quote yourself, my pet, there is no risk in it. Nothing in my life ever felt so right.'

The following weekend, Twice and I begged off work and, starting early in the morning by car, we arrived at Reachfar about four in the afternoon. My uncle, by this time in his life, had retired from work at Dinchory, but this did not mean that he was in any sense old or outworn. He was in his late sixties and My Friend Tom was now in his mid-seventies, but they were both as young of heart and mind as ever and were at the granary gable to meet us as we drove up the steep, rough approach to the house.

'It is myself,' said Tom, shaking hands with Twice, 'that is sorry that I was not here the last time you came north, and me away there in Inverness for my holidays and wearying for home all the time.' As Twice stepped out of the car, Tom surveyed him from head to toe. 'Not what I would be calling a ta-all man – aboot five foot eleven, maybe,' he said thought-fully, 'aye, but a fine pair o' shoulders. Maybe you'll manage to keep her in order. And did ye drive all the way from doon yonder in the car?'

'Doon yonder' I remembered, I had been very confident of my ability to 'fix' my family, but now, as Tom spoke his mind aloud, I felt very shaky and much less sure of myself.

'Where's Dad?' I asked a little breathlessly.

'He went round the sheep on the east moor,' said George. 'He should soon be back. My, it's fine to see you both. Come on into the house. Or will you walk out to meet your father, Janet?'

'How long can you stop?' my aunt asked.

'Only till tomorrow,' Twice told her.

It made my talking-to-convince time seem very short. 'You

go along in,' I said to Twice, 'I'll walk out the east roadie and meet Dad.'

I found my father about a quarter of a mile from the house, stopped him, sat down on a boulder beside him and lost no time in telling my story. He heard me through in silence, while he stared away to the north, over the firth, towards the Ben.

'A bad business,' he said when I had finished. 'What are you going to do, Janet?'

'I'm not going to lose Twice, anyway,' I said, and told him of our plan. 'You see, Dad,' I ended, 'there is one thing I have learned and know with every certainty and that is that a legal or religious contract does not make a marriage. Twice left Dinah in spite of the contract. Oh, she can claim money from him, but I am not going into this for my financial upkeep. I don't want or need that kind of contract. The kind of contract that I want and need I have already got with Twice. I have got absolute faith that, in the words of the marriage service, he will love and cherish me for all the days of my life. That's all I want and need.'

My father turned his head and looked into my face. 'You know,' he said, 'I believe you are right, Janet. Twice is a good man.' He rose. 'And you are right about what marriage should be. You are both old enough to know what you are doing and it is nobody's business but your own. Come on back to the house. Is the tea ready?' He stopped for a moment on the narrow track through the heather. 'What about George, Tom and Kate?'

'I'll tell them, Dad. We don't want to deceive anyone who matters, but we'll tell nobody else. Besides –' I laughed – 'George knows already that there is something strange in the wind – he knew it the minute we got out of the car. You know what he is. If all the world were as perceptive as my uncle George, you couldn't work a thing like this.'

My father laughed too. 'No. That's true enough.' He jerked his head in the direction of Achcraggan.

'We'll have to watch Jean. If *she* got hold of something like this—'

'We've thought of that too,' I said. 'The thing to do with

197

Jean is give her a talking-point. Just you give her the idea that I am being married in a Register Office and not all dressed up in a church and she'll be so scornful and indignant she won't even think of asking when and which Register Office.'

'Aye. Maybe you're right.'

'Be a little angry yourself when you get my letter saying that Twice and I took an hour off from work and got married. She'll be as mad as a shad and have herself a grand time calling me for everything. And she has never seen Twice anyway—'

'She's wild about that already,' said my father.

'All the better.'

'It's a funny thing,' he said in his old, wondering way, 'that whatever *you* do, you can't please Jean. Now, with myself, there's never an ill word out of her and she likes Jock and is very good to him. But when you first brought Twice here a short time ago, even although she was away south at the time, she said you needn't come to the cottage with your fancy friends because she was sure she wouldn't be good enough for them. I'm just fair beat to understand her sometimes. And of course she was fit to be tied when that Leddy Monica friend of yours came to Reachfar just after the war. Kate and the rest of us just never thought on taking the lassie down to Achcraggan.'

'It was Reachfar that Monica wanted to see anyhow,' I told him.

'Where is she now?' he asked as we went through the gate into the yard. 'My, but she was a nice lassie. Just as nice a lassie as I ever met.'

'I'm not sure where she is, but I'll have to write to the London address though, to tell her I'm getting married.' I winked at him over the bar of the gate.

'God, but you are like the Ould Leddy sometimes!' he said suddenly. 'You can make up that mind of yours and nothing will stop you – just the way Herself was.'

My family, led by my father, took my news in its stride. If I had paused to give the matter any thought, which I had not, I think I should have anticipated a certain amount of trouble with my aunt. In my experience, women take less easily to irregular matrimonial situations that do men, probably because of their traditional position as the submerged sex. But if I had indeed stopped to think that my aunt would disapprove, I should have been, as My Friend Monica would say, quite wrong. My father, at the tea-table, told them quietly of the situation and of our decision and he then expressed his own views before looking round at the others. 'Well – Kate?' he said then, and I felt that he, like me, anticipated most trouble and disapproval to come from this quarter and was therefore tackling the worst first, which is a trait in my family.

My aunt rose to her feet at the end of the table. We are a tall family, as I have mentioned before, and she is one of its most handsome women. She looked over all our heads at the wall on the north side of the big kitchen.

'Janet is quite right,' she said firmly. 'She is old enough to know the man she wants when she sees him and she has plenty of sense when she wants to have. I am proud to see that there's a woman left in this family with the courage to go her own way and be damned to what people say or think. You'll be happy, Janet.'

She went to the fireplace, picked up the big teapot and began to pour fresh tea for us all while I stared at her. Suddenly, the past unrolled before me. I remembered how, when she was young, my aunt had kept her young man Malcolm waiting and waiting while she looked after our home and my grandparents as the world expected her to do, until Malcolm went off and married somebody else. Later, after my grandparents died, my aunt had married another man, who had been killed in the war, but she had never left Reachfar and her marriage had caused hardly a ripple on the surface of life there. I now suddenly knew with certainty that that marriage had been no more than a ripple on the surface of her own life. In a few moments, while she poured tea from the big brown pot, I seemed to see the sacrifice that her life had been laid naked before me.

'Thank you, Kate,' I said.

She sat down in her place at the table again. 'We'll have to watch that one down at Achcraggan, though,' she said.

'For myself,' said Tom. 'I have never seen a great deal o' use in folk having these fancy weddings. If two people is going to come together, they will come together whateffer, whether a minister will be speaking words over them or not. And if they are going to part from one another, they will be doing that, too. Of coorse, there is the law, and a person would always rather abide by the law when reasonable. But in this case, where this woman in Belfast is apparently not reasonable, that makes the law not reasonable either. That's the way I look on it, whateffer.'

There was some further discussion to and fro and then I made a few comments and ended: ' – and we'll just tell the people around here that we were married in Glasgow.'

'For me,' said George, speaking for the first time, 'I wouldn't tell nobody damn a-all. There is far too much telling and speaking goes on in the world. Janet, when you and Twice is ready and can get a little time off from that place where you are working, chust get into the car and drive off. People is very good at making up their minds what other people will be doing. People will decide you are off to get married, without you telling them a damn word. Then, after a whilie, drive in here to see us and the people round here will make up *their* minds. They'll be telling Tom and me doon in Achcraggan the next week that we had the honeymooners at Reachfar for a night or two.'

We all began to laugh, as usual, at my 'clown' of an uncle, but we recognized the truth behind his words.

'I am a great believer,' he ended, 'in letting other folk tell *me* everything. It will save me a lot o' bother explaining lies to St Peter of Chudgment Day.'

'That's chust what I think too, forbye an' besides,' said Tom.

Twice and I acted according to the advice of George and, as he had foretold, we found our private life arranged for us out-of-hand. After we had turned aside one or two friendly remarks about the venue of our wedding with coy references to its being 'a quiet, family affair, for after all we aren't kids of twenty', all went as merrily as the proverbial marriage bell. We drove northwards out of Ballydendran one day, drove into Reachfar ten days later and then returned to the house we had found in Ballydendran to find ourselves inundated with wedding presents, which people had sent regardless of the fact that no wedding invitations had been issued.

'George was right,' said Twice, 'they've married us, Flash.'

'Don't you *feel* married?'

'If that's what I feel, it's wonderful,' he said.

It was, indeed, wonderful. Twice and I were very, very happy.

CHAPTER TWELVE

My marriage took place towards the end of 1947 and if it
did nothing else, my marriage had the effect of making Jean
bury the current hatchet and 'speak to' my aunt, George
and Tom again. I had been assured by my aunt and the rest
of my family that the breach between Reachfar and Jean
which had opened in 1945 was final and irremediable, but
I had always felt that this could not be so, for I knew that
Jean was ever at the mercy of that veering wind, while I also
knew that my aunt would never turn aside an approach that
would smooth the public face of the family unity.

Immediately after our honeymoon visit to Reachfar, therefore, Jean arrived, red-faced and panting from her hill climb
coupled with her indignation, in the Reachfar kitchen. To
my everlasting regret, I was not present, but from the faithful
and detached reportage of my aunt, George and Tom, I am
able to quote the following points from Jean's discourse.

a) Imagine any man marrying *her* at *her* age! She's thirty-
seven!

Nobody pointed out that Jean was thirty-nine when my
father married her.

b) Imagine getting married in an office place anyway, as
if she was a heathen.

c) And why did she have to go to Edinburgh for it?
Glasgow is good enough for ordinary folk.

d) And what is a young working couple like them wanting
with this 'great big hoose' they're building?

Nobody pointed out that, a moment ago, Jean had implied
that I was too old to get married, for now, my family realized,
the crux had been reached. Jean might have got over my

getting married and the 'office place' manner of it, but the 'great big hoose' of which she had had reports from friends commissioned by her to visit Ballydendran and inspect it from outside was to stick in her gullet like the solid lump of masonry that it was.

The house, in actual fact, was neither great nor big, but was a row of four old stone cottages, standing alone in an acre of ground beside a heap of stones that was the ruin of an old mill by a stream. When Twice bought this near ruin, Scotland was still in the throes of the postwar housing shortage and we would never have found a place to live, I fear, but for the intervention of My Friend Monica, who helped us obtain Crookmill, as it was called. To make it habitable, there had to be a certain amount of building and carpentering activity, but there is no doubt that Jean's reporting friends had made great exaggerations as reporters often tend to do, and my family, glad to get away from details of the 'marriage' itself, were nothing averse to engaging Jean's attention and indignation with fantastic descriptions of the 'great, big, hoose'.

'An' *two* bathrooms in it an' a-all!' said Tom.

'Aye and a man and three loons working in the garden to put it right,' said George.

'And an all-electric kitchen,' said my aunt.

They did not say that Twice himself did most of the plumbing, that the 'man and three loons' in the garden were an old neighbour and his grandsons who worked for nothing on certain afternoons and that the 'all-electric' of the kitchen consisted of a small, second-hand cooker so that, in the end, they sent Jean down to Achcraggan in such a fury of jealousy that she set about cleaning and repainting the cottage and rendered it uninhabitable for a fortnight.

By the time of my marriage, we have to remember that Jean had been at the cottage in Achcraggan for twenty-one years, from 1926 until 1947, and it is a matter of history that there were many changes in many lives in the course of that period. I think that the life of my family suffered less change than most lives. My grandparents died, but in a Ripeness-

Is-All un-sad sort of way, of old age and without pain, and my brother John grew up into a young man that I did not know, for that ten years of age stood between us like a wedge of time that was driven home by the hammer of space which kept him in the north of Scotland, while I was in London, and sent him to sea with the Navy for the war, while I was bound to Buckinghamshire by the Air Force.

Jean was fond of my brother, a thing which pleased me, amazed me, and at the same time widened the cleavage between him and myself, for the only way in which I could explain this bond between them was on the basis of some similarity in their natures. I distrusted my brother and, during the 1930s, when I went home on holidays, I would watch him covertly and find myself searching in him for some taint of Jean, which I felt must be there. It was not until much later that I came to know that the bond between Jean and my brother was basically sexual on her part and that she liked him because of his strong physical and character resemblance of my father, which became more and more marked the older he grew.

After our grandparents died, my brother left Reachfar and went to live at the cottage, because it was so much more convenient for the 'bus that took him each day to Fortavoch Academy, and he fitted into the life of the cottage and of Achcraggan in a way that I could never have done. I think that this was a happy time for Jean, but it did not last long, for in 1936 John, who was also 'clever at the school' as I had been and, indeed, cleverer, left Fortavoch and went to lodgings in Aberdeen that he might attend the university there, and Jean was thrown back on the solitude of the cottage, for my father continued to spend all his days at Reachfar.

By this time, Jean had antagonized the entire village and district, as well as most of the cronies from Cairnton who had been wont to come to visit her in the summer and have her to visit them in the spring, and the only friends that remained to her were two maiden sisters, named Teenie and Kirsty Graham, who earned a meagre living at Cairnton as dressmakers and who, I think, 'put up with' Jean's tantrums and her patronage which was almost insufferable, because she was their only means of a cheap change of air each summer. Each August, even throughout the war, these two would arrive at the cottage, wizened and sour-lipped and sycophantic, and give Jean all the gossip of Cairnton, admire the cottage fulsomely and allow themselves to be patronized and bullied by Jean in a way that made our flesh crawl. When this visit, the high point of the year, was over, Jean would clean and polish the bedroom they had used as if they had suffered from leprosy, call them by every insulting name she could think of and remark with enjoyable malice that they had only one comb between them. When that was over, she was alone again in the highly polished Castle Jemima with, as Tom put it, 'nothing to do but think on badness'. It was utterly natural, I think, that I should be the focal point for all this 'badness'.

Jean had never understood me any more than I had ever been able to understand her, and she understood still less my way of life after I left home and went away to the south of England and eventually to London to earn my living. For Jean, I can see now, the business of keeping body and soul together had always been the most important thing in life, a risky thing, full of pitfalls for a woman, unless she could find some 'good steady man' to marry her. It seemed to Jean not only unfair, but unbelievably improbable, that I should be able to strike out on my own, go from job to job earning what seemed to her to be fabulous amounts and achieving a way of life that was, to her, luxurious, without any apparent effort. I firmly believe, now, that, during the 1930s, Jean thought I was a prostitute, for she could think of no other way in which a young woman could have the clothes and the way of life which I had. And, with every year that passed, she became more cock-a-hoop because I remained unmarried and told George, Tom and Kate, with much gleeful malice at every opportunity, that she 'had aye kent that nae man in his senses wid hae onything tae dae wi' her'. This caused a lot of trouble and hurt feelings, for my family was like other families of our class and still believed that marriage was the best and most natural fate for any woman.

By 1945, when I was thirty-five, Jean was quite openly referring to me with delighted scorn as 'that auld maid'. My marriage in 1947, at the age of thirty-seven, was therefore more than a shock to Jean. It was a cataclysm, particularly as it had about it no air of 'any port in a storm', and here again, in describing Jean's reactions, I have to revert to the symbols by which she lived. Just as the cottage in Achcraggan with its polished furniture and gleaming paint represented all the security of life, so did a fur coat and a car represent wealth. In Cairnton, only the 'rich' quarry-owners had cars and only the 'rich' quarry-owners' wives had fur coats, and these two things, probably in childhood, had become never-changing symbols of wealth to Jean. Quality of coat and car did not come into the question. There were no degrees. Jean did not know, and would not have believed, that a good tweed coat from a famous house could cost more than a low-grade fur coat from a chain store, and Ford and Rolls-Royce were blood brothers of equal degree in her eyes. Fur coats and cars spelled riches and that was that.

At the time of my marriage, Twice owned an ancient and venerable car, and My Friend Monica, who was wealthy and fond of me, gave me, as a personal wedding present, a fur coat of her own which she had never liked and had had remodelled, because, with the clothing shortage that still persisted as an aftermath of the war, I was having difficulty in covering my nakedness. So, not only had I 'got a man efter a' ' in Jean's mind – I had also got a man that was 'fair rotten wi' money'. It was truly as if life in general set itself out specifically to create difficulties between Jean and me and, in spite of our best efforts, prevent us from ever reaching any common ground.

Other events, little and big, piled up as they tend to do. In 1948, I had a prolonged illness during which my family found in Achcraggan a widow called Daisy Ramsay who was willing to come to Crookmill to look after me and the house and, after I was well again, Daisy stayed on with us to caretake the house while Twice and I travelled on business.

Jean paid another call at Reachfar.

Imagine *her*, born an' bocht up on this hill at the back o' beyond, keepin' *servants* next as if she wis Lady Muck!'

Then My Friend Monica married young Sir Torquil Daviot and came to Poyntdale House where she began to use her money to pull the estate together. Monica did not know Jean and did not want to, but she knew and loved the rest of my family and would ride in about Reachfar, especially when Twice and I happened to be there. Jean sat at the cottage and brooded and, if I have described her at all, your guess is as good as mine as to how her thoughts ran.

My father was still spending his days at Reachfar, my brother had now become a schoolmaster and was established on his own in south Scotland, and Jean had nothing to do but polish Castle Jemima and 'think on badness'. I think it is no exaggeration to say that I became a sort of obsession with her, a focal point for all the frustration and loneliness of her life. I think, too, that, as a family, we were all guilty of selfishness, especially my father, who treated the Cottage as no more than a place where he ate his morning and evening meals and slept at nights. All our lives were full and we did not think of Jean, for, down the years, she had made of herself a thought that we all preferred to avoid. In particular, *I* did not think of her. I was very happy. My life was like a bright, broad plain, opening before me more widely and kindly beckoning as day followed day.

At the end of 1949, Twice and I went down to London for a few weeks and when we came back to Crookmill we were met by an indignant Loose-and-Daze as we called Daisy and her friend Lucy who looked after the house. Loose-and-Daze are regarded by Twice and myself, and many others, be it said, as a single, composite personality, largely because they think exactly alike about so many things and always express their thoughts in a sort of strophe and anti-strophe.

'That woman's been here— ' said Daze, almost before we had taken our coats off.

'Three times— ' said Loose.

'Poking into everything— '

'And asking—'

At this point, old Mattha who is our neighbour who insists on doing our garden and firewood and treating Twice and me as if we were half-witted, dumped Twice's suitcase in the middle of the floor and said: 'But Ah jist tell't her!'

'Coming here poking through the whole place—'

'And looking in the linen cupboard—'

'WHO WAS THIS WOMAN?' bellowed Twice, for a parade-ground bellow is the only means, frequently, of reducing the Crookmill household to order.

'That person from Ack-cracken!' said Loose, who is English.

'That woman from the Cottage!' said Daze, the Achcraggan native.

'The Mistress's faither's saykint wife, God help him, the pare sowl!' said Mattha who is always accurate.

'Jean! Good God!' I said.

'The damned bitch!' said Twice.

'Ye niver spoke a truer word,' said Mattha. 'That's jist whit Ah ca'd her tae her face!' and he carried the suitcase through to our bedroom.

At first, after we had heard the details of Jean's three visits, Twice and I were angry and indignant, but after we had had our dinner, to a Greek chorus accompaniment of Jean's iniquities and enormities from Loose, Daze and Mattha, we had begun to be amused. And there was little fear of Jean repeating her visits, it seemed, for, on the third occasion, she had been very summarily dealt with by old Mattha, who had given her his detailed opinion of her character, ordered her off the premises and threatened to call the police and charge her with unlawful entry if she did not go.

'The polis cannae touch me fur visitin' ma step-dochter, says she tae me,' Mattha told us, 'so Ah jist says tae her, Ah says: Ah only ken that the mistress o' this hoose is no' here the noo an' we are the caretakers an' Ah dinnae ken ye frae Adam, ye damnt auld bitch, Ah says, an' whit's mair Ah dinnae want tae an' jist you get oot o' this hoose, Ah says, or Ah'll send fur the polis. An' then she went.'

'I'm not surprised that she went, Mattha,' said Twice.

'Would you go and get us all a glass of beer?'

'I'm terribly sorry, Twice, and it's really dreadful,' I said, 'but I can't help laughing about it. Funny how one changes. At fourteen or fifteen, I would have been scarified by a thing like this happening in my family and in my home, but now it doesn't seem to matter a damn. I don't think it will worry Dad either, do you, if he hears about Mattha and so on?'

'Not a bit,' said Twice. 'He'll just read his paper and let Jean rave on. I bet she *is* raving too. What a fool that woman is! She knows perfectly well that she is a family joke – if not a general Achcraggan joke – and yet she can *not* snap out of it. What *is* this morbid jealousy of this house, anyway?'

'Just that. Morbid jealousy. So far, you see, until we got Crookmill, the Cottage was the best house, in Jean's opinion, owned by any of her intimate acquaintance. For myself, I prefer Reachfar, but Jean's taste doesn't run to farmhouses so much. Crookmill is in competition with the Cottage, she feels, but the worst thing about it is that she regards it as *mine. You* don't count, chum. It is I, Janet, who have got this wonderful 'big hoose' and Jean will never forgive me for it.'

'But *why*?'

'Because Jean never forgives me for anything, period. Oh, the hell with Jean. We've got other things to think about. What kind of clothes should we get for this trip to St Jago? Where *is* St Jago anyway? My geography of the West Indies isn't too strong.'

'It's doon Cuba way an' sooth-east a bittie, as Tom would say.' Twice laughed. 'I believe it is hottish in the days, but not too bad. If I were you, I'd carry as little as possible and buy what you need when you get there.'

'I suppose there will be shops of a sort?'

'Don't be so damned uppity! St Jago is a very up-and-coming, go-ahead, wealthy little island. Aren't I going out there to advise them on the latest in industrial plant? Of *course* there are shops! Indeed, I believe that St Jago Bay, the chief town, is developing into quite a fine city.'

'The truth is that I have never regarded the Golden Islands

of the West, the Hesperides – which is what the West Indies mean to me – as being real at all. Not real in the sense of having shops where you buy things. Even the word "Indies" doesn't sound real. It is a nostalgic word out of the past, like mariners and doubloons and pieces of eight.'

'You are quite right in a way,' Twice agreed. 'I'll tell you an interesting thing – the bills of lading for cargo going to that part of the world still refer to the "Spanish Main". That surprised me, somehow.'

'No! The Spanish Main is *poetry* real, not for ship's cargo! But wait a minute, bills of lading can be quite poetic things – I found that out long ago when I was a youngster and had a job as secretary to an old gentleman who was writing a book about the Port of London.'

'Ships themselves are very poetic sort of things,' Twice said. 'It's a pity that we have to go out by air, but the ships take about a fortnight.'

'However we go, it is going to be wonderful,' I said.

Before this time, I had travelled very little. Indeed, my travelling had been limited to a few short trips to the continent of Europe during the 1930s and Twice's recent promotion to the post of chief consultant with his engineering firm had opened up the whole world for me, it seemed. When, a week later, he and I arrived one morning at the Airlines Terminal in London, I could not believe that I was really about to cross the broad Atlantic in an aeroplane and I felt as I had not felt since, nearly thirty years ago, I had stood beside my father in Inverness Station on that morning in August.

There was a bookstall here too, and while Twice attended to the weighing of our luggage, I drifted towards it. Ahead of me at the counter was a distinguished-looking gentleman of about sixty in company with a small red-haired boy – grandfather and grandson, most likely, I thought, as one does.

'But, dammit, boy! You have an *Alice* already!' the old man was barking irascibly.

'I have *not*, sir!' the boy argued back. 'The two what is at home is the others's *Alices* and I've *never* had one of my own!' Clutching the book to his chest, he stepped backwards to look up at the old man and I, probably standing too close, was in the way, so that he cannoned backwards against me. He spun round and stared up at me with large, contrite, blue eyes.

'I *beg* your pardon! I hope I did not hurt you?'

The girl in the bookstall smiled at the heartfelt apology and I felt another upsurge of memory of Inverness Station.

'Not at all,' I said. 'Probably I was crowding in much too close. Are you going to have *Alice in Wonderland*?'

'He already has two copies of it, Madam,' the old gentleman said.

The boy looked up at me.

'They're my brothers's *Alices*. When you have six brothers all handing things down to you, you hardly ever have anything of your own!'

'Oh, all right, dammit!' said the old gentleman and turned to the sales girl. 'How much, me dear? For *Alice* and these?' He held out a copy of *The Times* and a bundle of magazines.

While the transaction was being completed, I said to the boy: 'And what is your name?'

'Alexander Macdonald Dulac Maclean, Ma'am,' he said.

'That's a fine Highland name,' I told him.

'Mostly they call me Sandy – except when Mother is angry and then she says Alexander.'

Looking at him, I found it difficult to believe that the mother of this seventh son could be angry very often, if he gazed at her as he was gazing at me with the large blue eyes in the stubby freckled face.

'Please find me the other half,' I said to the girl behind the counter. '*Through the Looking-Glass*.' Twice came forward as the girl handed me the book. 'Lend me your pen, Twice.' I opened the book and looked at the boy. 'What was that name again? Alexander Macdonald Black Maclean?'

'No, please – not Black. It's Dulac – D-U-L-A-C – like Sir Ian here – this is Sir Ian Dulac, Mrs—?'

'Alexander,' I said.

'Your name is Alexander too?' the boy asked Twice.

'Yes. Mine is Alexander Alexander, so they call me Twice,' Twice explained.

The boy gave a delighted crow of laughter and, while he chattered to Twice, I wrote on the fly-leaf of the book: 'A memento to Alexander Macdonald Dulac Maclean, a gentleman. London, January, 1950. Janet E. Alexander.'

'There,' I said, handing it to him. 'Two books of your own, now.'

'Thank you very, very much, Mrs Alexander,' he said gravely.

'And where are you headed for, sir?' the old gentleman asked Twice.

'An island in the West Indies called St Jago, sir.'

'God bless my soul!' said Sir Ian.

'You are going home with *us*!' shouted Sandy, clutching his books to his chest and dancing round in a circle on the concrete.

'Stop hoppin' like a chicken, boy! May I ask what part of the island?'

'St Jago Bay, in the first place,' Twice told him. 'I am an engineer and the Chamber of Industry for the island is calling me out in an advisory capacity. I gather we shall be in St. Jago for a month or so in all – but I don't know which parts.'

'You are the Allied Plant fellah?'

'That's right, sir.'

'Bless my soul! How d'ye do, my boy?' He shook hands with us both all over again. 'Delighted to meet you. Delighted! Been after these stoopid bastards – I *beg* your pardon, Madam – ever since the war to get an expert out. Chamber of Industry! Chamber-pot of hot air's more like it!'

'Sir Ian!' said the boy in a corrective tone. 'You know what Mother said about behavin' when she left us here in England by ourselves!'

'Dammit, boy, she ain't here now and you don't have to tell her!' the old man argued back and then, as if realizing that the boy was not his own age, he added: 'And hold your tongue and don't interfere!'

With the calm efficiency for which some airlines are justly famous, we were shepherded into the motor-bus, taken out through the grey London winter streets to the airport and loaded into the huge airliner that sat on the tarmac like a swan on an icebound lake. If all the truth were told, I had been a little nervous of this long flight, first to the Azores and then out west across the broad Atlantic to Bermuda, but Sir Ian and Sandy altered all that. It was their first Atlantic flight too, and it emerged that they were making it without the sanction of their families. Sandy and I sat side by side on one side of the aisle, while Sir Ian sat with Twice on the other and when, mercifully, we had gained too much altitude for Sandy to point out to me things on the earth, I sat back and tried to convince myself that the deep gap between me and *terra firma* was only an illusion.

'Mother will have got Sir Ian and me's cable by now,' said Sandy.

'You sent her a cable?'

'Yes, telling her we are flying home and to meet us at the airport.' He gave a giggle. 'She'll be hoppin' mad – so will Madame!'

'Who is Madame?' I asked.

'Sir Ian's mother.'

'His mother?'

'Yes. Madame Dulac, ye know,' Sandy explained, politely enough, but as if to an idiot. 'She is goin' to be somewhere in her eighties this summer.'

'Oh. Why will they be hoppin' mad?'

'Sir Ian an' me was supposed to come home in a banana boat. We're sick o' banana boats. They hardly ever let us do anything we want to by ourselves, so when we get a chance we just do it anyway.'

I glanced sidewise at the ruddy-faced, silver-haired man on the other side of the aisle and was suddenly reminded, as he laughed at some remark Twice had made, of George and Tom larking in the barn at Reachfar. I suddenly understood that 'Madame' and Mrs Maclean, like my grandmother when I was a child, probably often had good reason for being 'hoppin' mad'.

CHAPTER THIRTEEN

The terrifying journey passed like a dream and, all at once, it was dawn and Twice woke me by saying: 'Wake up, Flash, and get your first look at the Golden Islands of the West!' I looked out and down through the thick glass of the round window, through floating cream-puffs of cloud, at a sea of incredibly Wedgwood Blue that broke white over golden sand, to make a lacy frill round a piece of patchwork that was floating on the water. 'Bermuda,' said Twice. 'Next stop, St Jago.'

In the terminal at Bermuda, we all changed into thinner clothes, but when we landed, at noon, and stepped down on to the tarmac at Jago Bay, even my linen dress in which I had shivered in an over-heated London dress-shop seemed to have all the weight and warmth of a horse-blanket. The white concrete blazed, the red, purple and orange bougainvillaeas of a hedge flamed and burned and just as I felt that I must faint from the assault of heat and colour, Sandy's voice said: 'Gosh, Sir Ian! We're not half for it! Dad's here too!'

Sir Ian snatched Sandy's hand in a panic-stricken grip and said shakily: 'Keep quite calm, boy. Perfectly calm! No, no. You mustn't go, Alexander, my boy! Stay with us, Mrs Alexander. Must meet the Macleans – charmin' people the Macleans!'

Sir Ian and Sandy, hand in hand, stepped warily towards the airport building and Twice and I fell in behind.

'Those two youngsters are in trouble,' Twice murmured. 'We seem to be elected as the buffer state.'

I thought of my childhood, when I would retire from the family wrath with my back against the wall of My Friends Tom and George.

'Looks like it,' I agreed.

Sir Ian and Sandy waited inside the customs barrier until the officials released Twice and me and then, in phalanx, we stepped out into the hall to face the Maclean wrath.

'Well, well, well!' bawled Sir Ian heartily. 'And so you are here too, Rob! That's splendid! Splendid! Let's all go and have a drink!'

'Madame,' said Mrs Maclean in a portentous voice, 'is at Ike's.'

'God Almighty!' said Sir Ian and drew away, as if to run back to the aeroplane, before recovering himself. Then: 'Oh, well, must take things as they come.'

'Mother,' said Sandy, coming in with flank support, 'this is Mrs Alexander what we met in London what gave me *Alice Through the Looking-Glass* and this is Mr Alexander, Dad, and he's an engineer, too.'

I, being an old campaigner in this sort of situation, came in on cue and Twice, who is brimful of native wit, had Mr Maclean diverted into engineering talk in no time at all, but even after the luggage had been processed and we had all had a drink, we were not yet free.

'Come in our car,' said Sir Ian. 'Get a taxi for the bags, Rob. You have to go to Ike's anyway – only decent hotel in the place.'

'We are booked at a place called the St Jago Palace— ' said Twice doubtfully.

'That's Ike's,' said Sandy.

It seemed to be incontrovertible. We went to Ike's.

It was a delightful place, full of pillared patios, sunlit fountains, palms, ferns and lush, trailing vines, but as Ike himself, a fat Portuguese Jew, met us and conducted us into the main hall, the whole large white room seemed to be dominated by a little fat lady in black who stood leaning on a long-handled parasol and gazing upon us all with the cold, unfriendly eye of a mountain eagle.

'And what nonsense is this *now*, Ian?' she enquired in the unmistakeable accents of Victorian Edinburgh.

'Another edition of my grandmother!' I hissed at Twice.

This was the bare truth. My grandmother had been tall and spare while Madame was short and fat, but the dominating, matriarchal, majestic and frightening quality was in the one just as it had been in the other. And then she noticed that Twice and I had paused behind Sir Ian and the Macleans, and at once, as my grandmother would have done, she pushed aside the family affair until later – I felt that, like my grandmother, she was not dismissing it, but merely postponing it – and turned her attention to us with a grand graciousness, as if Ike did not exist and this hotel lounge were her own drawing-room.

'Mrs Alexander and Mr Alexander, Madame,' said Mrs Maclean. 'Madame Dulac. They were kind to Sir Ian and Sandy on the journey, Madame.'

'How d'you do?' She extended a white-gloved hand. 'That was very good of you. Rob, chairs, please. Ian, find Ike and tell him to come here.' She turned to the smiling, hovering, Negro waiter. 'Go away, boy. Find Mr Ike. And is this your first visit to St Jago, Mrs Alexander?'

Ike appeared and she ordered rum punch. 'And Paradise Rum, Ike. Don't let them try to serve me that vat-wash they make at Retirement. All right.'

Halfway through the second glass of this potent brew which Madame was drinking as if it were water, she said to me: 'You are a Highlander, aren't you?'

'Yes, Madame. From Ross.'

'What part?'

'The east. Near Achcraggan.'

'Near Poyntdale?'

'Poyntdale marches with our croft on our north side, Madame.'

'You knew Torquil Daviot, the one that married Lydia Marle?'

'Yes, Madame. I knew him when I was a child and remember him clearly.'

She smiled for the first time. 'An old flame of mine. But he preferred Lydia and I preferred Eddie Dulac. Oh, well, have a little more punch, my child.'

When we were having coffee after lunch, Twice and Mr Maclean were still talking engineering and Twice said: 'I've got a drawing among my papers. I'll get it.'

He rose to fetch his briefcase, but Sir Ian told a waiter to fetch it.

'Mr Alexander's bags have been taken up,' said the ubiquitous Ike, 'but I'll send for the case, sir.'

'Send for all the bags, Ike,' said Madame. 'Mr and Mrs Alexander won't be staying in this gin palace of yours. They are coming to Paradise.'

'Very well, Madame,' said Ike.

Protest was useless. At the end of half-an-hour, Twice and I set out with Madame in her Rolls-Royce for Paradise Estate and, to my knowledge, no further word was spoken to anyone by anyone about the illicit Atlantic flight of Sir Ian and Sandy.

I do not intend, here, to give a complete description of Paradise, St Jago, for it is the scene of other stories that I should like to tell and I am probably long-winded and repetitive enough by accident without deliberately being so. Suffice it to say here that Paradise came very near to living up to its grandiose name. It was the largest sugar estate on the island and consisted of a wide, basin-like valley, in the centre of which lay a small, by comparison, flat parkland dotted with trees, in the centre of which, again, stood the sugar factory and rum distillery. A half-mile to the east of this busy, hive-like heart, lay the 'Great House' of Paradise which had been the Dulac home since 1775; half-a-mile to the north of the hive or heart lay the 'Great House' of Olympus, an estate now incorporated in Paradise, where the Macleans lived, and half-a-mile to the west of the hive or heart lay the 'Compound', which was a group of some eight bungalows, occupied by the European factory staff, such as office manager, engineers and chemists. Rob Maclean, who was estate and factory manager, was regarded by Madame Dulac as a younger son of her own and the communion between Paradise and Olympus was very close indeed.

Twice, having hired himself a car and chauffeur, was of

necessity away from Paradise most days. Madame busied herself with her housekeeping – to which she still brought the meticulous pride and care of the Victorian Edinburgh in which she had been reared – and her garden which was large and of vast botanical interest and her interference by letter and telephone – she always spoke of the latter as 'The Instrument' – in the public life of the island. Sir Ian, the heir to the estate, who had earned his title by his service in the Army and in the Colonial Police, and who regarded sugar as a commodity that graced the table in a Georgian silver bowl, spent much of his time with Sandy, and when Sandy was at lessons of a morning with his tutor, he supervised, from horseback, the care of the polo ponies which he bred as a hobby. Most mornings, I typed the letters and reports that Twice had dictated to me the evening before, wrote a bit, explored the Estate lands and, in general, observed what went on, which has always been one of my favourite pastimes.

Life as lived at Paradise was so different from anything I had known before, or anything I had ever imagined, that it had a dream-like, Through-the-Looking-Glass feeling, which was exaggerated by the violent, exotic beauty of the place. In particular, the early mornings at Paradise were extraordinarily beautiful. The Great House stood on a slight eminence that the rooms might trap any cool breeze that might blow, and it was two stories high, with a huge dining-room, morning-room, library and several other rooms and the kitchens on the ground floor and a large drawing-room, sitting-room and some eight bedrooms with bathrooms on the upper floor. Twice and I occupied an enormous bedroom on the north-east corner of the building and, at six each morning, our tray with tea and fruit was brought to the verandah which ran round all sides of the house on both floors. The 'winter' sun would come up as we sat there in rocking chairs and the dew on the vines and shrubs in the garden would take on the scarlet of the hibiscus flowers, the yellow of the cassias, the blue of the potreas and the green of the leaves so that the drops became sparkling, many-coloured jewels, strung on platinum threads of gossamer.

'I was quite right,' I told Twice one morning towards the end of our stay. 'The Golden Islands of the West are *not* real. Anyone who had never seen this place would not believe in it. Even after nearly a month here, I don't yet quite believe in it myself.'

'True enough,' Twice said, and he stared through the door-way from the verandah into the enormous bedroom. 'I still can hardly believe in this acreage of mahogany floor. It seems sacrilegious, somehow, to walk on polished mahogany!'

'It is odd,' I said, 'that we should have come here through a copy of *Through the Looking-Glass*, for that's exactly how I feel. I feel that anything might happen — that the Queen of Hearts might come tearing round that corner through that screen of great big bell flowers, shouting "Off with his head!" at any moment.'

Even as I spoke, a branch laden with eight-inch-long, waxen-white datura bells was thrust aside and with a staccato tap-tap-tap of firm little heels Madame came through the aperture, followed by her old Negro butler, Nehemiah. With short, plump, beringed fingers, she poked around the stems of a potted fern and then drew herself up, very erect.

'Nehemiah, bring Samuel here at once!'

'Yes, Miss.'

Nehemiah disappeared and, for a moment or two, Madame examined a few more of her potted ferns and palms. Then she leaned over the verandah rail and, in a voice surprisingly commanding for its high pitch, she called: 'Sam-you-*elle*! Sam-you-*elle*!'

Sir Ian's face, in a froth of shaving soap, was thrust out of his bathroom window: 'Dammit, Mother! Stop howlin' like a banshee! Want me to cut me perishin' throat?'

'Ian! Retire to your toilet!' said Madame sternly and, as the face withdrew, she added: 'And mind your own business!'

Nehemiah now arrived, shepherding the hangdog Samuel who was already a-tremble in anticipation of the wrath to come, and no wonder. Madame wished to know why the plants had not been watered this morning. Madame wished to know whether Samuel understood plain English. Madame had given orders, had she not, that all verandah work was to be finished before the first tray was taken upstairs? And, furthermore, where were the table flowers for dinner this evening? They should have been cut before the sun was up as Samuel knew perfectly well, didn't he?

'Samuel, how old are you?'

'Twenty-two years, please, Missis.'

'Yes. Twenty-two years. It is over fifty years since I was twenty-two years and if I can see to the plants in the morning, so can you. Now, go away and cut the table flowers at once and then attend to these plants when my guests have finished breakfast. I will not tolerate lazy, sluggardly people about my house, you understand?'

'Yes, Missis.'

'All right. Go away and don't let this happen again.'

As soon as Nehemiah and the culprit had disappeared, Sir Ian's head came out of the bathroom window again.

'Shouldn't tell lies to the Negroes, Mother!' he said.

'Ian! I do *not* tell lies!'

'Tellin' that fellah you were only seventy-two – should be ashamed o' yourself! He'll think you had *me* when you were only twelve an' if that ain't an indecent lie, what is?'

'Get dressed at once, Ian, and don't be coarse!' said Madame and swept along to our end of the verandah.

It was a convention of Paradise that all exchanges between Madame and her son, such as the one I have quoted, went unheard by everyone except themselves, even when they indulged in them across the dinner-table, so that, by the time Madame had tap-tapped her way along to us, Twice and I had endeavoured to clear from our faces all trace of amusement.

'Well, well, good morning, my dears!' she said brightly, as if we had this second suddenly appeared before her astonished eyes. Trying to simulate a similar air of pleased surprise at seeing her right here on the verandah, we wished her good morning and Twice brought forward one of the wicker rocking chairs in which she liked to sit. The very high, carved back gave her an enthroned appearance.

'Thank you, my boy, but I mustn't stay gossiping.'

She sat down, her little fat feet swinging clear of the floor, and the chair began to rock to and fro as if actuated by the charge of energy that vibrated inside her stout, firm, little body.

'The servants become lazier day by day and we have this dinner tonight. Fifty years ago, I could give a dinner party or a garden party or even a ball here without the slightest trouble, but nowadays one has to stand over them constantly. It is all this trade union and political nonsense and queer American religions. It takes their mind off their work. No Negro has the brain capacity to think of more than one thing at a time and if they are thinking of politics or religion, they simply don't remember to do their work. I have been scolding Samuel, the boy who does this verandah, but scolding is quite useless, really, when they become Charioteers. You simply have to wait for them to get over it.'

'Charioteers, Madame?' Twice ventured, on a questioning note.

'Yes, the Charioteers of Jehovah,' Madame explained. 'It came in a year or so ago. It is all very silly and childish and makes them forget simply *every*thing, especially when they get a sinner or two following their chariot as Samuel has now. Samuel is towing his old grandfather and the girl who does the bathrooms behind his chariot to the throne of the Lord and it involves a great deal of prayer. It is very difficult to make them understand that they must do the towing and praying *after* they have watered the plants and not before. Still, the Charioteers is not as trying as the Trumpeters of Tomorrow. At one time, no less than seven of my house people were Trumpeters and it involved blowing hymns of praise on conch shells at dawn and dusk. The noise was a dreadful nuisance, but mercifully they soon tire of their religions, and of course, there's always a new one coming down from the United States. I hope this Mr Goldfine that the Chamber of Industry has asked us to entertain is not a Charioteer or a Trumpeter or anything. Oh, there you are, Ian. Do you know if Mr Goldfine is a Trumpeter?'

'Good God, no, Mother! Goldfine isn't a jazz-band fellah. Goldfine makes tractors an' those machines for diggin' mud an' that.'

'I meant his *religion*, Ian! I know perfectly well that the Chamber of Industry is making a fuss of him to get cheap machines to drain that swamp in Happy Grove. Waste of money and effort. There is rising water in Happy Grove.'

'What does his religion matter, Mother?' Sir Ian asked.

'Oh, it doesn't *matter*. But it is more comfortable to *know*, like when one has to attend a Jewish funeral.'

''Smatter o' fact, now that you mention it,' Sir Ian said, 'he has a damn' queer − well, you couldn't call it a religion, of course − more of a hobby. Aubrey Garson was tellin' me about it.' He turned to Twice and me.

''Straordinary fellah, Aubrey. Got a brain like that addin' machine thing over in the factory office. Runs the Island Bureau o' that word I can't say without spittin' − *you* know, all about how many cobs o' corn we grew last year an' how many babies got born with six fingers on each hand in the month o' November. Very interestin' thing that, the number o' Negro babies that have the beginnin's o' an extra finger. Aubrey was tellin' me that at the Bureau o' S-s-s−'

'Statistics,' said Twice.

'That's it! Well, they keep a record o' all these ones with the sixth digit as they call it an '−'

'Ian, we are not talking about Negro babies' fingers. What is this hobby of Mr Goldfine's?'

'Oh, that? Brothels.'

'Ian!'

''s a fact, Mother! Old Aubrey says you could have knocked him down with a perishin' feather when his secretary told him Mr Goldfine was askin' to see him an' Aubrey gets out the cigars an' the rum an' in comes this old cove that says he doesn't smoke or drink but how many brothels are there in the Island an' where are they? Dammit, I don't blame Aubrey. Neither'd you, Mother, if you'd ever seen Goldfine. He looks like a Baptist parson, only rich, of course. However, it turns out that he ain't interested in the brothels in the ordinary way

222

that fellahs are interested in brothels, 'specially Americans. He's president o' some anti-vice outfit in the States as well as bein' president o' the mud-diggin' machine concern.'

'He's sort of *for* mud with one hand and against it with the other, you mean, Sir Ian!' Twice inquired.

'An' his right hand don't know what his left is doin'!' bellowed Sir Ian. 'By jove, jolly good! Old Pro-an'-Anti Goldfine!'

'Ian, that will do! I take it that he won't discuss this — this *hobby* of his at dinner?'

'Never can tell with a chap like that, Mother,' Sir Ian said. 'An' Americans are always so enthusiastic about their hobbies, an' that.' He ruminated for a moment. 'There's another queer thing about him,' he said then.

'Ian! Why wasn't I told of Mr Goldfine's eccentricities before? I am willing to do all I can for the welfare of the Island and entertain *any*one who can help the coloured people in *any* way, but brothels at my dinner-table—'

'Dammit, Mother, he don't carry the actual brothels round with him! An' I've heard queerer things than brothels discussed at your dinner-table when I think of it!'

'Ian, what else is odd about this Mr Goldfine?'

'He wears square glasses,' said Sir Ian.

'Ian! *Dozens* of people wear odd-shaped spectacles these days!'

'That don't stop it bein' queer,' Sir Ian argued. 'I can't see why a man with egg-shaped eyes like anybody else has to go wearin' square glasses. Silly, I call it.'

While Madame and her son glared at one another, I attempted a change of subject. 'And there is a Mrs Goldfine, isn't there?' I asked.

'Yes,' said Madame, 'but she is illiterate.'

In a frenzied way, I looked at Twice and from him to Sir Ian and found that they were both staring in puzzled amazement at Madame.

'What are you talkin' about, Mother?' Sir Ian barked.

'She can't write, apparently, poor thing,' said Madame, rising and going to the verandah rail to look down upon

Samuel the Charioteer on the lawn below with a glance that seemed to prick him like a sword-point from behind, for he at once became violently active about his work. 'She did not reply to my dinner invitation. Mr Goldfine informed me of their acceptance – on The Instrument.'

She tap-tapped away along the verandah on her firm little heels and it was not until she was beyond the screen of datura bells and round the corner that any of us spoke, so strong was the wash of disapproval that she left in her wake.

'Mother's gettin' old,' Sir Ian said then. 'She don't feel it and won't admit it, but she's gettin' on all the same. Can't take in new ideas any more, ye know, like people acceptin' for dinner by telephone. Can't move with the times.'

'Or won't,' I said. 'And I don't know that I don't agree with her. She wasn't brought up to be casual about behaviour and she has every right to stick to her standards. Age has nothing to do with it.'

'Maybe there's something in that,' Sir Ian admitted, 'but it makes things damned awkward now an' again. We get all sorts here at Paradise. House has always had a reputation for hospitality – 'specially since my old grandfather's time. An' when the agricultural people or the industrial people or His Excellency want to sweeten some fellah up, they ask Mother to entertain him. Last year, we got some sort o' dago from Latin America that asked for ice in his port. 'Straordinary the things some fellahs think of! Mind you, I hope Goldfine don't get goin' on his brothels at dinner. The Honeymans are comin' an' old Mrs H wouldn't like it at all. Think I'll advise Mother to put you on his other side, Missis Janet.' He turned to Twice. 'An' *that* means that you'll get the wife, me boy. Don't take any notice o' Mother an' the woman bein' illiterate an' that. 'Smatterofact, she's probably a bit o' a flier, Mrs Goldfine. French, ye know.'

'French?' Twice said. 'Then count me out. The only French I know consists of a few words I learned when I was being chased out of Dunkirk during the war and they're not dinner-party words.'

'Oh, she speaks English, I should think. Old Goldfine

224

ain't got the brains to get married in a foreign language. Ever notice how damn' stoopid so many millionaires seem to be? All these meetin's I been goin' to at the Chamber of Industry, I ain't heard old Goldfine give a straight answer yet. All he does is make a note an' say: "I'll check back on our policy on that," – only he says it "pawlicy". The truth is the old perisher don't *know* the answer. It was Aubrey Garson that told me about the wife bein' French. If it had been anybody else, I would never have believed that old Auntie Goldfine had a Fifi for a wife, but if Aubrey can't be accurate to the last digit an' that, he acts as if he's dumb.' He suddenly frowned at Twice. 'Here, you not goin' to town today?'

'No,' Twice said. 'It's Saturday and nobody seemed to want to be bothered with me.'

'Well, what we sittin' here for? Let's go over to Olympus an' get Sandy an' all go down to the beach for a swim!'

After a forenoon of lazing on incredibly white sand, by an incredibly blue sea, under an incredibly blue and distant sky, and an afternoon of reading in long chairs in the cool shade of our creeper-hung verandah, Twice and I had leisurely baths and began to dress for Madame's dinner-party. The evening breeze from the hills had risen, the moon was hanging like a large white plate against the matt black of the sky which was criss-crossed in a modernistic design by the moonlit-to-silver trunks of the palms, and the tray with the whisky, soda, ice and glasses was standing on the table at the end of the mahogany four-poster beds with their great shell-carved head-boards. I had put on my dress and had sat down at the dressing-table to put up my hair when Twice, in shirt and trousers, began to pour us a drink.

'I don't know,' he said, standing behind me and smiling at my reflection in the looking-glass. 'You look very elegant, my pet. And very luxurious, very expensive, with your white skin and black velvet – it seems a pity to take you back to the kitchen chores of Crookmill. But you fit in very well there too. Are you sorry this is nearly over?'

'In a way, I am,' I said, pushing pins into my hair. 'I've loved every minute of it, but I don't think I could take it indefinitely. It has too dreamlike a quality. I feel that my feet are off the ground. I think that one has to be born to this sort of thing, or come to it at nineteen, like Madame. I am too old to accept it as my way of life now. I might feel more real in one of the staff bungalows round in the Compound, but *this* house and its wealth, combined with the climate, the colours, the exoticism of the vegetation, and so on, are far too much for me. I feel that if this is real, nothing else that I have ever known can be real. The real world can't contain both, I feel. Yet obviously it does. But for me this is a lotus dream or, like the heroes of old, I have died without knowing it and have made a landfall in the Golden Islands of the West.'

Twice put a drink on my dressing-table and laughed. 'Well, here's to old Goldfine! His brothels will bring you down to earth. Actually, I hope he does bring his anti-vice views to dinner. After all, we are leaving on Wednesday and Madame's reactions would make a happy memory!'

As he picked up his own drink from the tray, I rose to my feet and turned round and he put his head on one side to say: 'Darling, I must say you do one credit the few times you take the trouble to make a real slap-up job of dressing-up. You look quite extraordinarily handsome!'

'Thank ye kindly,' I said and glanced at my reflection in the long glass in the corner. 'How one *feels* has a lot to do with a woman's appearance. The way I live here at Paradise, I feel like a pet concubine most of the time, lying about on shaded verandahs and fanning myself. It's a good job you can't afford to give me scads of diamonds. With diamonds on this black velvet and how I feel, I'd *look* like a kept woman. But wait till you see Mrs Goldfine. You won't even notice *me* when she comes in!'

'Have you met her, then?'

'Lord, no! But the gossip column of the *Island Sun* has done nothing but report her wardrobe ever since they arrived in the island – and *I* have nothing better to do than read the gossip column in the *Sun*.'

Twice and I went along the verandah round two sides of

the house to the drawing-room where Madame, in blue-grey lace and a collar of pearls, looked like a stone statue of Queen Victoria miraculously come to life and, almost at once, the cars with the sixteen guests began to arrive. I now had the feeling that I had been transported back through time by about a hundred years. The drawing-room itself had stopped in time, as it were, with the few Victorian items that Madame had superimposed on it when she arrived as a bride at Paradise some sixty years ago. The grand piano stood in a corner, decently clad in its magnificent, fringed, Indian shawl; on the walnut whatnot the pampas grass reached from a Wedgwood urn towards the ceiling, and in the main vase of a many-branched epergne that stood on a Hepplewhite table, an ostrich egg reposed, smugly shining of dome like the bald head of a prosperous Victorian paterfamilias.

The main entrance to the drawing-room was at the top of a broad flight of steps that led up from the front drive to this first floor, so that the arrival of the guests had all the formality of arrivals at some great reception in the heyday of Victorian London, and there was no fuss of leaving outer wraps or removing goloshes. Each lady guest had everything in her favour for making an entrance through the wide porch-way at the top of the steps into the lights of the large room with, behind her, the dead black back-drop of the tropic sky.

The Goldfines were the last to arrive and Mr Goldfine the first to appear at the top of the steps, a portly man of about sixty-five, with white hair, the 'square' glasses to which Sir Ian had taken exception and pasty-coloured skin that hung in squarish folds from the temples, round the angle of his jaws to his chin, giving him the look of a jaundiced bloodhound.

In the wide doorway of the drawing-room he paused, and, half-turning, he extended his right arm in the gesture that an impresario might make on presenting some brilliant new discovery to a waiting audience, and no wonder. Into the frame of the doorway stepped – not a woman – but a creation of an elegance that was breath-taking. I use the word 'creation' because she looked, not as if she had been born

227

and had grown and developed by the normal process of time, but as if, as she stood there, she had been specially created for this moment, to step into this lighting, between these long pink damask curtains, and stand, smiling faintly, upon this pink carpet that came to life as a stage upon the dark mahogany of the floor. Her dress was of white, luminous satin, held up by a single narrow hyacinth-blue strap over one shoulder, and from behind her shoulders there hung a long cloak, also of the white satin, but lined with blue, so that the shape of her exquisite body stood outlined in its luminous sheath of white. And all about her, it seemed, the diamonds winked and blazed – from the long drops in her ears to the great spray brooch on her breast to the bracelets on her forearms to the rings on her fingers so that the air around her seemed to be alive with flashes of blue and white light.

At the far end of the room, while Madame greeted the Goldfines, I said to Twice: 'See? I *told* you so!'

'Nobody could tell the like of that!' he replied. 'You have to see it!' And we moved forward to be introduced.

When the formal meeting was over and I turned away to reply to some remark made by old Mrs Honeyman, I had a curious feeling of being suspended in a vacuum and, throughout dinner, while Mr Goldfine told me in refined language of the vice that was rampant in Tokyo and the slum conditions in Calcutta, I was haunted by this feeling of having come against a subtle barrier of nothingness in that moment when the fair, blue-eyed woman looked at me, gave me her faint smile and at once transferred her strangely limited attention to Twice. That was it, I decided. She was like an automaton; nothing emanated from her, so that at the moment of meeting there had been the feeling that her real attention was concentrated elsewhere. And it was not concentrated upon anything in the room, on anything that could be shared with her. All of her that one could see was the outward seeming – the beautifully-dressed fair hair, the wide, expressionless blue eyes, the glow of the satin and the blaze of the diamonds. And especially the diamonds. I

228

thought of how My Friend Tom would say of her: 'To tell ye the truth, I couldna' *see* her for diamonds!'

And, while I thought of all this, Mr Goldfine's voice was drawling on as he gave his hobby its evening canter between Madame at the head of the table and myself. He and his wife, it appeared, had been on a tour of the world which, perhaps, would be more accurately described as a vice survey. We were now being given the tour in retrospect and, with the advent of the savoury, he brought us to London.

'But I don't feel I've gatten dahn ta bed-rawck in London,' he said. 'I don't feel completely can-fident that I saw the right places. I wanna go back there sometime an' have another look-see.'

Madame and I set up a condoning murmur at his disappointment at London's deficiency in vice and pestilence and he continued: 'I gat in the wrong comp'ny in London, see? Yes, sir. I gat in the comp'ny of a friend of Mrs Goldfine's.'

He paused and, from some mutation that came over his loops of putty-coloured skin round his jowls, I realized that I was in the presence of the Goldfine humour. I made an attempt at a laugh and Madame joined in with a tight-lipped little ha-ha-ha.

'Yeah!' said Mr Goldfine with satisfaction at our response. 'Mrs Goldfine had me meet an old friend of hers that's a big shat in medical circles in London – Sir Hugh Reid. Yes, sir. Sir Hugh Reid. He's a great guy an' a great dactar, but when it comes ta vice he don't know the haff av it. Gat me inta all the haspitals an' everything but it was all very V.I.P. if ya get me, Mrs Dewlack, but nat dahn ta bed-rawck. You take it fram me, Mrs Dewlack, if ya wanta get ta vice ya gotta be prepared ta get right ta battam – ta bed-rawck!'

'Quite,' said Madame and, at a glance from her, I rose from the table and the other women followed suit.

As I stood waiting for the old lady to precede me down the long room and lead the way to the drawing-room, my glance went back to Mrs Goldfine at the other end of the table and, in that moment, I saw her cross the room to the door, against the background of the potted palms that stood

229

banked against the wall. Sir Hugh Reid— In a flash, I saw the café-bar of the cheap hotel in Sauchiehall Street and Annie Black crossing the floor between me and a potted palm to sit down at a table beside a fat man with a purple face and small, piggy eyes.

'Dreaming again, Flash?' Twice's voice asked.

I started, and then, with a laugh at the men standing round the table, I hurried after the rest of the women and out of the room.

The dining-room being on the ground floor of the house, plans for dispersal for powdering of noses were made on the way upstairs and, shamelessly, I headed Annie off, cut her out from the others and took her to my own bedroom.

'I had a feeling I knew you when we met, Mrs Goldfine,' I said at once. 'But it wasn't until your husband mentioned Sir Hugh Reid that it came back to me.'

The wide blue eyes gazed at me, beautiful and expressionless as a calm sea under a cloudless sky, eyes as innocent as a child's eyes, but without that searching wonder that is in the eyes of all children.'

'Remember Cairnton?' I said. 'I was Janet Sandison.'

'Oh, Cairnton. And Janet. Yes.' She laid her jewelled bag on the dressing-table, sat down and gazed at her beautiful reflection in the glass. 'That's a long time ago.'

She showed no reaction of surprise or of any other kind. She was quite uninterested in me, in Hugh Reid, in Paradise, in this dinner-party, in everything except her reflection in the glass. She opened the bag and laid out a complete make-up outfit in miniature, a row of little jewelled cylinders and phials, and set to work on her face. Absurdly, it crossed my mind that she was nearly three years my senior but that she still had this childlike, flower-like freshness. The word 'flower-like' has become, by usage, a symbol of innocence, but it was in no way inapplicable to Annie. She had a strange quality which I can describe only as being beyond the descriptive bounds implied by words like innocence or evil, as if she had been created thus and had lived in accordance with how she had been created, without making any attempt to modify herself to conform to any humanly conceived morality or standard. Having removed her make-up and having dropped from rose-tipped fingers a soiled tissue into the waste-basket, she put on a foundation cream and was then free to devote to me, politely, a little of her time.

'Is your home still at Cairnton?' she asked.

'Oh, no. My father went back to the north early in 1927. As you say, it's all a long time ago. We are getting old, although I must say you don't show your age much, Annie.'

'They call me Annette,' she said, but quietly, without any undue emphasis.

'Annette,' I corrected myself. 'A pretty name.'

The cream-foundation having 'set', if this is the correct expression – I know very little about the higher flights of maquillage – she began, with concentration, to apply a layer of powder.

'I met Duke in Paris,' she said.

'Duke?'

'Duke Goldfine.'

'Oh.'

With speed and skill, she replaced the make-up on her face, packed away the little cylinders and phials and patted the fair curls into their sculptured positions on her perfect skull. Then she rose, went into the bathroom, came out to the long glass and, twisting this way and that, smoothed the luminous satin over her hips, ending with a long, satisfied stare at her reflection. Coming back to the table, she picked up the bag and looked once more at her face. She might have been quite alone in the room until, as she turned away from the dressing-table, she seemed to become conscious of my presence again.

'Yes. I met him in Paris. In '45. The war made everything very difficult. As you say, Cairnton is a long time ago and we are getting old. Duke's all right.'

I was fascinated. It was strangely like speaking to a statue. The ordinary rules of conversation did not seem to apply, as if, with Annie, no rules of any kind existed at all and none of the normal reactions to anyone or anything could occur.

She was neither surprised that I should be here, like a ghost from her past, nor pleased to see me nor discomfited at being recognized.

'How did you meet Duke?' I asked.

'I was in hospital at the time. Touch of T.B. He thinks I am a refugee.' She looked back at her reflection, straightened the great spray of diamonds on her breast so that the stones blazed in a sudden frenzy of fire. 'He's all right. It was high time somebody turned up.' She turned away from the glass and went to the door and, weakly, I followed her along the verandah to the drawing-room.

She had spoken to me throughout with a pretty French accent which, in an accomplished actress, would have been extremely clever in its naturalness and lack of exaggeration, but I do not think that, in Annie, it betokened that cleverness of brain which it would have signified in an actress. I had a curious impression that, like the taste and quality of her clothes, the restrained style of her hair-dressing and make-up, the accent was something instinctive that had grown upon her to fit her into this new background that had 'turned up', her position as Mrs Goldfine, the beautiful victim of total war that a wealthy American had rescued and married. The symbol of the wild flower again crossed my mind as we sat down in the drawing-room, Annie on a Chippendale sofa that made an elegant framework for the luminous satin. She seemed to choose that seat instinctively, as a wild violet will grow against a background of moss, soft and green, or a primrose will open its pale, trusting petals against the barren ground under a beech tree, where the withered leaves of last year throw its fresh newness into even higher relief.

Throughout the remainder of the evening, she spoke very little, as if merely by being present, in her beauty, she were contributing enough, and I found myself wondering what happened in the brain behind these soft, wide, expressionless eyes. And I came to the conclusion that nothing happened. Nothing at all. I thought of the lines:

'The summer's flower is to the summer sweet,
Though to itself it only live and die—'

This expressed something of Annie's quality. She was different from all other people and the difference lay, I thought, in the fact that, in the ultimate sense, nobody mattered to her except herself. Mr Goldfine was somebody who had 'turned up' in time to provide for her old age. That was all. Annie was not conscious of hard times in the past or of present good fortune. I found myself smiling inwardly and a little ruefully as my mind played round the words 'My Friend Annie'. Annie was not thinking of me as 'My Friend Janet'. Annie was not thinking of me at all or of her husband or of anyone. Elegant and luxurious, on her Chippendale sofa, she was rapt, flower-like, in her own secret self, the self that even she was not aware of, a deep, unknowable essence once called Annie, now called Annette.

Close to eleven o'clock, Mr Goldfine came to the end of a discourse he had been giving us on teen-age drug-addicts in the United States and turned to Madame.

'Well, Mrs Dewlack, this has certainly been a great pleasure and I have been very interested to see and hear all about this beaurryful ol' place ya have here. Yes, sir. But this is only one side of the picksher. Vice is rampant among the Negroes an' prahstitootion is eating like a cancer at the vitals av their marrality. But right now, Mrs Goldfine and I have ta get back ta tha hotel. Mrs Goldfine has delicate health and I have ta take care with her. Come, hon.'

Annie rose, he adjusted the blue-lined cloak about her shoulders and, with an angelic smile at us all, she turned away and preceded him down the steps to the waiting car.

The other guests left immediately and, when the last car had driven away, we returned to the drawing-room and Madame picked up the cushion against which Mr Goldfine had sat and shook it violently, as if to rid it of the clinging crumbs and strands of vice and pestilence that must be upon it. She did not speak in words, but her whole demeanour spoke volumes. Sir Ian, however, had fewer conventional inhibitions about discussing his newly-departed guests.

'I wonder,' he said thoughtfully, 'how a fellah gets so

interested in syphilis? 'Straordinary the things fellahs get to thinkin' about!'

Madame hurled the cushion back into its chair. 'I was informed by the Secretariat that Mr Goldfine was an agricultural expert,' she said viciously. 'The man doesn't know a sugar cane from a potato!'

'Can't quibble about that, Mother. Dammit, he's from the middle o' Chicago!'

'And he calls it Chickawgo!' snapped Madame.

'That's probably the Red Indian way o' sayin' it, Mother.'

Madame drew herself up and glared at her son. 'From the shape of his nose, Ian, Mr Goldfine is certainly *not* a Red Indian!'

'Never said he was, Mother. Red Indians got more sense than to travel about Paris lookin' for syphilis. Imagine goin' to Paris for that! Can't see what he gets out of it. Must be an awful bore for that little wife o' his, livin' with a fellah like that!'

'Oh, she doesn't seem to mind,' I said.

'She seemed sort of dull for a Fifi,' Sir Ian ruminated. 'They're usually pretty talkative. Some of our French cousins'd talk your ears off.'

'I'm going to bed,' said Madame shortly. 'Goodnight, my dears. Sleep well.'

Sir Ian watched her tap away along the verandah and then said: 'Knew from the start it'd be a stinker of a dinner. The only French thing Mother likes is being called "Madame". The Dulacs have been marryin' Scots wives since 1725 but they've all been called "Madame". An' of course that perisher Goldfine has to go callin' her *Mrs* all night. 'Straordinary how stoopid some fellahs are! Oh, well, like a nightcap?'

'No, thank you, sir,' Twice said. 'I'm a little worn out with all the red-light areas. I feel I've had quite a night of it.'

'By Jove, jolly good!' bellowed Sir Ian. 'I must say I've been to some dull dinners in my time but never one with so much disease. Think I'll have a bath before bed.'

When Twice and I were in our bedroom, although I was

234

bursting with my dramatic news, I waited for the first comment to come from him.

'Well,' he said as he untied his tie, 'I always thought it was the modern legend, the equivalent of the sirens of the early mariners, but now I've seen it with my own eyes.'

'What?' I asked.

'The Dumb Blonde. All the blondes I've ever seen before had an underlying cunning, but that one hadn't. She is really and truly and exquisitely just plain dumb.'

'Dumb blonde nothing,' I said. 'That was my friend Annie.'

'What d'you mean, your friend Annie?'

'Annette Goldfine née Annie Black of Nethercairn, Cairnton.'

'The Negroes' duppies have got you,' Twice said. 'That woman never came out of Scotland.'

'Oh, yes, she did. She and I had a little chat about old times right here in this room after dinner.'

Twice, in his shirt-sleeves, sank on to the bed. 'Say, I take back that that I said. Yes, sir, as her sugar-daddy would say, dat dame ain't all dat dumb! I'd have sworn that the sound-box that produced that voice and accent had been made in France!'

'I know. No, Annie is not just any ordinary blonde.'

While the crickets chirped and the frogs held a choral service around Madame's lily pool on the lawn below, and the white moon continued on its uncaring course across the black sky, I told Twice all I knew of Annie.

'If old Goldfine's snob instinct hadn't made him mention Hugh Reid, I'd never have recognized her,' I said at the end. 'Usually, when you meet a person after a lapse of years, the first thing you recognize is some trait of character or of speech, or a glance or some mannerism. Like that time I recognized Andrew Boyd in the pub at Achcraggan by the likeness in his eyes and glance to his father. It wasn't like that with Annie tonight. I didn't recognize anything positive – it was rather the *negative* thing about her that made me recognize her. Old Goldfine had just mentioned Hugh Reid, and with my mind on Hugh, I happened to look down the

235

room and see Annie outlined against a palm in a pot, just as I had seen her, in the same unexpected way, in that café in Sauchiehall Street. She was moving then – and tonight too – as if she were fated to move just in that direction, without her own volition, just as – just as that white moon out there is moving across that sky. I must write to Hugh. He'll be interested to hear that I've met her out here.'

'And that brings me to something else,' Twice said. 'Annie may not be so dumb about looking after herself, but for a fairly clever woman you are about the dumbest thing that ever walked.'

'Me? Why?'

'Tonight, you suddenly tell me you know Sir Hugh Reid, one of the foremost nerve and muscle men in the world. Not so long ago, you were in bed with paralysed legs for over a year and we didn't know if you would ever walk again and you never even muttered the name of Hugh Reid.'

I stared at Twice. 'I never even thought of Hugh that way,' I stared.

'No. You wouldn't. Get into bed afore Ah get sweerin' at ye as old Mattha says.'

He stood for a moment looking out at the black sky and then, frowning, got into his bed.

'What's wrong, Twice?' I asked. 'What's worrying you?'

'Nothing. Why?'

'Don't be stoopid, as Sir Ian would say. Come on, what's up?'

He leaned on one elbow and looked across at me.

'Do you realize that of you and that blonde at the table tonight, the blonde is socially the more acceptable one and you are beyond the pale if all were known?'

I looked back at him. 'I realise it now that I think of it, but what of it? All is never known, good or bad, until it is too late for it to matter any more. Read your book and go to sleep and don't be a dope. I don't mind not being respectable, as long as you don't take me on a vice tour.' He smiled very faintly. 'And you haven't got square glasses or dyspepsia.' His smile became more distinct. 'And if all were known, which is never until it is too late as I said, Paradise prefers us to the Goldfines.'

Twice laughed outright and picked up his book from the table between the beds. 'I am very, very devoted to you,' he said, 'but I will never, never address you as "Hon". Good night!'

CHAPTER FOURTEEN

A few days after the dinner-party, Twice and I left St Jago for Scotland amid a babble of protest from Madame and Sir Ian, when they became aware that, now that Twice had done the survey of the island, Allied Plant Limited might send out another engineer to supervise the installation work on the plant that had been ordered.

'I do not *want* some other engineer,' said Madame categorically.

'But you see, Madame, the firm uses me mostly in a consulting and advisory capacity,' Twice tried to explain. 'When the plans are drawn and the equipment supplied, a younger man could—'

'Some young whippersnapper who would get into trouble with the coloured women!' snapped Madame. 'I won't have it! I shall write to them!'

And she did, too, 'write to them', and not by dictation either, but in her own large, bold, copperplate handwriting. Three days after we arrived back at Crookmill, Twice came home from the Works and told me that a 'snorter' of a letter had come in to Head Office from Paradise, which informed Allied Plant Limited that, unless Mr Twice Alexander was sent out to supervise the installation of the new plant on order for the Paradise interests, to wit: Paradise Sugar Factory, the St Jago Soap Factory, the Santa Anna Laundry and Paradise Wharves Limited, Messrs Allied Plant Limited could consider the orders to be cancelled. Madame was, she informed them, theirs faithfully, Charlotte Gertrude Dulac.

'Oh, lord, Twice! What did Head Office say?'

'I explained about her to old Hertford and he laughed like

a drain. In point of fact, they intended to send us back out to St Jago anyway.'

'Good. When?'

'When the first of the plant is shipped, which should be about June. The stuff for the Retirement Factory should be ready by about mid-May.'

'Will we be out for long?'

'A year at least, if they keep me on the St Jago assignment, that is. We ought to try to rent a house. Would you write to Marion Maclean, maybe?'

'That's a good idea. I will. Twice, can we go up to Reachfar before we go abroad again?'

'Oh, surely, my pet. I'm due some leave if I'm for overseas again. When would you like to go?'

'It doesn't matter. Any time that suits you.'

'Late in May then. By then, I'll have all the St Jago stuff in process and we could go up for a week or two before we leave for the Island.'

'That will be fine. I had a letter from Hugh Reid this morning. He was thrilled to hear that we had met Annie. I'd like to see Hugh again. You'd like him, Twice. I wonder if he'd be able to come up to Reachfar?'

'That's an idea.'

'Ever since we were kids, Hugh has been supposed to come to Reachfar with me, but somehow, something always stopped it. At first it was the paper round – he had to deliver the papers from his grandmother's shop. Then there was that drama about his bursary that I told you about. Then, when we were both at the university, we drifted apart and he went away to London. It would be fun if he could come to Reachfar after all, don't you think?'

Twice grinned at me. 'Iphm, I see. Determined to bring life to heel, aren't you?'

'What do you mean?'

'I wish-t I had a pencil that would write red!' he teased, quoting a phrase with which I had worn my family down at the age of six till they were all on the verge of dementia.

'How long is it since you started to wish-t that Hugh could come with you to Reachfar?'

'Since I was about eleven.'

'And you are still at it?'

'Twice, there's nothing *wrong* in that, is there? That phrase you used about bringing life to heel makes me sound arrogant and – almost sacrilegious, somehow. It is just that – well–'

'You wish-t Hugh could come to Reachfar!' he finished for me and laughed. 'No, I don't see that there is anything *wrong* in it, but doesn't it strike you that you are extraordinarily persistent?'

'Not particularly. If one wants a thing, one wants it.'

'But to want the same thing for about thirty years?'

I laughed at him. 'That only indicates that it was a good thing in the first place. Age has not withered nor custom staled its infinite desirability!'

'You're hopeless. All right, you'd better write to Hugh and find out what his plans are.'

In the end, this time, my 'wish-t' came true, for during April and early May, Hugh had engagements to speak at Edinburgh and Aberdeen Universities and also to visit a number of hospitals in northern Scotland, after which he would be free to join us at Reachfar for a few days.

It was not until Twice and I had been at Reachfar for a week and Hugh's arrival became imminent that it was borne in on me that Hugh was that extraordinary sort of personality which is known as 'news'. The tempo of life at Reachfar is slower than at other places, so that, as I have already mentioned, people have more time to think or, as the poet put it, 'to stand and stare'. Reachfar takes fewer newspapers than most houses, but yet, paradoxically, its people are remarkably well-informed on general affairs, because the *Weekly Scotsman* and the weekly northern counties newspaper are read from front to back, as is any odd daily paper that anybody happens to bring home.

'It is myself,' said Tom, 'that will fairly enchoy meeting this Sir Hugh Reid, him being such a wonderful doctor and him with only chust the one arm.'

'And to think of Janet knowing him since she was a bairn and never telling us!' my aunt said and, turning to Twice, she added: 'You'll have noticed that she's so slow-witted in some ways that she's nearly foolish.'

'But I *did* tell you!' I protested. 'Ever since I was a kid coming home for the holidays, I have told you about Hugh and Granny Reid!'

'How were we to know that your friend Hugh was the Sir Hugh that was helping all the crippled polio bairns?' my aunt asked indignantly. 'You never *said* anything!'

'I didn't know you were so interested and knew so much about Sir Hugh that is helping all the polio bairns as you call him!' I bellowed. 'I didn't know he was so famous! I hardly ever read the gossipy bits of the newspapers!'

'Gossip! And why *wouldn't* he be famous?' my aunt bellowed back at me. 'And the Air Force boys in the war and everything! And him collecting money for the poor little bairns that that man Hitler had shut up in concentration camps and them starving!'

'And him speaking on my wireless boxie about them,' Tom joined in, 'and the next day George going down to the Post Office and sending him a pound each from the whole of the three of us!'

'I'm SORRY!' I bawled. 'I just didn't realize he was so famous!'

'You have to mind,' George told my aunt and Tom, 'that Janet herself was sick in bed with her legs paralysed for a big bit o' the time that we were hearing so much of Sir Hugh.'

'Don't raise that side of it,' Twice said. 'I never knew either that Sir Hugh Reid was a friend of hers until a man we met in St Jago mentioned him and then she announced that she went to school with him. Bloody fool!'

I felt, now, that everybody was going much too far.

'Don't you dare call me a fool, Twice Alexander! And, anyway, my legs got all right without Hugh! Why *should* I have thought of him? You don't have friends for what you can get out of them! You – oh, horsefeathers! I'm going up for a walk on the moor!'

241

Hugh arrived at Reachfar on a Wednesday evening, still wearing the formal clothes that he had worn for his tour of a hospital near Inverness, and this in itself was a matter of extreme gratification to my family, especially my aunt. As he stepped out of the black, chauffeur-driven limousine at the granary gable, she whispered: 'He looks just like what he *is*, doesn't he?'

I knew what she meant. Hugh, with the greying hair, the formal, superbly-tailored air of distinction, the thin face with the thoughtful eyes, was my childhood conception of a 'specialist', as contrasted with Doctor Mackay of Achcraggan and Doctor Blair of Cairnton, who were 'family doctors' in their comfortable, baggy suits. My family were a little distant and shy of Hugh to begin with, a little awed and afraid in the presence of what they recognized, instinctively, as the great, but after a day or two of hearing of fights with Teenie Mathieson and tales of the paper round told by a Hugh dressed in flannel trousers and a tweed jacket, they were calling him plain 'Hugh' and Tom was addressing him as 'Hugh, lad'.

He liked Reachfar, as I had always known that he would, and I think the remote peace of the place was a boon to him, for on that very first evening, after supper, he drifted to the door to stand gazing up at the moor above the house and then, as if sleep-walking, he went on up the yard, through the gate and disappeared among the dark fir trees. My aunt, at the kitchen window, watched him go and said: 'What there is about that moor up there for some folk I will never understand. Janet was in it from morning till night, as a bairn, and plenty of other people are just the same. Mind you, the ones that like the moor are usually nice people, although I don't see anything much in it myself.'

'Och, it's aye an outing!' said my mischievous clown of an uncle.

'Herself doonbye will be wild when she gets back from her holidays to the south and finds that we've had Hugh here,' said Tom.

'*Sir* Hugh, when you are speaking in the same breath

about him and *that* one!' said my aunt. 'For myself, I think it's a good job she's away. We would have had to take Hugh down to see her just to keep the peace and he wouldn't be needing to go visiting, likely.'

'Nor it wouldn't keep the peace likely, when all was said and done,' said George.

'She would probably tell him he was only Auld Sweetie Maggie's Hughie,' I contributed. 'Is she *no* more reasonable than she ever was?'

'Not a bit,' said my aunt.

'It's worse she's getting, if anything,' said my uncle.

'As thrawn an' twisted o' the temper as an ould crooked stick,' said Tom. 'A person chust never knows what badness will come out of her next. But, mind you, she is very civil with your father, and as for young Jock, he can do no wrong.'

'Aye, that's true,' my aunt and George confirmed.

The next morning, Twice drove my father to the cattle-sales in Dingwall, while Hugh and I spent the bright day helping George and Tom to hoe turnips, and my aunt, as usual, attended to the house. Hugh and I, being much less expert than George and Tom, and Hugh working one-handed into the bargain, were soon left behind on the long rows, while the two practised hands, who seemed to move much less energetically and much less in every way than we did, drew quietly and unspectacularly away from us.

'Chust take your time,' Tom called back when he and George began to draw ahead. 'If it is only a little bittie you will be doing, it is always a bittie that won't have to be done again.'

Hugh and I relaxed our efforts to keep up and began to plod along at our own slower pace.

'The thing I like so much about Tom,' Hugh said, 'is that the simplest thing he says always seems to have the broadest base of wisdom in it. If it is only a little bittie you will be doing, it is always a bittie that won't have to be done again,' he repeated.

'Yes.' I leaned on my hoe and gazed out over the firth. 'There has always been something like that about Tom.'

Hugh looked at my stationary hoe. 'Of course,' he said,

'you have to do a *little* bittie. Just leaning on the hoe is no good at all!'

I laughed and we started to work again.

'I hope it's true about the little bittie having a value,' he said next. 'I was thinking of Annie. Hers has always been a very small contribution to the common weal.'

In the old days long ago, I had always been quite sure about the essential worthlessness of Annie, but I was less sure now.

'I am not going to commit myself about the size of her contribution,' I said. 'We simply don't know, Hugh, do we?'

He looked at me for a moment and we both began to work again.

'I suppose not,' he said. 'Did you know her really well as a child, Janet?'

'Not really. I used to go to her parties, because I had to. You know how children have to do things willy-nilly. But Annie and I never liked one another – we simply had no common ground, Hugh. Then, later on, when I was about sixteen or so, I discovered that she was a prostitute. I knew it long before the big *débâcle* when she and Tommie left Cairnton, you know. The thing I could never understand was *your* interest in her. I – well, I resented it. I suppose I was jealous and, of course, I was full of smug, womanly virtue. I've got over the jealousy and that sort of so-called virtue, but I still don't understand about Annie. I don't understand what makes a woman take to that sort of life. I don't see what they get out of it.'

'With Annie, I think it was a desire for luxury, for money and the things that she liked that it could buy. She had beauty, you know, and she loved her own beauty.'

Instead of the young green turnips before me, I could see the ringleted little girl posing before the looking-glass at Nethercairn and the luminous figure on the Chippendale sofa at Paradise.

'She has beauty still,' I said.

'And then, she has practically no intelligence,' Hugh went on. He gave a little laugh. 'On the night that Willie Black begot Annie and me on two different women, he gave an incomplete brain to one and an incomplete body to the other, it seems.' He waved his one-handed hoe at me with a smile. 'She could not earn the pretty things she wanted with her brain, so she found another way of getting them. That is simplifying the thing to an absurdity, of course. There were all sorts of influences – the twopenny novelettes the schoolgirls used to read and Miss Hadley used to confiscate – remember them?'

'And the vamps at the pictures on Saturday afternoons.'

'And of course the fact that prostitution was so rife in Cairnton.'

Startled, I dropped my hoe, picked it up again and stared at him.

'Ninety per cent of the Cairnton women were tarts,' he said, 'if you think of it in honest terms. They were born and bred to grow up and go to bed with the man that could give them the nicest house. The idea was in their minds from birth and in the background of all their training. It was like that in most of these little towns in those days – it is *still* fairly persistent as an idea, in fact. Annie simply took on the colour of her upbringing and her locality. Given a little more brain, she'd have been all right. She went after Tommie Hill – the richest bloke with the biggest house in the district, but she made one brainless mistake.'

'What?'

'She let her virginity go before the ring was on her finger. She lost it in a third-class railway carriage with Tommie between Glasgow and Cairnton, when she first started at the commercial college. Poor Annie. If she had held on to that one thing, everything would have been different, but that was where the landslide started.'

'Was she in love with Tommie?' I asked.

'Oh, I don't think so. A lot of muddled thinking goes on about love and a lot of very loose talk. Comparatively few people are capable of love – I think the true lover is about as rare as the true painter or poet. No, but if Annie and Tommie had married, they would probably have shaken down into some mode of living, you know, like thousands of other people, but after the big moment, Tommie wouldn't marry her. She was cheap, damaged goods. He told her so and she believed him. Her heart didn't break – hearts are tough, you know – and she decided to make the best of a bad job. Again this is a reduction of it all to the absurd. There were other factors. But Annie reasoned that what was lost was lost, it couldn't be lost a second time, and she went out to get what she wanted out of life. And she got it, too. In her heyday, in the thirties, she was the toast of a certain section of London and Paris. And, I suppose, she did a bittie for something or somebody, even if it was only a little bittie as Tom puts it. She did quite a lot for *me*, when I think of it.'

'For you?'

'Well, she hammered the Cairnton out of me,' he laughed. 'I was full of rescuing her from Tommie and saving her from herself and all that.'

'My father threw Tommie in the quarry loch over her!' I said, remembering.

'That was probably just as well. If he hadn't, Tommie would probably have killed me that night. He was pretty drunk. But if your father and I had never interfered, Tommie and Annie would have settled their differences all right. She was furious with us for poking our noses in, as she called it. I suppose she and Tommie were fond enough of one another in their own way.'

'They gave Cairnton something to talk about anyway,' I commented. 'I'll never forget all the outraged virtue around our house – poor Annie's ears must have burned.'

'Not they! Annie wouldn't have given a damn!'

I remembered my 'poem' of long ago; I remembered Annie making up her face in my room at Paradise. 'No, I don't suppose she would have,' I agreed. 'She was – and is – remarkably single-minded. She doesn't seem to care for anybody or anything except Annie.'

'That's fairly true.'

'Hugh, what was it about her that made you so fond of her – when you got over the sentimental, missionary stage, I mean? What sort of person *is* she, really?'

'I was drawn to her in the first place because of the blood relationship – when Granny told me about it, you know.' We had reached the end of a furrow and stood leaning on our hoes. 'It didn't take me very long to tumble to the fact that that secretarial job she was supposed to have in Glasgow was a myth and when I realized what she was up to, I was full of this missionary zeal to save her soul. Annie laughed in my face and told me to mind my own business. In Cairnton language, I "took the huff" for about a year and *minded* my own business, but that took the missionary out of me. I came in the end to the great conclusion that Annie's soul was indeed and in truth her own business and that it was sheer interfering impudence on my part to go messing about with it.' He laughed quietly. 'So, I came out of my huff and made friends with her again. I came to love her after I had learned to appreciate her. It is difficult to express. You know what happens when a new school of painting develops – the first reaction of everyone is to take a look and say that they don't like these new pictures. Then, after they have become more familiar with the technique and have learned how to look at them, they change their minds and decide there is something to like in them after all. If Annie had not been my half-sister, I would never have bothered to learn how to look at her, because she was too different from the ordinary run of people that I know. You see, when Annie tossed her bonnet over the windmill with Tommie on the five-ten train from Glasgow to Cairnton, she tossed the only little bit of tradition that was in her out of the window at the same time. She stepped out of the framework of Cairnton to which she had been bred, she developed a technique of living that was personal to herself – a new technique that owed nothing to tradition. To appreciate her, you had to learn to look at her as she looked at you – with complete and utter sentimentally-nil detachment. When you learned to do that, you came to admire her and I went on into loving her. I have not seen her for five years, but I don't imagine that she has changed.'

'But didn't you see her in London?'

'No. I only saw old Goldfine for a few minutes at ten in the morning. Annie hasn't got up at ten in the morning since she left Nethercairn!'

'Oh, Hugh! I wish you could have seen her at Paradise! And this wonderful detachment of hers – or is it a sort of innocence? It did not seem to occur to her that as Mrs Anti-Vice Goldfine, with her particular past behind her, she was in a false or vulnerable position of any kind. She didn't turn a hair, when I recognized her as Annie Black. She merely said: "They call me Annette".'

Hugh chuckled. 'What did *you* say?'

'I told her that it was a pretty name. What *could* I say?'

'Exactly. Her change of name was her own business and all you could do was respect it and address her by that name. She'd do the same for you in similar circumstances. Annie expects life to run smoothly. Shortly after she went over to Paris in 1945, she got ill and one of her girl friends happened to tell me about it so I went to her and got her into a sanatorium. Do you know how she greeted me? She said: "Hello, One-Wing – it's high time somebody turned up." That was all. She had a bad spot on her lung, she was helpless, alone and broke, but life turned me up to help her. That is what life is *for*, in Annie's mind, to turn up people at the right moment to help her and take her as they find her.'

'It must have been in that sanatorium that she met old Goldfine. He's mad on drug addiction and disease and the seamy side of life generally – but you know that. It's a sort of mental morbidity he has, probably due to being born with a gold-plated ice-cream-soda-straw in his mouth. She used exactly the same phrase of him. She said she was getting old and that he was all right and it was high time somebody like him turned up. In fact, that was about all she *did* say. She hardly spoke at all.'

'She never has talked much,' Hugh said. 'I don't think she is sufficiently interested in you or me or anybody to talk to us.'

'And, of course, that will suit old Goldfine down to the ground. *He* will talk about famine in China and venereal disease in Africa until all's blue, and when he gets going on what he calls "prahstitootion" he'd curl your hair – everybody's hair except Annie's. At Paradise he had us all wriggling in our seats but Annie just sat, dreaming on, serene and placid as a flower in the sun.'

Hugh gave a shout of laughter. 'Good for Annie! Janet, I think the whole thing is the most joyous joke I have ever heard!'

'There *is* a satisfactory feeling that it serves that old busy-body Goldfine right,' I agreed. 'Mind you, I hope that he never finds out the whole truth about Annie. That would be too cruel to both of them.'

'I wonder what he imagines her past to be?' Hugh said.

'Oh, I forgot that. Her words were: "He thinks I am a refugee". It is odd, but I feel that I have to quote Annie absolutely verbatim. I feel it would be wrong to say that she *told* him she was a refugee.'

'It probably would be. Probably Goldfine made up his own mind about that and Annie played along. You see, that's the other half of her character, as it were. She expects you to take her as she is, and *she* takes *you* as you are. If this man Goldfine finds it pleasant and comfortable to think that she is a refugee, Annie will let him think it. What he thinks is his own business. Annie is not going to draw him a diagram to prove that she is a Scottish tart, and the thing about it is that she doesn't remain passive like that primarily for the profit of being Mrs Goldfine. To go back to this technique of living that she has developed, the best way that I can put it is that she is utterly unafraid to expose the truth of herself. She likes men, she likes pretty things, she likes indolence and luxury and she is going to have these things by the easiest means in her power and she doesn't care who knows it. She paints her intention in raw colours for everybody with eyes at all to see. Those who don't like the picture can turn away and pretend to be blind or they can whitewash her in their minds like old Goldfine – Annie doesn't care. The picture of life as she sees it is that you go out to get what you want and she paints in her life what she sees life to be.

Most people don't. Most people live within a framework of technique by which they draw a line of sexual morality here and a line of religious feeling there because their tradition has taught them that these lines *should* appear in the picture of a life. The technique comes to dominate the picture and they wonder why the picture brings them frustration instead of satisfaction. Annie's picture isn't like that. Annie has always had a whale of a time, the picture she draws always pleases her in every detail, it hasn't a line or a brush-stroke in it that isn't all her own work and her own truth. She was always – even in her most unfortunate moments – enfolded in a security and happiness of her own. I hope she still is.'

'She still is,' I confirmed. 'A remote, detached sort of happiness.'

'I'm delighted she has got hold of this dotty old American provider. I am delighted that life has put him in her way. She *expected* life to provide for her and, you know, people tend to get what they truly expect. Annie expected to get what she wanted out of life and she helps herself to what she wants and leaves it to life to do the rest. There is a resemblance between Annie's attitude to life and your own, you know, Janet.'

I stopped hoeing to stare at him. 'Mine?'

'Yes. You have faith that life is basically a good thing, that the right thing for you will turn up, that everything will be all right. You have fought your way through the fear and distrust of life that seems to be born in most of us to a faith in its goodness. Most people don't. They come to distrust it more and more and fear it more and more and they become more and more unhappy and insecure on a deep level. But Annie has got you, me and everybody else licked – Annie never went through any phase of fear or distrust. There is no question of any fight through to a philosophy or a faith. Annie lives as a new-born baby lives, instinctively confident that the next meal will turn up from somewhere. When it doesn't come on time, or she is in any way uncomfortable, she bellows for help, just as a baby does. Until the arrival of Goldfine, she used to bellow for *me* and I always went to her. What did you think of Goldfine by the way?'

'I thought he was an atrocious old man, Hugh,' I said, as we began to hoe our slow way up the field again. 'What did *you* think of him?'

'I only saw him for a minute or two, but I thought him a bit terrifying. I was leaving for Germany that morning Annie rang up. I do wish I had seen her.'

'I am most awfully sorry that you didn't. As Mrs Goldfine she's terrific. Never miss another chance. She drips with diamonds, her French accent is delicious, and old Goldfine is so proud of her that it's pathetic. He brings her into rooms like an impresario presenting a prima donna. Then he raves on about disease, drug-addiction and prahstitootion and Annie sits there serene and calm as a visiting angel. It is simply enthralling – it has a sort of mesmeric, poetic quality. Even now, I find it difficult to believe that that evening happened. The whole visit to St Jago had a dream-like feeling that started right at the airport before we left.' I told Hugh of the meeting with Sir Ian and Sandy Maclean and how, after that, life became a pageant of the exotic and fantastic. 'Until that moment at the airport, when I gave the boy the book, because of the memory of old Lord Farness which he had brought back to me, Cairnton had been a closed chapter in my life – so unreal that I might never have lived there. My only real contact from those days was with *you*, and I have never regarded you as being really part of Cairnton. But that the person that should arise out of my Cairnton past should be *Annie* is the most extraordinary thing of all. I know that the West Indies are a cross-roads of the world these days of air travel, but I don't connect Annie with cross-roads, either parochial or inter-national. Annie, in my mind, belongs on the main streets where the gayest lights are.' Hugh laughed and I then said: 'She is an extraordinary product to have come out of Cairnton, isn't she?'

'She is indeed,' he agreed. 'The Cairnton tradition of that time was a tough technique to break through.'

'The truth is that Annie didn't break through it, Hugh,'

I told him: 'She was never inside it, any more than I ever was. I was insulated against it by being born and living for ten years up here and Annie was insulated by her own character. Annie's selfishness – for want of a better word – her interest in herself was so strong that she was not susceptible to influence even by her own mother. The very first time I saw her when we were both small children, I became aware that Annie was not equipped with a normal set of feelings at all. She was born free of them. It's the feelings that are the devil and cause all the hell. If we could all swim about in an emotional void and think about nothing but our appetites, like Annie, everything would be fine.'

Hugh laughed again. 'Maybe, but I don't entirely agree. Without feelings, a person is incomplete – Annie is incomplete. The feelings are splendid in a person and splendid for a person to have until they get warped and twisted out of true – that's when the hell sets in – and the technique of living tends to do the warping and twisting, as if a picture were being squeezed or stretched into a frame that doesn't fit. It is remarkable how, with all the study that's gone on down the ages, people have developed so little intelligence about the basic business and technique of living. In this year of grace, 1950, we ought to have a neat set of rules as in chess, don't you think?'

'Bishops, knights and pawns have no feelings,' I pointed out.

Again Hugh laughed. 'It does seem to get back to the feelings,' he agreed.

'You can't get away from them in life, unless you are born an Annie. Look what happened to Alice when the Red Queen came alive!'

'True enough. Talking of red queens, how is your step-mamma?' Hugh stared into the distance for a moment. 'I'll never forget her face that last prize day at the Academy as long as I live. I always think of her like that – red as a boiled lobster and shaking with rage.'

'It isn't inaccurate. She still gets like that at the mere sight of *me* in particular.'

'Still? One would have thought that she would have simmered down through the years.'

'Not over me. I don't think she ever will. We are like two forces that are diametrically opposed or oil and water or something. And life doesn't help. It keeps giving me things – such as Twice – that Jean doesn't think I deserve and so on. I have never understood Jean and I don't suppose I ever will, now.'

'That business of deserts is all wrong,' Hugh said with an emphatic push of his hoe. 'No wonder Jean is in a muddle if she expects people to get what – by Cairnton moral standards – she thinks they deserve. If we all got what we deserve, it would all be very dreary. Jean ought to take a leaf out of Annie's book and expect a bit better of life than Cairnton moral deserts. Serve her right if she ended up with Cairnton moral deserts herself. By the way, have you told her about Annie and St Jago and so on?'

'Good God, no! To start with, I haven't seen her. She's not here – she's down round Glasgow somewhere on a holiday. Otherwise, I suppose I'd have to take you down to the cottage to call on her.'

'God forbid! But when you *do* see her, you should tell her about Annie and Goldfine – it may change her views on moral deserts!'

'I have no interest in trying to change Jean's views on anything. Not that I could if I tried. And she couldn't change mine. We only make each other more so, if you see what I mean. When she says black, I almost *have* to say white. I despise myself for it, but I can't help it. And I don't know what makes me do it and I can't stop doing it. Maybe she makes me mad because she puts me into a ridiculous position with myself. But, anyway, I am not going to raise a thing like Annie having caught a millionaire. I can get into enough trouble with Jean without going about it deliberately and scientifically!'

'It's a question of knowing enough,' Hugh said, in his thoughtful way, as if he were talking mainly to himself.

'How d'you mean – knowing?' I asked.

'If you knew a little more about what makes Jean tick, you'd get on with her better. You are good at getting on with people when you want to.'

'Maybe your theory about knowing is right,' I said, 'but I'll never get to know what makes Jean tick. She dislikes me too much to tell me and she is too quarrelsome to let me come near enough to study her and find out for myself. I'm afraid I'll have to go on as I'm doing – seeing as little of her as I can and forgetting about her as much as possible. It isn't difficult. Over the years, I have built up a little prison in my mind – made of Cairnton stone – and I keep her in there. Masses of the people who know me don't even know she exists. I never let her out.'

We both laughed, went on hoeing and began to talk of our schooldays at Cairnton and of Annie again.

CHAPTER FIFTEEN

The turnips were in the Long Park, a long, narrow field immediately to the north of the house at the top of the long slope that led down to the firth, and, at mid-afternoon, when we all sat down to have the afternoon tea which my aunt had carried out to us, half of Ross-shire lay spread before us in the sunshine.

'This *is* a beautiful place!' said Hugh.

'It's bonnie enough the-now,' said George, looking out over the firth, 'but it's a devil in the winter time.'

'I can imagine that. What is that place down the hill, among the trees?'

'That's Poyntdale House, Sir Torquil Daviot's place. In the old days, when we were bairns,' George told him, 'aye, and till after the '14-18 war, it was a biggish estate. You see yon church steeple west yonder beside the road?'

'Yes.'

'Poyntdale went west to there, north to the shore of the firth, south to our march dyke down there and east to the sea, taking in Achcraggan.' As he spoke, all our eyes followed his pointing finger. 'And then the boundary came up on a south-west line from − who the devil is that coming over the roadie from the burn, Tom?'

All our eyes focused on the figure following the field path.

'God Almighty!' said Tom. 'It is herself from doonbye that is in it!'

'Mercy on us! She's coming here!' My aunt was panic-stricken and glanced wild-eyed from me to Hugh.

'The hell with it, Kate!' I said. 'Don't worry! Hugh knows Jean and all about her, don't you, Hugh?'

'I do indeed,' said Hugh. 'But would you like me to disappear, Kate? I know how embarrassing she can be.'

'No! No, Hugh. That would make it worse. It'll be *you* she's coming to see. I didn't even know she was back!'

'Nor us neither, did we, George?' Tom asked.

'No, dang it!' said George.

'What a hell of a lick she's coming at for an ould fat wifie!' said Tom. 'You'd think the devil himself was after her!'

'More likely the devil himself is *in* her!' said my perspicacious Uncle George.

As soon as Jean had puffed and blown herself within speaking distance of us, she said: 'Whaur's Duncan?'

'At the sales in Dingwall,' my aunt said. 'You'd better come into the house and have a cup of tea, Jean. I hope nothing is wrong?'

'Ye micht weel hope!' said Jean.

'This – this is Sir Hugh Reid,' my aunt said, grasping at some straw of convention.

Jean looked at Hugh. 'Ah heard ye wis here. Quite the toff these days, aren't ye?'

I stood speechless and at gaze. Hatred is indeed akin to love, in more ways than people tend to think, and at each fresh meeting after long separation from her, Jean's crudeness could take my breath away exactly as the breath of a lover can be taken by the first sight of the beloved after absence.

She turned away towards the house and the rest of us followed her, carrying our teacups and the basket.

'And how are you, Jean?' I said when we were in the kitchen and my aunt was putting the kettle on the fire. 'If I'd known you were back, I'd have been down to see you.'

'Ye wid, wid ye? Weel, ye can jist alter ye mind. The likes o' *you* will niver set fit in *ma* hoose!'

My aunt, tall, pale and in fighting fettle, swung round to face Jean. 'What do you mean?' she asked.

All of us except Hugh knew what was coming. Somehow, Jean had ferreted out the existence of Dinah.

'Ah'll sune tell ye whit Ah mean, an' jist wait till Duncan hears aboot it! Aye, an' *Sir* Hugh here an' Lady Monica an'

256

a' her fancy freen's! A fine thing, livin' wi' a man an' gaun aboot a' ower the warld wi' him an' her no' mairrit tae him! She's waur nor Annie Black! A fine thing fur the stuck-up Sandisons o' Reachfar. *Mrs* Alexander! Ye're jist plain Jinnit Sandison like ye aye wur for a' yer pride an' yer big hoose an' servants at Ballydendran!'

'Hold your tongue, woman!' said Tom.

'Ah will *nut* haud ma tongue! It's a cryin' scandal, that's whit it is, gaun aboot amang decent folk an' her nae better nor a strumpet! Ah'll come doon an' see ye, she says!' She glared at me, the light in her eyes snapping on and off. 'Ye'll not darken the door o' *ma* hoose, that Ah'm tellin' ye! Ye're nae better nor a street wumman like that Annie Black an' ye'll come tae the same bad end! The same riff cannae cover the likes o' you an' Annie Black an' decent folk like me!'

She stopped talking, panting for breath, and her eyes snapped triumphantly from face to face round the room, gloating over our discomfiture. She jerked the big armchair by the fireplace – the chair that my grandfather had always used and in which no woman of the family ever sat – into a different position by a few inches and went to sit down in it, in a triumphant fashion, like militant virtue settling upon a throne. The old chair, on well-oiled castors, was accustomed to the gentle easing down of the rheumaticky joints of Tom and not to this sudden clumping down of heavy virtue on its venerable horsehair seat and, as if it were a live thing, inspired by the Sandison enmity to Jean, it moved away backwards over the polished linoleum at the crucial moment and, completely off balance, Jean sat down with a resounding thump on the floor, her fat legs rising until her feet were on a level with her face, her arms flailing in the air.

George, Tom, Hugh and Kate are imprinted on my mind as they stood by the table, their four faces forming a semi-circle of utter astonishment; I looked from them to Jean who was rocking to and fro on the floor on the axis of her own buttocks, and burst into half-hysterical laughter, and at that moment my father and Twice, home from Dingwall, appeared in the doorway.

'What the devil's going on here?' my father asked and then he and Twice began to laugh too, the others joining merrily in the chorus.

I think it was Hugh, in the end, who helped Jean to her feet and to attempt to describe her rage and humiliation would be absurd. She had grown very fat with age, her face was scarlet with rage. She stamped, raved, screamed imprecations against me and Annie Black and ended by throwing herself in hysterical abandon at the treacherous armchair which, at the first assault, rushed away and crashed against the wall, leaving Jean once more on the floor, face downwards this time, her toes drumming on the hearthrug. 'Jist wait till Ah tell folk!' she was yelling. 'Jist wait till Ah tell folk about the strumpet that she is!'

Once more, Hugh, with Twice to help him, got her up from the floor and into a wooden chair without castors, while the rest of us hiccuped ourselves into some semblance of calm and my father, his ruddy old face under its white hair, looked 'worried', as he had been wont to do away back in the old days at Cairnton, as if events were away beyond his ken and control, as indeed they were.

My aunt made a fresh pot of tea and, at long last, Jean became sufficiently coherent to speak again and she poured out with dreadful malice, the light flashing on and off in her eyes as on that prize-day long ago, the intelligence she had gathered in the course of her holiday, ending with the venom-laden glance at me and the repeated: 'Jist wait till Ah tell folk aboot her!'

'What good will that do you?' my father asked, in the tone of a reasonable man asking a reasonable question, while the rest of us, who knew better than to expect reason from Jean, looked at him in amazement.

'Folk should *ken* aboot the likes o' her an' him!' she said, her glance flickering towards Twice. 'She shouldnae be amang decent folk! She's nae better nor a street wumman like Annie Black!'

'Hold your tongue, Jean!' my father said.

'Ah will *nut* haud ma tongue! It's the truth Ah'm speakin'

258

an' the truth should be tell't!' Her eyes, small and sharp as the eyes of a snake and full of that dreadful malice in her red, rage-swollen face, snapped back towards me. 'An' don't ye *dare* to set fit in ma hoose again, ye dirty prostitute that ye are!'

'Jean!' My father went towards her, his eyes blazing.

Jean became afraid, became hysterical and began to yell. 'That's a' she is, livin' wi' a man an' her no' mairrit! She's no' bringin' her sin intae *ma* hoose!'

I believe that my father would have struck her, had it not been for my uncle, the family 'clown', who stepped between them, very calmly, his pipe in his hand, a frown on his forehead as he peered down into its bowl.

'I doubt, mistress,' he said very softly, 'that as long as you live in *Janet's* house, you'll have to let her come into it as often as she likes, that is, if she doesn't order you to clear out of it altogether.'

Do you know what it is like when the naked truth is suddenly spoken, like a stone being thrown into a pool? My uncle's words had an effect, similar in quality, though less in scale, to that of a new planet sailing past the window, a picture by Leonardo suddenly appearing on the wall or a symphony by Beethoven sounding out of the air about us. We all stared at him, transfixed, as at the source of some wondrous miracle, as we frowned at him in our efforts to comprehend what he had said. Twice and Hugh had never known of my ownership of the cottage and the rest of us had long since forgotten that technically, and legally, it was mine. There was a long silence, which Jean was the first to break and she spoke in the merest whisper. 'That's no' true! It's no' true! It's *no'* her hoose!'

Defeat and the inner knowledge that her own statement was false were in the tone of the spoken words as she looked with appealing, frightened eyes at my father. 'Is it, Duncan?' she asked.

I think that my uncle and I were the only people among those present who had any appreciation of what the answer meant to her.

'Och, aye,' my father said easily, as if the point were of the most minor importance. 'Old Aunt Betsy willed the house to Janet – Janet just lends it to me, ye know.' Then his face suddenly became stern as the import of what he was saying dawned upon his mind in all its force. 'And if she orders us out of it after this, I won't blame her and it will be your fault, with your dirty evil tongue!'

Into the silence, the old clock with the rose-painted panel below its dial ticked away above the scar on the mantel-board that Jean had made with the knife so long ago.

'It's no' fair!' she screamed, and then her voice died to a defeated sobbing wail. 'It's no' richt an' it's no' fair. Everything aye comes her way an' ither folk get naething! She disnae need the hoose an' she disnae deserve it! Oh, ma hoose! Ma *Hoose*!' She laid her arms on the table and her head on her arms and began to cry as if her heart would break.

I found it unbearable. I walked out of the house and on up to the moor and I began to cry as I went through the gate from the yard on to the heather.

I was still crying when Twice found me and sat down beside me on the trunk of the rotten tree that we had felled for firewood the day before.

'It was bound to happen, you know,' he said. 'It's something that we've always expected. It's no use bawling about it.'

'I'm not bawling about Jean knowing about us, if that's what you mean,' I sobbed. 'Don't be a fool! I don't care if she publishes it in *The Scotsman*!'

'She won't.' His mouth twisted into a sneer. 'You should have heard her grovelling about that bloody house. You know, it's the first time I've watched somebody selling her soul – it was singularly unattractive.'

'Don't, Twice,' I said.

'It's very odd,' he continued, as if he were talking to himself as much as to me. 'I understand now why you always behave as if those six years of your life at Cairnton had never happened. And I don't blame you. If there was much of Jean as she was today in them, your memories must be mostly scar-tissue. Has she always been like that?'

'I don't know,' I told him. 'Besides, what do you mean by "like that"? You see, it is only in relation to *me* that she is like that, really. With Dad and Jock and other people she is quite different – a bit of a bitch with some, but not as she is with me. No matter what Dad and Jock say or do, she never gets angry though, but no matter what I say or do, she is bound to get angry. I am not saying that I have never been at fault – I often have – but there have been dozens of things I have had no control over, like this thing of Jemima Cottage, for instance. I don't even know when things began to go wrong between us – I think it started the very moment we laid eyes on one another. Strangely enough, the first major row I can remember was over Annie.'

'Annie? You mean the Goldfine blonde?'

'Yes. You see, Annie was a very pretty little girl – she was Jean's idea of an ideal child and Jean was always wanting me to play with her, walk to school with her and *be* like her.'

'Good God!'

'Annie and I could not have been more different as children. There was simply no basis for anything between us and there was nothing to be done about it and Jean could never understand it. And, of course, Annie was by miles the more attractive child from Jean's point of view. But the whole thing goes far deeper than poor Annie. Actually, I have more in common and am more in sympathy with Annie than I could ever be with Jean. It's all very queer, Twice. I don't understand any of it. I wish Jean hadn't said that thing, though.'

'What thing? About prostitutes? You don't have to—'

'No – not that. Don't be an ass! No. That thing about everything always coming my way and she having nothing. It must be terrible to live, feeling like that all the time – no wonder she hates one, if that's how she feels. Have she and Dad gone home?'

'Lord, yes, in Hugh's car. I said I thought I could persuade you to let her have the house for as long as she wanted it and she couldn't get away fast enough before I changed my mind.' Twice began to laugh.

'Twice, don't laugh! Please don't laugh! It isn't funny.'

'Darling, don't be stupid! If I don't laugh, I'll be sick. *You* didn't see her grovelling, hear her promising not to say a word about you if she could go on living in that bloody house. It was the most revolting thing I have ever seen! Coming after all that stuff about strumpets and prostitution – it was horrible. No wonder she's miserable – she'll never be anything else. Bloody old hypocrite! No wonder you hate the sight of her!'

'There is a peculiar thing,' I said. 'You know, I don't hate her now as much as I did.'

'God knows what made you change your mind,' Twice said. 'I should have thought that ordinary vanity, if nothing else, would stop a woman behaving as she did today.'

I was not really paying attention to what he said. 'Hugh and I got talking over the turnip-hoeing today, Twice,' I said. 'Hugh was telling me about Annie and then we got to talking about Jean. I said I was fundamentally opposed to Jean in a way that I could not help and Hugh said it was probably because I didn't know her enough. You know that's true?'

'I should have thought you knew her only too well. She doesn't hesitate to speak as a plain woman in a plain way, does she? I feel she has a gift for making her point of view more than clear.'

'You are in the trap I have been in for about thirty years,' I told him. 'All that strumpet stuff is not a point of view – that's a lot of sound and fury, signifying nothing. I have never heard Jean state a definite feeling of her own, something that came straight from her own heart and her own brain until today, when she said that thing about the cottage being mine and my not needing it and not deserving it. It's quite true. I *don't* need the cottage and I have done nothing to deserve it.' Twice stared at me as if I were crazy and I grinned at him as I went on. 'Don't look so startled. I don't intend to present the darned thing to Jean! I don't see that *she* deserves it either. The point is that deserts don't come into it, but Jean believes that they do. She has always gone on the assumption that wealth, a fur coat, a car, a nice house – all these are the *good* things of the world to her – come as a reward for being a good girl by Cairnton standards. No wonder she always distrusted – and came to hate *me*. What she said is true. Everything *has* come my way and I've made no effort to deserve any of it. Anyway, I'm glad you told her that she could still have the cottage, Twice.'

'It's not going to make her love you any better, you know,' he said.

'I don't give a hoot about that. I don't care how Jean feels about *me*. The important thing to me is how *I* feel about *her* and I like her better today than I have ever liked her before, but not well enough, of course, to have to see her if I can possibly avoid it!' I laughed. 'Hugh asked me today if I had told her about St Jago and Annie. Poor Jean, to be told that Annie's wages of sin was all those diamonds and Goldfine would just about finish her.'

'That's a point that I didn't quite get,' Twice said. 'How she came to drag the blonde into the diatribe at all.'

'Pure chance, that's all. To Jean, Annie is the symbol of the scarlet woman because she is the only strumpet that Jean has ever actually known. But it was sort of uncanny today, the way she brought her name in, as if Annie were some queer link between Jean and myself – or a charge that explodes us or something. Maybe I ought to tell Jean about Goldfine and make Annie respectable for her after all.'

'So that everybody will be an honest woman except yourself, you strumpet, you?' Twice inquired. 'No. You'd better leave it. It would be a terrible blow to Jean to discover that Annie had climbed right up and into and beyond her own class.'

At his words, I began to laugh and went on laughing until I had some difficulty in controlling myself. Twice, who had been beginning to smile a little at the whole absurd situation, stared at me and began to look angry again.

'What the devil's so funny?' he asked.

I spared a thought of commiseration for him, remembering that this was the first time that he had seen Jean in full action – he had hitherto witnessed only a few minor tantrums – and that he could not have enjoyed it.

'Darling, I'm sorry,' I said. 'You are taking all this far too seriously. Console yourself that no-one else who discovers our guilty secret will be half as unpleasant as Jean was.'

'I still don't see any reason to scream with girlish laughter,' he said. 'What *was* so funny?'

'You saying that about Annie being in Jean's class. I told you that the first major row I can remember between Jean and me was about Annie. It happened on the evening of the first day I went to Cairnton Academy. Both Annie and I went into the First Year of the Higher School, but I was in A Section and Annie was in E Section. When Jean asked if I had seen Annie at school, I said that I wasn't in Annie's class. She argued that Annie was in the First Year, just as I was, and I wouldn't explain about the sections system because it meant telling Jean that Annie was among the duds and I was afraid that she would say something nasty that would cause a fuss at the supper table and generally worry and annoy Dad. Later on, she got me alone in the scullery and read me a virtuous lecture and called me a little liar. I was probably an arrogant little brat, for, after that, I *would* not explain about the sections. I told her that she was an ignorant fool, talking of something she knew nothing about, and marched out of the back door, and I remember her calling after me: "You're a thrawn, bad wee besom, an' ye are *so* in Annie's class!" I thought no more of the whole thing except that Jean's calling after me had been very undignified but she went on believing that I was in the same class as Annie. But it wasn't true, you know. It was just another of these things that grow into deceptions between Jean and me. Annie and I weren't really in the same class.'

I was staring down the long tunnel of time when a note of mock solemnity in Twice's voice made me look at him and see the grin on his face.

'No,' he said. 'No, I quite believe you weren't. Not really.'

I grinned back at him. 'No,' I said. 'I don't think I have ever really been in quite the same class as My Friend Annie.'

THE END

MY FRIENDS THE MISS BOYDS
BY JANE DUNCAN

The My Friend books tell the story of Janet Sandison, of her Highland family, and of the fascinating and varied friends who shaped her life.

MY FRIENDS THE MISS BOYDS is the story of her family home, Reachfar, a Ross-shire farm run by her stern grandparents. It tells of life in a Highland village before the first World War and of the shocked consternation caused when the Miss Boyds, frivolous, men-mad old maids, bring their scandalous behaviour into the community.

This is the first of the My Friends books.

'An enchanting novel. It is a full, rich life that Miss Duncan describes, and her characterizations are sharp and sometimes poignant.'
The Times

'It grows on you uncannily. This is only the first of the happy saga.'
Manchester Guardian

0 552 12874 0   £2.50

MY FRIEND MURIEL
BY JANE DUNCAN

The My Friend books tell the story of Janet Sandison, of her Highland family, and of the fascinating and varied friends who shaped her life.

Janet Sandison first met My Friend Muriel when, as a brash determined young woman of 20, with a degree from Glasgow University in her pocket, she went South in search of a job. As well as a job she found Muriel, ordinary to the point of oblivion, but who was to prove a catalyst in Janet's life. For it was Muriel – and her slightly shady husband – who suggested Janet should come back to Scotland and work at 'Slaters', and it was at Slaters that Janet met Alexander Alexander, a Scot in whom she had met her match.

This is the second of the My Friends books.

'It is beautifully written, full of moving and funny incidents, and highly entertaining.'
John o' London's

0 552 12875 9 £2.50

MY FRIEND MONICA
BY JANE DUNCAN

The My Friend books tell the story of Janet Sandison, of her Highland family, and of the fascinating and varied friends who shaped her life.

Janet and Monica became friends during the war. They didn't meet again until Janet and 'Twice' Alexander were about to marry, and then Monica, with her flaming red hair and aristocratic manner, burst on post-war Scotland determined to become a permanent part of their lives. Throughout the renovation of their old stone cottages into a home, through Janet's tragic illness, Monica clung close, creating problem upon problem in their stormy lives.

It wasn't until they all went back to Reachfar, to the family in Ross-shire that the old values of friendship were re-established.

This is the third of the My Friend books.

0 552 12876 7   £2.50

A SCATTERING OF DAISIES
BY SUSAN SALLIS

Will Rising had dragged himself from humble beginnings to his own small tailoring business in Gloucester – and on the way he'd fallen violently in love with Florence, refined, delicate, and wanting something better for her children.

March was the eldest girl, the least loved, the plain, unattractive one who, as the family grew, became more and more the household drudge. But March, a strange, intelligent, unhappy child, had inherited some of her mother's dreams. March Rising was determined to break out of the round of poverty and hard work, to find wealth, and love, and happiness.

The story of the Rising girls continues in The Daffodils of Newent and Bluebell Windows.

0 552 12375 7   £2.50

THE DAFFODILS OF NEWENT
BY SUSAN SALLIS

They were called the Daffodil Girls, spirited and bright, enduring, loving and dancing their way through the gay and desperate twenties.

APRIL   who married the tortured and sexually suspect David Daker, convinced she could blot out his memories of the trenches.

MAY   pregnant by her handsome music hall star husband who didn't want to settle down.

MARCH   loved and betrayed by the man who had fathered her child, and who still wanted her.

The Daffodils of Newent – three wonderful girls whose story began in A SCATTERING OF DAISIES.

0 552 12579 2   £1.75

BLUEBELL WINDOWS
BY SUSAN SALLIS

The Rising sisters – the 'Daffodil girls' – were older now. The anguish of growing up in the twenties had gone. All three were – apparently – happily married and there were children to swell the vibrant Rising family. But the problems that had begun in youth still remained.

March, the eldest, the most difficult, loved but could not trust her clever manipulating husband. He had deserted her once and she could never quite forgive him.

May had her own worries – a son who seemed more than usually promiscuous, and a husband who grew more attractive and handsome even as she approached her fortieth birthday.

April had a husband she loved, and two small gentle daughters. But she was the only one who knew that Davinia was not her husband's child.

BLUEBELL WINDOWS takes the Rising girls – whose story began in A SCATTERING OF DAISIES and THE DAFFODILS OF NEWENT into the turmoil of the Thirties.

0 552 12880 5   £2.50

COPPER KINGDOM
BY IRIS GOWER

The Llewelyns lived in Copperman's Row – a small
backstreet where the women fought a constant battle against
the copper dust from the smelting works. When Mali's mam
died there were just the two of them left, Malia and her
father, sacked from the works for taking time off to nurse
his wife. Mali felt she would never hate anyone as much as
she hated Sterling Richardson, the young master of the
Welsh copper town.

But Sterling had his own problems – bad ones – and not
least was the memory of the young green-eyed girl who had
spat hatred at him on the day of her mother's death.

COPPER KINGDOM is the first in a sequence of novels
set in the South Wales copper industry at the turn of the
century.

0 552 12387 0   £2.50

A SELECTION OF FINE NOVELS
AVAILABLE FROM CORGI BOOKS

☐	12874 0	**MY FRIENDS THE MISS BOYDS**	*Jane Duncan*	£2.50
☐	12875 9	**MY FRIEND MURIEL**	*Jane Duncan*	£2.50
☐	12876 7	**MY FRIEND MONICA**	*Jane Duncan*	£2.50
☐	12720 5	**LEGACY**	*Susan Kay*	£2.95
☐	12387 0	**COPPER KINGDOM**	*Iris Gower*	£2.50
☐	12637 3	**PROUD MARY**	*Iris Gower*	£2.50
☐	12638 1	**SPINNERS WHARF**	*Iris Gower*	£2.95
☐	10249 0	**BRIDE OF TANCRED**	*Diane Pearson*	£1.75
☐	10375 6	**CSARDAS**	*Diane Pearson*	£3.95
☐	10271 7	**THE MARIGOLD FIELD**	*Diane Pearson*	£2.50
☐	09140 5	**SARAH WHITMAN**	*Diane Pearson*	£2.50
☐	12641 1	**THE SUMMER OF THE BARSHINSKEYS**		
☐			*Diane Pearson*	£2.95
☐	11596 7	**FEET IN CHAINS**	*Kate Roberts*	£1.95
☐	11685 8	**THE LIVING SLEEP**	*Kate Roberts*	£2.50
☐	12579 2	**THE DAFFODILS OF NEWENT**	*Susan Sallis*	£1.75
☐	12375 7	**A SCATTERING OF DAISIES**	*Susan Sallis*	£2.50
☐	12880 5	**BLUEBELL WINDOWS**	*Susan Sallis*	£2.50